blue
rider
press

ANGEL CITY

ALSO BY JON STEELE

The Watchers

War Junkie

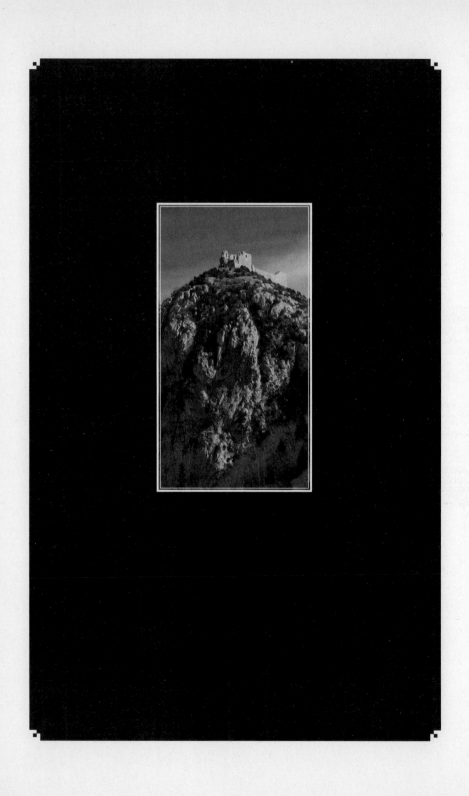

ANGEL CITY

Part Two of The Angelus Trilogy

❧

JON STEELE

BLUE RIDER PRESS • A MEMBER OF PENGUIN GROUP (USA) INC. • NEW YORK

blue
rider
press

Published by the Penguin Group
Penguin Group (USA) Inc., 375 Hudson Street,
New York, New York 10014, USA

USA · Canada · UK · Ireland · Australia
New Zealand · India · South Africa · China

Penguin Books Ltd, Registered Offices: 80 Strand, London WC2R 0RL, England
For more information about the Penguin Group visit penguin.com

Lyrics from "South City Midnight Lady" by Patrick Simmons, © WB Music Corp. and Lansdowne
Music Publishers, used by permission of Alfred Music Publishing Co. Inc. Lyric to "The Wheel" by
Robert Hunter, copyright © Ice Nine Pub. Co. Used with permission.

Library of Congress Cataloging-in-Publication Data

Steele, Jon, date.
Angel City : Part two of the Angelus trilogy / Jon Steele.
p.   cm
ISBN 978-0-399-15875-9
1. Murder—Investigation—Fiction.   I. Title.
PS3619T4338A54   2013   2013009626
813'.6—dc23

Printed in the United States of America
1   3   5   7   9   10   8   6   4   2

BOOK DESIGN BY EMILY S. HERRICK

for
Juanita Hedlund

❧

LES CARRIÈRES (OFTEN REFERRED TO AS "THE CATACOMBS") ARE the tunnels and quarries that run for hundreds of kilometers beneath the streets of Paris. They were begun in the twelfth century by miners following limestone deposits to be used for building materials. The Great South System under the Left Bank of Paris is the most extensive section of *les carrières*. It is deeper than the present-day subway, rail, and sewer tunnels. The German Luftwaffe used a section of *les carrières* (near Luxembourg Gardens) as a bunker during the Nazi occupation of Paris.

THE CATHARS WERE A CHRISTIAN SECT, MOST ACTIVE DURING THE eleventh through the thirteenth centuries. They believed in the duality of the universe. To them, pure immaterial spirits (souls) were created by a Good God and dwelled amid the stars with angels, while the material world was created by an Evil God who sought to entrap pure spirits in the forms of men on Earth. And though the Cathars believed Jesus Christ to be a "pure spirit," they did not accept him as the Son of God, nor did they believe he died on the cross. The Cathars did not practice the Catholic sacraments of baptism or Communion; their one sacrament of Consolamentum was offered near death as preparation for the soul's return to the realm of the Good God. In keeping with their beliefs, the Cathars considered the Catholic Church, particularly the physical wealth and power of the Papacy, to be a creation of the Evil God. For these reasons, the Cathars were condemned as heretics.

MONTSÉGUR IS THE NAME OF BOTH THE GEOLOGICAL FORMATION OF igneous rock (called *pluton*) located on the north slope of the southeast Pyrenees and the medieval fortress atop it. It is thought there was a previous structure atop the pluton in the pre-Christian era; most possibly a temple of sun worship. The temple was replaced with a stone fortress during the eleventh century and later abandoned. In 1204, the fortress was refortified by a local noble who opposed the expansion of the Kingdom of France into Occitania (what is now the department of Midi-Pyrénées in southeast France). The noble allowed the Cathars to take refuge in the fortress to escape the slaughter of the Albigensian Crusade, initiated by Pope Innocent III in 1209. In 1233, the Roman Catholic Church ordered the extermination of the "Cathar heresy" through the Office of the Inquisition. In 1243, French Crusaders acting in the name of the Pope laid siege to the last redoubt of the Cathars at Montségur. The fortress of the Cathars was destroyed by the Crusaders at the end of the ten-month siege. The current structure atop the pluton was built over the ruins of the Cathar fortress at the behest of the King of France. It served as a military garrison until the eighteenth century.

THE DOMINICANS ARE AN ORDER OF PRIESTS ESTABLISHED BY SAINT Dominic in 1215. The order was known as Ordo Prædicatorum, the Order of Preachers. They encouraged devotion to the Virgin Mary through the recitation of the rosary; they were also fiercely loyal to the Pope and many became feared throughout southern France as Inquisitors. With the blessing of the Pope, Inquisitors had the power to subject anyone suspected of heresy to trial by torture and death by burning.

PARADISE: Planet Earth, where the Unknown Creator has set in motion an evolutionary process affecting the future of the universe.

HARPER'S KIND: referring to small creatures born of light and without free will, sent to Earth two and a half million years ago by an Unknown Creator to hide in the forms of men and defend the evolution of Paradise.

THE ENEMY, GOONS: referring to those creatures born of light who preceded Harper's kind but rejected the divine will of the Unknown Creator, first taking the forms of men and breeding with human females to create a new race of physical beings, thereby bringing "evil" to Paradise.

SUTF, OR SPECIAL UNIT TASK FORCE: the top-secret division of the Swiss National Police under the command of Inspector Gobet.

HALFBREEDS: children of the enemy who infected Paradise with greed and fear. A term also used by Jay Harper to describe the children bred by Harper's kind in a now abandoned experiment to replenish their numbers in the wake of severe losses.

PARTISANS: human beings in secret service to Harper's kind.

TIME WARP: a defensive maneuver in which Harper's kind isolates a small geographical area by locking it in a moment in time.

THE FIRST FIRE: the flame remnant used in the creation of the universe, brought to Earth by Harper's kind two and a half million years ago to trigger the evolutionary process as planned by the Unknown Creator.

RADIANCE: the potion mixed with a special blend of tobacco and used by Harper's kind to prevent the physical weight of the human form from crushing out the light of their being.

DEAD BLACK: an injectable potion used by Goons to create a feeling of euphoria while committing acts of evil.

FLASH: the ability of Harper's kind to "see" past events in their eyes, as if reliving the event.

SCAN: the ability of Harper's kind, and the Enemy, to check another's eyes for levels of pure light or traces of dead black.

IMAGINING: a process of conceptualization shared by Harper's kind and human beings.

THE WAR, ETERNAL AND FOREVER: the two-and-a-half-million-year-old battle for Paradise, fought in the shadows between Harper's kind and the Enemy.

In my ears are the cries of the stricken;
and I can see, as I have seen in the past,
all the marring and mangling of the sweet,
beautiful flesh, and the souls torn with violence
from proud bodies and hurled to God.

JACK LONDON
The Iron Heel

Prelude

❦

IN ÆTERNUS

FORTRESS MONTSÉGUR, OCCITANIA, MARCH 15, 1244

WHEN THE KNIGHT REACHED THE STONE STEPS TO THE RAM-
parts, he realized he was walking in circles. He stopped, looked
around the courtyard. Till then there had only been the sensation of a
staggering, forward motion; now came an awareness of the world
around him. It was the tower he recognized at first, rising like some
singular presence against the late afternoon sky. It was badly damaged
during the bombardment, as were the battlements. In the early days,
when French catapults were still halfway down the mountain at Roc de
la Tour, the stone missiles did no more than bounce off the outer walls
of the fortress. The knight made sport of collecting the stones, calling
them "the Pope's turds" and bringing them into the courtyard where
the fighters of Montségur built their own catapult. After writing curses
on the stones, the fighters returned them down the mountain from
where they had come. But in February the French broke through the
lower defenses and scaled the cliffs, securing a foothold on the summit.
Their catapults found their range and the final assault began. They leveled the terraced village on the north cliff in three days, forcing the folk

who lived there to seek refuge within the fortress. Still, the fighters of Montségur would not surrender. The French adjusted their targeting and launched stones, a hundredweight each, into the courtyard.

Just now, seeing the crumpled shelters in the courtyard and the pools of blood on the ground, terrible images came to the knight's eyes. There was no defense from the bombardment, not even in the lower chambers of the tower. Fighters and folk were crushed to death. The French then attacked with infantry and captured the barbican a mere thirty chains from the fortress gates. It was Montségur's last line of defense. All was lost unless the Crusaders could be repelled.

The knight felt a cold wind at his back.

He turned to the smashed open gates, and for a moment he was confused. He couldn't remember what had happened next. But as he felt the wind on his face, more images came to his mind. He saw the fighters of Montségur mustering in the courtyard at evening, preparing for the last battle. Two young boys stood nearby, holding torches so the fighters could see as they dressed in chain mail, coifs, and helmets. There were but a handful left now: nineteen knights with swords and shields, five crossbowmen and archers, twenty sergeants and infantrymen with lances and war hammers, a few Basque mercenaries with axes and cudgels. The knight remembered the fighters speaking quietly among themselves.

"What is the day?" one said.

"Why should you care?" another answered.

"Because I should like to know the day of my death, if this is to be the day of my death."

"Then, it is a Tuesday, I think."

Such fateful words were a soldier's words, the knight remembered thinking. And he remembered how he, too, tried to recall the day just in case this would be the day of his own death. The fighter was correct, it was a Tuesday; first day of March. The day was named after the Norse god of war, Tiw; the month was named after the Roman god of war.

"Not a bad day to die, then," the knight said to the fighters, fitting his helmet to his head and securing the chin strap. The fighters laughed.

About the courtyard, the three hundred folk seeking refuge within the fortress had gathered to watch the preparations for battle. Farmers and shepherds from the surrounding valleys, craftsmen and merchants from nearby towns, dispossessed nobles from Languedoc. Many of them credents to the Cathar faith, all of them sympathetic to the cause of the Cathars. The leaders of the faith watched, too; the ones who called themselves "the good men." They stood at the entrance of the tower, somber and silent in their black robes. The knight could see their lips forming words of silent prayer as was their manner.

The knight bowed to them, the good men continued to pray.

The knight turned to the fighters, the fighters fell quiet.

"Brothers in battle, I salute you this fine evening. For ten months, we have held an army of ten thousand soldiers at bay. Not just any soldiers, but soldiers of France. At our greatest strength, we were two hundred fifty fighters. I ask you to think on it. Outnumbered more than sixty to one, yet we have not been shaken from this rock. We are told, tonight, there is a full company of infantry at the barbican awaiting our surrender. We are told two more companies are making their way up the mountain and will be here by the dawn. They say Louis IX—"

Some of the fighters cursed, the rest of them spit.

"They say that Capetian donkey, then—"

The fighters laughed.

"—they say he commands us to kneel and swear an oath of fealty to France. But I say as we live and breathe, this rock beneath our feet is all that is left of Occitania. It is our land, and I say free men do not kneel on their own land. And His Holiness the Pope—"

More curses and spit.

"I mean that evil son of Satan—"

Laughter.

"—has blessed the French soldiers, calling them Crusaders, warriors of Christ. He has decreed these Crusaders to be doing God's work in slaying the Cathars."

The knight pointed to the folk.

"His Holiness therefore orders us to surrender these men and women to the Inquisition, that they may be investigated for the crime of heresy. But I say these folk have fed us, tended our wounds, washed our braies and leggings, kept our worn shoes bound together with scraps of cloth torn from their own tunics. I say these folk have done all in the defense of Occitania but wield a weapon."

He nodded to the good men at the tower.

"More, we are ordered to surrender the leaders of the faith to be burned at the stake unless they repent. But I say these good men have prayed for us, offered our dying brothers the sacrament of Consolamentum. I say we are bound to these good men and them to us. I say we will not surrender one pure soul to the tyranny of a corrupt and sinful Church."

The fighters agreed with grunts and snorts.

"Brothers in battle, mark my words well: This alliance of Pope and King howling at the gates craves more than our lands to make them France. Pope and King crave our absolute destruction so that all memory of this place, all memory of us, will be wiped from the face of the Earth."

The knight pulled his sword from its sheath. He could see the chinks and nicks of battle on the blade. He admired the markings by torchlight.

"So, with apologies to the good men for my foul tongue, I say we tell Pope and King to go fuck themselves in the arse."

There was no laughter this time; only the sound of weapons being drawn and raised. The folk in the courtyard parted to let the fighters pass. The boys, bearing torches high, led the way to the north gate. As the fighters had arranged themselves in formation, the knight nodded to the boys.

"Douse the fires. Get you both to the tower."

The boys lowered the torches to the soggy ground. The fires sizzled out, the boys dashed away. The knight stood quietly, watching the sky, waiting for his eyes to open to the stars. There was the Great Plough of the heavens, there was Polaris. There was Draco and Cassiopeia. A voice whispered to him from behind:

"And what have to offer the stars this fine evening, Oh noble knight?"

It was Jean de Combel, crossbowman from Laurac. Always good with a mocking word before battle to cheer the men. The knight turned back to him, touched the flat of his sword to the crossbowman's shoulder.

"I pray, 'Whatever you do, let me live one day longer than that ugly bastard de Combel.'"

The crossbowman laughed.

"Then you shall live forever, knight, for I will never die."

The knight nodded.

"Done. Now open the gate, de Combel, and let's put the bargain to the test."

Jean de Combel stepped forward with his archers. They lifted the cross brace, set it aside. The doors moaned and creaked open on iron hinges. The knight stared ahead, imagining . . .

If they could retake the barbican and dislodge the forward company of French Crusaders, drive them over the cliffs, the fighters could capture the catapults. The machines could be turned around, used against the enemy soldiers scaling the mountain, and those encamped at Roc de la Tour. Two more catapults stood there. And in capturing those, the fighters would have enough firepower to break the siege. The folk could descend along hidden trails and disappear into the shelter of the Pyrenees, then over the peaks into Catalonia. But the French were dug in too well, and when the King's crossbows opened at the flanks, the fighters of Montségur were caught in crossfire.

The knight winced, remembering a long bolt howling through the battle. He remembered hearing the killing thing before it hit him. Knowing the moment he heard its voice, it was meant for him. The bolt hit with the force of a war hammer, the tiny blades cutting through his chain mail, digging into his chest. He saw himself dropping his sword and shield, falling to the ground. He lay amid the battle tasting his own blood in his mouth, knowing the blade had missed his heart but pierced his lung. The attack withered, the fighters fell back. Jean de Combel picked up the knight's sword, pulled the knight's arm around his own neck, lifted the knight to his feet. They hurried to the fortress.

The knight pulled away from de Combel, fell against the stone arch of the gate.

"My sword! Give me my sword!"

Jean de Combel handed it to him.

"*Va be, esta be!*" the knight cried. "This is it! Stand at the forecourt! The bastards must not enter the fortress or the folk will be slaughtered!"

The fighters formed a line at the gate, drawing the French soldiers onto the narrow strip of land between the fortress and the sheer cliffs. There was little room to maneuver, and when the French pressed at the gate, the fighters forced them back with lances. The knight heard the screams of King's men at the rear falling to their deaths. He raised his sword and cried again:

"*Va be, esta be!*"

Then he collapsed again to his knees and could not rise. Folk appeared in the courtyard to drag away wounded. Two folk grabbed the knight.

"No, I will stay!"

Jean de Combel turned quickly. "You are finished here, we will hold. Take him!"

The folk carried the knight to the infirmary below the tower cellar. A dank and hellish place stinking of blood and pus. Torches formed a pool of light around two wooden tables. One table was empty, dripping with blood; a fighter was strapped to the second table, screaming through the leather strap clenched between his teeth. The screams became shrieks as a surgeon, a barber from Carcassonne, sawed off the fighter's leg. A boy working with the barber removed an iron rod from white coals and cauterized the bloody stump. The boy had done it many times and he was good at it.

The barber saw the knight, nodded to the folk.

"On the table. Remove his chain mail and gambeson," the barber said.

The folk did it quickly. The barber wiped his filthy hands on his tunic, hurried to the table. He tore open the knight's linen shirt, probed the wound.

"It's a three-sided blade," the barber said. "I'll try to dig it out, but you will not live, I think. Do you wish to receive Consolamentum?"

The knight looked around the infirmary. More wounded coming in.

"Tell the good men to see to my brothers first."

"As you wish."

The barber turned to collect his knives.

The knight felt dizzy. The flame and smoke of the torches seemed to slow and take strange shapes. His eyes began to lose focus and close . . . He felt an arm slip under his neck, raise his head. The knight opened his eyes, saw a fighter in chain mail and coif emerge. The fighter held a clay cup to the knight's mouth.

"Quickly, drink of this."

The knight looked at the fighter's armor. It bore no coat of arms, and the chain mail was stained with blackish blood.

"Who . . . who are you? Bring your face into the light that I may see you."

The fighter leaned forward. The knight saw a battle-hardened face, oddly painted with streaks of mud.

"I do not know you. Have reinforcements broken through? Are we saved?"

"There are no reinforcements, and there will be none."

"Then . . . who are you?"

"Someone who's been at your side these ten months, fighting the evil that surrounds this sacred ground."

"What evil do you speak of?"

"The enemies of light, the devourers of souls. They know I'm here, they're hunting for me."

"Your words are strange."

"Drink of this cup and sleep. When you wake, you'll understand."

The knight felt his consciousness slipping, then a flash of fear . . . He tried to raise himself.

"No, this is a trick, you are a poisoner."

The fighter held him down.

"You are mortally wounded and already falling into death; but you must live for one hundred more days. Look into my eyes, listen to my voice. It cannot end here; it must not end here."

And when the fighter offered the cup again, the knight did not resist. There was a bitter taste, warmth, falling into light.

And now . . .

. . . the knight was healed, standing in the courtyard of the battered fortress. He looked down at himself, saw he was wearing a plain wool tunic and coarsely woven leggings. He thought he looked very much like one of the folk, then wondered which of the dead folk's clothes he was wearing. He pulled the tunic away from his neck, saw the bloodied scraps of linen bandages tied around his chest. A voice called:

"So it's true. You're alive."

The knight looked up to the battlements, saw a shadowed form at the ramparts.

"Who's there?" the knight said.

"Jean de Combel, best crossbowman in the fortress, that's who. Come up, the air is fresh up here."

For a moment the knight was taken aback by the crossbowman's familiarity. Then he remembered that was the way within the fortress. Nobles and peasants, knights and infantrymen, men and women even; all were equal before the Pure God of the Cathars.

"What about the others?" said the knight.

"What others?"

The knight had difficulty remembering who "the others" were. He tried to see them in his mind. Soldiers of France, arse-lickers of the Pope; yes, that's them. He nodded to the walls.

"The ones beyond the walls, the French."

"Oh, them, the Crusaders. They're far too busy roasting a boar to care about fighting. Besides, there's been a truce for two weeks."

"A truce?"

"From the day you were wounded."

"It's been two weeks?"

"It has. We fought them back to the barbican, as you commanded.

But we couldn't drive them off the mountain. It went back and forth all night. At dawn, we'd had it and called for a truce. The Crusaders could have stormed the courtyard and slaughtered us all; but they were in a hurry for their breakfast and accepted the truce instead."

The knight looked around the courtyard again. The fortress appeared to be abandoned.

"Where is everyone?"

"In the tower, watching the remaining folk and fighters receive Consolamentum. The ones that stayed, anyway. I was asked to keep an eye on the Crusaders, make sure they keep to the truce."

"Did many leave us?"

"More than half."

"Half?"

The crossbowman shrugged.

"Can't blame them. The King offered safe passage to all who promise to become good little Frenchmen."

"Fighters, too?"

"Fighters, too, including you and the rest of the Avignonet assassins, if you choose."

"Avignonet?"

"You remember; you and your merry band, slaughtering those seven Inquisitors in their beds last year. The very deed that brought us to this happy day."

The knight tried to remember it. He looked at his hands. *Yes,* he thought, *the hands of an assassin.*

"What are you thinking?" Jean de Combel said.

The knight looked up.

"Has there been any word from those who left? Have the Crusaders kept their word?"

"Some of the folk were paraded around the fortress this morning. The Inquisitor ordered them to sew a yellow cross to their tunics, to show the world they are heretics returned to the teats of Whoring Mother Church. There was a priest with them—one of the Inquisitors, I'm sure. A fat slob of a Dominican, he was. He called to me. Promised the wearing of the yellow cross would be the extent of my punishment if I would surrender to him."

"And will you?"

"I showed him the crack of my backside and shouted, *'Vai t'escoundre!'* "

The knight laughed. Jean de Combel certainly would shout *go fuck yourself* to a priest. And he would shout it in Occitan, refusing to even curse in the tongue of the French King.

"How many of us are left, then?" the knight said.

"Fighters?"

"Yes."

"Twenty-six. Many with wounds."

"And folk?"

"One hundred ninety-two Cathars."

The knight stood still a moment.

"So, it is true. We are defeated in this place."

"Yes, we are defeated. Come up and take the air, enjoy the truce while you can."

"Yes, I will," the knight said. "I'd like to see what a truce looks like. I don't recall ever seeing one."

He climbed the stone steps, used his left arm to balance himself against the wall. There was some pain still, but he felt almost disconnected from it. As if it were happening to someone else, not him. Closer to the ramparts, he had a better view of Jean de Combel. The crossbowman was wearing a bloodied gambeson over a linen shirt. His leggings and shoes were bloodied as well. The crossbowman reached down, gave the knight assistance up the last steps.

"I was told you had died three times," Jean de Combel said.

"I'm not as fast on my feet as I used to be, if that makes you any happier."

The knight stepped onto the ramparts and he felt the warm sun on his face. He looked beyond the battlements to see the lands of Occitania. Mountains like citadels, thick forests of pine and oak, meadows of poppy. Farther were sunlit rivers winding through maquis scrublands; and above it all, great winged vultures soared in loping circles. He closed his eyes and breathed. He smelled wildflowers, sage from the maquis, snow and ice from Mont Canigou. And Jean de Combel was right; there was the scent of roasting meat. The knight saw fifty or so French soldiers at the end of the summit. They wore swords at their belts, but appeared relaxed.

"So, this is what a truce looks like," the knight said.

"It is."

The knight sniffed at the scent of meat.

"Smells good, doesn't it?" he said.

"What are you saying? Only the French could waste perfectly good boar over a spit. I've half a mind to march down there and make those bastards a proper *sanglier* stew. We still have a few onions and garlic in stores. Some carrots, too. And the French have the boar. And the fat Dominican is with them, see him? Probably has a boy under his robes, pulling at his fat dick. I promise you, *that* papist will have a skin of wine for the sauce."

The knight looked at Jean de Combel.

"They might toss you a foot if you beg."

"Perhaps. But as the Pure God would have it, it's too late."

"Why too late?"

The crossbowman laughed.

"Because I've received Consolamentum."

"When?"

"With you, two days ago."

"Me?"

"Yes, well, you were delirious with fever. Not surprised you don't remember it. Your fellow assassin de Lahille was there, too. Took us some fakery to get you through the ceremony. We held you up and poked you in the back when you needed to reply. None too coherently, but you grunted well enough, and the good men took pity on you."

"You tease me, de Combel."

"Not at all. I speak only truth now. I have to. Comes with receiving the one and only sacrament of the Cathars. And a serious business, it is. It means that for the rest of our lives, there is no meat. Has there ever been a troubadour with a more woeful tale? Locked up with these pacifist vegetarians for ten months; not a scrap of meat to eat for the fighters. Do you know how hard it is to do battle without meat in your stomach? What am I saying—of course you do. Anyway, look out there. Crusaders cooking boar, so close we can smell it. And yes, they probably would toss us a foot. A hairy back foot, if we begged. But alas, it's forbidden to us both now."

The knight tried to imagine the sight of receiving Consolamentum in a delirious state. He didn't remember it—he had lost touch with the real world after someone held a cup to his lips.

"Something amuses you?"

"Twice so."

"Tell me."

"I'm amused that I've become one of the good men through the fakery of my brothers in battle."

"And good at fakery we were."

"I'm sure of it."

"And your other amusement?"

The knight smiled.

"I'm amused a killer like me can now be considered one of the good men."

"And good at killing you were."

The knight looked at the French soldiers on the plateau, then beyond to where the shadows of hills began to creep over the land.

"Do you believe in the faith of the good men, de Combel?"

The crossbowman sighed.

"I believe that these good men believe it, and I believe it is a comfort to these gentle folk."

"So what is to happen to them?"

"You don't know?"

"You're the first person I've seen since I woke up, or the first I can remember seeing. I'm not even sure how I made it to the courtyard."

The crossbowman chuckled.

"You'd best come with me, see for yourself. Make your own choice about going or staying, now that you're on your feet. It's still not too late to leave the fortress and become a good little Frenchman."

The knight followed the crossbowman along the ramparts, careful not to trip over rubble and spent missiles in his path. At the southwest wall, Jean de Combel leaned through the battlements and pointed down.

"That is what happens tomorrow."

Five hundred meters down, in a clearing at the edge of the forest, hundreds of French soldiers appeared small as ants. They were busy as ants, too, carrying tinder and buckets of pitch to a large square palisade. There were wooden ladders at the walls and the soldiers took turns climbing the steps to empty their burdens. Soldiers inside the walls spread the stuff over a thick flooring of straw.

"They will burn us, as heretics," the knight said.

"They will."

"When?"

"Tomorrow, at dawn. And that will be the end of Montségur and the good men, I think. And a foul end it is. I'd hoped we could do more for them. But, alas, there is no choice but to watch them marched to their deaths."

The knight looked at Jean de Combel, never before having heard such a sadness in the crossbowman's voice.

"How do you mean, de Combel?"

The crossbowman's eyes betrayed a secret knowledge, one he tried to conceal with a mocking smile.

"Why I . . . why I only mean these Cathars are a gentle folk, they deserve better than extinction."

The knight stared at the crossbowman.

"You fought bravely as anyone to defend them, de Combel. You will burn with them at the dawn, will you not? What more could you do as a fighter?"

The crossbowman turned his eyes from the knight, looked down on the palisade. The French soldiers were done with their work and drinking wine from skins. After a long silence, the crossbowman looked at the knight.

"You said it yourself before the last battle. Pope and King wish to wipe all memory of this place from the face of the Earth. I feared your words as you spoke them. I fear them now more than any words I've heard from a man. Shall I tell you why?"

"Yes."

"Because more than battle, more than what will come at the dawn, I fear a world without the Cathars."

The knight nodded, looked up to the sky. There was Saturn, there was Mercury, there was Mars hanging at the edge of the falling dark.

"Fear not, de Combel. It cannot end here; it must not end here."

BOOK ONE

GO, SET A WATCHMAN,
LET HIM DECLARE WHAT
HE SEETH

❧

ONE

I

Radio Intercept, Paris: September 9, 2013, 19:30 hours.
Groupe d'Intervention de la Gendarmerie Nationale: Code Red
Alert.

> ". . . Batobus Manon *dockside at Musée d'Orsay. Several bodies
> seen floating in river.* Manon *heading east on river. Anonymous tip
> reports area of Notre Dame to be target of attack by Muqatileen
> Lillah. This is a GIGN Code Red Alert. Engage Operation Dragon
> Fortress. Repeat: This is a GIGN Code Red Alert. Engage Opera-
> tion Dragon Fortress. Level A terrorist strike in progress. Six men
> wearing black jumpsuits and balaclavas, carrying light automatic
> weapons have hijacked Batobus* Manon *dockside at Musée
> d'Orsay. Several bodies seen floating in river . . ."*

Harper's mobile reconnected to Operations Control in Berne.
"Did you copy that transmission, Mr. Harper?"
"The enemy tipped off the police."
"Indeed, they plan to make a show of it. The world's news media will
be all over the story in a few minutes."

"You're sure the bomb is on board?"

"Affirmative."

"How many goons?"

"Standard kill squad of six."

"Time to target?"

"Tactical gives it eighteen minutes at present speed and course."

"Can the mechanics shift the time warp?"

"Negative. It's locked over Saint-Sulpice."

Swell, Harper thought. Plan A looked great on paper. Goons attack, Inspector Gobet's time mechanics drop a warp over Saint-Sulpice. Harper sorts the goons, cleanup crew secures the bomb. Just another night in paradise. None of the Parisian locals the wiser as they take aperitifs in nearby cafés.

"Then now's the time for suggestions, Inspector."

"Tactical is transmitting a counterattack to your mobile as I speak."

A map of Paris appeared on Harper's mobile screen, zoomed in on the border of the 6th and 1st arrondissements. Two dots appeared marking Pont Alexandre III and Notre Dame; a third dot triangulated Harper's position at Rue de Mézières, then a line appeared marking a track to l'Académie française on the Left Bank.

"Double-time it, Mr. Harper, and you'll reach the river ahead of the *Manon*. From there you'll have an opportunity to intercept."

"Just how am I supposed to get aboard, swim?"

"Tactical suggests something more along the lines of flight."

"What?"

"Old tricks being what they are, Mr. Harper."

The map zoomed into a footbridge above the river Seine, directly in front of l'Académie française. *Manon*'s course would bring her directly under Pont des Arts. The map flipped to side view and an arrow marked height from bridge to river. It was a thirty-five-meter drop; winds: southwest at nine klicks per hour.

"You can't be serious."

"In the last few minutes, SX sweeps have popped hot with chatter on

4

the Internet. Signals decode the chatter to read the bomb is worse than suspected."

"Define 'worse.'"

"The enemy has successfully bonded the Ra-226 with agony potion."

Harper worked the chemistry. Ra-226: radium, rare earth metal. Number 88 on the periodic table of elements, highly toxic. Pack enough of it with explosives, you've got a dirty nuke. Bond it with agony potion, you've got a fucking nightmare.

"Christ, they'll turn the center of Paris into a dead zone."

II

THE PILOT OF THE *MANON* FELT THE BLADE SLICE ACROSS HIS throat and he watched his blood spill down his chest. In the last moment of his life, he heard voices and screams . . .

"We bring you forever death!"

"No, please!"

"Oh, God! Help me!"

"Get the skins together!"

The hostages fell atop one another as they were herded to the center of the cabin. They huddled between the benches and watched six hooded men move quickly to take control of the boat. Four of the men squeezing the hostages together, another carrying a large backpack and rushing to the outer deck at the stern, one more taking the helm and hitting switches to kill the cabin and pilot lights. The *Manon* was cast into darkness. Abu Jad, at the outer edge of the hostages, held his daughter close to his chest to hide her from the hijackers. It was her ninth birthday and this was to be her present: a trip to Disneyland Paris and a night cruise of the river Seine to see Notre Dame Cathedral in Paris. It was all the little girl dreamed about since seeing *The Hunchback of Notre Dame* on DVD last year in Beirut. She knew all the songs from the film. She was singing her favorite of the songs to her father as the boat docked near Musée d'Orsay to take on a family of German tourists. That's when the hijackers appeared from the shadows. Long knives in their hands, machine guns strapped across their chests. And though Abu Jad heard the hijackers' leader shouting his commands in Arabic, there were French and Americans and Asians on board, too, all of them seeming to understand the leader's commands.

"Get down on your knees! All of you!"

The hostages sank to the deck. Abu Jad felt his daughter's face against his chest; her eyes squeezed shut, her voice singing quietly:

"*But suddenly an angel has smiled at me, and kissed my cheek without a trace of fright.*"

Abu Jad stroked his daughter's hair. He whispered in her ear.

"Yes, my darling Rima, God will send an angel to protect us."

Abu Jad felt the tip of a bloodied blade under his chin, forcing him to look up into the leader's eyes.

"Perhaps you should pray to me, little man."

"I . . . I pray only to God."

"*Hal ante muta'aked wa ana al lathy mumsek bi rouh ibnaitka alkhalida ayuha al rajul?*" the leader said.

"I hear your words as Arabic, but you are not speaking Arabic. How can this be? Who are you?"

The leader moved the blade from Abu Jad's chin and traced it through Rima's long hair.

"Aren't you the clever little man?"

Abu Jad pulled Rima to his chest.

"I beg you to have mercy on my child."

The leader set the tip at Abu Jad's throat.

"Tell me who I am, clever little man, tell me and I will be merciful to the little skin."

The black eyes staring at him, Abu Jad thought, were not even human. No, they were the eyes of the evil jinn.

"You are not a man, you are a demon escaped from hell!" Abu Jad cried. "May God send an angel to crush you and protect the innocent!"

The leader's evil eyes glared with hate.

"Tsk, tsk, little man. Haven't you heard? There is no heaven, there is no hell. There is only this place."

By the time he finished the words, the demon had buried his blade in Abu Jad's throat.

III

HARPER RAN UP RUE DE SEINE, CRASHED THROUGH THE TABLES at Café La Palette. Just after Place Gabriel Pierné, he cut through the passageway off Rue des Écouffes and came onto the esplanade of l'Académie française. At first sight things were as they should be of an autumn night. Traffic speeding down Quai de Conti, *bouquiniste* stands along the embankment walls, people crowding around. Traffic lights turned red and cars and buses stopped. Pedestrians hurried to and from Pont des Arts, the footbridge stretching above the river to le Louvre.

Harper checked his watch: four minutes to intercept.

He moved into the shadows along the limestone façade of l'Académie. He stood motionless and unseen, watching Pont des Arts. The footbridge was one of the city's favorite gathering places. And tonight, hundreds of locals had come to sit on the wooden planks and picnic and wave to the tour boats passing below. Words flashed through Harper's eyes. Words he'd read somewhere . . . *For the world's more full of weeping than you can understand.*

A local wrote those words, Harper thought. *A poet, maybe.* Harper reached under his coat, unhooked the lock straps of his killing knives. He drew his SIG Sauer, loaded a 9-millimeter hollow-point into the firing chamber. He pulled the decocker, eased down the hammer, imagining what he'd tell the poet over a pint: *It's the war, mate, eternal and forever . . .*

"But it wasn't supposed to be this way."

An EC135 police chopper dropped from the sky with a growl, skimmed the heads of the locals on the bridge before racing downstream. It hovered over Pont Alexandre III, searchlight switching on, lighting up the dark river below. *Airborne French coppers,* Harper thought, *searching for the* Manon. Another chopper roared in from over the Tuileries, searchlight already blazing. It circled above Pont de la Concorde, drifted slowly upriver toward Musée d'Orsay. The locals on the Pont des Arts fell quiet, all eyes following the two shafts of light like moths to flames.

Sirens.

Harper looked upriver, saw the spinning blue lights of police vans turning onto Pont Neuf. The vans skidded to a stop, doors burst open, and a company of GIGN deployed across the length of the bridge. Snipers armed with M82s took positions in the downstream bastions. The rest of the company draped a curtain of heavy chains over the bridge's arches. The chains reached down into the river. *And that would be Operation Dragon Fortress,* thought Harper. Meaning no matter what, Batobus *Manon* was not getting beyond Pont Neuf.

He checked his watch again: three minutes.

"Right then."

He stepped from the shadows, marched toward Pont des Arts. He saw a platoon of French police storm Pont des Arts from the Right Bank. They were decked out in body armor and helmets with blast shields. They were armed with PSR assault rifles. The locals on the bridge made way for the platoon, many of them capturing the action on their mobile phones. The platoon's lieutenant raised his mask and yelled through a loudspeaker:

"Évacuez le pont! Évacuez le pont!"

The locals were hesitant to leave the bridge till the lieutenant pulled his sidearm and double-tapped the sky with warning shots. Civilians ran without thinking, bodies were pushed back onto Quai de Conti. Tires screeched as cars and buses plowed into one another trying to avoid the crowd. One taxi lost control and ran onto the sidewalk. It crashed into the embankment wall and rolled. A man and women, too slow to escape, their terrified faces caught in the headlights, were crushed. Panic took hold, and the locals stampeded straight at Harper. He pushed against the mob, headed for the dead and dying. He pulled his mobile, connected to Control in Berne.

"Casualties on the Left Bank at Pont des Arts, Inspector. Request comforters on site."

"Negative. All comforters have been evacuated from the target zone."

"Say again?"

"We cannot afford to lose comforters in the blast."

Harper looked up, saw long shreds of black mist race through the sky. They caught the high turrets of the Louvre and slithered down the limestone walls.

"The devourers already smell death," Harper said. "They're closing in."

The inspector's voice was steady. "You are ordered to disregard casualties and continue with intercept. You know how it is."

Harper watched shreds of black mist claw their way over the river, following the scent of dying souls.

"No choice?"

"None. Good luck, Mr. Harper."

Harper saw the lieutenant setting his platoon across Pont des Arts. The barrels of their rifles balancing on the guardrails, taking aim at the *Manon*.

"Hate to tell you this, Inspector," Harper said, "but good luck just got harder."

He dropped the mobile in his pocket, raised his SIG above his head, and forced his way through the locals.

"Move! Get out of the way!"

He jumped onto the hood of a crumpled van, looked downriver again. Searchlights on the police choppers had found the *Manon*. The boat's speed now cut to a crawl. Good news: Slowing down buys a couple of minutes. Bad news: It gives the police on Pont des Arts plenty of time to lock sights on the target. The lieutenant took his position behind the firing line, his voice screeching through the loudspeaker: *"A mon ordre, ouvre le feu pour éliminer!"*

"For Christ's sake, wait!"

Harper fired a round into the sky. *CRACK!*

The lieutenant turned to see a man in a beat-up coat, pistol in hand, jumping from the top of a van and running toward the bridge. The lieutenant turned, raised his sidearm, drew a bead on Harper. So did three police with assault rifles. Harper froze in his tracks, slowly pointing his SIG Sauer to the ground. He spoke calmly. *"Écoutez, Lieutenant, il y a une arme nucléaire à bord."*

The officer wasn't impressed. He ordered Harper to drop his weapon. *"Posez votre armes!"*

"Lieutenant, listen, you kill the bomber, the bomb still activates."

An earsplitting growl buried Harper's voice as the two choppers swooped in and hovered three meters above the bridge. The downdraft knocked the police off balance and Harper to his knees. Searchlights bore down with an otherworldly light that crawled over the wooden planks. The light broke into streaks and illuminated the Plexiglas-topped boat passing slowly beneath the bridge. One half-breed in the pilot's cabin, three more taking firing positions at the bow, surviving hostages gathered in the center of the cabin. All the half-breeds armed with UZIs and AKs . . . *Where's the fucking bomber?* Then Harper saw him. He was crouched at the stern, shooting up a hypo's worth of dead black potion. Harper saw the deadman's switch in the goon's left hand, saw the goon's fingers twitching against the trigger pad. Standard bad-guy slaughter kit. Release pressure, the device begins a nonstop ninety-second count-down. Gives the rest of the kill squad time to transmigrate into shadows and escape before the blast. The goon dropped the hypo, kicked back its head, ready to check out to the big nowhere.

"Bloody hell."

Harper grabbed the meshed fencing of the bridge, struggled to pull himself up against the downdraft. He felt the barrel of a gun at the back of his neck, heard the French lieutenant scream through the choppers: "Drop your weapon, English bastard, or I'll fire."

"Mate, what part of nuclear fucking weapon *don't* you understand?"

"Drop it!"

Harper dropped his SIG on the planks.

"Hands to your back!"

Harper did as ordered, watching the *Manon* clear the cutwaters of Pont des Arts and crawl toward Île de la Cité. The French police on Pont Neuf had a clear shot at the Batobus, and they opened up with a hail of bullets into the pilot's cabin. The *Manon* stalled, then the night exploded as the goons returned fire. Tracer rounds ripped through the dark at seven hundred meters per second and ricochets sparked on the bastions of Pont Neuf. Rapid-fire reports echoed through the heart of Paris like jackhammers on speed.

The lieutenant turned his eyes to the firefight for a second. It was all the second Harper needed. He scooped up his SIG, knocked the lieutenant to the floorboards, saw the boat pulling farther away, saw half the police on Pont des Arts taking aim at the *Manon* . . .

"Shit."

He reached inside his coat, pulled a small glass vial from his weapons rig, and smashed the vial onto the wooden planks of the bridge.

"Et facta est lux."

There was a blinding flash of blue light before Pont des Arts disappeared in thick, churning fog. Harper tossed the SIG to his left hand, pulled a killing knife with his right. He jumped for the guardrail—at least where he remembered it to be before it disappeared in the fog. He caught the rail with his foot, balanced for the hundredth of a second it took to work trajectory . . .

"Old tricks being what they are and all."

He jumped into the fog.

IV

THE GOON AT THE STERN OF THE *MANON* SAW THE FLASH OF LIGHT and the fog envelop the bridge; it was drifting toward him now. But with 30 cc of dead black rushing through his blood, it was all part of the groove in knowing mass death was about to be unleashed at his hand. The human skins would inhale the agony potion, blisters and burns would form in mouths and tracheae, they'd choke to death. And now, bonded with radium, the agony potion would kill for a thousand years. The goon pulled off his balaclava and cursed the searchlights glowing weirdly in the fog.

"See me, watch me! I bring the world forever death!"

Soon he would be free. Soon he would be one of the devourers, roaming the world, feeding on the dying souls of men. He raised his fist to the searchlights.

"Tonight, tonight! I will feast!"

The dead black pumped harder through his veins. He began to let his fingers slip from the trigger pad . . . but he stopped . . . to behold a wondrous vision. A winged form in silhouette, descending through the churning and glowing fog. One arm rising with a small sword in hand, the other hand pointing down to him. The goon's eyes widened.

"Yes, yes! My Lord and Father! You have come to carry me to the darkness! Father, I open my arms to receive your blessing!"

V

HARPER CRASHED DOWN, SLAMMED THE GOON TO THE DECK. HE swung his killing knife, sliced off the goon's trigger hand, rammed the SIG's barrel into the unbelieving thing's gaping mouth.

"Receive this instead, pal."

He pulled the trigger, blew apart the goon's skull. He flipped the dead thing onto its belly, sliced open the backpack. The bomb was in a sealed plastic box, one meter long by half a meter wide. Inside: a shape-charged, high-explosive device surrounded by aluminum tubes. Try and fuck with it, it'd blow. His eyes followed the jumble of wires to a small isolated compartment where a digital timer counted down bad news.

"Seventy seconds."

Quick scan of the cabin.

Hostages amidships, out of their minds with fear, screaming as bullets ripped over their heads. Three goons firing off the bow toward the police on Pont Neuf, one more crouched behind the controls driving the boat ahead . . .

One goon missing.

Then a form rushed from starboard, an UZI blasting from its hands. Harper ducked behind the dead bomber as thirty rounds ripped off in three seconds. The cabin's Plexiglas shell shattered to bits. Harper raised his eyes—the goon had been targeting police speedboats off to port. Harper raised his SIG, the goon caught the move and turned to fire. Harper beat him to the trigger with two rounds to the head. The goon dropped.

"Fifty seconds."

Harper looked for a way to get at the bomb. Plastic casing, quarter inch thick. He dug at the corners with his killing knife. He heard the hostages scream, saw another goon coming straight at him. Harper threw his killing knife. The blade caught the thing in the stomach. It squealed, stumbled ahead, fell on Harper. Harper pulled the knife from its guts, the goon crumbled to its knees. Harper rammed the knife into the back of its neck, severed spine from brain. He kicked the dead thing over the side.

"Twenty seconds."

He smashed at the bomb casing with the butt of the bloodied knife.

10, 9, 8 . . .

He lifted his SIG from the deck, set the muzzle on the casing, pointed it at the timer.

. . . 5, 4, 3 . . .

"Welcome to Plan B."

He closed his eyes and squeezed the trigger. He heard the report of the bullet, waited for the blast of the bomb. It didn't happen. He opened his eyes. The bullet had blown the timer to pieces.

"Zero."

The searchlights blinked off and on. Harper looked up to the choppers. The police had been watching him struggle with the bomb and blow its brains out. He raised a thumbs-up to the light. As if getting the message, the choppers pulled away and the snipers on Pont Neuf sent a volley of fuck-this-shit into the *Manon*. *CRACK! CRACKCRACK!*

The boat lurched ahead and turned in a wide loop. Harper saw the hostages' faces, the sudden speed like mainlining terror. He rolled over, saw one bullet-ridden goon dead at the controls, another in the same condition nearby. Then on the bow, caught in the glare of searchlights, the last goon rising without a shadow to piss in. Harper squeezed the grip of his SIG to activate the laser sight and light up the kill spot between the goon's eyes.

"So, hotshot, any last words?"

The goon slowly raised its hands in surrender, turned around. Harper saw the half-dead eyes under the balaclava break into a smile.

"Acta est fabula, plaudite."

Harper ran the words: *The play is over, applaud* . . . last words of Emperor Augustus. Harper squeezed the trigger.

"Not bad."

The back of the goon's head blew apart in a spray of blood and brains. Harper crawled ahead, fired rounds into the skulls of his pals.

"Now stay dead."

Screams again.

Harper turned, saw two passengers pointing off the bow. The Batobus had come around, heading for Pont Neuf. In the searchlights Harper saw the chains hanging from the bastions . . . laden with four-sided hooks and razor wire. The chains wouldn't just entangle the *Manon*, they'd rip all human flesh to shreds. Harper rushed to the pilot house, pulled the dead goon from the controls. He tried to pull back on the throttle and shut down the engine, but it was jammed. He scanned the riverbanks. Stone embankment to port, wood-hulled barge tied up to starboard.

"Swell."

He turned the wheel to the right, pulled the dead goon back over the wheel to hold it in place. He dove back toward the hostages.

"Hold on!"

The boat rammed the barge with a sickening crunch. Benches ripping from planks, shards of Plexiglas cutting through the air, hostages skidding over the deck. The *Manon*'s hull rose from the water, slammed down, and shuddered as if hitting concrete. And with engines running full speed and the rudder now jammed to forty degrees, the stern came about wildly and rammed the chains hanging from the bridge. The *Manon* struggled like a fish on a line till the razor wire caught her propellers. The engines shrieked, sputtered to a stop. The *Manon* was dead in the water.

VI

T HE HOSTAGES LAY SCATTERED ABOUT THE CABIN LIKE BROKEN things. Harper scanned their eyes. He could already see the nightmares that would haunt them the rest of their lives. He got to his feet, holstered his SIG. The hostages stared at the bloodied knife in his right hand. Harper pulled the knife to his back.

"It's over. Help will be here soon."

He hurried aft, sliced the shoulder straps of the backpack from the headless bomber. He sheathed his knife, pulled off his coat, and lay it on the deck. Carefully, he slid the bomb from the bomber and lay it on his coat. He tied the coat's arms into a sling, lifted the bomb, and hurried to the bow. Here he could jump onto the barge, slip away in the shadows. He heard a voice:

"And kissed my cheek without a trace of fright."

Down at his feet, a little girl clinging to the body of a man.

Harper saw the gash across the man's throat. He checked the man's eyes for light. The man was dead, but his soul held on to the last breath as desperately as his daughter held him. Rules and regs flashed through Harper's mind. Stopped cold on *Do nothing to reveal yourself to men, even if it means abandoning a dying soul.*

Then came the sound of steel-toed boots pounding along the embankment heading for the *Manon*. *French coppers in full battle array*, Harper thought. He turned, walked away from the little girl and the dying man. He hurried past the hostages and jumped the rail and landed on the barge. His eyes followed the shadows, saw where he could move into them and slip away. He looked back over his shoulder at the wreckage of the *Manon. Could have been worse,* he told himself. He headed for the shadows, stopped . . .

"Sod it."

He jumped back aboard the *Manon.* The hostages, thinking the killing had returned, screamed with fright. Harper raised the palm of his right hand to their eyes.

"Transit umbra, lux permanet."

They quieted. Harper rushed through the cabin, knelt next to the little girl. Her head was resting on the man's chest, and her eyes stared blankly ahead. Harper knew she'd slipped into that terrible place of numbness human beings go when their souls are battered by unknowable things. He passed the palm of his hand before her face.

"Et non somnia visitet te."

She took a sharp breath, released it slowly, and fell to sleep.

Harper leaned over the dead man, called to his soul.

"Your daughter is safe now. The nightmares will pass her by. You can let go now, you're finished here. Be not afraid, this is how it happens."

TWO

HARPER HEARD TWO SETS OF STEPS MOVING DOWN A LONG HALL. His and whoever it was pushing him along. No use resisting. He had a black bag over his head and his hands were bound at his back with nylon cables, so the one guard pushing him had the power of fifty. At the end of the hall the guard pulled at Harper's shoulder.

"Arrêtez ici."

Harper stopped, heard a door slide open . . . *whoosh*.

The guard pushed Harper ahead two steps and told him to stand still; the door closed. Five beeps, then the sound of a second door sliding open in front of him. The guard pushed Harper ahead and told him to stand still again. Same drill two more times till he was guided into what smelled like a room of polished wood and pipe tobacco. An office or a study. And whoever occupied it was locked up behind four hermetically sealed doors. Harper felt himself led across a wooden floor, then onto a carpet. The guard ordered him to sit. Luckily, there was a chair waiting for him. The guard cut the cables from Harper's hands, pulled the bag from Harper's head.

He was in a room of cream-colored walls and furniture that looked like it'd been seconded from Versailles. There was a crystal chandelier hanging from the ceiling and it filled the room with warm light. There was a Persian carpet under Harper's feet and a Louis XIV desk facing him. An empty armchair was parked behind the desk. It was embroidered with gold thread. No telephone or computer or papers on the desk. Just Harper's overcoat and sports coat lying in a lump. Three delicate chimes filled the room. Harper saw a gilt-bronze clock on an ornate side table. The base of the clock was cloudlike, and the clock itself was held by two cherubs as if in flight. The sound of the chimes faded away, then there was just the ticking of the clock.

"So where the fuck am I?"

Whoosh.

Harper looked back over his shoulder; the guard was gone. He stretched his arms, noticed the gold emblem on the wall behind the desk. Scottish thistle in the center, the words "Brigade Criminelle" curving above it. His mind scanned episodes of the History Channel. Half a second later he knew where he was. Brigade Criminelle, 36 Quai des Orfèvres, Île de la Cité. HQ of the French police once known as la Sûreté, the model for Scotland Yard and every hard-nosed cop squad in Europe. Words curved below the thistle: *Qui s'y frotte, s'y pique.*

Harper ran the words: *If you rub against it, it will sting.* A quaint expression French mothers told their children to warn them about the obvious dangers of life. Like playing with fire, or crossing a road without looking both ways. From the lips of Brigade Criminelle, Harper imagined the warning to translate more like: *Screw with us, you'll get one of these up your arse.*

"Even more terrific."

To the right of the desk, a leather-backed door was cut into the wall. Looked like any door till it clacked and thunked and opened on hydraulic hinges. A small gray-headed gent in his late sixties stepped through the doorway and entered the room. He was dressed in a rumpled suit, carried a stack of files under his arm. There was a briar pipe anchored between his teeth, and a trail of smoke followed him as he shuffled to the desk. That's when Harper noticed the man was wearing bedroom slippers instead of shoes.

The steel door eased closed automatically and locked.

Thunk. Clack.

The man pushed Harper's coats aside and dropped the files onto the desk. He took his time arranging them side by side before sitting in his armchair and emptying his pipe into an ashtray. Harper watched the man open a drawer, rummage through the contents, pull out a pouch of Bergerac tobacco. The man reloaded the pipe and lit up. Harper heard a voice emerge from the cloud of smoke that had swallowed the man's head.

"Mon nom est Bruno Silvestre. Je suis le juge d'instruction spéciale pour . . ."

The introduction continued according to the French tradition of never using three words when twelve will do. Gave Harper a moment to think. Any minute, Inspector Gobet's time mechanics would drop a time warp over the place and the cleanup crew would move in. They'd sort the bomb, they'd make any sign of Harper having been there disappear. Nothing to do but stall.

"Sorry, gov, I don't speak French."

"Non?"

"No."

The man opened the file farthest to his left. He flipped through the first three pages. Harper saw a gold signet ring on the little finger of the man's left hand. He couldn't make out the insignia.

"In the arrest report, the GIGN commander at the scene states you spoke French on Pont des Arts, with an English accent."

"He's mistaken," Harper said.

"How could he be mistaken, monsieur?"

"There was a chopper a few meters above our heads. Two of them, in fact. It was loud. Understandably, your GIGN commander at the scene got it wrong."

"Choppers, monsieur?"

"Helicopters."

"Ah, je comprends."

The man took a fountain pen from his jacket and made a notation in the margin of the page, mumbling to himself.

"... *les hélicoptères ... à quelques mètres ... au dessus des têtes ... très fort.*"

He tapped the page with an emphatic period and closed the file.

"*Alors.* I am Bruno Silvestre. I am the special investigating judge for the Brigade Criminelle. Because of the unique nature of the evidence collected so far, I requested to review certain facts in your case. Do you understand what I am saying to you now?"

"Sure."

"*Bon*, then we may begin."

The man who called himself a judge removed a set of mug shots, held them up for Harper to see.

"Is this you, monsieur?"

Head-on and profile shots of a bloke with light brown hair, green eyes, a handsome enough face to suggest someone of well-bred English stock. Other physical characteristics were listed at the side of the photos. Height: 1.95 meters, estimated weight: 80–85 kilos, estimated age: 36–39, name: blank.

"I'm sorry, gov. What was the question?"

"Is this you, monsieur?"

"In a manner of speaking."

"*Pardonnez-moi?*"

"I said, in a manner of speaking."

"That this is you in the photographs?"

"It's complicated."

The judge nodded, puffed on his pipe, lay the mug shots on the desk.

"Who are you, monsieur?"

"Me? I'm a tourist. In town to see the sights."

The judge opened the next file, pulled out a handful of photographs, fanned them across the desk like a deck of cards. All of them tinted with the green glow of a night vision lens. POV said the photos were taken from the police choppers tracking the *Manon*. Harper scanned the shots. Him blowing the bomber's brains out, him slashing open a goon's throat and tossing the dead thing over the side, him drilling bullets through the skulls of two more dead goons and summarily executing the last goon standing.

"For a tourist in town to see the sights, monsieur, you have had a very busy night. By the way, how did you know there was a weapon of mass destruction aboard the *Manon*? I only ask because the police did not know this. There was no mention of it in the original tip-off."

Harper didn't answer.

The judge pulled out a white card and held it up. Harper saw ten black smudges all in a row.

"Your fingerprints were taken immediately after you were brought to the Brigade Criminelle at twenty-one hundred hours this evening."

Harper flashed back.

Bagged and tagged by the police aboard the *Manon*, dragged up the embankment steps, thrown into the back of a police van. Facedown on the floor, heavy boots on his back and neck. Van sped through the streets, sirens screaming till it slammed to a stop. Hauled out, dragged into a building, and shoved up against a wall. Police pulled the bag from his head. "Smile, roast beef," one policeman said. They snapped the mug shots, bagged him again. Not daring to let him loose, they twisted his bound hands, inked his fingertips, and pressed them to paper. Then one of the police grabbed him, led him down concrete stairs, tossed him into an isolation cell. Quiet. The kind that'd drive a man insane if he stayed in it too long. Harper slowed his heart rate to hibernation mode. Slow breaths, stillness. Wasn't a sound till five hours later when the cell door opened and a lone guard led him to the judge's office. The whole trip through beforetimes took a half second.

"Yes," Harper said. "I seem to recall something like that."

The judge tossed fingerprints onto the desk. They skidded to a stop in front of Harper.

"Your prints have been reviewed by every police department and security agency in Europe and North America. Several times, with no result. We expanded the search worldwide. As yet there has not been a single match; not even a possibility of a match. The odds of such a thing for a European male of your age and race, not to mention your obvious special forces training, are less than zero."

Harper gave it five seconds.

"I'm not European."

"Pardonnez-moi?"

"I'm not European. I'm British."

The judge took his pen and made a note in the file.

"Le suspect . . . dit qu'il est . . . britann . . . ique."

The judge opened the next file, pulled out six more fingerprint cards, dealt them onto the desk.

"These fingerprints belong to the men who carried out the attack aboard the *Manon*. They have proven to be slightly more interesting than yours."

"How's that?"

"Because there are no fingerprints."

Harper shrugged. "Wouldn't be the first criminals to have their prints surgically removed."

"Very true. And it is a known practice by members of Muqatileen Lillah before a suicide mission. But this is the finest work I have ever seen. Not the hint of a loop, or a whorl, or a ridge. It is as if these men were born without fingerprints. Either way, you may appreciate my problem."

Where the hell is he going with this?

"Depends. What's your problem?" Harper said.

"Monsieur, there was a battle in the center of Paris tonight. A battle that saw nine innocent human beings slaughtered. But none of the combatants, including the one survivor, can be identified."

"I had nothing to do with the civilian deaths, gov."

The judge looked back through the arrest report.

"Non, you are only a British tourist in town to see the sights, who appeared from nowhere and attempted to stop the French security forces from the exercise of their lawful duty on Pont des Arts. You then disappeared in an unexplained flash of light and fog, only to reappear aboard the *Manon* where you disarmed a weapon of mass destruction in the

most reckless manner possible, then executed six men dressed in black jumpsuits and balaclavas. You then attempted to remove the WMD from the scene, but were subdued and arrested by the French police. Would that be an accurate description of what you did do?"

Harper sat still for a long moment, analyzing the man's voice. The old gent was bland as Muzak and couldn't be read.

"Speaking of the bomb, gov, where is it?"

The judge took a considered puff from his pipe.

"It was placed in a hazardous containment unit and is now in the process of being transferred to a secure location."

"A military base, you mean. Where a pack of generals is waiting to get their hands on it, see what makes it tick."

The judge's silence was an affirmative.

"Mind if I give you a little advice, gov?"

"I welcome it, monsieur."

"Tell your generals not to open it. Better yet, tell them not to even look at it."

"Why not, monsieur?"

"Because it isn't a bomb. It's Pandora's fucking box."

The judge nodded, wrote slowly in the file.

"Pandora's . . . fucking . . . box."

Harper heard the ticking of the clock. He checked it; twenty after the hour. The inspector's time mechanics were taking their bloody time. He rubbed the back of his neck, feeling the weight of his form pressing down.

Need a hit of radiance, boyo.

"You are expected somewhere else, monsieur?"

"Sorry?"

"I notice you watching the clock."

"Just passing the time. Listen, I've got some fags in my coat. Mind if I grab one?"

The judge sucked on his pipe, filled the room with smoke.

"I am afraid smoking is forbidden in the office of Brigade Criminelle, monsieur."

"Of course it is."

The judge opened file number four, laid out individual shots of the dead goons.

"Would you please confirm these are the men you killed aboard the *Manon*?"

First up: a slashed throat under a face that had been chopped to pieces by the *Manon*'s propellers after Harper threw him into the river. Next five shots: one goon each, skulls blown open by multiple head shots.

"Sure, that's them."

"Who are they, monsieur?"

"Terrorists. From Muqatileen Lillah."

The judge shook his head.

"Members of Muqatileen Lillah are exclusively South Asian. Their manifesto decrees them to be the chosen race of God. Never has a person of another race been included in their number. Despite your handiwork in deconstructing their skulls, initial examination suggests the men are not Asian. These men appear to be Caucasian of undetermined ancestry."

Harper shrugged.

"Would've thought if it looks like a terrorist and kills like a terrorist, it's a terrorist," Harper said.

The judge waved the mouthpiece of his pipe over the dead goons.

"Monsieur, you and I both know these men were not terrorists. These killers were only posing as terrorists."

Harper read the man's eyes. Pale blue, normal luminance levels in the irises, clear of dead black. The man was human, nothing more. *How in the hell can he know?*

"Not sure I follow you, gov."

"*Non?*"

The judge pulled a series of photos from the next file, laid them on the desk. They'd been blown up ten times. Grainy as hell, but clear enough. Harper with the bomb wrapped in his coat, jumping for the railings to escape the *Manon* like a crook on the lam; then returning. A white grease pencil circled Harper raising the palm of his right hand before the eyes of the survivors, then the little girl. Another circle targeted Harper leaning over the dead man.

"At first, I was ready to accept the supposition of the Interior Ministry that you are a paid assassin working for a foreign government. The Israeli Mossad, most probably, as they have recently been quite active in assassinating members of Muqatileen Lillah. In line with that supposition, I assumed this dead man with the little girl was part of the plot. Someone evil enough to sacrifice his own child to achieve his ends. And I thought you had returned to the *Manon* to be assured he was dead. But this man is identifiable, and he has fingerprints. His name is Abu Jad, a cardiac physician from Beirut. He was taking his daughter on a birthday cruise."

"So?"

"Monsieur. You are a highly skilled killer. I am very sure your mission was to escape with the bomb so that it would not fall into the hands of men in search of more efficient ways of destroying one another. Yet you gave up your one chance of escape to offer comfort to a little girl and a dead man."

Harper stared at the judge. "So?"

The judge tapped the photos of the dead goons. "We both know these terrorists are not human. We both know they are evil made flesh, hiding among men as they have done through the ages."

"Is that a fact?"

"*Oui, monsieur,* and it is a fact that has revealed to me who, and what, you are. And I have been waiting for your return to Paris many, many years."

The clock chimed three thirty. Harper listened to the sound circle the room like it was looking for a way out. Then he noticed the lack of windows in the place, then the carefully fitted acoustic panels in the walls. And getting into the office was like breaking into a bank vault. The office had to be a shell within a shell, with phase cancellation frequencies blasting between the walls maybe. Harper added it up: By accident or design, the inspector's time mechanics couldn't get a track on him. Harper leaned forward in his chair, trying to lock his eyes on the judge;

trying to figure if the setup was an accident, or if the elderly gent in bedroom slippers knew what he was doing.

"Listen to me, gov; whoever, or whatever, you think I am, you've got the wrong man."

Harper watched the judge pull the last file to the center of the desk. It was thick and yellowed with age. It was bound with blue ribbon, and the ribbon was secured with a red wax seal. The judge blew away a layer of dust and opened the file, slowly sorted through the onionskin pages. Harper saw the words were handwritten with a fine script. When the judge found the page he was looking for, he began to read aloud.

"Your name is Jay Michael Harper. Your father was a lawyer at Gray's Inn who paid his way through law school working as a bartender in the West End. It was during that time that your father met your mother, the daughter of a member of the board of Coutts and Company. She was an only child. Your parents fell in love, and you were conceived early on in the relationship. They planned to marry. Your mother's parents did not approve of the match and disowned her. Your parents married in a civil court and lived above a grocer's shop on Tottenham Court Road. You were born seven months later at University College London Hospital. The following Christmas your mother's parents saw you, and as it often happens upon seeing a grandchild for the first time, they reconciled with your mother. They bought a house for your parents on Carlingford Road, very close to Hampstead Heath. This is where you were raised . . ."

Harper saw a little boy running up three flights of stairs, then climbing the ladder to the attic. Building a fortress of crates and cardboard boxes to hold off Mau Mau attackers. Harper could smell the dust, see the boy standing on the boxes, wooden stick as a righteous sword in hand and rallying his imaginary army: "To the last for Queen and Country!"

He blinked, the judge still reading.

"You were educated at Highgate School, where you distinguished yourself as a rugby left wing. You went on to the University of St. Andrews, where you distinguished yourself at right wing and geography studies. During your graduate year, your parents were killed when a gasoline delivery truck plowed headlong into their car. Your maternal grandparents died of cancer within six months of each other in your fourteenth year. You had no siblings, no aunts, no uncles or cousins. You quit university and traveled through Europe. You were left a sizable inheritance, so money was not a problem. But you sensed your life to be in need of direction and you obtained a commission in the Coldstream Guards through Brigadier Sir Malcolm Holloway, a close friend of your parents. You began your military career with No. 7 Company, but had yourself transferred to 1st Battalion. You distinguished yourself in reconnaissance skills. You were also rated as an exceptionally good shot. In April of 2004, you were tapped by the director of Special Forces to join the newly formed Special Reconnaissance Regiment as an intelligence officer. You were involved with the Jean Charles de Menezes shooting at Stockwell tube station in 2005 from the standpoint that it was you who warned your superiors the Metropolitan Police had misidentified the target. Unfortunately, your warnings were not acted upon and an innocent man was shot dead. You were kept from testifying before an inquiry and you resigned your commission in protest. Your resignation was not accepted. In the following month you were seconded to a top secret search-and-destroy unit known as Foxtrot 9. The unit was based at Al Minhad Air Base in the United Arab Emirates and referred to in all communications as the Gulf Institute for Agricultural Security and Sustainability."

The judge looked at Harper.

"Une histoire intéressante, non?"

Harper stared at the judge, trying not to give away the fact that he was bloody well gobsmacked. He'd just heard more about Captain Jay Michael Harper than he'd ever been allowed to know since he was awakened in the dead man's form. And hearing it, Harper knew it was all true, not because he could remember it, but because he could feel the weight of the dead man's flesh and blood press down on his eternal being. He tried to shake it off. *Christ, what's keeping the inspector's lads?*

"Rather run-of-the-mill tale for an English schoolboy," Harper said.

"Then you will not be surprised to hear what happens next?"

"What's that, then?"

"You die."

The weight pressed down.

"A misprint, I'm sure."

"Let me see . . . *a été tué* . . . *Non, c'est très clair,* you are quite dead. You were killed in the northwest tribal regions of Pakistan."

A burst of images rushed through Harper's eyes: Lights out on a chopper. Take off from Bagram Airfield, Kabul, Afghanistan. Night mission to infil target, ten klicks west of Af-Pak border. Dismount. Chopper breaks off. Quiet. Double-time it up and over the mountain, cross the border into Pakistan.

The judge's voice:

"You and three men from Foxtrot 9 were involved in a covert mission with orders to track and eliminate Taliban assets in the Parachinar Valley . . ."

Skirt the villages, crawl through farms, find an abandoned farmhouse before dawn. Five hundred meters south of Burgi, fifty meters off Boarki Road. Place stocked with food, gas, local dress. There is a gassed-up Toyota pickup truck hidden under a tarp. The mission is go.

"What you did not know was that the mission was doomed from the start, betrayed by a high-level member of ISI, Pakistan intelligence . . ."

Waiting for the contact to show. Pak spook assigned to drive and translate. Men changing into salwar kameez and sandals, then cleaning their weapons. One of them, ginger-haired lad from Cardiff. Ellis is his name, checking the five-round magazine of his L115 sniper rifle. Looks silly as hell with a taqiyah cap on his head. Good lad. Wasn't going to take Ellis this time because of his hair, till Ellis said, "Beggin' your fuckin' pardon, sir, but there's plenty of ginger heads in Pakland courtesy of the Raj. Your bloody lot couldn't keep it zipped around all those dark-eyed beauties."

Just now, Ellis singing a Welsh lullaby: *"Huna blentyn ar fy Mynwes . . ."* Hear a racket outside . . . fifteen pickup trucks packed with heavily armed Hajis. But instead of continuing along Boarki Road, they turn up the dirt track, head straight for the farmhouse.

Captain Jay Michael Harper: "We've got company, lads."

Hajis circle the house, blast away. One Haji with a video camera, standing on the back of a truck, filming the action. The assault is overpowering. Two of his men dead in the first five minutes. Ellis takes a shot in the chest. Cease-fire. Haji, with very proper Brit accent, calling over a bullhorn: "Surrender, we will not harm you. You have three minutes to decide. Live or die."

Captain Harper crawls to Ellis. The lad's life slipping away . . . "Don't want my mum to see my body tied to the back of a truck and dragged through the streets, Captain." Then he's gone.

Captain Jay Michael Harper: "No worries, mate."

Pulls the dead men together. Covers them with their uniforms and boots, blankets and mattresses. Dumps two cans of gasoline over the lot, sets it alight. Flash of fire, room fills with smoke. Voice with the bullhorn still calling: "You have one minute. Will you live or will you die?"

Grabs the L115, crawls to the next room, aims through a glass window, and drills an 8.59-caliber round through the bullhorn and into the loudmouth's head. Drops the rifle, crawls to the back of the house as the Hajis open up again. Sits in the corner, watches the fire down the hall. Pulls his sidearm, sets the death end in his mouth, points it to his brain . . . Almost laughs remembering a little boy atop a cardboard fortress in the attic of Carlingford Road . . . *To the last for Queen and Country!*

The judge's voice coming around again . . .

"Two days later, a Taliban website posted video of what it claimed to be a firefight with British forces on the sovereign soil of Pakistan. The house was consumed by fire in the battle. So much so that all the Taliban had for proof were the charred remains of humans and British weapons. Upon analysis of the tape, British intelligence realized one of their soldiers had escaped the fire . . ."

Finger on the trigger.

Captain Jay Michael Harper: "Do it, boyo! Do it!"

RPG crashes through the window, explodes, knocks the gun from Harper's hands. Door at the back of the house breaks open. Hajis charge in, grab Captain Harper, drag him outside, throw him in the back of a pickup, and speed away.

"There was a mystery as to what happened to the fourth man . . ."

Beatings. Sleep deprivation. Grinding out cigarettes in his flesh. Screams. Holding him, keeping his existence secret, waiting for the Holy One of God to come from Rawalpindi to torture and slay the infidel personally. Video camera already set to film the slaughter. Can't take much more. Hajis go to pray, leave one guard. Pretend to sleep . . . Lone guard sets his AK-47 on the ground, kneels to pray. Gather what strength is left, jump and snap the fucker's neck. Grab the AK, crawl into the dark.

The judge's voice again:

"Six weeks later, a farmer found a shallow grave containing human remains, burned beyond recognition. In a gesture of cooperation, the ISI of Pakistan notified the British Embassy of the discovery and invited their council. DNA tests were inconclusive, but the MOD judged the remains to be yours and declared you dead."

Harper blinked, found himself back in the judge's office. He tried to lift himself from the chair, couldn't move. The weight . . . crushing down . . . the judge staring at him.

"But here you are, alive and well and killing in Paris."

Harper felt the phantom of a dead man begin to stir.

He looked down at his hands.

They were shaking.

How the hell can he know this, any of it? Every trace of the man should have been destroyed. Slowly, like a dead man rising, he lifted his eyes to the judge.

"Who the hell are you, and what the fuck do you want?"

The judge closed the file. Puffed from his pipe before laying it in the ashtray.

"Mon nom est Bruno Silvestre. Je suis le juge d'instruction spéciale pour la Brigade Criminelle. And what I want, monsieur, is to help you."

The clock chimed four a.m. Then came the sound of both doors opening at once. *Whoosh, thunk, clunk* . . . Four French GIGN police marched in, dressed for a riot. Two with submachine guns pointed at Harper, one with plastic ties and a black hood in his hands. The last one laid an official document on the judge's desk. A set of gloved hands grabbed Harper's shoulders and pulled him to his feet. Two seconds later, Harper's own hands were bound at his back. The copper began to pull the black bag over Harper's head, but Harper shook him off. The copper rammed a Taser into Harper's back and let go with fifty thousand volts. Harper's muscles seized up and he dropped to his knees. The copper grabbed him and hauled him to his feet again. Took Harper a few seconds to get his mouth working.

"This your idea of offering help?"

The judge looked up from the document. "I regret we could not understand each other earlier. Any help I may have been able to offer has been superseded by a development, monsieur."

"What sort of development?"

"Pandora's fucking box has disappeared."

"The bomb?"

"When the containment unit arrived at its destination and was opened, the bomb from the *Manon* was gone. You are suspected of knowing how such a thing could happen."

So that was the order of battle, Harper thought. The inspector's lads went for the WMD first, leaving him holding the shit end of the stick. Leaving Harper to wonder how shitty it could get.

"And what happens to me?"

The judge read from the paper in his hand.

"By order of the president of the French Republic, you are hereby denied due process under the Code of Criminal Procedure, and all rights guaranteed under Article Nine of the Declaration of the Rights of Man and of the Citizen are rescinded. You will be transferred, without delay, to La Santé Prison to be subjected to enhanced interrogation at the hands of the Direction Centrale du Renseignement Intérieur."

"Sounds like a place where the screws punch first, ask questions later."

The judge looked at Harper.

"I'm afraid, monsieur, you will find the conditions at La Santé extremely difficult."

"How hard can it be, gov, if you're already dead?"

The black bag came down on Harper's head.

THREE

MAX WAS SLEEPING. THOUGH EVERY ONCE IN A WHILE HE'D SUCK at the sippy cup and the milk would leak onto his lips. Katherine eased away the cup, dabbed runaway drops from Max's chin. She carried him to the crib, laid him down for a nap. He shuddered, then settled. She covered him with a blanket, blew out the candle, and turned on the crib monitor. She left the room, pulled close the door. A fat ball of gray fur was waiting in the hall, its tail plopping from side to side, blocking the way forward.

"Hello, fuzzface. Suppose you're hungry, too?"

Mew.

"C'mon."

Monsieur Booty followed at Katherine's ankles as she walked down the hall. She passed Officer Jannsen's room. She was sitting on her bed, tapping the keys of a laptop. A Glock pistol was strapped to her hip. Katherine stepped into the room. She caught the scent of Chanel and gun grease.

"Chatting with your boyfriend?"

"Filing today's stat report with Berne."

"I hope you're telling the inspector I've been a good girl."

"*Bien sûr.* I also told him you qualified on the firing range. How was the shop this morning?"

"Making more candles than I'm selling, but who cares?"

"Max asleep?"

"Yeah, he'll be out for a couple hours. I'm going to have a hot bath."

Officer Jannsen checked her watch. Katherine shrugged and walked off. Their voices chased each other back and forth down the hall.

"I know, tea before bath."

"See, you are a good girl."

"This must-be-punctual-in-all-things stuff makes me want to scream sometimes."

"It's good for you. Builds character."

"You say that about everything I hate doing."

"I know. It's the best part of my job."

Katherine walked down the stairs and into the sitting room. It was a large open space with a high timbered ceiling, floor-to-ceiling windows looking out to the edge of a forest. Mount Hood, across the river in Oregon, peaked above the trees and pointed to that glowing spot in the clouds where the sun was hiding. It was a nice view. Sometimes she'd see a deer walking through the trees. Sometimes a small black bear or a fox; sometimes it'd be one of the Swiss Guards patrolling the perimeter with a Brügger & Thomet submachine gun in his hands. But now, there were only the trees.

She picked up a copy of *The New Yorker* from the sofa. She thumbed through the pages on her way to the kitchen, checking if there were any cartoons she'd missed. Monsieur Booty was already sitting by his food dish. If the beast had fingers instead of claws, they'd be tapping the floor.

"Oh, get a grip."

She dropped the magazine on the kitchen table, opened a cabinet, and pulled out a bag of cat food. She fed the beast, scratched it behind the ears, then walked to the sink and turned on the water pump. She picked up the kettle and filled it from the tap. She looked out the window, saw the small garden at the back of the house. The garden, like the front of the house, backed up to dense forest; in fact, the whole place was surrounded by dense forest. And each time she looked at it, she felt safe. She switched on the kettle, opened her box of magic teas. That's what she called them, anyway.

They were from a health food shop in Grover's Mill and they came in mason jars. Her doctor in Portland prescribed them as part of her recovery. This one in the morning, that one at midday; this tea for afternoons, that one before bed. It was part of her daily regimen. Along with no cigarettes, no alcohol, no drugs. Then again, with a box of magic teas, who needs dope? Especially when the teas had names sounding like the exotic strains of weed she used to buy at her favorite head shop on Santa Monica Boulevard. Morning Light, Midday Buzz, Night Clouds. She prepared the afternoon blend, Violette's Garden. Something for the remembrance of pleasant memories, the man at the shop told her. There was a quote from some dead poet on the back label:

> *Each violet peeps from its dwelling to gaze at the bright stars above.*
> *—Heinrich Heine*

The kettle clicked off. Katherine saw rain pelting the kitchen window.

"Not here, Heinrich old boy. This is the land the stars forgot, and the sun most days."

She poured the boiling water into the teapot to brew. She inhaled the fragrance and a feeling of calm came over her, the way it always did. She arranged the pot and cup and saucer on a tray, and she carried it to the table. She lit a candle, sat down. She curled up her legs and pulled her bulky sweater over her knees. She watched the candle burn.

When she first came to the house, this comfy cabin in the middle of a wooded nowhere, nine and a half kilometers from the nearest town, she was in a daze. The last thing she remembered from back in Lausanne was telling Inspector Gobet she wanted to see the cathedral once more before leaving Switzerland. And she could remember standing on the esplanade, looking at the tower for a few minutes . . . Then Inspector Gobet took her by the arm and led her back to the car. They gave her a shot on the way to the airport, one of those shots that sent her off to Neverland. She didn't even remember boarding an airplane. Next thing she knew, she was here. And if they told her "here" was Miami Beach instead of the boondocks of Washington State, she wouldn't have known the difference.

She remembered wandering upstairs and downstairs and through the halls. The fat furry cat she'd carried all the way from Switzerland was still in her arms. She found her way to the kitchen. A small wooden table stood in the center of the room, two wooden chairs tucked under it. She walked around the table, counterclockwise, three times before dropping Monsieur Booty to the floor and pushing the table and chairs to the side of the room, blocking a counter and some cabinets. She had no idea why she'd done it, other than the table felt out of place where she'd found it. The next morning Katherine returned to the kitchen to find someone moved the table and chairs back to the center of the room. Katherine shoved them back to the wall. It went on like this for a week, till she wrote a note and tacked it to the kitchen door:

Whoever the fuck you are, leave the fucking table where I fucking put it.

The next day, the table was left against the wall. And every day since, Katherine would sit alone at the table with a pot of tea, watching a candle burn. One day, after a long week of rain, her eyes were drawn to a ray of light passing through the open door. She looked out to the garden, saw the clearing sky, saw the snow-covered peak of Mount Hood glowing in the light, and she realized why she needed the table to be here. It reminded her of the small table jutting from the wall in the belfry loge of Lausanne Cathedral. And some afternoons, sipping her tea, Katherine could almost see the crooked little man who lived in the loge . . . and after a time she remembered his name: Marc Rochat. Then she remembered how he found her running through the streets, knowing she was hunted by a pack of killers. He brought her into the cathedral to hide her because . . . because the crooked little man thought she was an angel who needed to find a way home. She remembered how he'd sit with her at the table and stare at her with a half-mad look in his eyes, telling her he was back with her in "nowtimes," and that he'd been in "beforetimes." And he had the funniest stories about the people he'd met along the way. She remembered how the belfry loge shook at the ringing of the hour, how it scared her to death at first. Rochat told her it was only Marie-Madeleine telling Lausanne the time. She remembered how on that last day, amid the cacophony of all the bells, the crooked little man saved her life, saved the cathedral he imagined to be a hiding place for her and all the lost angels in the world. She remembered looking down from the belfry and seeing him dead on the ground. She remembered calling his name, begging him to come back.

And there was another man, she thought, but she could never remember who he was, or if he was even real. As if the man was there and not there at the same time. Sometimes she thought she could almost see him, but each time her memory searched for a name, the man disappeared.

The clock above the kitchen door chimed four times.

Katherine stared at it, feeling something very strange, as if coming back to nowtimes. She looked at the calendar hanging from a hook on the wall.

"Two and a half years ago. Two and a half fucking years."

She poured a cup of tea and inhaled the fumes, wishing to remember more, but she couldn't. That's what made her feel she was still losing her mind—what was left of it, anyway. She talked to her doctor about it. He told her the depth of her trauma had altered her memory of events. Rewritten them into a scenario that made it easier for her to accept. The doctor told her it would be best to just let go of them. Better for her, better for the child growing within her body.

Katherine sipped her tea, laughed to herself.

"And wasn't he just the little surprise?"

Max Taylor.

Not Maxwell, no middle name, just Max. Six pounds, four ounces of screaming joy. Katherine took one look at him and called him Max, thinking the gooey runt was going to need all the help he could get. She sipped her tea and the memories continued to play through her mind like a film.

It wasn't till she got to Grover's Mill that she even realized she was pregnant. And not just a little pregnant, but four and a half months' worth of pregnant. At first, she thought she'd been putting on weight from the medications her doctors had prescribed, not to mention her appetite suddenly knowing no bounds. Then came the morning she stepped from the shower and saw herself in the mirror.

"Wait a minute—no way in hell is *that thing* my butt."

The more she studied her body, her breasts and her hips, the more she tried to remember the last time she had a period. She couldn't.

"Oh. My. God."

She threw on a robe, stormed out of the bathroom, and marched down the hall for a *what the fuck?* session with Officer Jannsen.

"Anne!"

Officer Jannsen ran up the stairs, her sidearm drawn, ready to fire.

"What's wrong?"

"You know damn well what's wrong."

Officer Jannsen holstered her weapon, leaned against the wall.

"Someone move the kitchen table again?"

"Fuck the kitchen table."

"All right then, what's the problem?"

"Problem? What could possibly be a problem? Everything's just so fucking fine. By the way, when were you planning to tell me about *this*?" Katherine said, pointing to her belly.

Officer Jannsen led Katherine to her room and sat her on the bed.

"You were brutalized, Katherine. You suffered severe mental and emotional trauma."

"Yeah, yeah, it's all about me. But in the middle of all this caring and sharing, why didn't anyone bother to tell me I was fucking pregnant?"

"The doctors in Switzerland, your doctors in Portland, all thought it best you discover it on your own. It would be a positive sign that you were reconnecting with reality. Telling you sooner would have created more shock and stress harmful to you and the baby."

"The baby? What makes you guys think I even want a baby? What makes you think I don't want to call Abortions-R-Us and get rid of it, like right fucking now?"

"Is that your choice, Kat? Is that what you really want to do?"

"What? Four and a half months gone, and *now* you offer me a choice? Why didn't all those fucking doctors in Switzerland make the decision for me? I was crazy, I was certifiable, wasn't I?"

"None of us is allowed to make that kind of choice."

"Why the fuck not? You choose everything else about my life. Where I live, who my doctors are, what I eat and drink. Jesus, I don't even know who the father is. I was gangbanged . . . How am I supposed to . . ."

Katherine felt a jolt, and she touched her belly. Officer Jannsen watched the look on Katherine's face.

"What is it?"

"The little bastard just kicked me."

"Are you sure?"

"Yeah. I mean, I think so."

Officer Jannsen sat next to her and rested her hands over Katherine's belly. There was a kick, then another, as if demanding to be part of the conversation.

"Seems to be of an opinionated mind. Like his mother, I'd say."

"You think?"

Officer Jannsen nodded.

"Listen to me, Katherine: We've monitored the baby from the beginning. You were given everything you needed to make sure the baby would be healthy. He's fine."

"It's a boy?"

"Yes, Kat, it's a healthy boy."

That night, after a triple shot of Night Clouds tea, Katherine lay in the moment of half sleep and she imagined herself standing in the nave of Lausanne Cathedral. It had been one of her favorite falling to sleep dreams. Light pouring through the giant leaded-glass window in the south transept wall. Bright, warm . . . like standing in the middle of a rainbow. She could feel the colors seep into her body. But that night, falling to sleep, she heard a voice in the dream. A voice telling her to be not afraid, that the life within her was pure, that she was the bearer of the light. Katherine knew it was a crazed imagination. But just now, drifting deeper into sleep, it was comforting.

Early the next morning, she decided to sneak out of the house for a walk. She wasn't twenty steps before Officer Jannsen stepped out from behind a tree.

"You're not supposed to leave the house alone."

"I'm not alone, I'm carrying a passenger, remember?"

"Where are you going?"

"I don't know. Town, I guess. It's only nine kilometers."

"Nine and a half. I'll go with you, Kat."

"I don't want you to go with me."

"Too bad."

Katherine watched Officer Jannsen pull a cell phone from her belt, dial some numbers, hit send. Then came the Glock from under her coat. She checked the magazine. That done, she pulled two matching gold rings from her pocket. She held one out to Katherine.

"Cripes sake, Anne, it's just a walk."

"You want to walk, this is how you walk. You don't like it, we go back to the house."

Katherine held up her left hand.

"Okay, I do."

Officer Jannsen slid a ring on Katherine, then herself.

They walked down the wooded drive to a narrow road. The road wound down a hill, not passing another house or driveway till they reached Carson Highway. They stopped at the edge of the road and waited for a timber-laden eighteen-wheeler to come and go. Katherine looked at Officer Jannsen, noticed the backpack over her shoulder was rather large.

"What's in the bag, a bazooka?" Katherine said.

ANGEL CITY

"One ballistic blanket, spare nine-millimeter clips, four stun grenades, one field medical kit, two liters O-neg blood."

Katherine rolled her eyes. "Jeez, Louise."

They crossed Carson Highway onto Rainbow Falls Road for six more kilometers before it ended at Grover's Mill; population 970, not including the bus tours to Rainbow Falls that passed through town, twice a week on Tuesday and Friday afternoons like clockwork. Officer Jannsen turned to Katherine.

"All right, we walked to town. Now what?"

"I'm hungry."

"There's food at the house."

"If I wanted food at the house, I would have stayed at the house."

They walked along Main Street to a place called Molly's Diner. Katherine had seen it in passing once, after a trip to the doctor down in Portland with Officer Jannsen and two bodyguards. Katherine remembered asking if they could stop and go in and have a cheeseburger and Coke. The answer was NO. The answer was always NO. And now, damn it, Katherine was going to have it *her* way.

The place was filled but for a corner booth. Katherine walked to it and slid in. Officer Jannsen followed her, took off the backpack, and set it on her side of the booth. There was a small jukebox mounted to the table. Katherine flipped through the selections.

"See, that wasn't so bad. Nobody even tried to kill me."

Officer Jannsen pulled out her cell, hit a few keys, pressed send.

"I'm not against you going out, Kat. But we have to be with you."

"Every minute of the day?"

"Yes."

Molly herself came over wearing a tie-dyed dress and a necklace of amber stones and peace symbols. Her hair looked like it had been born free and stayed that way all her life.

"Howdy, ladies. New to town or just passing through?"

Officer Jannsen delivered the cover story. She was from Quebec, Katherine was from North Carolina. They met at Mount Holyoke in an art history class and had been together ever since. Katherine was expect-

41

ing a baby, and they moved to Washington to take advantage of the state's domestic partnership laws; that and to get as far away as possible from Katherine's right-wing nutter family who didn't approve of her lifestyle choices.

Molly thought that was just fine, because she was all for women doing whatever the hell they wanted in this man's world, and she said they'd have plenty of quiet in Grover's Mill since the town was full of old hippies growing medical marijuana and other related artsy folk who just wanted to keep to themselves and live quietlike.

"So what can I getcha, girls?"

Officer Jannsen ordered a coffee. Katherine wasn't sure what she wanted till Molly said her homemade flapjacks with natural maple syrup were just the thing for a woman with child. Katherine said that sounded perfect and asked for a glass of water to wash it down.

"No problem, honey," Molly said, heading for the kitchen.

Officer Jannsen pulled a bottle of water from the backpack.

"Here, I brought water from the house."

Katherine watched her set a bottle on the table, push it across. One liter, no label. Katherine unscrewed the cap, took a sip.

"We use well water at the house, don't we?"

"Yes."

"Where's it come from?"

"Where does what come from?"

"The water. Does it come from a spring, a lake?"

"It's water."

"Don't bullshit me. Not today."

Officer Jannsen spoke softly.

"Lausanne."

Katherine belted out her surprise. "Lausanne, as in fucking Switzerland?"

"That's right. And how about keeping your voice down?"

Katherine dropped the decibels.

"Are you telling me tap water from Lausanne gets shipped halfway around the world and we fill our well with it? That's fucking crazy. I mean, what's the matter with the water that was in the well in the first place?"

"The chromium levels were too high."

"For a woman who's knocked up, you mean."

"Knocked up?"

"Pregnant. Bun in the oven. In the female way."

Officer Jannsen scanned the diner, then leaned across the table.

"Lausanne's water has certain minerals you can't get anywhere else. The doctors say they're necessary for the baby's development."

"I bet they do."

Officer Jannsen stared at Katherine.

"What's on your mind, Katherine?"

"You knew I was pregnant from the beginning. You never told me."

"Those were my orders."

"Do you know who the father is?"

"It's not my concern who the father is."

Molly delivered the espresso and flapjacks, talked about the weather a minute, and left. Officer Jannsen looked around the diner again.

"Once more, what's on your mind, Katherine?"

"How long do I have to stay in Grover's Mill?"

"Until Inspector Gobet says otherwise."

"Why? You told me the bad guys were dead."

"They were part of a much bigger organization, a very deadly organization. Our intel says you're still in the gravest of danger if you try to live in the open."

"Bullshit."

"It isn't bullshit, it's real. You know how real it is. And you know it's as deadly as it is real."

"Then how come you guys are here and not the FBI, or the CIA, or the fucking YMCA?"

"What?"

"How come there are no American cops protecting me? Why you guys?"

Officer Jannsen smiled.

"Do you think we could be here, in America, without the permission of the American authorities?"

"I don't know what to fucking think. I haven't been thinking for myself for four and a half months. And when I got switched on again, whoopee, I'm pregnant."

Officer Jannsen sat silently.

Katherine looked out the window.

It was pretty here, she thought. There was a town hall, a tree-lined square, a fire brigade, B&Bs, shops and restaurants catering to tourists. The firemen had rolled out the antique hook and ladder and were giving it a wash and shine. And beyond them, at the corner of Main and Elm Streets, Katherine saw the black Ford Explorer parked with a clear view to Molly's Diner. The four men inside watching her watch them.

"The day shift is here."

"We go where you go, Katherine."

"So who's watching the house?"

"The night shift."

"So me taking a walk to town is screwing up everyone's schedules."

"Not really, there's a swing shift squad. Besides, keeping you safe is our job, Katherine."

"Me and the baby, you mean. Let's not forget the baby no one bothered to tell me about."

Officer Jannsen looked at her watch.

"Why don't you eat your breakfast, then we'll go home."

"Oh yeah. Can't be late for my Midday Buzz teatime, can I? Not by one fucking minute. Know what? After breakfast I might just keep walking. All the way to the next county and get a bikini wax. How about that for an idea?"

Officer Jannsen's face became expressionless. Katherine knew the look. It meant she'd gone full-tilt Swiss cop.

"I want to make things as easy for you as I can, Madame Taylor—"

"'Madame' is it now? When did that happen? Oh, that's right, I'm pregnant. Fuck the 'mademoiselle' routine. And 'madame' has that nice hooker ring to it, doesn't it?"

"If you make things hard for me or any of the protection unit, I'll have no choice but to keep you confined to the house."

Katherine smiled.

"I really like it when you talk tough. Makes me go all tingly inside."

She dug into the flapjacks. After a few bites, she leaned back across the booth.

"C'mon, Anne, you have to admit, going through all that . . . that stuff and finding out I'm going to have a kid is a mindfuck."

"I understand, Katherine. And I'll do all I can to help you."

"Call me Kat. After all, we're married and expecting a baby. Might as well get friendly about it. You do know how to be friendly, don't you?"

"My job is to protect you, not to be your friend."

Katherine sighed, combed her hand through her hair.

"Know what? Let the guys in the Explorer protect me twenty-four/seven. I need you to knock off a couple hours a day and just be my friend, someone I can talk to. Can you get it through your head that I need you to loosen up once in a while and be a pal? Because if you don't, I swear, magic teas or no magic teas, I'm gonna lose my friggin' mind once and for all."

Officer Jannsen nodded. "As long as it doesn't compromise my job."

"Really?"

"Really."

Katherine picked up her fork, jabbed another chunk of flapjacks, and mixed it through the syrup.

"So, now, let me ask you a favor. You know, girlfriend to girlfriend. Three favors, to be exact."

Officer Jannsen gave it that half smile of hers. *Looks damn cute when she does that,* Katherine thought. Officer Jannsen raised her hands in mock surrender.

"*D'accord.* What's number one?"

"Give me fifty cents."

"Now?"

"Right now."

Officer Jannsen reached in her pocket and found the coins, dropped them on the table. Katherine picked them up and slid them into the jukebox, pressed a button. The Doobie Brothers: "South City Midnight Lady." Officer Jannsen watched Katherine bop her head to the beat and sing along:

> *"Up all night I could not sleep.*
> *The whiskey that I drank was cheap.*
> *With shaking hands I went and I lit up my last cigarette."*

Katherine got to the chorus. Something about a hooker with a golden heart. Officer Jannsen crossed her arms.

"And what's favor number two? Or is it me sitting here listening to you sing badly?"

"This is a great fucking song and this jukebox has all my favorites. So you know what? We're going to have date night, once a week, right here in this booth."

Katherine bit into the flapjacks, talked with her mouth full.

"Okay, favor number two is, we open a candle shop in Grover's Mill."

Officer Jannsen shook her head. "We talked about that when we first got here. Inspector Gobet doesn't think you're ready for that kind of exposure."

"Well, Inspector Gobet is going to have to live with it if he wants me to play ball. Just tell him to send over my candle-making stuff from Switzerland the next time they make a water delivery."

She held up her left hand, flashing the wedding ring.

"Besides, it'll add to the whole two hot lesbians living together and having a baby thing. You heard Molly, we'll fit right in in this town."

She watched Officer Jannsen raise an eyebrow, and not in a completely objectionable manner, Katherine thought.

"Well?" Katherine said.

"I need to get it cleared with Berne, but I'll ask. What's number three?"

Katherine opened the bottle, swallowed some more Lausanne tap water that had been shipped halfway around the world.

"There's nothing around our house but a bunch of evergreen trees, is there? No nosy neighbors, no kids looking for their lost dogs, no Jehovah's Witnesses who'll come knocking at the door to save an ex-hooker from her sordid past?"

"No neighbors, no Jehovah's Witnesses. Just you, me, and the rest of the protection detail."

"Good. Because after I order another stack of flapjacks and we play just about every song on this jukebox, we're going to walk home and do some girlie stuff."

"Girlie stuff?"

"You know, sit in the garden, talk about clothes. I give you a pedicure, you show me how to shoot a gun."

Officer Jannsen took a moment to replay the last bit.

"I don't think Inspector Gobet would classify weapons training as girlie stuff."

"We're in America. What wholesome girl doesn't know how to shoot a gun by the age of ten? Not that I fall under the heading of wholesome, but you get the idea."

"Katherine—"

"It's Kat."

Officer Jannsen sighed. "Kat. First of all, you can't go shooting in the woods at the back of the house."

"Where do you guys practice?"

"We have an underground firing range."

"Where?"

"Out in the woods."

"Cool, let's get going. I can hardly wait to shoot stuff."

"Kat, people who get off shooting stuff are usually the people who should never touch a gun."

"Meaning?"

"Meaning you're going to have to give me a better reason if you want me to consider asking Inspector Gobet about it."

Katherine pushed her plate aside and drilled Officer Jannsen with algid eyes.

47

"Okay, how about this, best girlfriend ever? It's really nice having you and the Swiss Guard protecting me and all. But if what you're telling me is true, that there's some international gang of bad guys still after me, then I don't want one of those motherfucking creeps coming anywhere near me. And if one of them does, I want to know how to blow his fucking head off, all by myself."

FOUR

The best thing about nowtimes in the great American Northwest, Katherine liked to tell herself after afternoon tea, was her bathtub. The kind a girl could stretch her legs in, Jacuzzi jets on demand. With a few inches on either end, she could do laps. She climbed in. The water was hot and it felt good, and there was a window at the foot of the tub with a view of the rainy world outside.

She thumbed through *The New Yorker* again. Satisfied she'd read all the cartoons, she dropped the magazine on the floor and slid down into the water. She lay there a moment, thinking about . . . about nothing. She held her breath, closed her eyes, and let her head sink underwater. She forced herself to stay down, fighting the urge to come up for air. When her heart began to pound, she tried to slow it down. *No fear, no fear* . . . She sat up and gasped, wiped the water from her face. Officer Jannsen was sitting on the stool next to the tub.

"What are you doing, Kat?"

"Meditating."

"Underwater?"

"Dolphins do it, sometimes days at a time. I read it in *The New Yorker*."

"No you didn't."

"No?"

"Dolphins are mammals; they can't spend days at a time underwater. And, you set off the pulse monitor."

Katherine looked at the green rubber bracelet she wore 24/7 like a piece of hipster jewelry. That's what Katherine thought it was when Officer Jannsen strapped it to her wrist just before they left Lausanne. Turned out it was a gadget to monitor her well-being. Max had one, too.

"Oops."

Officer Jannsen stood, pulled a bathrobe from the wall hook, and set it over the stool. Katherine saw the Glock on Officer Jannsen's hip. Then she saw the swelling of breasts under the sleeveless T-shirt, then the nice shoulders. Katherine was aware of a sensation she hadn't felt in a long time.

"Anne?"

"Yes?"

Katherine bit her lip. "What's for dinner?"

"The boys are going to town to pick up pizzas. You want to share one with me?"

"Oh, yes, please. With anchovies."

Officer Jannsen bowed.

"*Je vous en prie, madame.* Anything else?"

Katherine slid down into the water again. "Nope."

Officer Jannsen left and closed the door behind her. Katherine watched her toes wiggle in the water.

"Such a stupid girl you are, Kat Taylor."

She opened the drain, climbed out of the tub. She threw on the bathrobe, grabbed a towel.

"'What's for dinner?' Jesus, how lame can you get?"

She wrapped the towel around her hair and walked into her bedroom. She could see Max's room through an open door. He was still down for the count. She stood before the mirror, her mind wandering. More like wondering where the hell that little buzz in the tub came from. Must bring it up at her next meeting with the shrink, she told herself. She remembered the last session, last month. The shrink asked if Katherine had experienced any sexual feelings. Had she masturbated, for example, or thought about masturbating? Katherine, never shy about sex in her life, went ballistic.

"Are you out of your fucking mind, you fucking freak?"

It took a healthy shot of whatever it was the doctors put in the needle to calm her down. Then, a few weeks later, she's staring at Officer Jannsen's breasts under a sleeveless T-shirt and feels a rush of *oh, yes, please, and don't forget the anchovies.*

"Really, really stupid girl."

Katherine pulled the towel from her hair and ran her fingers through it like arranging her thoughts. She and Officer Jannsen had been together since she'd left Lausanne. They had grown to be friends, even though Anne Jannsen was first and foremost a Swiss cop in girl's clothing.

Katherine's mind wondered and wandered a bit further. As in how close they might be, even though neither of them had said a word about it. After all, Officer Jannsen never took vacations. And she never went out on her own, and she most definitely did not fool around with the hunky Swiss Guard boys.

And then there were the rings.

At first, Katherine would take off her ring when returning to the house from the candle shop, or the doctor, or one of their long walks together. Katherine noticed Officer Jannsen kept hers on all the time. Not like she'd ever forget to put it on or take it off, Katherine thought. Anne Jannsen wasn't just a Swiss cop, she was part Saint Bernard and never forgot a thing. And then there was the way Officer Jannsen looked at her with that half smile of hers. *As if she* likes *looking at me,* Katherine thought. Katherine slowly opened her bathrobe and took a look at the goods.

Her breasts had dropped a cup size since she stopped nursing. They still had great shape and didn't sag. Her nipples had changed for sure.

They'd become . . . well, nipples that looked like they had been sucked on by a hungry critter for months. But they were kind of cute the way they poked out from the areolae of her breasts. The rest wasn't looking too bad, either. The boys had set up a gym in the garage, and Katherine worked out with them three times a week. Real Swiss Army grunt and sweat stuff that turned her into something of a hard body. In fact, she was in the best shape of her life.

She pulled her hair into a clip, let the robe fall to the floor, and sat at her dressing table. She rubbed lotion over her skin. She remembered Officer Jannsen's half smile, then the solid shoulders, then the breasts under the sleeveless T-shirt. Katherine shook her head.

"Forget about it and get dressed."

She threw on a pair of panties and a bra and went to the closet. She put on the usual baggy sweats. She saw herself in the mirror.

"You look like a sack of potatoes. And you've been a sack of potatoes for too long."

She kicked off the sweats, pulled on her favorite pair of Levi's. She slipped on a cashmere sweater, the one she thought went well with her hazel-colored eyes. She took another gander at herself in the mirror. Better, but something was missing. There was a scarf somewhere. A birthday present from Officer Jannsen, as a matter of fact. She went through the chest of drawers looking for the damn thing. In the bottom drawer, buried under her collection of mismatched socks, she found a makeup bag. She couldn't remember ever buying makeup, not since she'd come to Grover's Mill, anyway. She opened the bag. Eyeliners, lipsticks, mascaras. All unopened and unused. And it was the good stuff.

"Huh."

She picked up the Lancôme mascara and worked the brush through her eyelashes, just a touch. Then she began to trace a line of Armani red across her lips. There was a knock at her bedroom door.

"Kat?"

The lipstick skidded over her lips.

"Oh, fuck!"

Another knock.

"Kat? What's going on?"

"Don't come in!"

She dropped the lipstick and ran to the bathroom. She quickly washed her face and grabbed a towel. She ran through the bedroom and opened the door, saw Officer Jannsen standing in the hall, taking in the curious expression on Katherine's face.

"Are you feeling all right, Kat?"

"Yeah, fine. What's up?"

"Max is up."

"Is he?"

"They hear him babbling in Control."

"Oh, yeah, Control."

Officer Jannsen stared at Katherine. *And damn,* Katherine thought, *she's flashing that cute half smile of hers again, and her eyes are smiling even more.*

"What are you up to, Kat?"

"Just, you know, finishing up."

"*D'accord.* I'll change Max and take him downstairs and get him started with dinner."

"No, that's all right, I'll get him."

"You sure?"

"Yeah, no problem."

"Pizzas will be here in thirty minutes. I like your sweater, by the way."

"Huh?"

"Your sweater. It's cute. It goes with your eyes."

"Thanks."

"See you downstairs."

Katherine eased back into her room and quietly closed the door. She slumped into the chair at her dressing table and looked in the mirror. Her eyes were flared and her skin was flushed and she felt her stomach doing the kind of flip-flops she hadn't felt since she was sweet sixteen and never been kissed when Janice Binkley, Emerson High School's hottest cheerleader, took Katherine under the grandstand at halftime to smoke a joint and said, "Open your mouth, pretty girl," and blew dizzying smoke into Katherine's body and kissed her long and deep.

"The shrink is so going to love this one. He'll fucking cum in his trousers."

She opened the drawer and shoved the makeup back in.

She walked to Max's room, saw him standing in his crib, holding on to the rail. He saw her and went quiet. Against the last of the light bleeding through the sheer white curtains, he was shadowlike and still.

"Well, don't just stand there, buster, say something."

Max gurgled and bounced up and down on his legs. She switched on the lights and Max squealed excitedly, as if he'd just seen a rabbit pulled from a hat.

"Yeah, yeah, you love that trick."

She walked toward him and he stared at her with that intense look of his, as if he were trying to read her face. She stopped in front of him and stared back. It was the same game each time Max woke up: the two of them standing like gunfighters at the O.K. Corral, waiting to see who'd make the first move. Katherine threw up her arms in surprise.

"What?"

Max squealed and gurgled and bounced up and down some more. Katherine lifted him from the crib, kissed the top of his head.

"And you love that trick, too, don't you?"

She carried him to the changing table, laid him down, and unsnapped his pajamas. His cloth diaper was soaked in the front, loaded in the back.

"And this is your favorite trick of all."

She undid the pins and turned up her nose.

"Whoever said your own baby's poo doesn't stink was lying through their teeth because, buster, you stink to almighty heaven."

Max had a vocabulary of six or seven words in varying languages courtesy of Officer Jannsen and the multilingual Swiss Guard protecting the house and grounds. *Mommy* was often the French *Maman*, *milk* was the German *milch*, his pacifier was the Italian *ciuccio*, even though Katherine always called it *Mister Gummy*. But for the most part, Max chose to express himself with a word he made up himself. It covered everything and anything that might be running through his little boy brain.

"Goog."

"Oh, goog yourself."

Katherine dipped a soft cloth into a water basin and washed him. She used another cloth to apply lotion to his skin. She powdered him and dressed him in a fresh diaper and T-shirt.

"There you are, fresh as a daisy. Let me get rid of the evidence and we'll go downstairs."

"Goog."

"No, I'm having the pizza. You're having a tofu burger."

"Goog, goog."

"Tough."

She dressed him in fresh flannel pajamas with little blue bears printed on the material, lifted him from the table, and set him back in his crib. He looked at her with a frown and uttered another of his favorite words, in French.

"*Non.*"

"*Pas de panique.*"

She handed him a small rubber hammer and a Whac-A-Mole game. Hit one on the head here, another one pops up there. Repeat until sleepy.

"Bang on this awhile. I'll be right back."

"Zeug."

That one came from *spielzeug*, German for *toys*, but *zeug* was close enough for Max. He attacked the contraption vigorously.

Whack, whack, whackwhack.

"Zeug!"

Katherine went into the hall and opened the closet. She tossed Max's T-shirt and used pajamas into a laundry basket. The soiled diaper and washcloths went into a sealed bin. All the laundry was taken care of downstairs, even Max's diapers. Problem was, laundry day was every day with Max. And as much as she loved the little squirt, and as much as Officer Jannsen kept telling her doing laundry builds character, Katherine sometimes felt she was trapped in a B-movie prison flick (starring Katherine Taylor as Prisoner 99 doing a ten to twenty stretch for grand theft auto). About six months into diaper duty, she asked Officer Jannsen (starring as the Warden Bitch of Cell Block 4) if she could get a lighter sentence and switch to disposable diapers. Katherine was told it was a security measure to use cloth.

"Not the best idea to be seen with boxes of disposable diapers," Officer Jannsen said.

"Anne, the locals all know Max. The kid could get elected mayor by a landslide."

"There are other concerns."

"Like what?"

"The plastic shell used in disposable diapers negatively affects the testicular cooling mechanism necessary for spermatogenesis in baby boys."

Katherine's jaw dropped.

"You made that up just to scare me, didn't you?"

"It's scientific fact."

"Okay, ouch to that idea."

And that night in bed, sipping her Night Clouds tea, she wondered where Officer Jannsen ever learned such a thing as "testicular cooling mechanism," because it sure as hell didn't sound like something they teach at Swiss cop school. Then again, having met Inspector Gobet, maybe they did. Then Katherine began to think that actually a testicular cooling mechanism sounded like some adult *spielzeug*. And if there wasn't such a toy, then maybe Katherine should invent one herself and sell it on eBay. Make gazillions.

Remembering it, Katherine laughed to herself, thinking how much her life had changed since Lausanne, thinking it wouldn't be a bad movie after all; starring Katherine Taylor as Katherine Taylor, and Brad Pitt as anyone as long as he was in it. She laughed again. From lesbo lust to dirty diapers to gorgeous man meat fantasy, all in a day.

"The shrink is so going to crap himself."

She walked back to Max's room. He was sitting now. Rubber hammer in one hand, other hand reaching through the bars of the crib and holding on to Monsieur Booty's tail.

"Boo," Max said. Max-speak for Monsieur Booty.

The beast always showed up this time of day to jump on the nearby stool for a bit of manhandling by Max. Whether it was having its ears pinched or whiskers twisted or tail pulled, Monsieur Booty always came back for more. The two of them seemed to have the most intense conversations, even if the entire vocabulary between them consisted of *mew* and *Boo*.

"Okay, gang, let's eat."

She lifted Max from the crib and carried him into the hall and down the stairs. Max pointed the way as they walked—sort of. His fist did well, but his little finger always veered off at a twenty-degree angle. Monsieur Booty followed at Katherine's heels to halfway down the stairs, where he squeezed through the balusters and jumped to the ground floor and dashed ahead. Katherine went into the kitchen and dropped Max into his high chair. He still had his rubber hammer and proceeded to play Whac-A-Mole on the tray, using imaginary moles.

Whackwhack, whack.

"Go get 'em, tiger. It's the ones you can't see that'll bite your butt."

She took Max's dinner from the warming oven. Dinners at the house were catered from Molly's Diner five nights a week. Turned out Molly had studied at Le Cordon Bleu College of Culinary Arts in Chicago. Even had her own two-star Michelin restaurant on North Halsted, till she realized she was only a dope-loving hippie at heart. She sold the place, moved to Grover's Mill, and opened a diner just before Katherine arrived. Which was fine with Katherine, as cooking was never a required skill as a high-priced hooker.

"Look what Molly made for you, Max. Tofu burger with mushy peas."

Whack.

"Goog."

"You bet, and doesn't it look yummy?"

Katherine chopped up the food into tiny bites with a small rubber spoon. She scooped up a spoonful and lifted it to Max's mouth.

"Loff," he said.

"That's a new one. Sounds German. Try it in English."

"Goog."

"Whatever. Open wide."

Max loved Molly's cooking. He never spit up a morsel and he took his time with every spoonful. Savoring it like some food critic for the high chair and diaper set.

"Nnnn." Max-speak for Officer Jannsen, just now walking in the kitchen.

Katherine felt herself blush.

"What's on the menu tonight?" Officer Jannsen asked.

"Tofu burger and peas."

"He loves that one, doesn't he?"

"Sure does. And if the pizzas don't show up soon, I'm going to start sneaking bites. Is that okay with you, Max? Can I steal some of your dinner?"

"Goog."

"Know something? You're getting to be a big boy now. You need to add a few more words to your vocabulary." Katherine looked at Officer Jannsen. "Don't you think he should be reciting the Gettysburg Address by now? Or is all this English, French, German—"

"And Italian."

"Yeah, that one, too. Is it all confusing him?"

"Don't worry, Kat. He's very busy internalizing linguistic patterns into a holistic structure."

"What the heck does that mean?"

"It means he's exceptionally intelligent."

Katherine gave Max another spoon of mushy peas.

"Okay, me no worry."

Officer Jannsen sat next to Katherine. Max smiled at her, and mushy peas tumbled over his lips. Katherine scooped them up and held the spoon to his mouth.

"Why don't you let him try holding the spoon?" Officer Jannsen said.

"Are you kidding me? He'll put his eye out."

"Actually, I was watching him play with crayons the other day. He has well-developed primitive tripod grasp skills."

Katherine looked at Officer Jannsen a second.

"Do you just make stuff up to trick me into doing what you want?"

"What stuff?"

"'Internalizing linguistic' things and 'primitive tripods'?"

"I studied human development at EPFL."

"Cop school?"

"École Polytechnique Fédérale de Lausanne."

"Oh, yeah, I remember. It's on the lake. Full of geniuses and stuff."

"Stuff?"

"Yeah, you know, scientific stuff."

"Oh, that stuff."

Katherine nodded to the gun on Officer Jannsen's hip.

"So how'd you end up a cop?"

"I wanted to make a difference in the world."

"And here you are, stuck with Max and me in Grover's Mill. That's one big difference you're making in the world."

"What makes you think I would rather be anywhere else?"

Their eyes met for a moment.

"Anne?"

"Kat?"

"I'm going to Control to check on the pizzas."

"I can go."

"No, that's okay. I'll do it. You teach Max about primitive tripod whatever. I'll be right back."

Katherine hurried out the door and into the garden. She stopped a moment, took a breath of crisp evening air.

"Okay, that one was *not* an imagination. Must talk to the fucking shrink, like, tomorrow."

She walked toward the garage, saw three Ford Explorers parked in the driveway. The pizzas had landed.

"Swiss Guard, big deal. Can't even deliver a pizza."

She followed the flagstone path to the log cabin hidden in the trees. The front of the cabin had a screened-in porch, and she saw the door to the sitting room was open and the lights were on. She knocked on the screen door.

"*Allez!* We're hungry!"

No one answered.

She went inside, through the porch and into the sitting room and down a hall. She heard a voice:

"*. . . details are still sketchy, and French police were seen confiscating press video and camera equipment, as well as the mobiles and cameras of onlookers in the name of national security. However, one piece of video has emerged on the Internet . . .*"

She rounded the corner into a small room made even smaller by all the thirty-six-inch monitors on the walls, all displaying different angles of nearby roads, the grounds, hallways in the main house, Max's bedroom. Five large men, pistols strapped to their belts, crowded together in the middle of the room watching one monitor. On screen: a wobbly wide shot of a bridge above the river.

"*. . . and again, this is amateur video, but you can clearly see members of the police on the Pont des Arts as the tour boat approaches . . .*"

News, no thanks, Katherine thought. Same shit, different day, over and over again. She saw a pile of unopened pizza boxes on a table just inside the door. She sorted through them looking for the one with anchovies. She found it at the bottom and was going to tell the boys thanks for nothing, but realized they wouldn't notice anyway. She headed for the door.

"*. . . and there, that's it. A blinding flash of light and the bridge disappears in a cloud of fog, and look, look there. You can see the shadow of a man falling, almost flying, through the fog. He doesn't appear to be one of the police, and he appears to have a long knife in his hand . . .*"

She turned toward the monitor, saw a fuzzy image on the screen. Zooming in, coming into focus. Katherine tipped her head to look at it.

"*. . . jumping onto the tour boat, where police report they later found grue-some scenes . . .*"

Another voice cut through the room:

"*Schalten sie den fernseher!*"

The TV shut off, the men turned to the voice, and so did Katherine. It was Officer Jannsen, standing in the doorway with a happy-to-see-everyone Max in her arms. Took a few seconds for Katherine to realize the only sound amid the sudden silence was that of Max sucking on his Mister Gummy. She looked at the Swiss Guard, then back to Officer Jannsen.

"What's wrong?"

Officer Jannsen shifted Max from one hip to the other, his diapered rear end now resting on the butt of her Glock.

"Nothing's wrong. I was wondering what took you so long."

"You just barked at the boys in German."

"I'm Swiss-German. German is the official language of the Swiss Guard."

"It's also the language you bark in when you're officially PO'd."

"PO'd?"

"Pissed off. I was trying to watch my language in front of the you-know-what in your arms."

"I'm hungry," Officer Jannsen said, "that's all. And you don't need to be watching the news."

"I may be certifiable, but I'm with-it enough to know . . ."

She stopped talking, and her eyes took in the faces watching her. She looked at the darkened screen. Something felt familiar; something terrible. She looked at Officer Jannsen.

"This stuff on the news, does it have something to do with me?"

"How do you mean?"

Katherine felt a flash of rage. She tossed the pizza box on the table, walked over, and took Max from Officer Jannsen's arms.

"Don't give me that Swiss cop shit."

"Kat—"

61

"No. You tell me what's going on. What's the big fucking secret?"

"Watch your tone of voice, Kat."

"Don't fucking tell me to watch my fucking tone!"

She saw an expression on Officer Jannsen's face, saw her eyes pointing toward Max. He'd stopped sucking on his pacifier. He was staring at Katherine, holding his breath—he was frightened.

"Oh, crap, Max. I'm sorry."

Officer Jannsen looked at the men, kicked her head to the door. They were gone without a sound. Katherine began to cry.

"I'm so sorry, Max. I'm so sorry."

Max tipped his head to the side as if to study the tears in her eyes. Katherine took a quick breath and smiled and gently bounced him, trying to laugh.

"It's okay, Max. Don't pay attention to silly Mommy. Mommy's just a little cuckoo sometimes. You know, like the funny clock in the house . . . cuckoo, cuckoo."

Max smiled, took the pacifier from his mouth, pressed it to her lips.

"Ciuccio."

"No, not like Mister Gummy. *Cuckoo*, like the bird."

"Ciuccio," Max insisted.

Katherine took the pacifier between her lips. She opened her eyes wide like she was tasting chocolate fudge ice cream. "Mmmmm." Max pulled away the pacifier and reinserted it into his own mouth. He began to suck happily. Katherine kissed his forehead, crying and laughing at the same time.

"Oh Max, you've gotten stuck with such a lousy mother."

Officer Jannsen stepped close to Katherine.

"No, Kat, you're a wonderful mother."

"Oh yeah, scare my child to death. I'm so perfect."

Officer Jannsen reached over to rearrange a few strands of Max's black hair.

"Yes, you did scare him at first. Then you guided him through his fear and gave him confidence. You taught him fear can be controlled."

"You think?"

"*Observed Maternal Behaviors in the Transference of Human Emotions* was the title of my PhD thesis."

Katherine rolled her eyes. "Of course, genius with a gun that you are." She glanced toward the monitors. "And all that? What was it?"

"Kat, you know the doctor wants your Internet and TV screened."

"Yeah, I know. But humor me, I'm nuts."

Officer Jannsen nodded. "There was a terrorist attack in Paris. Nine people were killed. The news is full of pictures you don't need to see."

"And that's it? Nothing to do with me?"

"That's it."

"Okay."

Max sensed a change in Katherine's mood. He broke into a drooling smile.

"Are you laughing at your cuckoo mommy for being afraid of the boogeyman?"

"Cuckoobug!"

"Yeah, cuckoobug for Cocoa Puffs. That's me."

"Goog."

"Oh, goog yourself."

She tickled Max's belly. He squealed and giggled.

Officer Jannsen picked up the pizza and took Katherine's arm.

"Come on, Kat, let's go back to the house. I'll make you a cup of tea."

✤

FIVE

Monsieur Dufaux worked the tables in Café du Grütli, chatting with his customers. He checked table six at the windows. The fellow sitting there had finished his dinner, pushed his plate aside, and was now leaning over the front page of *24 Heures*. Dufaux walked over, picked up the fellow's plate and cutlery, and saw the empty glass on the table.

"*Voulez-vous une autre carafe?*"

"Just a glass, *s'il vous plaît.*"

"*Et l'addition?*"

"Put it on the inspector's tab."

Monsieur Dufaux picked up the carafe.

"And perhaps one day the inspector will grace me with a visit to pay this tab? I mean, yes, you only come in a few nights a week, but after a couple of years, a tab adds up. It's now longer than the Book of Numbers."

Harper flipped over the newspaper. "Sorry?"

"Inspector Gobet's tab and the Book of Numbers. From the Bible. They both go on and on."

Harper thought about it.

"Let me know when it's as long as the Book of Psalms."

"*Quoi?*"

"One hundred fifty chapters. Longest book of the Bible."

Dufaux scratched his chin.

"*Pas mal.* I must remember that one. I'll bring you a fresh glass, on the house. I'll join you, too."

Harper watched Monsieur Dufaux make his way through the tables, the man's shoulders bouncing with chuckles. Harper made a mental note: Crack a joke in this joint, get a free glass. He turned his eyes to the windows. Outside, evening had given way to the dark. He focused on the pools of light beneath the streetlamps along Rue Mercerie. Unbeknownst to the locals, the streetlamps in the protected zone had been fitted with Arc 9 filters. Part of Inspector Gobet's plan to beef up security around Lausanne Cathedral. The filters slowed the speed of artificial light by fifty thousand microns per second. Didn't matter to the locals, but with Arc 9s, Harper's kind could detect minute spikes of black body radiation in the light. Or so went the theory. He flashed the light mechanic from Berne, six months ago, positively giddy explaining how the filters worked.

"You see, when applied to sodium vapor lamps in areas sealed with a level four time warp, such as the protected zone, Arc 9s will allow you to see around corners and back over your shoulder at the same time. We're very excited about it."

"You don't say."

The filters still had some kinks, the mechanic chattered on. Something about certain meteorological conditions interacting with negative resistance ions.

"As a result, a spike in black body radiation could be either a mortal threat moving through nearby shadows or a cat falling at terminal velocity."

Harper stared at the mechanic.

"A cat. Falling at terminal velocity."

"Cats, yes," the mechanic replied. "You see, cats reach terminal velocity at one hundred kilometers per hour. That's a speed they reach when falling at a distance greater than one hundred feet. The *Felis catus*, or common domesticated cat as it's known, then has the ability to stabilize and spread its legs, forming itself into something of a parachute. Fascinating stuff. Did you know a cat has a better chance of surviving a fall from forty floors than four?"

Harper considered the mechanic's enthusiasm regarding the topic.

"Mate, are you telling me you've been tossing cats from windows to test your bloody lamp filters?"

The mechanic appeared pained.

"Why, no. It's only based on computer simulations. Goodness, I love my cats. I have two of them. Would you like to see their pictures?"

Harper blinked and turned from the window. He saw Monsieur Dufaux setting two fresh glasses and a carafe of white on the table. Dufaux sat across from Harper and poured.

"*Santé.*"

"*Et toi.*"

They touched glasses and sipped.

"So how have you been?" Dufaux said. "You haven't been in the café for, what, a week or two?"

Harper thought about it. He couldn't quite see his timeline. Mission debrief always included a memory scrub. Delete this, trim that. Made a jumble of things for a few days. He flashed the medics in the white coats at the Vevey infirmary. They checked, they scanned, they didn't like what they'd found. They strapped him to a stretcher, shoved him into a regenerative stasis tank for days. Today was only Harper's second day out.

"Had a bit of a holiday," Harper said.

"Holiday. Good, very good. Need one myself. So, what's happening in our crazy world?" Monsieur Dufaux said, turning over the newspaper and looking at the front page. "What on earth?"

Oddly enough, that was Harper's reaction on seeing it, too. A grainy, backlit, and shadowy image of a winged form falling through the fog at Pont des Arts, side by side with a four-hundred-year-old painting of

Saint Michael the Archangel. The headline above the pictures read: "Was This the Angel Who Fell from the Sky to Save Paris?"

"Good Lord," Dufaux said. "Can you believe this?"

"Not sure what it's all about. Haven't been following the news of late."

Dufaux took a sip from his glass.

"Well," he said. "Let me tell you what you missed while on vacation."

Seems while Harper was in the tank, the world's newspapers went heavy on Paris. The usual hard news up front: pictures of the *Manon*'s wreckage, backstories about the dead and survivors. And, of course, the one picture of the man who fell from the sky at Pont des Arts. The French government's line was that a foreign power had conducted an illegal counterstrike against Muqatileen Lillah on sovereign French soil. After rounds of finger-pointing at London and Washington, D.C., with no joy, the French government then pointed to the Israeli Mossad. The French president referred to the Mossad's scorecard in assassinating Iranian nuclear scientists on Tehran's streets in broad daylight as a case in point. The Israeli government wouldn't comment, but seemed perfectly happy for the world to think, *Of course Israel did it. Israel is very good at this sort of thing. Don't fuck with Israel.*

In answer to press queries regarding the type of WMD captured in the attack, the government would only reply, "We cannot comment at this time for reasons of national security." The French press began to sniff out that the government was hiding something. Then came a scandal of lip-smacking proportions when it was learned the chief suspect in the counterstrike—the man falling from the sky at Pont des Arts—had escaped from La Santé Prison two days after being arrested. The French press went mad.

"Où Sont les Responsables?!" the headlines read.

The press went from mad to crazed when the head of the French police held a press conference to announce he'd issued an arrest warrant for a man no one could describe with any accuracy, and that "the suspect's mug shots, fingerprints, and other relevant details have gone missing." In an attempt to get a detailed description of the culprit, the twenty-one survivors from the *Manon* were reinterviewed by police sketch artists. None of the survivors could remember the man clearly.

"A normal reaction to a terrible shock," the top cop said.

And with that, political commentators had a field day guessing the counterstrike was actually the work of France's own Direction Générale de la Sécurité Extérieure, who—in their greatest screwup since the 1985 *Rainbow Warrior* incident—had not bothered to inform the French police of the operation. After all, the press concluded, who but the DGSE could arrange "an escape" from La Santé Prison? Then came the front page of *Le Monde*, suggesting that since the "unknown man who fell from the sky" had, in fact, saved Paris, the French president was duty-bound to identify the man and present him with the Legion of Honor. But with only nine dead in the attack, the press quickly lost interest and the world's headlines returned to a civil war in Syria, where pictures of slaughter were plentiful. By the end of the week, the attack in Paris had moved to page three. The final "all is well" story came in a fluff piece about Parisians returning to their beloved cafés for aperitifs and conversation. The man who fell from the sky was forgotten. Monsieur Dufaux paused for breath and took a sip of wine. He pointed to the front page of today's paper.

"And now comes this nonsense."

Enter one Mr. Geoffroy de Villehardouin, blogger and amateur art historian from Dijon (where the mustard comes from, the *Daily Mail* was happy to mention). Mr. de Villehardouin recognized the similarity between the blurry image of the man falling from the sky and Guido Reni's seventeenth-century painting of Saint Michael the Archangel. Mr. de Villehardouin wrote:

"Of course, one must admit the 'wings' I have highlighted in the photograph are, surely, no more than the tails of the man's coat flaring upward as he fell. Still, overall, the similarity to Reni's image is more than remarkable."

Mr. de Villehardouin then posted the images side by side on his blog (a space usually reserved for discussions of religious architecture in the

Medici era) and wham. The blog became an overnight sensation, with more than fifteen million hits. And today, the side-by-side images were making the rounds of the world's newspapers. Monsieur Dufaux pushed the paper aside with amusement.

"First he's a Jewish James Bond, then he's a beloved hero of France, now he's Saint Michael reborn. Oh, I tell you, people do see what they need to see."

Harper pulled the newspaper from the table, dropped it facedown on the empty chair next to him. He jumped on the man's last words, happy to change the subject.

"What do you mean?"

Monsieur Dufaux laughed.

"Three years ago, I had a tour group from Mexico in the café; they came for fondue. I gave them a few lessons. You know, here's the fondue fork and here's how you spear the bread, so on and so forth. They were soon dipping their bits of bread in the pots and sopping up the cheese, having a real fiesta. I left them to it and went back to my kitchen. Not ten minutes later I hear a shriek from the dining room. I run back and see the lot of them on their knees, praying to my fondue pot."

"What?"

"They were praying. To my fondue pot."

Monsieur Dufaux paused for effect, took a sip of wine. No doubt he'd told the story a hundred times, Harper thought. No doubt it got better each time in the telling.

"So . . . what happened was one of them saw the face of the Virgin Mary in the crusted cheese at the bottom of the pot. My God, they were besides themselves, waving rosaries and singing 'Ave Maria.'" They offered me a thousand Swiss francs for the fondue pot, on the spot."

"What did you do?"

"What could I do? I gave it to them. For free."

Monsieur Dufaux pronounced the *F* word in a manner that suggested it wounded him deeply.

"And did it?" Harper said.

"Did it what?"

"Did it look like the Virgin Mary?"

Monsieur Dufaux finished his wine, refilled both glasses.

"You know, everyone in the café came over for a look and agreed it was the face of the Virgin Mary. Only Marc Rochat said differently, after studying it from every angle."

It'd been a long time since Harper had heard the lad's name. His face flashed through Harper's eyes for a second, then it was gone. One of the side effects of the memory scrub he'd gone through after the cathedral job. He could remember events on his timeline, but certain faces and names were redacted. A little something to remind Harper of one of the bigger rules and regs of his kind in paradise: *They are not us, and we are not them* . . . so get on with the bloody job, boyo.

"So, what did the lad say?" Harper said.

Monsieur Dufaux laughed.

"He said, very slowly and very deliberately, 'It looks like the crusted cheese at the bottom of a fondue pot.' I tell you, the things that would pop from that boy's mouth!"

"Sounds like him, from what I can remember."

Monsieur Dufaux sighed.

"*Mon Dieu*, I miss him. He always laughed at my jokes, even if he didn't understand them. Which was all of the time, come to think of it."

Harper watched feelings of loss pass through the man's eyes. He tried to imagine what such a thing felt like.

"Came here a lot, did he?"

"Every night before he went to the tower to call the hour. He liked the food, he liked the crowd."

Harper scanned the room. Everyone settled into their evening debate on the important affairs of the day, sans cigarettes. A smoking ban had taken effect in the bars and cafés throughout Switzerland. Many of the locals were unhappy.

"Such nonsense!" Madame Budry complained. "What will be next? Invading my home to test my bathwater to assure themselves it does not exceed the temperature decreed by some faceless *fonctionnaire*?"

Everyone nodded in agreement. Even the small white dog on the stool in the corner wagged its tail with a hearty "Hear, hear."

"It is quite the crowd," Harper said.

Monsieur Dufaux lowered his voice. "I've been meaning to ask you. I heard you were with him when he died."

Harper scanned the man's eyes. Dufaux was ex–Swiss Guard, and his café was a live drop site for partisans in service to Harper's kind. Two of them, the Algerian street cleaners, were coming into the café, just now, for espresso. The older one, the one with the white scarf around his neck, signaled Harper that all was well in the Saint-François quarter. Yes, Monsieur Dufaux would hear things. Didn't mean Harper could add to them, even if he wanted to.

"Sorry, there's nothing I can tell you, Dufaux."

Dufaux raised his glass.

"To absent friends, then?"

Harper tried to see the lad's face. He couldn't.

"Sure."

They drank.

"Does the new one ever come into the café?" Harper asked.

"The girl, you mean."

Took Harper a moment to recall it was a young woman calling the hour now. She was from Iceland. She played classical guitar next to Marie-Madeleine to keep the old girl company. That's what Harper had been told, anyway.

"That's right, the girl. Does she ever come to the café?"

"Not yet, but Monsieur Buhlmann says to expect her soon."

"Buhlmann?"

"You know, old fellow from the cathedral. *Le guet* before Marc Rochat. Buhlmann says the girl is still living at the school."

"Mon Repos?"

"*Oui*. But she's just turned eighteen and they're letting her roam about town. And get this, she's a vegetarian. Can you imagine it? A vegetarian in Switzerland? Like an Eskimo lost in the Sahara. Then again, we've never had a girl calling the hour before. Anyway, old man Buhl-mann asked me to add a few plates of rabbit food to the menu to attract her attention. Give her a safe place to spend her evenings. I hear she's quite pretty, but very shy."

Harper looked down into his glass.

"Wouldn't know. I've never seen her."

"Up close, you mean."

Harper felt something, as if something dark had passed through the room. He scanned the locals; nothing. He looked at Dufaux. The man was smiling.

"Sorry?" Harper asked.

Monsieur Dufaux nodded out the windows to Escaliers du Marché and the wooden steps leading up the hill to Lausanne Cathedral. He spoke softly.

"Your new flat is up those steps and just behind the cathedral on Rue Vuillermet. Top floor studio, little balcony with a view of the belfry. And you've been living there for the last nine months."

Something moved in the corner of Harper's eye. Heavy curtain at the door billowing, someone coming in. He looked at Dufaux, the man's face still smiling. Ex–Swiss Guard or not, no bloody way the man should know that one. Harper reached for the killing knife under his sports coat.

"How do you know where I live, Dufaux?"

Monsieur Dufaux shrugged, emptied the carafe into their glasses.

"Because I own the building, monsieur. Which reminds me, when you ask the inspector about the tab, tell him to not forget the rent. *Bon*, back to my kitchen. I need more practice with my bulgur, lentil, and tofu casserole. *Le guet*'s favorite dish, Buhlmann says. *Bonne soirée, monsieur.*"

"Right. Cheers for the glass."

Harper watched Dufaux hurry around the tables and disappear into the kitchen. Harper looked toward the door, saw two regulars coming in. The professor from the university and his wife, both of them with books under their arms. For a moment, Harper couldn't find his breath.

He released his grip on the killing knife. He looked down at his hand . . . trembling. He rolled his fingers into a fist and squeezed till the trembling stopped.

"Fuck sake. What the hell was that?"

He drank the last of his wine, put on his coat, and eased through the tables. The locals had come to accept Harper's presence in the café, especially after Monsieur Dufaux passed the word that the tall, quiet Englishman worked as a security consultant for the International Olympic Committee in Lausanne. Made Harper something of a celebrity in the café. Harper shuddered to think what the locals would've made of him running a killing knife across Monsieur Dufaux's throat for no apparent reason. No doubt Madame Budry would have fallen into paroxysms of disquiet.

He pushed through the curtains, pulled open the door, and stepped outside. He walked along Rue Mercerie and ducked in the first shadow he could find. He found a loose gold-tipped fag in his coat and fired up. It tasted bitter, but he drew on it anyway, waiting for relief. It was slow in coming.

Nine deep-throated bells sounded in the night.

He looked up the wooden steps of Escaliers du Marché. Saw the trees along Rue Viret, saw the floodlit belfry of Lausanne Cathedral. An illuminated, solitary pile of rock. He imagined the new one, the girl from Iceland, already standing on the east balcony, waiting for the last bell to fade, waiting to raise her lantern and call the words of comfort over Lausanne. If he waited long enough, he'd see her round the tower and come to the south balcony, and he'd hear her call the hour. Harper lowered his eyes, dropped his smoke on the ground, kicked it down a drain.

"Cras credemus, hodie nihil."

He walked across Place de la Palud toward the Saint-François quarter for a bit of look-but-never-touch at GG's nightclub. The barkeep always poured a healthy splash and the scenery was good, especially the midnight show. And in one darkened corner there was a table with a good view of anyone, or anything, coming through the door.

Just ahead, around the corner at Rue Madeleine, Harper saw something flutter in the light. His eyes registered a spike in black body radiation. He opened his coat, pulled his SIG Sauer. The closer he got to the corner, the more the spikes modulated heavily in the six-hundred-nanometer range. He raised his SIG, pulled the slide, loaded a round into the firing chamber. Whatever was waiting for him was bloody big.

"Here, kitty, kitty."

He lunged around the corner, smack into the death end of a gun. Make that two guns. One for each of his eyeballs.

"Good evening, Mr. Harper."

"Did we startle you?"

Harper tilted his head and looked beyond the barrels. Two bulldozer-sized men at the trigger ends. *No doubt about it,* Harper thought; *the light mechanic's Arc 9 filters need work.*

"Well, well. Mutt and Jeff. Long time no see. What brings you boys to town, besides trouble?"

"Inspector Gobet requests that you join him presently."

"Would you come with us, please?"

Mutt and Jeff hadn't lost their talent for speaking in double-tap.

"Where?" Harper said.

"He's waiting for you outside the protected zone."

"His motorcar is just around the corner."

Harper made his SIG safe, holstered it.

"Sorry, lads, I'm on mandated medical leave. In fact, I was just on my way to GG's to fill a prescription. So if you'll excuse me."

Harper took a step. Mutt and Jeff's guns followed his head.

"Am I missing something?" Harper said.

"Just a precaution. We were told you're not quite yourself these days."

"Now get the fucking lead out and get in the fucking motorcar, *s'il vous plaît.*"

The Merc was parked on Place de la Riponne. Jeff opened the rear door for Harper, then took the front passenger seat. Mutt climbed in behind the wheel, gave Harper the brief.

"We'll be leaving the protected zone at Pont Bessières and join real time."

"How far back are we?" Harper asked.

"Standard five-minute lag."

"Time to destination?"

"Twenty-one minutes."

Harper thought about it.

"And what is our bloody destination?"

"You'll find out when you get there," Mutt said, turning over the engine.

"Of course I will."

Jeff reached down and lifted a Brügger & Thomet machine gun. It was fitted with red dot sight and sound suppression. He looked back over his seat.

"Fasten your seat belt, Mr. Harper."

"Sorry?"

"All passengers, including those in the rear seat, must wear seat belts. It's the law in Switzerland."

Harper pulled the shoulder strap and locked himself in.

"Of course. Wouldn't want to break the seat belt law as we blast our way through the streets, would we?"

The Merc headed to the traffic circle at Avenue de l'Université, rounded onto Rue Viret, and passed under Lausanne Cathedral. Mutt pressed one of the control buttons mounted in the steering wheel. Jeff's side of the windshield became a heads-up display of Lausanne in 3-D. A shimmering blue dome marked the protected zone around the old city and the cathedral. Jeff touched the windshield at Pont Bessières, and a series of blips and beeps sounded as the image spun around to display a POV shot of the bridge. A red line plotted a point at the far end. A woman's voice filled the car:

"You are attempting to exit the protected zone on a heading of one hundred and sixty-three degrees. Please render your access code."

"Baker-six-Sierra-Golf-Zulu-five," Jeff said.

"Access code accepted. Please select time differential equation for your present GPS coordinates."

A stream of equations that would've made Einstein's head explode appeared on the windshield. Jeff tapped one of the shorter ones.

"Thank you. Please engage time warp modulators."

Mutt pressed a switch that would've turned on the air-conditioning in a normal car. In the Inspectormobile, it generated a subharmonic frequency Harper couldn't hear, but he could feel it vibrating through the car.

"Time warp modulators engaged," Mutt reported.

The Merc rounded the Lausanne Museum and lined up with Pont Bessières.

"Bridge and intersection cleared. Required speed for exit: one hundred ten kilometers per hour. Please stand by."

"Standing by."

Mutt eased off the accelerator, giving the traffic lamp across the bridge time to flip to green. When it did, he tore over the bridge at speed.

"Gate activated in five, four, three . . ."

The Merc followed the trajectory plotted on the heads-up display.

". . . two, one, contact."

For a moment, nothing moved. Silence. Then came a ripple of light and rush of wavelike sound, and Harper watched the slow bending of buildings and streetlamps till the Merc caught up with real time and things snapped back with a jolt.

Mutt shut down the heads-up display, and Jeff checked in with HQ in Berne.

"Berne, we are clear in real time. Package on board. Proceeding to rendezvous with Dragon Six."

"Roger. Will advise. Enjoy your evening."

Harper settled in his seat, lamenting the fact he could've been well into his second vodka tonic by now. Then again, with Monsieur Dufaux's description of the screwup that was the Paris job, Harper wasn't surprised he'd been summoned by the cop in the cashmere coat.

The Merc cruised out of Lausanne and through the small towns along Lac Léman till Mutt turned off the main road and the Merc's headlights were swallowed in the dark up ahead. A train flew across the sky and a long stream of illuminated windows whipped by in a blur. Harper thought it a swell trick and was somewhat disappointed to see the earthen embankment supporting the railroad as they drew closer. There was a tunnel through the embankment, and it opened to a shadowed somewhere. Instinctively, Harper sat up. His eyes followed the headlights along a narrow road bordered by stone walls, and beyond the walls he saw row upon row of ascending vines. The headlights caught a road sign—Appellation du Villette—and when the Merc rounded a turn and climbed a steep hillside, he saw the expanse of Lac Léman curving to the west and her dark currents running in willowy streaks. France rose on the south shore, and looking east, the blue-white peaks of the Alps sparkled with moonlight.

The road wound its way higher and cut through vineyards and skirted cliffs. It ran through the village of Aran before winding higher still. The Merc's headlights panned the hillside and lit up the stone terraces. Harper saw clusters of green and red grapes glistening on the vines. The Merc rounded a bend, and the headlights caught some stone houses gathered on a cliff, then another sign at the side of the road: Grandvaux, Canton de Vaud. At the turnoff to the village, a metal fence blocked the road. Two men in reflective vests stood behind the fence. They watched the approaching car slow to a stop. Mutt shut down the engine, Jeff secured the Brügger & Thomet. They both turned back to Harper.

"You'll need to get out here and walk. Inspector Gobet is waiting for you at *les caves Duboux.*"

"We apologize for the inconvenience, and the guns in the face thing. Nothing personal."

"No worries," Harper said.

He reached in his sports coat, pulled his SIG.

"You won't need your weapon, Mr. Harper."

"We failed to mention this is a social occasion."

Harper flashed Montreux, two years back.

"You boys remember the last social occasion the inspector invited me to? In Montreux? The guest of honor was a hotel night clerk who'd been nailed to the wall and left with his guts hanging out."

Mutt smiled with the sincerity of an insurance salesman.

"Rest assured, this is nothing of the sort."

"Besides," Jeff said, "the village is surrounded by a tactical unit of the Swiss Guard."

Harper took another look at the men at the fence. The both of them with MP5 machine pistols under their reflective vests.

"Of course it is. Thanks for the lift."

He got out of the car. The men retracted the fence without a word, and Harper walked toward the village. The buildings were old stone things from the fifteenth century. They had flower boxes and painted shutters at the windows, and the doors were marked with names. Crausaz, de la Grille, Léderrey. All the names were followed with "Vignerons et Encaveurs." Seemed Grandvaux was a winemaking village.

"My sort of town. Where's the bar?"

He came to a fork in the road where the closest thing to a bar was a stone fountain topped with a bronze spout. He leaned over for a drink. The water ran clear and it was cold. He straightened up, wiped dribbles from his mouth. He rounded a corner and walked down a curving lane. Blocking the way were six stainless steel vats as tall as him, all of them filled with freshly cut grapes. The grapes were green and moist and they made the air smell sweet. Harper squeezed between two vats, saw three locals in a wine cellar. They wore blue overalls and were shoveling clumps of grapes onto a treadmill that went *clank, clank, clank*. The grapes bounced along the treadmill to an auger, where they were crushed and separated from their stems. The men took frequent breaks to sip at their *vin blanc*. Each time raising their glasses to the light to admire the wine's color. One of them noticed Harper, then they all noticed him. They didn't speak, they just stared.

"*La cave Duboux?*" Harper asked.

"*Nous sommes Palaz et Fils, monsieur. La Famille Duboux c'est tout droit.*"

"*Merci.*"

He walked on, heard a slow waltz in three-quarter time.

He followed the music to where light poured from a cellar door and fell upon a handful of locals dancing in a narrow street. More people were gathered around watching the dancers, all of them with glasses of *vin blanc* in their hands. In the window just above, an old man operated a hand-cranked Victrola. He'd turned the fluted horn toward the street and it filled the night with music. Harper backed into the shadows and watched. Something struck him as odd. Not the Victrola, not the dancing. It was the gentleness of the scene. He couldn't remember the last time he'd seen such a thing in paradise. The waltz ended, and the couples stopped dancing. Harper stepped from the shadows, and all the locals turned their eyes to him.

"Bonsoir," he said.

The locals didn't speak. They stepped aside, watched him pass. At the open door, Harper saw more locals sitting at tables made of wine casks. And at the edge of the crowd, sitting alone, was the cop in the cashmere coat.

"Ah, good evening, Mr. Harper. Would you care to join me?"

✤

SIX

HARPER DIDN'T KNOW WHAT TO MAKE OF THE LOCALS STANDING as if someone who mattered just walked through the door. The inspector pointed to the empty stool next to him.

"I'm so pleased you could come, Mr. Harper. Do sit down."

The inspector's tone said there wasn't a choice in the matter, anyway, so sit and enjoy it. The locals settled in their own seats, continuing to stare at Harper.

"You must wonder why I asked you to meet outside the usual haunts. As it happens, today marks the beginning of *la vendange* in Grandvaux."

Harper stared at the inspector, trying to make sense of the words.

"The harvest . . . the grape harvest?"

"The very thing. There's always a fête at the end of the first day. I never miss it and thought you'd enjoy seeing it."

The inspector's explanation didn't help.

"You dragged me out of the protected zone to talk about grapes?"

"Indeed, I have. Allow me to introduce Monsieur Duboux. His family, like all families in the village, has tended the vineyards of Grandvaux for six hundred years. He also tends a section of vines I am fortunate enough to own."

Harper turned to a man in work trousers and a blue flannel shirt. He wore an old Swiss soldier's cap on his head. Midsixties, face tanned from a life of working in the fields. The man set a bowl of freshly picked grapes on the table along with two glasses and a bottle.

"C'est la dernière bouteille de 2010, Inspecteur."

Inspector Gobet bowed his head.

"Vous êtes trop gentil, Monsieur Duboux."

"En fait, I would like to offer it to your guest."

"Néanmoins, my dear sir, I will partake of the honor. And perhaps, now, you might ask old Fournier to play a bit of *le Ranz*. I'm sure Mr. Harper would enjoy hearing the villagers serenade the cows."

Monsieur Duboux tapped his nose and winked, gathered fresh bottles, and invited the happy crowd into the street.

"Mes amis, il est temps de chanter!"

Harper watched the locals collect their glasses and follow Monsieur Duboux out the door. He heard Duboux call to the old chap with the Victrola.

"Allez, Fournier. Donnez-nous une pour les vaches!"

When the music played, the locals sang a lullaby that echoed down the street and into the night. Harper looked at the inspector.

"They're out in the street, singing to cows?"

"Very old Swiss tradition," the inspector explained. "Keeps the beasts calm and happy."

"There's nothing in these fields but vines."

"Mr. Harper, the cows may have moved farther afield, but in Switzerland, traditions linger. Passed down and cherished from generation to generation like the family watch."

Harper thought about it.

So far, Inspector Gobet was batting for six on the no-bloody-idea meter. The inspector smiled, opened the bottle, poured.

"I must say, Mr. Harper, you've made quite the impression in the village. It's quite the honor to be presented with a bowl from the first day's harvest, not to mention the last of the 2010. A near perfect vintage."

"Raises a question: What have I done to deserve it besides show up?"

Inspector Gobet set his nose in the glass and breathed the bouquet.

"Simply put, the good citizens of Grandvaux have an awareness, shall we say, of who and what you are. Try it."

Harper picked up his glass. Nice color, good nose.

"It's swell, and what the hell do you mean?"

"The wine, of course."

Harper scanned the cellar. There was no one around.

"Look, Inspector, I just got out of the tank yesterday. My timeline's well scrambled. I'm really not in the mood to follow-the-leader till he gets to the bloody point."

The inspector picked a grape from the bowl, popped it in his mouth. He slid the bowl across the table.

"Try one of these, Mr. Harper. They were picked this very morning at dawn. From my private vineyard, as a matter of fact. You may find they have a particular zing. Good for what ails you."

Harper pushed the bowl away.

"What's ailing me is your lads in the white coats seem to have been a little heavy-handed with the memory scrub. Took me an hour to find Café du Grütli tonight, and it's around the bloody corner from my flat."

The inspector returned the bowl to Harper.

"Please, do have a grape."

"No fucking thanks."

A pale fire burned in the inspector's eyes.

"Mr. Harper, I gave instructions that you were to be told this was a social occasion. If you'd prefer me to remind you that you are *not* a creature of free will, then I'll be more than happy to do so."

Yes, fucking sir, Harper thought. He picked a grape, tasted it. The skin seemed to melt and a sweet liquid washed over his tongue, then came a rush of light to his eyes. Warmth, weightlessness.

"Radiance?"

The inspector nodded. "The very thing."

"It comes from grapes?"

"Not just any grapes; these grapes, picked at dawn on the first day of *les vendanges*. A bit of distillation, then a blending with the leaves of certain Moroccan tobaccos, et voila. A pleasant smoking experience necessary to the well-being of our kind in human form."

Harper looked outside, watched the locals swaying and singing still. He flashed coming into the village, seeing the curious looks on their faces. Half joy, half wonder.

"It isn't supposed to affect them."

The inspector pulled another grape, bit into it, and savored the taste.

"In its raw form, a little goes a long way. So much so that after eating a few handfuls, the locals are induced into a transcendental state that allows them to see, in a manner of speaking, the light that dwells in the eyes of our kind."

"What about you? Do they recognize you?"

"Me? Oh, I'm something of an old hat in the village. You, however, are quite the new boy."

Harper popped two more grapes. The inspector was right; good for what ails you.

"Christ, no wonder you've got a tactical unit surrounding this place. Keep the locals under lock and key."

"More along the lines of mutually assured security. The villagers present us with the first day's harvest, as they have for thousands of years, and we see to it they are not disturbed by any unpleasantness during this happy time."

Harper held his glass against a candle, saw particles of perfect light shimmering in the wine.

"How long does the effect last for them?"

"Only for a few nights. Then they'll begin the fermentation process and carbon dioxide will be released into the air. Among other things, the process causes them to forget about the likes of you and me, till the next *vendange* comes around. Another glass? I'm afraid it's another of those quaint Swiss traditions that an opened bottle must not be left unfinished."

"Quite right, too."

Inspector Gobet poured.

Outside, the Victrola played another waltz, Viennese this time. The locals shaped into couples and began to spin themselves silly. Harper saw the inspector's fingers tapping in time to the music. For half a second, Harper thought, the cop in the cashmere coat looked positively human. Harper plucked a few more grapes and popped them in his mouth . . . *ziiiinnng.* The music wound into a dizzying coda, and the locals laughed and applauded and shouted to the old man with the Victrola: *"Encore, Fournier! Encore!"*

The inspector finished his glass and stood.

"Well, this has been pleasant. Care for a stroll?"

Harper knew the social occasion portion of the evening had concluded. He took a last swig from his own glass.

"Sure."

They went into the street and walked into the shadows.

They turned down Rue de l'Église, walked past the Riccard and Bougnol cellars. More locals making merry over bowls of grapes and glasses of wine. At the Genévaz cellars, some locals sat at a long table in the middle of the road, raising glasses and singing a tune about a fair young maiden who kissed all the boys from Fribourg to Lausanne and back again.

At the edge of the village, Harper followed the inspector onto a grassy path bordered by fieldstone walls. A hundred meters on, they came to a stone arch fitted with an old iron gate. Inspector Gobet removed a key of similar vintage from his coat and opened the lock.

"Let me guess," Harper said. "Your own private vineyard."

"Let's just say I'm the latest in a long line of *propriétaires*. It was on this very patch of land that our kind inspired the Romans to cultivate the Chasselas grape. There are some wonderful writings in the Lausanne Museum you must read sometime. Lots of reports to the Emperor from the commander of the legion, explaining how the soldiers enjoyed working in the vineyards at harvest time. Lots of *in vino veritas*, that sort of thing."

Harper looked back at the village. Locals had gathered on the village square overlooking the lake for another round of singing to the cows, this time to the cows across the lake in France.

"Not surprised."

The inspector pushed open the gate and they walked down the field-stone steps leading through the vineyard. A third-quarter moon gave enough light to guide them in the dark, and at the end of the steps there was a small stone hut sitting amid the vines. The inspector turned to Harper.

"Please, take a seat on the bench. I won't be a minute."

Harper watched the inspector open the door. Moonlight spilled through the doorway, and Harper saw the sniper team inside. The spotter checking his sector through binoculars, the shooter adjusting the sight of his Barrett anti-material rifle. The door closed behind the inspector. Harper sat on the bench, scanned the hillside. He saw stone huts scattered through the vineyards. He did a recon of the layout. There wasn't a square meter of ground surrounding Grandvaux that couldn't be seen by one of the huts. All together, the huts triangulated a series of impenetrable kill zones. No doubt the inspector's snipers could make a head shot from a thousand meters. And with a 12.7-millimeter explosive round, the hit would be impressive. Harper laughed to himself. An hour ago he'd arrived and found himself bemused by the transcendental gentleness of the villagers. Now he was in a vineyard surrounded by shoot-to-kill snipers.

"Switzerland, land of enchantment."

The inspector emerged from the hut and joined Harper on the bench.

"My apologies, I needed to check in with our command post on Chemin de Baussan. Lovely view from here, don't you think?"

Harper gave it a glance.

Moon, mountains, lake.

"It's swell."

The inspector had a cigarette case in his hand, and he offered it to Harper.

"I have," Harper said, patting his pockets. "Somewhere, I think."

"Actually, I'm switching you to a new blend. Keep the case as a token of my appreciation for a job well done in Paris."

Harper flashed back to the café, getting up to speed with Monsieur Dufaux.

"Can't remember much of it. But from what I saw on the front page of the newspaper, and from what Dufaux tells me, it looks like cleanup in Paris was a bloody mess."

The inspector dropped the cigarette case in Harper's lap.

"You made six confirmed kills, we made the bomb disappear, all with minimal collateral damage. In our line of work, we call that a good day."

Harper took the cigarette case.

"Cheers then."

He opened it, saw twenty gold-filtered fags all in a row. He took one, and the inspector had a burning match at the ready. Harper nodded toward the stone huts scattered throughout the vineyards. "Lighting me up for your snipers?"

"More like giving them an opportunity to align their sights."

"Right."

Harper touched the tip of the cigarette to the flame and drew in the smoke. He felt a warm rush of radiance as the weight of his form melted away. Christ, he thought, it had been a long time since it was that good.

"Mind if I ask a question, Inspector?"

"Go ahead."

"Just how did my picture end up on the front page of every newspaper on the planet? Thought your clever lads in the SX squad were supposed to take care of that sort of thing."

"As they did, as the cleanup crew did. Every shred of tape or image of you caught in a camera or mobile was tracked and deleted. We decided to leave that particular image in the public domain."

"Figured as much. It's the *why* I'm wondering about."

"Well, firstly, you aren't identifiable to any great degree to the general population. Secondly, HQ likes a bit of stoking the angelic legend now and again. Thirdly, we'd very like to locate the one responsible for it."

"Sorry?"

"The picture appeared the night of the attack as part of a videotape that was released before the battle was even over. By the time it was spotted on the Internet, it'd already been seen by millions of people around the world. Given that everything sent on the Internet is routed through our SX squad before delivery, it was quite the trick."

"Any idea who did it?"

"We can't trace the source. Nor can we trace who it was that hacked Monsieur Geoffroy de Villehardouin's blog."

"Geoffroy de what?"

"The art historian who allegedly posted the pictures on his blog. He died ten months ago. His blog has been inactive, till yesterday."

Harper took another hit. He saw himself on the Pont des Arts, saw himself jumping from the bridge into the fog.

"What are you imagining, Mr. Harper?"

Harper smiled.

"Couple of hits off a new blend and you're checking the manner of my thinking already?"

"Yes, as a matter of fact."

Harper took another drag.

"Whoever took the picture knew where the attack was happening before we did. Someone who knew I'd be there. Couldn't be the enemy, they'd have used the intel to put me down."

"What else?"

Harper flashed the front page of 24 Heures.

"Someone knows who I am, who we are. Knows how to cover his tracks."

The inspector nodded approvingly.

"Not bad for a first go out of the tank. Continue with the imagination, Mr. Harper."

"Anything specific?"

"Let's try the events of the Paris operation."

Disconnected fragments of time floated through Harper's eyes. Now and again he saw a sequence, the *wham* . . . he flashed the Paris job. Jumping from Pont des Arts onto the *Manon*. Screams, cries, blood. Whacking the goons, defusing the bomb. A dead father, a young girl singing a song. French police coming on board, slamming Harper to the deck. Then a blast of white noise, then seeing himself climbing out of the tank at the Vevey clinic ten days later.

Harper blinked, looked at the inspector.

"There's a hole in my timeline."

"You cannot upload any images from the last ten days?"

"That's how long it's been?"

The inspector nodded.

"Two days in La Santé Prison, eight days in the tank."

Harper tried again. Zip.

"Sorry, only thing I know about the last ten days is what I read in *24 Heures*."

"Because HQ ordered everything from the point of your arrest, up to your being released from the tank, deleted."

Harper took a hit of smoke.

"Why?"

"You were exposed to specific information regarding the life and death of Captain Jay Michael Harper. You had a rather bad reaction to it, especially at the hands of the French secret police who subjected you to enhanced interrogation in prison. Which explains the rather heavy-handed manner of your memory scrub, and your current state of confusion."

Harper thought about it.

"Feedback?"

"I'm afraid so."

"How bad?"

The inspector found his own cigarette case in his cashmere coat. He took a cigarette, had a match at the ready, and lit up. He took a long pull, then released the smoke.

"By the time we pulled you from La Santé, you were clawing at your skin, trying to dig your way out of your form."

Harper saw himself climbing out of the bloody tank, saw the gashes and scratches on his stomach. Thought it was from the battle on the *Manon*. He snapped back, chuckled to himself.

"This conversation's getting better by the bloody minute, Inspector. Can't wait to get the punch line. Wouldn't mind having another drink before you spill it."

The door of the hut creaked open. One of the snipers stepped out with two steaming mugs and a bowl of grapes on a wooden tray.

"Ask and you shall receive, Mr. Harper."

"Not exactly what I had in mind."

The inspector took the tray, set it on the bench. He lifted one of the mugs, popped a few grapes.

"*Merci, Corporal,*" the inspector said.

"*Voluntier, Inspecteur.*"

Harper looked at the soldier's face. A young woman of Asian descent, nineteen or twenty years old max, dressed in military camouflage. Her black hair pinned to the back of her neck, her emerald green eyes staring at Harper. For long seconds, Harper returned the stare.

"Something is wrong, monsieur?"

Harper took the other mug.

"No. Cheers, Corporal."

She returned to the hut, quietly closed the door. Harper looked at the inspector.

"She's one of them, isn't she?"

"If you mean is Corporal Mai one of my Swiss Guard tacticals, yes."

"Inspector, I know my brains are fried at the moment, but I can still spot one of your recognition tests well enough. She's one of *them*, from your school at Mon Repos."

The inspector sipped his tea.

"Very good. How did you know?"

Damn good question, Harper thought.

"It's . . . her eyes."

"Why?"

Harper thought about it some more.

"Back at the café, Dufaux said the lad's name. I saw him for a second. Hat, lantern."

"Marc Rochat, you mean."

Hearing the name again, Harper saw him again, but only for a second.

"Yes, that's right."

"And?"

Harper nodded to the sniper hut.

"The corporal's eyes are the same as the lad's."

"The color, you mean."

"They're the same color, yeah, but so are yours and mine. It's everything else. The shape and separation. They're exactly the same as the lad with the lantern."

The inspector drew on his smoke.

"It's a genetic trait."

"All of them?"

"Yes, all of them."

"Does she know?"

"Does she know what?"

"Does she know she's a half-breed, bred by our side?"

The inspector pulled another grape and ate it.

"I suggest you drink your tea, before it gets cold," he said.

The inspector's tone had all the politeness of a good and gracious host. Still, Harper knew if he didn't shut up and drink, the inspector would see to it the tea was poured down his throat. He almost sipped, looked at the inspector instead.

"What's yours?"

"Earl Grey, with a dash of milk."

"What's mine?"

"Does it matter?"

No, Harper thought, it didn't. He sipped. Whatever it was, it had the delicate flavor of jasmine.

"Not bad as potions go, Inspector. What will it do?"

"It should better regulate random electrical impulses as they interact with the hippocampus region of your brain. Specifically those you were exposed to in Paris."

"Memories, you mean. Captain Jay Michael Harper's memories."

"Yes."

Harper took a grape, sipped his tea.

"Everything was deleted, plus I've just had the mother of all memory scrubs. Not to mention eight days of regenerative stasis. I should be good to go."

The inspector reached inside his cashmere coat again. He removed a manila envelope, handed it to Harper.

"What's this?"

"Your regenerative stasis results."

Harper rested his mug of tea on the bench. He took the envelope and opened it. Two sheets of paper. List of tests and procedures on page one; page two listed the results.

"Nothing here but zeros," Harper said.

"Because there are no results. The process was canceled."

"Canceled?"

The inspector drew on his cigarette.

"Always been a tricky business, our hiding in the forms of men. Now and again, a phantom manifests itself and searches for a soul no longer there. Our beings enter a state of feedback. Unregulated, the consequences can be most severe."

Harper flashed back to Café du Grütli. Reaching for his killing knife, ready to slice open Monsieur Dufaux's throat for no reason at all. Then Mutt and Jeff with their guns in his face . . . *We were told you're not quite yourself these days . . . and get in the fucking motorcar,* s'il vous plaît. No bloody wonder.

"I know what feedback is, Inspector. I also know the only way to fix it is regenerative stasis. So when do the medics fix it?"

"As yet, they can't."

The inspector tapped his cigarette. Harper watched the smoldering ash sink to the moonlit ground, all the while listening to the inspector's voice.

"What happened?" Harper said.

"When the medics began to extract your eternal being, your form went offline. Extraction was abandoned."

"I died, you mean, in my form."

The inspector didn't answer.

"How long?"

"Fifteen hours, fifty-eight minutes, nineteen seconds."

Harper thought about it. A human soul could hang on for three days until dissipation of rigor mortis, waiting to be comforted and guided to the next life. For Harper's kind, it was three minutes.

"Not that I'm complaining, Inspector, but why the hell am I still here?"

"Best guess: At the moment of extraction, a phantom electrochemical signal from your host's hippocampus region jumped the firewall and made contact with your eternal being."

"Best guess, you say."

"Affirmative."

Harper felt something crawl over his skin. Then again, it wasn't his skin.

"Are you telling me my host is still alive?"

"'Alive' is not a word I would use in describing the condition."

"No? What word would you use? Take your pick, there are a quarter million words in the *Oxford English Dictionary* alone."

The inspector regarded the view.

"'The formation of heavenly bodies according to the received theory which supposes it to have taken place by the concentration and consolidation of cosmic matter.'"

"That's twenty-five words, Inspector."

"Yes. From *Views of the Architecture of the Heavens*, by the ninth-century astronomer and opiate addict John Pringle Nichol. A Scot, you know. Curiously enough, his words serve as a rather good definition of the word *evolution* in the *OED*."

Harper added it up: $2 + 2 =$ no bloody way.

"Locals evolve, Inspector, not our kind. Not you, not me, not the handful of us who are left. Not in two and a half million years. We die in our forms, we die forever."

"So it would seem. However, in your case, at the very moment the medics were about to pull the plug on you, a luminance burst was registered in your eyes at a factor of 1.6×10^9 cd/m²."

"Sounds rather bright."

"One way of imagining it would be to imagine the brightness of the midday sun pouring through the rose window of Lausanne Cathedral."

"What's the other way of imagining it?"

"It matches the luminance level of the first light of creation hidden beneath Lausanne Cathedral."

Harper heard the inspector's voice, then saw himself and the lad in the cavern beneath the cathedral, saw a fire burning in a small bush. They transferred the fire to the lad's lantern, carried it back to the nave to hide it from the bad guys.

"You're telling me something happened to me during the cathedral job. Being exposed to the light . . . changed me."

"Actually, I'm not saying anything of the sort, Mr. Harper. I merely lay out the facts."

"What facts? That I bloody rose from the dead? That's not evolution, Inspector, that's a . . ."

"A what?"

"A miracle. And you and I know there's no such thing in paradise."

The inspector sipped his tea.

"Yes, so for the moment, let's call it an undefined metaphysical condition as a result of your form being exposed to the first light of creation, two and a half years ago."

Harper flashed through the cathedral job. Landed on the messy end with the lad killed, himself half dead, bad guy corpses everywhere . . . and someone else.

"I wasn't the only one exposed to it."

"Me and those members of the Swiss Guard associated with the Lausanne operation, you mean. We've been running tests on anyone exposed to the light. Luminance levels are all normal, so far."

Harper looked at the inspector.

"That's not who I'm talking about."

"I beg your pardon?"

"There was a woman, a local. I can't see her, but I can see her shadow on the timeline. She was there with me and the lad. She was exposed to the light, too. What was her name?"

The inspector smiled.

"Nice try, Mr. Harper, but you know you are forbidden to hear the name, as she is forbidden to hear yours."

Harper thought about it. The medics couldn't make her, or any local, completely disappear from a timeline, but a local could be *shadowed out* from the second level of consciousness. Standard procedure after a tough job. Kept a lock on any feelings or emotions that might have been generated by "extreme contact." That's what HQ called it. Given time, shadows became forgotten things. And plenty of time had passed for her to have become well lost, Harper thought. Still, like the lad with the lantern, the woman in the shadows lingered.

"There's something about . . ."

She was there, just out of reach.

"You were saying, Mr. Harper?"

Harper blinked, looked at the inspector.

"Nothing. I was saying nothing."

He sipped his tea, scanned the view again.

Moon, mountains, lake.

"Tell me, Inspector, why aren't we in Lausanne, or at the clinic in Vevey? Why are we having this swell conversation in the middle of a vineyard by the light of a waning moon?"

"A somewhat lyrical notion, Mr. Harper."

"Maybe it's the smoke, maybe it's the grapes, maybe it's the tea. All I know is there's no way in hell you should be telling me a word of this. HQ ordered my timeline trashed for a reason, but here you're poking through my brain and looking for clues that aren't supposed to be there anymore."

The inspector took a puff off his smoke, popped a grape, regarded the night sky. Harper watched him, waited.

"You know, I often come here to have a good long gaze out there. Only natural, as the locals would say. After all, we're creatures born of light from somewhere out there; from a time we only know as the unremembered beginning. Our eternal beings only exist in this place by maintaining a resistance to the gravitational forces of the very cosmic matter in which we hide. In that way, we're very much like the stars themselves."

They sat silently for a moment.

The inspector looked at Harper.

"Since coming back online, your eternal being is devouring radiance at an unsustainable level. Under normal circumstances it wouldn't be a problem; we'd pull you out of Captain Harper, get you into a new form. There's one standing by right now. A Canadian from the Joint Task Force 2 unit."

"But you can't do that."

"No, we cannot."

"How long do I have?"

"Six weeks. Eight, if you're lucky."

"Then what?"

"Quantum mechanics."

Harper thought about it: *very much like the stars themselves.*

Burning fuel so fast its hydrogen core fuses into inert matter, unable to maintain enough degeneracy pressure to counter the gravity of its own mass. Inert core expands to 1.4 solar masses—the Chandrasekhar limit, it was called . . . Harper flashed back to an episode on the History Channel telling him all about it, along with a rather spectacular animation of a star the size of Earth exploding, then reversing and collapsing in on itself at 135,000 meters per second. In the blink of an eye, the star is squeezed to an infinitesimal point of compressed matter from which nothing, not even light, can escape. Harper looked at the paper in his hands, the report with his regenerative stasis results; the one with all the zeros telling him he was royally screwed. He folded the paper and returned it to the manila envelope. He handed the envelope to the cop in the cashmere coat.

"You know, Inspector, on a scale of one to ten, your idea of a social occasion is absolute shit."

The inspector raised an eyebrow. "In any army on this Earth, such a comment would land you in the brig, Mr. Harper."

"Except you, me, and the rest of this bloody salvation army aren't of this Earth, are we?"

The inspector took the envelope, returned it to his cashmere coat.

"Orders from HQ are that you be dropped back in the tank and locked down until the medics find a solution to your situation."

"And what are the odds of the medics finding a solution to my situation in six weeks—eight, if I'm lucky?"

The inspector shrugged. "I would've thought you'd have a better chance of hitting the numbers in the EuroMillions lottery two months running."

Harper rubbed the back of his neck.

"I suppose this is payback for my sins."

"Your sins?"

"If I'd made a break from the *Manon* with the bomb. When I had a chance and jumped back . . ."

He didn't finish the thought. The inspector finished for him.

"To comfort a passing soul and a frightened little girl."

That's right, Harper wanted to say, but he looked at his watch instead: 23:35 hours.

"So into the tank, wait it out till lights-out," he said.

"Those are your orders. My orders are to make sure you follow yours this time."

"How about this: How about Mutt and Jeff take me back to Lausanne and lock me down in GG's? There's plenty of booze, and the scenery would be a hell of a lot better than the tank. Might as well get all the look-but-not-touch I can before quantum mechanics kicks in. With a little luck I can still make the last act of the midnight show."

"Or you could go back to Paris on tomorrow's afternoon train and avoid the whole thing."

It took half a second more than it'd take a star to implode before the words registered. Harper looked at the mug of tea in his left hand, the smoldering stub of his smoke in the other. A new blend, the inspector called it. Harper had to admit, the manner of his own thinking was much improved.

"HQ doesn't know you're juicing me for a mission, do they?"

"No, they do not. Nor does anyone outside my personal detail."

"A bit out of character for you, isn't it? Breaking a direct order from HQ?"

"Mr. Harper, please. My orders are to assure you are picked up tomorrow evening and see that you are locked down in the tank. My detail will be arriving at your flat at seventeen hundred hours to do just that."

"And if I'm not there?"

"Well, we'll begin a search of your haunts in an attempt to locate you."

Harper looked across the dark vineyards toward the village. The fête was winding down, and the locals were drifting off to their cottages. He watched one couple walking slowly, unsteadily. They were laughing and holding hands.

They are not us, we are not them . . .

So much for the last act at GG's, Harper thought.

He took a last hit from his smoke, released it slowly. He dropped the butt into the dark earth and ground it into dust. He stared at the grapes in the bowl, watching them glisten in the moonlight. He selected the biggest, juiciest-looking grape and popped it in his mouth . . . *ziiinng.* He joined the inspector in scanning the night.

"So, Inspector, what the hell is happening in Paris? And what has it to do with the price of beans?"

"Beans?"

"Me and my undefined metaphysical condition."

✿

SEVEN

I

KATHERINE WAS IN THE BACK ROOM OF THE CANDLE LODGE, pouring wax into star-shaped shells, when she heard the bell above the entrance door. She checked the monitor connected to the hidden camera out front. Rule number one, as handed down from Officer Jannsen: Anything looks out of place, hit one of the panic buttons located about the shop. A couple of the Swiss Guard boys were always staked out around the corner. Rule number two: All else fails, there was a loaded Glock under the counter.

Katherine stared at the guy in the monitor.

Usual clients to her candle shop were customers from Molly's Diner or familiar faces she had seen about town, or the tourists in buses on their way to Rainbow Falls. Katherine's best clients were the local marijuana growers, who said her candles held magical properties that made their plants grow bigger, yummier buds.

But the guy on the monitor, the guy standing amid the candle-laden tables, was none of the above. He was in his late sixties, he was bald, he wore a wool topcoat over a pin-striped suit. He carried a briefcase, and there were pince-nez on his nose. The topper was he was standing perfectly still, staring into the lens of the shop's CCTV camera. Thing was, the camera was hidden behind a small mirror. Katherine removed her safety glasses and gloves, and she walked to the front of the shop. The man bowed.

"*Bonjour, Madame Taylor. J'espère que je ne vous dérange pas.*"

Katherine almost answered before she realized no one in town knew she spoke French. She jumped for the Glock.

"I am here by the permission of Inspector Gobet, Madame Taylor. And your protection detail is aware of my presence. There is no need to call for assistance, or shoot me, for that matter."

Katherine pulled her hand away from the gun. She looked at the man, then over his shoulder, then through the shop window and out to the street. There was a Mercedes S600 parked in front of the shop. A white-gloved, black-suited chauffeur stood next to it. With the bowler hat on his head, the chauffeur looked seven feet tall. Katherine looked again at the man standing in her shop.

"Who the heck are you?"

"I am Monsieur Gübeli, Madame Taylor. I am a private banker from Lausanne representing the estate of Marc Rochat."

Katherine lost her breath a moment.

"Marc?"

"*Oui.* I am here to advise you that you are the sole beneficiary of Master Rochat's estate."

If there weren't a wall behind her, Katherine would have fallen over.

"What? I mean . . . what?"

"His estate, madame." He looked around the cluttered shop. "If we could sit somewhere, perhaps I could explain the details."

"Details?"

"It's just that Master Rochat was rather well-off. The amount left to you is considerable."

Something wasn't right, Katherine thought. She stared a minute, seeing if he'd flinch. He didn't.

"Marc could barely write his own name, he wouldn't even know what a will was . . ."

"Madame?"

"And what is this *Master Rochat* stuff?"

The man took a step forward.

"Of course, madame, excuse me. You see, 'Master Rochat' was the proper form of address among those in the service to the Rochat family. The family's financial matters were my particular concern. After his father and grandmother died, I took over all of Master Rochat's affairs. As far as his will, a note was recently found in one of his sketchbooks. The note made it very clear that in the event of his death, all his possessions were to become yours."

"A sketchbook?"

"Yes, madame. A book he titled *piratz*, misspelled with—"

Katherine saw herself in the belfry that last day. Rochat handing her a book with the title written on the cover. He'd written it in his own hand.

"With a *z*," Katherine said.

"Yes, madame. With a *z*."

Katherine shook her head as if waking from a dream.

"What did you say your name was?"

The man stood still as a coatrack.

"Gübeli, madame."

Katherine stared at him, still not trusting him.

"Yeah, I remember that name. Marc told me about you. You're the one that brought him to Lausanne from Canada after his mother died, aren't you? From Toronto, wasn't it?"

Monsieur Gübeli smiled.

"Yes, I brought him to Switzerland. Though I'm sure you know as well as I, Master Rochat was from Quebec City. He was ten years old when I brought him to Switzerland. He lived with his grandmother at Vufflens in a large house he imagined was a castle. He went to a school in Lausanne with children like himself. He worked as *le guet de Lausanne* until he died saving your life, and the cathedral."

Katherine smiled.

"Jesus, you're telling me the truth. You did know him."

"Yes, madame, for fourteen wonderful years."

Katherine looked over Monsieur Gübeli's shoulder for another peek at the chauffeur. The more she looked at the two of them, the more they looked like a couple characters from Marc Rochat's imaginary world. Katherine sat on a stool behind the counter.

"How much money?"

"Pardon?"

"The considerable amount of money Marc left me. How much?"

Monsieur Gübeli answered with the efficiency of a calculator. "At the current exchange rate, it would be eighty-five million, four hundred twenty-three thousand, two hundred thirty-seven American dollars."

"What?"

"Eighty-five—"

"No, it's okay, I heard you the first time. Jesus, that's not considerable, that's a shitload."

"Uh, well, as I said, I tended to Master Rochat's business affairs and was somewhat successful in managing his investments. I would be happy to continue in that capacity on your behalf."

Katherine stared at him, imagining the shopping rage she could unleash upon the world with that kind of cash. She laughed to herself.

"Something amuses you, madame?"

"Yeah, me."

"I don't understand."

"Not sure I do, either. Once upon a time money was . . . everything. Now I'm here in a candle shop and I've got this great kid, and life is . . ."

She waved her hand like pushing away the thought.

"Wait a second," she said. "Why me?"

"Madame?"

"Why would he want me to have all his money?"

"The exact wording in his will states: 'Because I'm very sure she will need some money when she gets home.'"

Katherine could almost hear Marc Rochat's voice saying the words.

"He had no idea, did he? Marc, I mean."

"I am afraid I do not comprehend your thought, madame."

101

"The money. Eighty-five cents or eighty-five million bucks, it was all the same to him, wasn't it?"

"*C'est vrai, madame.* In many ways, it was a reflection of his true nature."

"Meaning what?"

"I mean to say, Master Rochat was sensitive to the needs of others, and that sensitivity had a remarkable effect on people."

Katherine turned in a small circle, thinking, remembering . . . She sighed, looked at Monsieur Gübeli.

"No."

"Madame?"

"I'm not interested in Marc's money. You must be able to do something with it. What about that school he went to in Lausanne—Mount Somethingorother, I think. There must be lots of schools for people like him."

"Mon Repos, madame. But as that school is fully endowed by the Rochat family already, as are similar schools around the world, perhaps I could suggest the establishment of a new foundation to assist children with brain injuries, born into families of lesser means, in less developed countries?"

The Marc Rochat Foundation. Katherine liked the sound of it.

"Yeah, that's good. And you know what, how about old people with no families, or homeless kids, and . . ." She combed her fingers through her hair. "Jesus, so many people need help, don't they? And I know Marc would've wanted to help as many as he could. So tell you what: Why don't I leave it up to you? Marc trusted you, that's good enough for me."

Monsieur Gübeli smiled and bowed his head.

"Your generosity is noble, madame. I am sure Master Rochat would have been very happy with your decision."

Katherine rocked on her heels.

"Yeah, well, I'm sure I'll regret it someday, but there you go. I would like his sketchbook, though."

"Certainly, and there are several sketchbooks."

Katherine could see them on the shelf of the belfry loge. She remembered looking through them that first day he'd taken her into the cathedral to hide her from the killers.

"Yeah, I remember them. Three or four, I think. You have them, all of them?"

Monsieur Gübeli nodded, stepping closer again.

"Madame will also be interested to know he included other items in his will."

"Yeah? Like what?"

"The black felt hat he wore while calling the hour, his lantern, a few boxes of candles from the cathedral."

"Really?"

"He asked that they be passed on to you, so you would always remember living in the tower. Certain Lausanne authorities responsible for the cathedral have decided to honor Master Rochat's request. If madame would sign a few papers, I can release the items to you forthwith."

"You have them? Here?"

Monsieur Gübeli pointed outside to the Mercedes. "I took the liberty of bringing the items with me, assuming you would wish to have them."

"What about the cash?"

"*Pardonnez-moi?*"

"Did you bring the money, too? Just in case I decided I wanted it?"

"Uh, well . . . no, madame."

Katherine sighed and laughed again.

"Yeah, well . . . probably better that way."

She looked at the clock on the wall; it was just after noon. She was suddenly famished. *Surprising what tossing away eighty-five million will do for an appetite,* she thought. She jumped from the stool.

"You like tuna-noodle casserole, Mr. Gübeli?"

"I beg your pardon?"

"I'm hungry and it's Tuesday. In this town, that means tuna-noodle casserole for lunch."

Monsieur Gübeli brightened.

"Why, it would be a great pleasure."

Katherine took a long black cloak from a hook on the wall and tossed it over her shoulders. She led Monsieur Gübeli out of the shop. The chauffeur in the bowler hat had the rear door of the Mercedes open and ready. Katherine looked at Monsieur Gübeli.

"Uh, dude, we're just walking across the street."

Monsieur Gübeli turned to the chauffeur and addressed him in French, telling him to wait. The chauffeur bowed and closed the car door. He then removed a white handkerchief from his pocket, unfolded it, and proceeded to dust the Mercedes of any offending particulates. Katherine shook her head in disbelief and started across Main Street. Monsieur Gübeli followed close behind.

"You know, you and your chauffeur didn't make the most subtle of entrances."

"Madame?"

"In this town, nobody'd be caught dead in a vehicle without four-wheel drive and mud flaps, preferably with a freshly killed deer across the hood. You drive into Grover's Mill in a hundred-thousand-dollar Merc with Lurch at the wheel."

"Madame?"

"The butler from *The Addams Family*. American TV sitcom. I was raised on reruns. Lurch reminds me of your . . . never mind. Point is, the two of you are sort of hard to explain. I mean, I am supposed to be hiding out in this town."

"Ah. Yes, of course. Officer Jannsen and I have already prepared a cover story that fits with your current arrangement."

Katherine stopped in the middle of the road, turned around.

"What story?"

Monsieur Gübeli looked up and down the street with concern.

"Don't worry," Katherine said. "The only real traffic we get in this town is when the tour buses come through. So what's your idea of a reasonable cover story when you're trying to explain a guy in a suit who wears funny glasses, who's just been driven into town by a six-foot-plus other guy who spends his downtime polishing a spotless Merc with a handkerchief?"

Monsieur Gübeli adjusted his pince-nez.

"Ah. Well, that your family is extremely wealthy and that I am the family lawyer, as well as your godfather. I have been asked by your parents to persuade you to abandon your current living arrangement and to return to your family in North Carolina, where your illegitimate child may be put up for adoption."

Katherine shrugged.

"Damn if that doesn't sound exactly like something my parents would do. Not bad, Monsieur Gübeli. You got a first name, seeing as you're my make-believe godfather?"

"I am afraid that would suggest an informality I could not presume."

"Huh?"

"It is not our way, madame."

"Whose way?"

"The firm I represent."

"Suit yourself." Katherine spun on her heels and led the way to Molly's Diner. She went immediately to her favorite booth, undid her cloak, and let it fall down from her shoulders. She flipped her way through the jukebox.

"Molly's on a mission to widen my musical tastes. She's loaded the box with Grateful Dead and Jerry Garcia tunes. Says they'll cleanse my spirit. Molly's a genuine child of the sixties."

Monsieur Gübeli removed his topcoat and took the bench opposite, rested his briefcase on the seat. Molly came over.

"Howdy, sugar. Who's your friend in the suit? And who's the funny-looking character in the street dusting the limo?"

Katherine rolled her eyes. "The family lawyer and his driver. Sent by Mommy and Daddy to bring me home to Jesus."

Molly set her hands on her hips.

"Is that so? Well, let me tell you, it's a free country, and your parents can choose to be old sticks-in-the-mud and you can just go on choosing to live your life the way you want it. Isn't that so, Mr. Lawyer-Person?"

Monsieur Gübeli cleared his throat.

"I assure you, madame, I am only a messenger. I do not pretend to affect opinion."

"Say, you are a lawyer, aren't you? No matter, we serve all kinds here. What can I getcha?"

Katherine slapped the table.

"Two blue plate specials and two iced teas, Molly."

"I'll make it three and send a plate out to the chauffeur, seeing as he's working up an appetite being so funny-looking. Back in a jiffy."

Molly walked away. Katherine leaned over the table and whispered, "How'd I do on the cover story?"

Monsieur Gübeli smiled and whispered back, "Very well, madame. Most convincing."

"Great."

She found two quarters in her blue jeans, dropped them in the jukebox, and punched C-13. A seventh chord hit on a downbeat and rippled along till the band fell into a slow-rolling rhythm with a faraway voice:

> *"The wheel is turning and you can't slow down,*
> *You can't let go and you can't hold on,*
> *You can't go back and you can't stand still,*
> *If the thunder don't get you then the lightning will."*

Katherine watched Monsieur Gübeli stare at the jukebox and saw the look of amazement on his face.

"Welcome to the great Pacific Northwest," she said. "Stay awhile, you'll get used to it."

Monsieur Gübeli looked at Katherine.

"To tell the truth, madame, I was recalling a time from my younger days. May 26, 1972, to be exact."

"Wow, that's pretty good recall. What happened?"

"I took two hundred fifty micrograms of lysergic acid diethylamide and attended a Grateful Dead concert at the Lyceum Theatre just off the Strand."

Katherine studied Monsieur Gübeli's bankerlike appearance.

"You. Dropped acid. And went to a Dead concert?"

"Oh, yes. I remember how that evening's performance of 'Morning Dew' affected me. It had the quality of a lament for all mankind. I was very moved."

Molly arrived with the plates and a pitcher of iced tea.

"Molly," Katherine said, "you won't believe this, but the family lawyer here was an acid-tripping Deadhead back in the seventies."

"Of course he was." Molly laughed. "I had him pegged as a fellow traveler the minute I laid eyes on him."

"Yeah? How?"

Molly set the plates on the table and poured the iced tea. She put her hand on her hip and waved her finger at Katherine like she was teaching a lesson.

"Once a Deadhead, always a Deadhead, sugar. Dress him up in a suit and he'll still be tripping his way through life with a good and honest heart because he has seen the light. Ain't that right, Mr. Lawyer-Person?"

Monsieur Gübeli nodded graciously. "An excellent way of imagining it, if I may say so."

Molly winked at him and walked away. Katherine looked at Monsieur Gübeli, and she couldn't help giggling.

"Well, that was one of the weirder things I've ever come across in this town."

"I'm pleased it amuses you, madame."

Katherine picked up her fork and dug in.

"Anyways, this is good old North American food, the real thing. Hope you like it."

"Oh, I have had this very dish before," Monsieur Gübeli said.

"No way."

"Indeed, madame, with Master Rochat. He said it was a secret—"

Katherine sat very still. Not noticing the music had stopped, not seeing the man across the table from her. Not hearing her own voice complete Monsieur Gübeli's sentence . . .

". . . recipe. From his mother."

Monsieur Gübeli waited a moment before speaking softly.

"Are you all right, madame?"

Katherine blinked, refocused her eyes.

"Yeah, it's just you were talking about Marc and his mother, and I remembered he was telling me about his mother's secret recipe. No . . . something's not right."

"Not right?"

"Yes—I mean, no. I mean it was someone else who told me about it."

"Someone else?"

There was a quick flash through Katherine's mind. Almost a glimpse of the man who wasn't there. He was tall, he was waving to her, saying good-bye. She shook her head.

"No, it had to be Marc. It was only him and me in the cathedral. That's what the doctors keep telling me. So damn confusing."

"The confusion is understandable, madame."

"Yeah, they keep telling me that one, too. Thing is, sometimes, I can see things, like I was there again."

"A bit of beforetimes, perhaps?"

The sound of the word sank deep into Katherine. She held on to it for a long moment.

"How do you know that word?"

"Master Rochat said it very often when talking about people he remembered. It was one of his endearing habits."

"Yeah, it sure was."

Katherine slowly twirled noodles with her fork. Her mind drifted again. Monsieur Gübeli coughed politely.

"I apologize if I have upset you, madame. It was not my intention."

"No, it isn't that."

"May I ask what it is?"

"It's really strange, you know. Sometimes, I feel like Marc's imagination, the way he saw things, I feel it rubbed off on me. Like you said, a bit of beforetimes. Silly, I guess."

"Actually, madame, I would call it a gift."

Katherine felt a chill. She lifted the black cloak and pulled it over her shoulders and wrapped it around her body.

"You know, he gave me this old thing the day he died. I don't remember much, but I remember Marc said I'd need it to keep warm. The doctors told me I slept with it for a month, wouldn't let anyone take it from me."

"Master Rochat was extremely sensitive to the needs of others. That sensitivity had a remarkable effect on people."

Katherine looked at Monsieur Gübeli.

"Did we already talk about this stuff?"

"*Pardon?*"

"Did you just tell me that before . . . about Marc being sensitive, the way he affected people?"

Monsieur Gubeli coughed. "No, madame, I cannot say I did."

"Really?"

"I'm quite sure."

"Huh."

They ate and the conversation turned to the weather and the candle shop. Molly came by to collect the plates and refill Monsieur Gübeli's glass with iced tea and tell him it was mighty fine he'd come to town and that he should come back real soon for some magic brownies and a perusal through her Grateful Dead bootleg tapes. Monsieur Gübeli said he would be delighted to do so. Molly looked at Katherine.

"I've got some of your Midday Buzz tea brewing in the kitchen, sugar. I'll bring it out when it's ready."

Katherine rolled her eyes.

"Jeez, between you and Anne, I'm gonna go berserk."

"You're living in a small town, sugar. We all take care of our own. And don't you even think about paying the bill. Let Mr. Lawyer-Person pick it up. If he can afford a limo with a funny-looking chauffeur, he can afford lunch."

"Will do, Molly."

Katherine sat back in the booth, closed her eyes, combed her fingers through her hair. She heard Monsieur Gübeli's voice:

"Remarkable."

She opened her eyes, saw him staring at her.

"What's remarkable?"

Monsieur Gübeli appeared embarrassed, quickly taking a handkerchief from his pocket and the pince-nez from his nose to wipe the indiscretion from his lenses. Katherine noted Monsieur Gübeli and his driver were both big on handkerchiefs.

"You must excuse me, madame. Normally, I am not one to stare."

"Hey, it's okay. I'm used to men staring at me. Well, not so much now, but back in the day when I was doing the hooker thing."

Monsieur Gübeli's eyes widened. Katherine covered her mouth.

"Oh, shit. You didn't know about the hooker thing?"

"Well, of course I knew, but . . . I would not presume to mention . . ."

Katherine lowered her face into her hands.

"Oh, shit."

"I assure you, madame, such a thing is of no concern to me or my firm. We are not in the business of making judgments regarding our clients."

Katherine peeked through her fingers.

"So, why were you staring at me?"

Monsieur Gübeli cleared his throat.

"It was the way you were sitting and touching your hair. I found myself drifting in beforetimes, as Master Rochat called it."

"Really? Where were you?"

"With Master Rochat, in fact. The afternoon I dined with him at his home, having tuna-noodle casserole. After our meal, he showed me a sketch he had drawn of you. I was stunned. It was a sketch worthy of a Renaissance master. And watching you in similar repose, just this moment, I understand how he was inspired to draw it."

Katherine saw herself in the cathedral in the middle of the night, watching the light of the candles Marc Rochat had set about the nave.

Hundreds and hundreds of candles. Listening to him tell her the story of the lost angels who'd come to Lausanne to hide in the cathedral because they had no other place to go. He took a folded paper from his coat and gave it to her . . .

"What's this?"

"It's the angel I saw in Lausanne."

Katherine blinked, took a slow breath.

"I remember it. He showed it to me in the cathedral."

"I am very happy to hear that you remember it, madame."

Katherine combed her hands through her hair again, her mind drifting.

"Mr. Gübeli, when Marc showed the drawing to you, did he say anything to you about it?"

"Why do you ask?"

"Like I said, Marc had one wild imagination. I was just wondering if it was a little, you know, less wild before I barged into his life. Do you remember if he said anything?"

Monsieur Gübeli sipped at his iced tea. He rested his glass on the table.

"It was the last day I was to see Master Rochat alive, madame, so I remember the day vividly. He showed me the drawing, and I asked him who it was. He said he was very sure it was a drawing of an angel who was lost in Lausanne."

Tears burned at the corners of Katherine's eyes, and she saw herself holding the drawing in her own hands, telling Rochat she wasn't an angel, telling him she was a prostitute. He stared at her, his voice was desperate, so wanting to believe . . . *Maybe you don't know you're an angel because you're so lost.*

"Madame Taylor?"

Katherine refocused her eyes. "Huh?"

"Are you unwell?"

"No, it's just . . . He knew the truth before he died. He knew I was nothing more than a hooker . . . then he died."

Monsieur Gübeli let Katherine sit with her thoughts for a minute.

"Perhaps, madame, you would like to see that drawing again, so that you would know what Master Rochat actually felt for you."

"You have it? Now?"

Monsieur Gübeli lifted his briefcase to the table, tapped a code into the keypad under the handle. The locks snapped open.

II

O FFICER JANNSEN HIT SPEED DIAL. THE LINE CONNECTED TO A recorded message.

"You have reached the twenty-four-hour help line of Guardian Services Limited. Please leave your message after the tone."

The tone came and went. She let her watch count down five seconds before logging in.

"Bravo-Delta-*neuf*-Zulu-Lima-*trois*-Echo-Echo-*cinq*-India-Foxtrot."

Then a blast of static as white noise analyzed her voice, then the ping of a seven-hundred-digit key unlocking a line to the communications grid of the Swiss Special Unit Task Force, then a familiar voice from Berne.

"Good afternoon, Officer Jannsen."

"Good evening, Inspector. Have you been monitoring the video and audio feeds?"

"Cameras in both the shop and the restaurant are picking up light fluctuations in the subject's irises each time Monsieur Gübeli mentions Marc Rochat's name. Your suspicions are correct, Madame Taylor's imagination is moving through time."

Officer Jannsen stared at the close-up of Katherine's face and the optical targeting locking onto her eyes and the cascade of numbers running down the side of the screen.

"How should I proceed, sir?"

"As planned."

Officer Jannsen didn't respond.

"Was my order unclear, Officer?"

"I'm not sure how she'll react to luminance probes being conducted on the child. Not this soon."

"We've already seen to it, Officer."

"Sir?"

"Her teas have been adjusted to keep her in check. As far as the tests on the child, she'll have no reason to think they are more than a required medical procedure. You'll reassure her that this is the case, of course. The equipment will be in place three days hence, in good time for the child's next checkup in Portland."

"Permission to speak freely, sir."

There was an icy pause.

"Go ahead, Officer."

"Luminance probes on the child weren't to be conducted for another six months. I'd like to know the reason for the change."

Officer Jannsen waited for Inspector Gobet to analyze the manner of her thinking. Even with years of training, it took getting used to. She remembered the many times a question remained unanswered for hours. This time it took less than thirty seconds.

"Our operations in protecting Madame Taylor and the child are based on the assumption she was raped and impregnated by the enemy. Whilst I cannot go into details, I can tell you evidence has come to light that may contradict that assumption. I need confirmation on the boy's status, one way or the other."

Officer Jannsen remained quiet, not wanting to give the inspector a clue to the terrible thought in her mind: If the boy turned out to be normal, HQ in Berne would drop all protection. Katherine and Max would be left on their own, and without a memory of what really happened over the last two and a half years. Officer Jannsen touched the image of Katherine's face on the monitor.

"Oh, Kat . . ."

"I beg your pardon, Officer?"

Officer Jannsen bit her tongue.

"*Je suis désolé.* I meant to say 'Madame Taylor.'"

"On the contrary, you present the opportunity to discuss your relationship with Madame Taylor."

"Sir?"

"In monitoring the house feeds of the public areas, I haven't failed to notice Madame Taylor has developed emotions of great affection toward you, and that she takes comfort in those emotions. I have also noticed what I consider to be a similar affection on your part."

Officer Jannsen looked at the screen. Katherine was looking at the drawing now and smiling; her eyes were bright.

"Sir, let me state for the record that nothing improper has occurred in the public *or* private areas of the house."

"You misunderstand my comment, Officer. There is nothing improper in the expression of human emotion between human beings. You are one of them, and not bound by our rules and regulations regarding familiarity with locals. I should think a natural development regarding such emotions might be helpful in Madame Taylor's recovery."

Officer Jannsen felt the blood rush to her face, like she'd been caught with her pants down. Then she realized it wasn't shame, it was rage.

"Sir, are you ordering me to sleep with Katherine Taylor?"

"Certainly not. I am simply reminding you how deep was the madness from which we rescued her. As long as she is under our protection, it is critical you do everything in your power to prevent her from falling back into the abyss."

"And if the time comes when we have to cut them loose?"

"Then you, and we, will do just that," Inspector Gobet said. "That's the way of things in our line of work."

If she could've reached him, she would've slapped him.

Then she remembered her oath: *To protect them, to die for them.*

❧

EIGHT

The TGV slowed where the French countryside gave way to the concrete slums surrounding Paris, some of the tenements standing so close to the tracks, the train seemed to pass through sitting rooms. Here was a woman reading a magazine, here was an old man staring at his television, here was a little boy watching the train go by. Crossing the trestle at Charenton-le-Pont, the train slowed again, and coming into the rail yard at Bercy, the train jerked and swayed over switches and tracks till it eased into Gare de Lyon. It groaned to a stop at Platform E. Harper looked at the clock above the station platform: 18:29 hours. He looked at his watch, still five minutes back. He adjusted his watch to real time.

"Easy peasy, lemon squeezy."

He stayed in his seat, watched locals struggle with bags and alight from the train and push their way through oncoming passengers headed for the 18:46 to Avignon. When he saw there were no French police on the platform looking for a man of his general description, Harper followed the locals to the arrival hall. The place was jammed with people looking for connections, bums looking for spare change, gypsies looking for suckers. He turned up the collar of his coat, lowered his eyes, moved unnoticed through the crowd. He climbed the iron staircase to Le Train Bleu restaurant. He took the table next to the tall windows, the one marked RÉSERVÉ. A waiter in a blue tunic arrived and bowed.

"Puis-je prendre votre commande, monsieur?"

Harper checked the waiter's eyes. They were clean.

"Vodka tonic. Sans vodka, sans tonic."

The waiter bowed and said, *"J'arrive,"* as if the order made sense. He returned two minutes later with a cheap mobile on a silver tray. He lay the tray on the table, did his bowing thing again, and left. Ten seconds later, the mobile rang. Harper picked it up and connected the line, didn't say a word. Then came a sepulchral voice wrapped in a French accent: "You were not followed?"

Harper looked out the windows. Hundreds of locals hustling through the forecourt of the station, hundreds more pounding the pavement along Boulevard Diderot.

"Only by you, it seems," Harper said.

"Then things are as they should be. See you in church."

"What church?"

Harper heard the clink of a glass down the line, then the voice.

"Le Monde taxi, ID number 3476. Outside, under the clock tower in five minutes."

Harper dropped the mobile on the tray and found his way to the gents. Clear. He reached for his SIG Sauer to load a round into the firing chamber. Ended up patting the place where his gun wasn't. So far, things were going according to plan. Not that he knew what the plan was, exactly.

"It's a recon mission, Mr. Harper, leave your kill kit behind," said the cop in the cashmere coat back in the vineyards of Grandvaux. "A Do No Harm order is in effect in this case for the moment. Are you clear on that point, Mr. Harper?"

"Crystal."

Harper ran through what he did know. Inspector Gobet's SX squad had been scanning through the events of the last two weeks—the enemy strike on the river Seine, his bloody photograph spread over the Internet, being exposed to the details of the life and death of Captain Jay Michael Harper—looking for intersecting lines of causality. Contacts with underground elements had been made and a person of interest popped hot, needed to be scanned for light. That's all the inspector would tell him, besides . . .

"Oh, there is one more thing, Mr. Harper; you'll be flying blind."

Harper knew the drill. No advance knowledge as to the identity of the target. No advance knowledge of his own bloody cover till it was revealed by the target. Some of the locals, the sensitive ones, could sense the presence of Harper's kind in their midst. Flying blind was a defensive maneuver; one more way of hiding among men. It was also a great way of crashing head-on into a wall named trouble. He deleted the thought from his mind, found another one sitting in its place: the last time he'd been in a church. It ended with the lad with the lantern, *le guet* of Lausanne Cathedral, lying dead on the esplanade beneath the belfry. Harper leaned over the sink and splashed cold water in his face. He looked at his reflection in the mirror.

"Living the dream, boyo, one day at a time."

He found his ride under the clock tower, climbed in, took a magical mystery tour around Paris for the better part of an hour. Must've crossed every bloody bridge over the river Seine, twice. And at each crossing, Harper lowered his eyes to avoid making eye contact with the French police patrolling the parapets. Crossing the intersection onto Pont de l'Alma and entering the taxi lane on Avenue Bosquet, Harper realized the taxi had yet to stop for a red light. He tried to figure the odds of such a thing in a town like Paris. He gave up, left it at "ever such a lot."

The driver made a quick left onto Rue Saint-Dominique. Harper saw a decent-looking *tabac* on the right, small café tables under an awning. As the evening so far had consisted of driving in ever lessening circles, Harper thought about asking the driver to pull over so he could grab a glass and a smoke. Maybe anticipating the question, the driver hit the accelerator, crossed through Les Invalides and ran onto Boulevard Saint-Germain. Sixty-seven seconds later, the driver cut a sharp left onto a cobblestone square and hit the brakes. Harper looked out the window. Up against the evening sky was the floodlit, limestone tower and the façade of a very old building. Late tenth century, from the looks of it.

"What do you know, it's a church."

"Monsieur?" the driver said.

"Out there. It's a church."

"Bien sûr, monsieur. C'est l'Église de Saint-Germain-des-Prés. It is the oldest church in Paris."

Harper looked around the square. Tourists with maps, Parisians with attitude. Whole scene read all's well. He spoke to the back of the driver's head.

"I don't suppose you'd have any idea what I'm supposed to do about it. The oldest church in Paris, that is."

"Mais oui, you are to go inside and find René Descartes, *monsieur."*

Harper's mind scanned episodes of the History Channel, landed on *Great Minds of the Scientific Revolution.* René Descartes: mathematician and philosopher. Born in Indre-et-Loire, France, March 31, 1596. Came up with the Cartesian coordinate system leading to analytical geometry and calculus. Came up with Cartesian skepticism leading to *cogito, ergo sum.* Died in Sweden, February 11, 1650.

"Correct me if I'm wrong, but Descartes has been dead awhile, hasn't he?"

The driver looked back over his seat. His shrug was perfect.

"Oui, monsieur, il est fucking *mort,* and I am late for my fucking supper. So how about getting out of my taxi before I ask you to pay the fucking fare?"

Harper did as suggested. He watched the taxi rumble away over the cobblestones and disappear up Rue Bonaparte.

"Et bon fucking *appétit."*

A cold breeze whipped his back. He checked the sky. Heavy clouds moving in from the northwest, pulling a veil across what was left of the

third quarter moon. He searched the pockets of his coat, found his cigarette case. He pulled a smoke and lit up. He drew a hit of radiance,
checked the sky again. Looked like rain, nothing more.

"So far, so good."

He did a slow three-sixty, took in the sights. There's Saint-Germain-
des-Prés Métro and Brasserie Lipp across the boulevard, there's Les
Deux Magots café just across the cobblestones. He was standing in the
heart of Saint-Germain-des-Prés. He was also standing barely a kilometer from where the Paris job went down on the river Seine, two
weeks ago.

Funny, he thought.

Then he thought, *Not really.*

He pulled another hit of radiance, checked the entrance of ye olde
church. A tramp sat on the steps of the portico. He was wrapped in a
wool coat, and his wool cap was on the ground next to him; over-
turned, waiting for donations. He was killing time reading a book.
Someone was behind the tramp, half-hidden in the shadows of the portico. Someone in blue jeans and a hooded black sweatshirt. The hood
was pulled over his head like a monk's cowl. A bell, a deep hollow
sound, rang the hour. Eight o'clock in the evening. Harper checked his
watch. On the dot, to the bloody second.

"Not bad."

Harper dropped his smoke on the cobblestones, crushed it into dust,
and walked toward the church. He passed the tramp, dropped a two-
Euro coin in the wool cap. The tramp looked up to Harper.

"Merci, monsieur."

The tramp's eyes were clean. Harper glanced at the tramp's book,
open to Canto X of Dante's *Purgatorio:*

WHEN WE HAD CROSSED THE THRESHOLD OF THE DOOR
WHICH THE PERVERTED LOVE OF SOULS DISUSES,
BECAUSE IT MAKES THE CROOKED WAY SEEM STRAIGHT,
RE-ECHOING, I HEARD IT CLOSED AGAIN.

"Don't mention it."

Harper passed the someone half-hidden in the shadows of the portico. He could just make out the face under the hoodie. The someone was a kid. Fourteen, fifteen maybe. He was staring at the ground.

"*Bonsoir,*" Harper said. "*Ça va bien?*"

The kid didn't answer, kept his eyes drilled to the ground.

"No worries, I know the feeling," Harper said.

He pulled open the door and stepped inside the church. He waited to see if one or both of the characters outside would be following him. Nobody. He went into the nave, gave the dimly lit place a recce. Same as walking into Lausanne Cathedral . . . the sensation of rising up to endless heights within an enclosed space bound by stone. It was a swell trick, Harper thought, given this space wasn't endless at all. Sixty meters long, maybe, twenty-some meters wide, nineteen meters high. Harper imagined the whole place would fit into Lausanne Cathedral four times over, and there'd still be room for a parking lot. But as his eyes adjusted to the sombrous light, colors began to emerge from the arches and columns of the nave. Reds and greens, blues and gold. The columns drew Harper's eyes upward to the ribbed vault where a skobeloff-tinted sky was filled with thousands of stars.

He looked back at the entrance door. No one coming in.

He walked east up the main aisle, saw a dozen locals scattered about the church. Some lighting candles before the statues of saints in the south aisle, some sitting on the side benches along the north aisle, some kneeling in the nave offering whispered prayers. Harper stopped at the crossing where the transept divided the nave from the chancel and main altar.

Here, the stone surfaces seemed to vibrate with color.

The columns and arches of the apse were decorated with geometric patterns of red and green, and the walls above the arches were painted like some Garden of Eden wherein dwelled the twelve apostles and the four winged creatures of the synoptic gospels. Closer to the crossing, either side of the chancel, two huge murals, more like medieval tapes-

tries than paint on stone. On the north wall, Christ the Triumphant en-
ters Jerusalem. On the south, Christ the Condemned drags his cross
down Via Dolorosa.

Harper stared at the murals, musing on a thought. Why did the target pick *this* place for a meeting? And what did a philosopher-mathema-
tician dead for the last 360 years have to do with it? And by the way,
where was the great dead man?

He looked left, right.

A darkened stained glass window and small altar were set in the north
transept, but it was the tomb in the south transept that Harper walked
to. A statue of a chap in dramatic pose topped the tomb. As Harper got
closer, he discovered it wasn't the great dead man he was looking for.
This tomb held the remains of one *Ioannes Casimirus, Dei Gratia rex Po-
loniae, magnus dux Lithuaniae, Russie, Prussiae* . . . The list went on to
mention the chap had also been the hereditary king of the Swedes,
Goths, and Vandals.

"Right, so where's the other guy?"

He walked along the ambulatory between the chapels built into
the outer walls and the high, wrought iron fence surrounding the
apse. He stopped at the easternmost point of the church, at the Lady
chapel. There was a statue of the Virgin Mother holding the Holy
Child. A hundred votive candles burned at her feet, and she appeared
to float on a cloud of light. He stared at the statue. Mother and child.
He felt a twinge of familiarity, as if he'd seen them before. Then
again, with a billion such statues in the world, crafted in everything
from medieval stone to glow-in-the-dark plastic, why should this one
be different?

He walked on past Chapelle Sainte-Geneviève, Chapelle Sainte-Anne.
Nothing. At Chapelle Saint-Benoît, he saw three marble slabs set in an
unpainted stone wall. Black, eight feet high, Latin lettering carved into
the faces of each slab. He walked into the chapel. Two long-dead monks
of the medieval abbey that was Saint-Germain-des-Prés lay entombed
to the left and right. In the middle:

MEMORIAE RENATI DESCARTES

RECONDITIORIS DOCTRINAE

LAVDE

ET INGENII SVBTILITATE

PRAECELLENTISSIMI

Harper ran the words: *In memory of René Descartes, famous through the praise of a better founded science and the sharpness of his mind. First to defend the right of human reason and . . .* He stopped, sensing a presence behind him, then the same voice he'd heard over the phone at Gare de Lyon.

"It is strange to think the man who first articulated the concept of human reason as a proof of physical existence has no head, *non?*"

Harper looked back, saw the form of a man standing in the shadows of the ambulatory. Everything about it read *target acquired.*

"Sorry?"

The form stepped from the shadows. He looked a big man, the kind who could take care of himself in a barroom brawl. He wore dark blue glasses over his eyes, and a ragged scar ran down his right cheek. He had a head of wild black hair with a Ho Chi Minh beard to match. He nodded toward the tomb.

"Him. The one in the middle. Descartes. When he died in Stockholm, he was buried in a graveyard reserved for unbaptized infants. The French, being French, demanded his remains be returned to the land of his birth so that they might honor him. It took some time for his body to make the trip, and along the way, pieces of him disappeared. Some of his bones were fashioned into rings to be worn as jewelry. But it was his head that suffered the greatest indignity. The soldier responsible for the remains cut off the skull and replaced it with another. Descartes's skull became quite the objet d'art among the enlightened wealthy of Europe. It was bought and sold many times. Each owner participated in the grotesque practice of inscribing his own name into the skull. It's at the Palais de Chaillot, in the Musée de l'Homme. The rest of him is here. Quite the honor, *non?*"

Harper had been staring at the man's mug since he stepped from the shadows, waiting for an image association to lock on. Nothing. He looked at Descartes's tomb, then back to the man.

"If you say so. By the way, who are you?"

The big man walked into the chapel and stood before the tomb. He traced his fingers over the black marble slab where it read, *Now he relishes the sight of truth . . .* The man turned and faced Harper.

"My name is Astruc."

Closer to him, Harper tried to read the eyes hidden behind the blue lenses. No luck.

"Astruc, right. And you know who I am, of course."

"I do."

A moment of silence passed between them.

"Right. So now that I'm here and you know who I am, perhaps you'd care to tell me why it is I'm here."

Astruc tipped his head and looked behind Harper. "Search him, Goose."

Harper felt a pair of hands run across his shoulders and down his back and sides. Feeling the pocket of his coat holding his wallet and cigarette case. The hands pulled them out quickly, tossed them to Astruc. The hands continued around Harper's waist and down his legs and ankles. They pulled away, and whoever owned the hands walked to the side of the chapel and into Harper's line of sight. It was the kid who'd been standing outside the church. The cowl of his sweatshirt was pulled from his head now. Harper stared at him.

Goose—the name fits, Harper thought. The kid's long neck poked from his sweatshirt and his underdeveloped ears were pinned to the sides of a small round head. Harper tried to get a read on the kid's eyes. The irises were opaque, colorless, and glassy as hell. The kid was on something. *Swell,* Harper thought. *One barroom brawler in blue shades, one kid stoned to the bloody moon. Can't get a read on either of them. Should be a swell evening.*

"Greetings, kid," Harper said.

The kid shifted his eyebrows downward and his hands made two quick, fluid moves. Middle fingers pointing to his chest and flipping up, then the three middle fingers of his right hand tapped the palm of his left. Took Harper two seconds to work out that the kid wasn't telling him to fuck off. The kid was deaf and aphonic; he was signing in slang, *What's up?*

Harper looked at Astruc, pretending not to understand the gesture.

"Goose is being polite in his own way," Astruc said.

"Sure he is."

Astruc tossed back Harper's wallet and cigarette case without opening them. Harper slipped them into the pockets of his coat.

"Not even going to check my library card?"

"Why should I? I already know who you are. And I apologize for the search. I'm sure it's not what someone like you expects in a church. But given the way you're dressed, I needed to make sure you were as advertised."

Harper waited for the big man to spill the rest of the advert; he didn't.

"I suppose you can't be too careful, even in a church," Harper said. "By the way, you haven't told me what it is you do, Astruc."

"No, I have not. And for the time being, you do not need to know. All you need to know is, from this moment, I am in charge. Is that clear?"

Harper nodded.

"Right. Well, now we've sorted that one, what's next?"

Astruc stepped closer to Harper, eyeing him from foot to head.

"Next? Next is easy. Next you take off your tie with whatever it is you had for lunch on it, and you come with me."

Harper followed the big man out of the church. The kid tailed after Harper. They crossed the road toward Les Deux Magots. The chatter of voices and clatter of plates seeped through lighted windows. Astruc pointed to an outside table where they could talk privately. They both sat with their backs to the café windows. Harper saw l'Église de Saint-Germain-des-Prés across the road. The limestone façade and bell tower made for a nice view. Astruc wasn't taking in the view of the church, though; his eyes were on the Saint-Germain-des-Prés Métro stop across Boulevard Saint-Germain.

Harper looked left, saw Goose in the shadows of a nearby doorway, watching passersby. Hoodie over his head, hands tucked into the pouch of his sweatshirt. *The kid is good with shadows*, Harper thought.

"How old is the kid?" Harper said.

"Twenty-six."

"You're joking."

Astruc kept his eyes locked on the Saint-Germain-des-Prés Métro.

"Along with being deaf, Goose suffers from a form of paedomorphosis. His facial features did not mature with the rest of his body. As you can imagine, he grew up being tormented as a freak of nature."

Harper threw a glance at Goose again. Still watching passersby from the shadows. *Maybe that's why he's good with shadows*, Harper thought. *Spent his whole life growing up in them, hiding from the cold gazes of strangers.*

"Sure, I can imagine it," Harper said.

Astruc looked at Harper.

"If you need to speak with him, look him directly in the eyes and speak normally. He'll read your lips. And don't underestimate him. His IQ is above two hundred, along with having a photographic memory."

"Impressive," Harper said. "What's the connection?"

"Connection?"

"You. Him. What's the connection?"

Astruc stared at Harper.

"He is my pupil. I am his teacher. It has been this way since I found him and saved him from evil."

"Evil, right."

A white-aproned waiter came outside. Astruc gave him the order: single malt, neat, *trois fois*. He turned his eyes back to the Saint-Germain-des-Prés Métro stop.

"Expecting someone else, then?" Harper said.

"What?"

"Three drinks."

"Yes, I am expecting someone. Someone you must meet. He'll be here shortly."

Harper checked his watch. Almost 21:00 hours. He was due to report back to the inspector at the bottom of the hour.

"Who am I meeting and why?"

"You ask many questions," Astruc said.

"Blame it on Descartes. All that Cartesian skepticism."

Astruc raised an eyebrow.

"I didn't realize your particular line of work allowed for sarcasm."

Harper didn't know how to answer that one. As yet he still didn't know what his particular line of work was supposed to be.

"Call it my amusing hobby, then. *Ergo*, who are we meeting, and why?"

Astruc found a cigarillo and lighter in the pocket of his coat. He anchored the smoke between his teeth and lit up.

"His name is Gilles Lambert. He's a *commis aux dossiers* in the mayor's office of the fourteenth arrondissement."

Harper ran the words.

"A file clerk?"

"Yes, a file clerk. One who spends his days in a small office making little tick marks along columns of tax revenues collected from local businesses. A very ordinary Parisian in every way, except for his own amusing hobby."

"Which is?"

"He likes to spend his weekends exploring *les carrières*."

Those words flashed Harper back to last night, returning from Grandvaux after his meeting with the cop in the cashmere coat. The midnight show at GG's had come and gone, so Mutt and Jeff dropped Harper at his flat. Went in, turned on the telly. Tuned to the History Channel, like always. Presently wrapping up episode six of *The Ascent of Man*. He mixed a vodka tonic, sat out on the small balcony with a view of the cathedral. He lit a smoke, listened to the bells ring for two o'clock. He watched *le guet*, the new one, round the tower with a lantern and call the hour over Lausanne. But with the wind blowing from the north, her voice carried the words of comfort out over the lake. Then, as if by wizardry, the voice on the telly said, "Coming up next on the History Channel: *The Underground Mysteries of Paris*."

Big surprise: Half the program deals with *les carrières*.

First century: Romans discover limestone deposits on the banks of the Seine and start digging. Fast forward: Paris is a city built of stone. Demand is high. Every official building, every palace, every church, is dressed in the limestone mined from the quarries of Paris. Miners spread out, follow the veins, excavating a maze of tunnels under the city. Seventeenth century: The veins are played out and the tunnels abandoned. They become the trading routes of smugglers and thieves trying to avoid the king's taxmen. Plague visits Paris. The city's streets are overrun with rotting corpses. Skeletons are dug up from the city's cemeteries and dumped in the tunnels to make room for the newly dead.

Harper snapped back to nowtimes.

"You're talking about the catacombs."

Astruc shook his head.

"The catacombs are barely a kilometer of the tunnels. Kept very tidy for the tourists. Skulls neatly arranged, dusted twice a month. The rest of the tunnels, all three hundred kilometers of them, are somewhat less welcoming. But there are Parisians who find them irresistible—they are known as cataphiles."

The waiter returned with the drinks. Harper watched Astruc lift his glass and check the nose. Harper didn't drink. He leaned back in his chair, tried to fade from Astruc's consciousness, get a read on the man's manner of thinking. As if sensing movement, Astruc turned to Harper.

"You do not care for the whiskey?"

Harper stared at the man's blue lenses. *Swell, the sensitive sort,* Harper thought.

"Just interested in knowing why I'm waiting to meet someone whose idea of fun is spending his days off underground, wandering through tunnels."

Astruc sipped at his drink and pointed his cigarillo toward the Métro.

"You're about to find out."

A tall, skinny chap was coming up the steps of the Saint-Germain-des-Prés Métro. He wore a blue windbreaker on top of a black shirt, and his workmen trousers were tucked into a pair of Wellington boots.

He carried a canvas backpack. He stood at the corner, waiting for the light to change. When it did, the skinny man stood a moment as if unable to decide whether to take the next step. He did, finally, only to find himself halfway across the boulevard when the lights changed again. He dodged an onslaught of unforgiving traffic and made his way to the cobblestone square of Saint-Germain-des-Prés. He faced the entrance of the church as the last bell faded away. He genuflected, bowed his head, made the sign of the cross.

"Your *commis aux dossiers* seems the religious sort," Harper said.

Astruc removed smoldering ash from the tip of his cigarillo.

"French Catholics can be sentimental when it comes to their faith. Especially when confronted with evil."

Harper heard something in Astruc's voice. Longing, maybe, not to mention it was the second time he was laying a riff about evil.

"What about you, Astruc? You the sentimental sort when it comes to faith?"

Astruc took another draw from his cigarillo. Words rolled from his mouth on a cloud of smoke.

"Once a Catholic, always a Catholic."

The tall skinny man named Gilles Lambert rose from his knee and turned toward Les Deux Magots. He spotted Astruc, stood still one more moment before deciding to cross the cobblestone square.

"And he's nervous," Harper said.

"Very. Which is why you are here."

"Sorry?"

"You're a comforter of men, are you not?"

Harper stared at Astruc, knew the man behind the blue lenses was playing him.

"If you say so."

There was no shaking of hands or formal introduction as Gilles Lambert reached the table; the skinny man simply shrank into an empty chair. Astruc nodded to Harper.

"Gilles, this is the one I told you about. He'll be coming with us, as I promised you, for the protection of your soul."

Lambert nodded. Astruc pushed a glass of whiskey to him. "Here, Gilles, take a drink."

"*Merci.*"

Lambert slowly sipped, then again. Harper saw the man's eyes were more than nervous; they were awash with fright. The kind that'd make a man kneel in front of a church to sign himself, then reach for 86-proof alcohol as backup. Harper watched him sip to the bottom of his glass.

"Could . . . could I have one more before we go?" he said.

Astruc gestured to the waiter at the café doors: *Encore, trois fois.* He turned to Lambert.

"We're grateful you chose to help us, Gilles."

"*Oui, mais . . .* though I'm not sure we should continue as planned. The police hacked into my website and posted a message to all cataphiles: '*Ne pas entrer les carrières. Danger de mort.*' They're saying anyone going down there could be killed. And that's not all. I saw municipal workers dumping cement down the access tunnels near Hôpital Cochin in the middle of the night. I've been told the same thing is happening near Montparnasse Cemetery. They're sealing off the center of the Great South System, and—"

Astruc interrupted Lambert.

"But you know a way in that doesn't use an access tunnel, don't you, Gilles?"

"*Oui, mais il est très dangereux.* We must crawl through tunnels that have not been reinforced."

Harper watched Astruc lean close to Lambert.

"Gilles, you know the police are trying to cover up what you found down there. But you are a man of faith, a believer in the teachings of Holy Mother Church. It is that faith that caused you to turn to your priest for guidance. He baptized you, gave you your first communion. I know he counseled you that for the sake of your immortal soul, you must trust me."

"*Oui.* He said these things to me."

Harper stared at Astruc. The big man in the blue shades was laying it on thick. Round two arrived, Lambert sipped slowly this time. Harper picked up his own drink and was mid-sip when he heard Lambert's voice:

"And you, you are a priest sent by His Holiness the Pope, truly?"

Harper's glass nearly dropped when he realized Lambert was talking to him.

"What?"

"*Pardonnez-moi, mon père,* I don't mean to be rude. Monsieur Astruc told me you would not be wearing a collar tonight. But must we really go back down there?"

Harper slammed back his whiskey, rested his glass on the table. *A priest? That's my bloody cover?* He looked at Astruc.

"Why don't you explain the details, as you're in charge?"

"Of course," Astruc said. "Gilles, Father Harper is a priest of the Dominican Order. He is also a professor of ancient languages at Lausanne University. In that capacity, he serves His Holiness as an advisor on matters of Church history. When I approached your confessor to discuss what you had found in the cavern, your confessor was concerned for the state of your soul, as am I. He insisted on contacting his superiors in the Vatican, and the matter was referred to the Congregation for the Doctrine of the Faith. This office reports directly to the Pope, and upon hearing of your case, His Holiness requested Father Harper be part of the investigation, for both the benefit of the Church and the protection of your soul. Is this not the truth, Father Harper?"

If Harper had a choice, he wouldn't believe a bloody word of what he was hearing. Flying blind, such a bloody thrill. No choice but to stay with the cover. Even if it meant furthering the torment of the skinny, frightened man looking at him and waiting for an answer. *Is that not the truth, Father Harper?* Harper leaned toward Gilles Lambert.

"I want you to listen to my voice. I have been sent here, and I'll be with you. I'll protect you. Do you hear me?"

Lambert nodded.

"Yes, yes, I hear you, *mon père.* And I believe you." He clutched his stomach. "But you must excuse me, my bowels haven't been well; not since I found them."

He hurried into the café and disappeared down the stairs to the toilets.

Harper thought about calling for round three. Deciding it might not fit his pastoral image, he studied Astruc instead. Didn't look the sort who could possibly have a contact in the Vatican, let alone a man who took his marching orders from the Pope, or anyone. Then again, once a Catholic, always a Catholic. Those were the big man's own words. Maybe that was *his* truth. Astruc gave a smirking excuse for a smile, as if reading Harper's thoughts.

"Something is on your mind, Father Harper?"

"Loads. For the moment I'd settle for finding out what that man found down there that's turned him into a nervous wreck."

"You were not informed?"

Harper shrugged. "You know how it is with Dominicans; our superior gives us an order, we don't ask questions. Besides, I was led to believe you'd be filling in the blanks. Or is that not the case?"

Astruc stared at Harper. Even hidden behind the blue shades, Harper could tell it was a cold stare. And the big man let it hang like an icicle till he turned and called to the shadows.

"Goose, donnez-moi la mobile."

Goose walked over, pulled an iPhone from the pouch of his sweatshirt, gave it to Astruc.

"Merci," Astruc said. *"Ramènez la bagnole."*

Goose double-timed it back to the shadows and disappeared.

Astruc tapped at the mobile screen with his thick thumbs.

"There is a network of quarries under Lycée Montaigne. They were used as bomb shelters during the Second World War by the Nazis. They're like most of the tunnels and quarries under Paris: forbidden to enter. Over the last six weeks, there's been a building project in the sixth, very near the Lycée. They were using pile drivers to lay the foundations. They hit a fissure between two adjoining plates of bedrock, sending a shock wave through the sixth arrondissement. It registered two-point-five on the Richter scale. Not enough to cause any real damage, but enough to make it onto TF1. Gilles was watching the news that evening and knew it had happened close to the quarries of Lycée Montaigne. He went down for a look the next day. He found a half-meter-wide crack in one of the walls of the bunkers. He looked in with his flashlight, saw it connected to a passage. He couldn't resist crawling in."

Astruc checked for Gilles Lambert through the windows of the café.

"I realize he doesn't look it at the moment, but Gilles is the best cataphile in Paris. He knows the tunnels like the back of his hand. His website is the Holy Bible of cataphiles. He knew the passage had never appeared on any map drawn up by *l'Inspection générale des carrières*. More, the passage followed a seam of crystalized magma."

"Meaning what?"

"In geological terms, the passage shouldn't be there at all."

Harper's senses sharpened.

"And?"

"The passage sloped down into the Earth, straight as an arrow, never turning."

"How far?"

"I don't know. But at the bottom of the passage, Gilles discovered a cavern carved from solid black rock. There were coves cut into the walls. It was there Gilles Lambert came face-to-face with evil."

"Define 'evil.'"

Astruc lay the iPhone on the table, pushed it across to Harper. On screen: close-up shots of a naked, headless corpse in a morgue. The body had been flayed, its arms and hands crossed over the chest.

"There were one hundred of them," Astruc said. "All butchered in the same manner. As you can see, they're quite old."

Harper continued to flip through the photographs. One hundred tables in a large open building, one hundred headless and skinned bodies on the tables. As he flipped through the photographs, Harper realized "quite old" was an understatement. The exposed muscles and tendons were leathered. Looked like a convention of mutilated mummies, all of them with their arms crossed over their chests.

"What is this place, where the bodies are?"

"Base Aérienne 442."

"Which is what?"

"A secret facility, twenty-one kilometers outside Paris. The mortuary of Brigade Criminelle was not large enough to house the bodies. After the escape of the terrorist suspect from La Santé Prison, the French president demanded better security."

Harper listened to the tone of the big man's voice. He was telling the truth and lying at the same time. More, the big man was teasing, taunting.

"I was told, as part of your holy work, that you had encountered this sort of thing before," Astruc said.

Harper looked at him, wondering which "sort of thing" the big man was talking about. A subterranean cavern carved from solid rock? Check. Dead forms with their arms crossed over their chests? Check. Both found beneath Lausanne Cathedral. Then the photographs of the bodies themselves. Beheaded and skinned. He flashed through the cathedral job again, landed on a woman hanging by her ankles in the sitting room of her Geneva flat. Same bloody MO. A few thousand years between them, but the same damn thing. More of those swell intersecting lines of causality spilling into the mix.

"Sure, I've encountered it."

"May I ask where, as I understand you to be a professor of ancient languages?"

"All you need know is I've seen it before."

"Of course," Astruc said. "The sanctity of your office would preclude you from divulging such details."

Harper looked at the shots again, this time noting the time and date stamps in the upper right-hand corners. August 16, 04:15 hours.

"These shots are official. How did they end up on your mobile?"

"It's no concern of yours."

"Sure it is. Especially if you want me to take a hike through the tunnels to some underground cavern and decode some scribble you found on a wall or a parchment. That is what you want me to do, isn't it? Or perhaps with all the evil you seem to encounter, maybe you want me to make the sign of the cross down there, splash around some holy water."

Astruc was silent for a moment. He picked up his glass, studied the contents.

"You would mock the sanctity of your holy office?"

"What I mock is being played for a sap."

Astruc drew on his cigarillo.

"I obtained them from someone within the French police."

"Stole them, you mean."

"They are not stolen. They were given freely."

"By whom?"

"Someone like Gilles Lambert."

"Meaning what?"

"Meaning someone who now fears for his immortal soul."

Harper analyzed the big man's voice. He was lying through his teeth. Harper closed the photos on the mobile, slid it across the table to Astruc.

"You know, for a man with a taste for single malt and cigarillos, not to mention a photo album of mutilated corpses on his mobile, you display a touching concern for the immortal souls of men."

Astruc eased off his dark glasses, looked down from Harper's gaze. But Harper could see where the thin scar along the right cheek met a disfigured eye, as if some beast had clawed his face. Astruc slipped on a new pair of glasses, raised his eyes.

"Then we both have our amusing hobbies, don't we, Father Harper?"

Harper stared at him. Clear lens over the left, shaded over the right. Harper tried to scan him for light . . . couldn't get a read with only one eye.

"Yes, I suppose we do at that."

A black Mercedes van stopped on the boulevard next to the café. The side door slid open, and Harper saw Goose at the wheel. Astruc drank the last of his whiskey, tossed his cigarillo onto the cobblestones, nodded toward the café windows. Inside, Gilles Lambert was coming up the stairs.

"Our transport is here, and so is our guide with the bad stomach. *Allons-y.*"

Harper looked at his watch: T-minus ten to check-in.

Inspector Gobet would have to wait.

❧

NINE

I

A HARD RAIN FELL AS THEY DROVE THROUGH MONTPARNASSE AND into the working-class neighborhoods of the 14th arrondissement. Gilles Lambert rode up front with Goose and directed their way through the streets. Lights in windows were few and far between. Early to bed, early to rise was the order of the day this end of Paris. At the intersection of Rue des Petits Arbres and Avenue Monforte, Lambert pointed to an empty lot off the road. Goose drove onto the pavement, then into the cover of low-hanging willows. He shut down the motor, killed the lights.

"Gilles, would you mind waiting outside with Goose? I'd like to make my confession to Father Harper before we go."

"Yes, yes," Gilles said, slipping the strap of his canvas backpack over his shoulder. "I did the same thing this evening, before I came."

"Good, Gilles, very good."

He climbed out with Goose, and they walked to the back of the van. Goose opened the rear door, hauled out his own backpack and a plastic shopping bag. He dropped them on the ground. When the door shut, Astruc took off his overcoat. He wore a black windbreaker over a black sweatshirt. Somehow, without his overcoat, the man looked two sizes bigger. He reached behind his seat, found a pair of Wellington boots. He kicked off his shoes, slipped on the boots.

"It's a constant sixteen degrees in the tunnels. Leave your overcoat and sports coat in the van."

Harper waited for more. Nothing.

"That's it? That's your confession?"

Astruc glanced out the windows. Goose was putting on a set of Wellingtons. Gilles Lambert was nervously watching the road for passing cars. There were none.

"I want you to keep an eye on Gilles. If he begins to panic, you must keep him under control. It's imperative we reach the cavern tonight."

"Why?"

"You heard him. They're filling the access tunnels with concrete. They're trying to seal the cavern from the world. I would have thought, having seen the photographs, you would want to examine the scene yourself."

"Sure. I'm just wondering what else it is you're looking for."

"What do you mean?"

"The bodies aren't there anymore. They were moved to Base Aérienne 442, no?"

"I'm not sure I understand what you are asking, Father Harper."

"I'm asking: What is it you're looking for under Paris?"

Astruc nodded.

"There is something else. Something that you must see with your own eyes to verify its credibility."

The words registered as truth.

"Ten Our Fathers and ten Hail Marys," Harper said.

"What?"

"Your penance."

Astruc's good eye drilled into Harper.

"The guilty one, Father Harper, is not the one who commits the sin, but the one who causes the darkness."

"Sounds like scripture."

"It is scripture," Astruc said.

No it isn't, Harper thought, *it's Victor Hugo. Les Misérables,* book one, chapter four. The musings of an old bishop who would not condemn a convict named Jean Valjean. Still, Astruc's gaze let it be known it was scripture enough for him, and that he believed it with the fervor of a fanatic.

"Must have missed that one in seminary school," Harper said.

Astruc slid open his door, jumped out. He stepped away a few seconds, then was back with a pair of Wellington boots and a hooded windbreaker. He tossed them into the van at Harper.

"Here, you'll need these."

The windbreaker was gray and the boots were black. All of it off the shelf, sales tags still attached. Harper removed his shoes, slid on the boots. Perfect fit.

"How did you know my size?"

"Goose spotted you at Gare de Lyon. He made you for an eleven and a half."

Harper looked back through the rear window. Goose was hiding from the rain with Gilles Lambert. The kid's glassy eyes stared back at Harper from under the cowl of his hoodie. He made those same quick moves with his hands: *What's up?*

"Clever kid."

"I told you, don't underestimate him."

Harper took off his overcoat and sports coat, slipped on the windbreaker. He stepped from the van, followed Astruc around the back. Gilles Lambert opened his backpack, handed out four Petzl headlamps.

"We will need these in the tunnels. Put them around your necks for now so you don't lose them. And don't switch them on till I tell you. We don't want to attract the attention of the residents. Follow me."

Lambert pulled up the hood of his windbreaker and stepped out from under the trees and into the rain. Astruc signed to Goose: *Follow him.* Goose hooked his arms through the shoulder straps of his backpack and walked after Gilles. Astruc put up his hood, looked at Harper, nodded toward the road.

"*Allez,* Father Harper."

Harper covered his own head.

"Sure."

They crossed the intersection, walked along Rue des Petits Arbres. With their hoods, Harper imagined they looked like a gang of monks up to no good. They came to an overpass crossing a ravine. Forty meters deep, thirty meters wide, rail tracks running through it. Lambert stopped, pointed down.

"That's what's left of *La Petite Ceinture*, the railway that once circled Paris. We need to climb down to it and follow the tracks for two kilometers. This way."

They crossed the overpass, turned down a dimly lit road, followed the pavement along a rusting chain-link fence almost hidden by tall weeds and wild bramble. A crooked elm tree, more dead than alive, stood on the other side of the fence. Coming close to it, Lambert checked the road and the few windows with lights. All clear. He stepped from the pavement and reached the weeds and grabbed hold of the fence where it joined a steel post. He yanked hard and peeled away the fence, just enough to squeeze by.

"Quick, before someone sees us. I will follow last."

They hurried through, pushed through the weeds, and came out at the top of the ridge. A manila rope, two inches in diameter, was anchored to the elm. The rope dropped to the bottom of the ravine. Harper saw knots tied in the rope every two meters. Looked military. He wondered if there was more to Gilles Lambert than met the eye.

"I'll go first," Lambert said. "Please, hurry after me. If a car comes, duck down into the weeds, wait for it to pass."

They lowered down in turn. Gilles, Astruc, Harper, Goose. They gathered around the rope. The high-above streetlamps offered enough light to make out their surroundings. They weren't far from the overpass of Rue des Petits Arbres, and the overpass cast a band of shadow across the width of the ravine. There were overpasses up and down the rail line and just as many bands of shadow.

"Which way are we going?" said Harper.

Gilles pointed south, away from Rue des Petits Arbres.

"That way. It's easiest if we walk along the tracks."

They moved to the center of the ravine.

Astruc looked at Harper and Lambert.

"Wait here. Goose and I will walk ahead and make sure the police aren't about."

"But the police don't know about this place," Lambert said.

"Just the same, we'll check. The two of you stay here where I can see you."

Astruc and Goose walked ahead without making a sound.

Harper looked at the ground. Rotting sleepers, corroding rails, broken bolts and shoulder ties. Beneath the lot of it was a thick layer of gravel that went *crunch* with the lightest touch.

"Pretty good."

"Pardon, mon père?"

"Them. Quiet as church mice," Harper said.

He heard a rustling sound behind him. He turned, saw three faces peer from makeshift cardboard shelters tucked in the shadow of the overpass, protected from the rain.

"And who might they be?"

"Tramps," Lambert said. "But don't worry, they're always here. This is their home. They fixed the rope to the tree."

"The tramps fixed the rope, not you?"

"I think so. It was never here before they made this place their home. I used to have to walk another three kilometers to get up to the street. One day I saw them coming down the rope and setting up their huts. They don't seem to mind me using it. I leave them food and wine sometimes. They prefer the wine."

Harper looked at the tramps. Too dark to scan their eyes.

"Do you ever talk to them?"

"Non. They keep to themselves."

Harper looked toward Astruc and Goose. They were standing still now. Astruc talking, the kid signing. They couldn't see the tramps from where they were. Maybe they didn't need to. Maybe they already knew the tramps were there, or maybe they didn't care. He turned to Lambert.

"Tell me something, Gilles: Was there anything down there besides the bodies?"

"*Quoi?*"

"In the cavern, was there anything else down there? Artifacts, pieces of metal, anything?"

"*Non*, there was nothing but the bodies. Not that I noticed. I ran away . . ."

A wraithlike light moved along the top of the ridge. It panned through the dark and illuminated the rain. Then came the sound of wheels rolling over wet asphalt before slowing to a stop. Doors opened and closed, the wheels rolled on. Harper listened for the sound of copper boots pounding on pavement. Nothing. A bus dropping passengers, he thought.

"Right. You went in, found the bodies, ran away."

Fear flickered in Lambert's eyes.

"*Non*, I ran away when . . . when . . . I heard voices."

"What sort of voices?"

"Moaning, as if they were in pain."

"Who?"

"The bodies. They were moaning, they were in pain."

Fear could drive human beings mad. Harper had seen it over and over again. Like some last place of refuge. Checking Lambert's eyes just now, Harper wasn't convinced the skinny man wasn't halfway there already.

"Gilles, those bodies were thousands of years old."

"I know, *mon père*. But I heard them. That's why I ran away. I didn't tell the police, I was sure they would have me committed. But I heard them, *mon père*. I'm not lying to you."

Tink, tink.

Harper looked down, saw a stone skip along the rail and hit his boot.

He turned around. Astruc had tossed it from twenty meters and was now signaling them to advance. Harper made a mental note: *And that one is a good shot.*

"We'd best go. One more thing, Gilles: When did you find the cavern?"

"August fifteenth. It was my birthday."

The date fit with the photos Astruc had of the bodies.

They followed the rails, caught up to Astruc.

"Everything okay up ahead?" Harper said.

"It's clear. Shall we continue?"

Half a kilometer up the line, the earthen sides of the ravine gave way to high concrete walls and an abandoned train station. Platforms and benches sat like ghostly things in the pale light. Harper watched shadows move over the walls, checked them against the motion of the weeds and trees along the ridge. They matched. Now and again he looked back over his shoulder. Nothing but straight lines of perspective squeezing down to a point of unseen singularity. And when he turned ahead, it was the same damn thing. So if this was the train line that once circled Paris, where was the bend in the line? Then again, if no one else saw it, why bring up the subject?

They kept walking.

Harper kept his eyes to the ground where he could watch the way Astruc and Goose walked without making a sound. He flashed back to learning the same trick, somewhere. Or maybe he was imagining it. Or maybe it was the dead guy in his head, Captain Jay Michael Harper, remembering it. The tracks disappeared into the gaping mouth of a railroad tunnel. Lambert stopped.

"We'll need to use our lamps from now on," he said. "Be careful not to trip over the sleepers. And don't worry if you feel something running around your feet. It's only the rats."

They each fitted their headlamps and switched them on. Four narrow beams of light shot through the rain and into the beckoning dark. They walked ahead, pulling the cowls of their windbreakers from their heads. Everyone but the kid, Goose. Even in the dark he kept his face hidden.

Harper counted his paces.

He hit four hundred twenty when Lambert stepped off the tracks and walked to the sidewall. He kicked away a pile of rubbish hiding a long piece of corrugated metal. He lifted one corner. There was a meter-wide hole in the ground. Lambert anchored a steel bar against a rock, braced the bar under the metal sheet to hold it up.

"It's best to go in feetfirst. It's very steep, so try not to lose your footing or you might break your leg, or your head. And whoever comes last, knock away the bar to cover the entrance."

He disappeared down the hole. Astruc followed. Goose removed his backpack, climbed in, pulled in the backpack. Harper looked back up the tracks. He could just make out the shapes of the tramps from Rue des Petits Arbres standing at the opening of the rail tunnel. Only now, there were four. Shadows in the rain, watching.

"Don't be shy, lads. We're all shadows here."

II

H E EASED INTO THE OPENING, KNOCKED AWAY THE STEEL BAR. The cover slammed down, and Harper half climbed, half slid on his arse down the hole. Kept thinking he'd pass a sign any second: *Abandon all bloody hope, ye wankers who enter here.* When he found solid ground under his feet, he was at the head of a horizontal shaft. Ceiling low as the walls were wide, which wasn't much. Gilles Lambert, Astruc, and Goose were crouched in the cramped space a few meters ahead, waiting for him.

"Did you cover the entrance?" Lambert asked.

Harper looked at Astruc, wondered if mention should be made of the fact they were being tailed . . . *Sod it.*

"Done."

They walked in a crouch, came to the end of the shaft. There was a roughly dug opening at the base of the wall. Meter wide, meter high. Lambert got to his hands and knees.

"This shaft was a storage area for the railway until 1916, then it was sealed. It was the only one on the line built like this, but there were no records of where it was. I searched for it for months. When I discovered it, I compared it to my maps of *les carrières* and realized there was only a separation of two meters. It took me three months to dig this passage. I hope no one is claustrophobic."

He got on his hands and knees and crawled in, Astruc followed. Harper looked at Goose.

"After you, my son," Harper said.

Goose shook his head, made a few quick movements with his hands, then pointed to the hole in the wall: *After you.* No doubt about it, Harper thought; Goose's hands were louder than words. Especially the *f* and *k* signs tagged at the end. Signing slang for *fucker.* Harper smiled.

"Whatever you say, kid."

He ducked down and crawled ahead. Kept his eyes on the ground, kept moving. Lamplight splattered the close-in walls and lit up bits of dirt falling from the ceiling. He cleared the passage, got to his feet, found himself in a tunnel with just enough room to stand. Sidewalls barely shoulder-wide. It stretched ahead into the dark.

"*Bienvenue aux les carrières, mon père,*" Gilles Lambert said.

"Cheers."

Goose emerged from the passage, his backpack lashed to his ankle and dragging behind. Whatever was inside went *clank.* Goose undid the lashings, and Harper reached for the backpack.

"Need some help with that, kid?"

Goose held on to it. Astruc saw the exchange.

"Just some technical equipment to assist in our investigation, Father Harper. Goose can manage it."

"Of course he can," Harper said.

Astruc looked at Lambert.

"How long will it take us to get to the cavern?"

"Two hours at the least. But I need to show you something. Please, all of you, turn off your headlamps."

Lamps switched off. Harper raised his hand before his eyes and couldn't see it. He heard Gilles Lambert's voice:

"The lamps reflect off the limestone walls and offer enough light for us to find our way. But if your lamp fails and you become separated from the group, you will become hopelessly lost. And the clay floors of the tunnels absorb sound waves, so you'll be deaf as well as blind."

Astruc's voice was next.

"Then we'll keep to the present formation. Gilles, me, Father Harper. Goose will bring up the rear to make sure no one lags behind."

Lamps switched on, and they marched ahead.

The tunnel ran straight as a Parisian boulevard for a kilometer. It joined a quarry filled with cataphile graffiti. Initials, dates, wild-eyed creatures that appeared in quick flashes of light, then disappeared. Other side of the quarry, the tunnel continued; they entered it and kept moving. All the walls tagged with graffiti, like the quarry. They passed smaller side tunnels to the right and left. A quick glance with headlamps illuminated the first ten meters, then all light was swallowed by the hungry dark. They came to a four-way intersection.

"Normally we would go that way, but I heard the tunnels have been sealed with concrete. We must go this way, the long way."

Harper wondered what the hell Lambert was talking about till he saw two signs carved into the walls: BOULEVARD JOURDAN, AVENUE DE LECLERC.

"There're road signs down here?" Harper said.

Lambert nodded.

"*Oui*, but only in the main tunnels. They follow the streets of Paris, twenty-five meters above. Once you branch off, it gets tricky without a map."

"And you have a map, do you?"

Lambert tapped the side of his head.

"It's all up here."

They marched up Boulevard Jourdan till Lambert led them into a low-ceilinged quarry, then through a maze of tunnels connecting to side tunnels leading to more quarries. An hour into it, Harper realized his sense of direction was shot to hell. There was no way of knowing north from south, east from west. And without Lambert and the map in his head, there would be no way of finding their way out. That was a good thing, Harper thought. Whatever Astruc and the kid were up to, they still needed Gilles Lambert to find their way back. And as Harper (*make that Father Harper, OP,* he thought) was Lambert's chief hand-holder, the same need applied—hopefully. He looked back over his shoulder. Goose was five meters back, his glassy eyes reflecting in the light of Harper's headlamp. The kid stopped walking, stood still, stared at Harper.

Astruc's voice called, "Let's keep moving, Father Harper."

Harper looked ahead, saw two headlamps shining back at him. Couldn't see Astruc or Lambert, just their lamps.

"Goose is lagging behind. We need to wait for him."

"Goose is fine. He likes to keep his distance from strangers. That's all."

Harper walked ahead, looked back over his shoulder. The kid was standing still, waiting for Harper to walk on.

"Right."

They met a series of low-ceilinged passages. They walked in a crouch through some, crawled on hands and knees through others, always moving through the dark in a battery-powered bubble of light. They came to a rusted iron door built into the tunnel wall. Harper saw the numbers *1643* etched into metal. A door built to lock out smugglers, Lambert said.

"Could someone help me move it?"

"Sure," Harper said.

He knelt on the clay floor next to Lambert, and they set their shoulders into the iron door and heaved. The door groaned on its hinges. Lambert was right, the sound didn't echo away. It just dropped dead in the tunnel. Harper illuminated the darkness beyond the door and realized the limestone walls ahead, like all the walls since they left the main tunnels a long while ago, were bare of graffiti.

"Somewhat off the beaten path, I take it," Harper said.

"Very much so, *mon père*. But it is the only way."

Lambert ducked in, and Harper ducked behind him, but a big hand grabbed his shoulder, stopped him.

"Stick to the formation, Father Harper."

"Of course. What was I thinking?"

Astruc went in. Harper looked at Goose. He was leaning against the tunnel wall like a teenager hanging outside a 7-Eleven, both hands in the front pouch of his hoodie, holding something.

"Don't get lost, kid."

Harper ducked into the tunnel. It was high enough to walk through, but the clay floor soon became damp, then muddy, then it was flooded. Lambert stopped.

"We're very near the water table down here. You need to brace your hands against the walls and keep your feet on the stone foundations at either side of the tunnel *comme ça*. Be careful not to slip—the water turns the clay floor into quicksand."

It was a long slog till the water receded and they entered a shoe box–shaped quarry supported by two limestone pillars. There was a small cove cut into the far wall.

"We should take a break here," Gilles Lambert said. "The next part is very difficult."

Harper looked at him.

"The next part?"

Astruc and Goose slumped to the ground, sat on either side of the tunnel entrance. Harper walked to the far wall, slid down next to the cove. Lambert sat on a chunk of limestone rock in the corner. Head-lamps crisscrossed the quarry and lit their faces. All of them covered with dust and grime. They sat quietly a moment, catching their breath. A soft sound rushed through the tunnel just outside the quarry: *whoosh.*

"That's the number four line of the Métro," Gilles said. "It runs directly above us, twenty-six meters up. The train's weight bears down on the earth and forces air to move through the tunnels."

Harper took another look at the limestone pillars in the center of the quarry. Not even pillars. Just a pile of mismatched rocks, like the one Lambert was sitting on, stacked and pinned between the floor and ceiling.

"That's what's holding up the number four line of the Métro?"

"And the water and sewer lines, and the sixth arrondissement of Paris."

"The sixth?"

"*Oui*, we are under Rue d'Assas now, in the sixth."

The location registered with Astruc.

"Then we're very close to the quarries beneath Lycée Montaigne?"

Lambert pointed to the opening next to Harper.

"Through there," Lambert said.

Harper leaned down and looked in. His headlamp lit up the cove, only it wasn't a cove. It was a narrow shaft with a great pile of human bones blocking the way. Harper looked at Lambert.

"It's full of skeletons, Gilles."

"*Oui*, they were dumped here—"

"During the plague, I know. I saw it on the History Channel. Question is, how do we get through?"

Lambert crossed the quarry and knelt next to Harper. He began to remove the skulls and bones from the entrance. He placed them carefully on the quarry floor. He reached deeper into the tunnel again and again, laying remnants of human existence on the clay floor of the quarry. At one point, he pulled out a broken skull, held it out to Harper.

"It will go faster if you help me, *mon père*."

"Sorry?"

"Could you help me?"

Harper looked back at Astruc and Goose. They watched. Maybe the big man was squeamish about skeletons. Maybe he wanted Harper to have another go in the pastoral concern department to keep Gilles Lambert in line. Maybe Astruc and the kid were sitting on either side of the only way topside for the sole purpose of making sure nobody tried to leave. Harper took the skull from Lambert's hand.

"Sure."

He laid it on the clay floor, then an ulna, then a femur, then a rib, then another skull. They were dry and chalky to the touch. And as he added vertebrae, sternums, tibias, fibulas, and skulls upon skulls to the pile, a cloud of fine dust hovered above the bones.

"So what is this passage, Gilles?"

"It must have been a service shaft to the Lycée quarries once, to pass tools through. But from my research, I found there was a massive cave-in during the sixteenth century, and it was sealed. It was never used again."

"A cave-in?"

"*Oui*. An entire street was swallowed as people slept in their beds. That's why no cataphiles come this way. On all the official maps, this is a dead end."

Harper looked at the bones he'd stacked on the clay floor.

"I'm not surprised."

Gilles Lambert backed out from the tunnel.

"You can see it now, the way me must go."

Harper looked in the shaft. His headlamp lit up a massive giant slab of collapsed rock ten meters ahead. He saw a gap in the lower corner. Looked fit for a large rabbit.

"Doesn't look too stable in there."

"It isn't. It's never been reinforced."

Harper looked back at the bones.

"How did you think to look behind the skeletons to find the shaft?" he said.

Gilles shook his head. "I didn't look behind them, I was coming the other way. I had to dig through the bones to get out."

"What?"

"I was so upset with what I heard in the cavern, I began to panic coming out. I lost my sense of direction. Instead of going back into the quarries under the Lycée, I came out here. It was an accident."

Astruc moved closer and looked into the tunnel.

"How far now?" said Astruc.

"Once we get through here, it's not far. But getting there is very difficult. Crawling under the rubble, there's not enough room to use your legs, and you can't raise your head to see where you are going. You must feel your way, reach ahead and pull yourself along. After a hundred meters the passage splits. To the right is the way to the Lycée quarries near le Jardin du Luxembourg, to the left the tunnel angles down and leads to the corridor and cavern."

"Good, very good," Astruc said, turning to Goose and signing for him to come. Goose rushed over, dropped his backpack on the floor again, and again it went *clank*. The two of them studied the way ahead. Gilles Lambert sat up, adjusted his headlamp, looked at Harper.

"But before we go, would you offer a prayer, *mon père*? For our continued protection?"

Harper had to remind himself, again, of his recent ordination into the Dominican Order. His mind raced through Catholic prayers, trying to find one for the occasion of being thirty meters under Paris with a pile of skeletons at your knees.

"Is there any particular prayer you have in mind, Gilles?"

"*Non, mon père.*"

Astruc straightened up.

"Perhaps, if Father Harper would allow, I could offer a prayer."

Harper nodded. "Go right ahead."

Gilles Lambert bowed his head with Astruc. The two of them closed their eyes. Goose caught the move and crossed the quarry. He knelt close to Astruc, locked his glassy eyes on the big man's lips. It was Harper's turn to watch.

"*Notre Père, qui es aux cieux . . .*" Harper listened to the sound of the voice. "*. . . délivre-nous du mal . . .*" Watched Goose's lips forming silent words in perfect unison with Astruc. "*. . . mais delivre-nous du Mal . . . Amen.*"

In the resultant silence, Harper looked at the two of them. *They believe.* Astruc opened his eyes.

"Are you ready to continue, Gilles?"

Gilles nodded, nervously.

"Yes, yes. I am ready now, *et merci.*"

Lambert crawled into the opening, hands and knees making small crunching sounds on bits of bones. At the collapse he lay flat on the clay floor, reached into the gap, and pulled himself ahead. Harper watched him disappear, then he looked at Astruc. The big man stared back.

"Something on your mind, Father Harper?" Astruc said.

"*Notre Père.*"

"What about it?"

"Haven't heard it in French in a long while."

Astruc looked at Goose and ripped off a few quick signs—*watch him, be careful*—then he got onto his belly and crawled after Gilles. Harper gave the big man time to pull himself under the rubble pile, and he stared at Goose. Goose signed his own version of Astruc's question: *Something on your mind, fucker?*

Harper gave the skeletons a once-over, then crawled into the shaft. At the face of the collapse, he lay on his stomach and targeted his head-lamp into the hole. *Like crawling into the belly of a worm,* he thought. He saw the two headlamps of Lambert and Astruc moving slowly forward. Then they began to turn and sink deeper into the Earth. Harper reached in, caught two outcrops of rock, and pulled. He dragged himself over rocky floor, reached ahead again, pulled. There wasn't enough room to raise his head to see the way, or to look behind himself to check if Goose was following him. He reached the bend in the tunnel, then it began to slope downward, then came the rumble of falling rock. A tremor rolled through the close-in walls, and a cloud of thick dust filled the tunnel.

"Oh, shit."

Harper hid his eyes in the crook of his arm, waiting for the tunnel to collapse on top of him. He heard Gilles Lambert's muffled voice calling back through the dust instead.

"We're at the place connecting to the Lycée Montaigne. The collapse has slipped a little, but I think we can still get through. I need to pull some rocks out of the way."

Harper heard Goose coming up behind him, felt the kid's hands tap at his legs as if asking what was happening. Harper wondered how the hell you tell a deaf person who can't see your lips or hands that presently, you're bloody well stuck.

The tapping came again, then a shove.

Harper pulled the lamp from his head; he pointed it back over his shoulder. His fingers found the on/off switch. He flipped the light on and off: *Dot, dot, dot. Dash. Dot, dot, dash. Dash, dot, dash, dot. Dash, dot, dash. S-T-U-C-K.* Harper was only half-surprised when Goose answered in dots and dashes: *Roger.* Then Harper wondered: If Gilles couldn't clear the passage and the only way to get through the tunnel was to pull yourself ahead with your hands and there was no way to turn around, how the fuck were they supposed to back up? Then he realized: They wouldn't be able to. He buried his face in the crook of his arm.

"This really is so bloody swell."

And he couldn't help but laugh to himself when he imagined the dead man who wasn't supposed to be in his head anymore joining in the conversation: *Tell me about it.* There was another shudder through the tunnel, not as bad as the last one, but enough for Harper to feel the walls close in just a bit more.

"It's all right," Lambert's muffled voice called back. "I've cleared the way."

Harper heard Gilles and Astruc crawl forward. He grabbed ahold of the sidewalls and pulled himself ahead. The tunnel turned at a sharp angle where it split right and left. To the right, the tunnel angled upward and it was filled with rocks and fresh concrete. Had to be the way to the caverns under Lycée Montaigne, Harper thought. He could raise his head a bit now. He saw Gilles and Astruc in the left tunnel. They were sinking down at a very steep slope. Harper followed. Fifteen minutes later, the tunnel ended at a hole in the wall. He crawled through and came into a corridor of black rock.

Harper got to his feet, stretched his arms and back for the first time since they'd gone underground. His headlamp caught Astruc and Gilles Lambert enjoying the same freedom. As they waited for Goose to clear the tunnel, Harper looked around. They stood at the end of the corridor, angling down at thirty degrees. He stepped closer to the wall. His headlamp caught the hundreds of divots in the stone, as if the tunnel had been hand-carved from solid rock.

Bloody hell, he thought. *Same damn stone, same damn construction, as the vertical shaft hidden under the well of Lausanne Cathedral.*

Goose clawed through the hole with his backpack still lashed to his ankle. He sat on the floor, undid the lashings. He hooked the backpack to his shoulders and got to his feet.

"How far to the cavern now, Gilles?" Astruc said.

"I'm not sure, but it goes quickly."

Astruc looked at his watch.

"We should hurry, then. We lost valuable time at the collapse."

Harper checked his own watch. They'd been down for four and a half hours.

"Right. Let's go, then."

Gilles Lambert led the way, then Astruc, then Harper. Goose kept his position five meters back at the rear. Harper listened to their steps echo off the stone walls, ceiling, and floor. Harper had thought about counting his own steps, passed on it, thinking if this tunnel really was like the tunnel under Lausanne Cathedral, then he already knew how deep it would be: two and a half kilometers. He scanned the dimensions of the corridor instead. The tunnel under the cathedral was rounded and went straight down. This place was a rectangle, angled down a slope. But he'd happily bet a round of drinks at GG's that the dimensions would yield a quotient of 2.5. Same as the Lausanne tunnel again.

He stretched his arms from his sides, his fingertips just touching the sidewalls, feeling those hundreds of divots per square centimeter. He remembered everything Inspector Gobet's research lads from Berne had learned from studying the Lausanne tunnel after the cathedral job. Nothing, *rien du tout*. No idea who built it, no idea how it was made. Only that it had been built long before Harper's kind had come to paradise to hide in the forms of men . . . and that the dimensions of construction, when divided any which way, kept yielding a positive or negative quotient of 2.5, like some mathematical proof of eternal occurrence.

Harper laughed to himself; talk about a higher power. His thoughts faded away, and there was only the sound of steps echoing off stone until Gilles Lambert stopped walking.

"We're here," he said.

III

A LOW OPENING CUT INTO A BLACK STONE WALL, STRIPS OF RED tape stretched across the opening. Words on the tape translated as "Crime scene" and "Do not cross." Astruc and Goose walked ahead, pulled down the tape. They ducked through the opening, disappeared. Harper looked at Gilles Lambert, saw fear flare in the man's eyes.

"It'll be all right, Gilles. I'm here with you."

"*Oui, merci, mon père.*"

Harper ducked through the opening, and Lambert followed.

Four narrow beams of light cut through the immense dark, reflected mirrorlike off the black stone walls and crisscrossed wildly. The effect was dizzying. Gilles Lambert lay his canvas backpack on the ground, pulled out four candles and a book of matches.

"*Attendez.* I found it's easier to see using candles."

He lit the candles, one by one, passed them out.

"You can switch off your headlamps now," he said.

The lamps went off.

Slowly, soft light swelled through the darkness and the cavern became visible. Six rectangular walls of equal shape and height were gathered around a conical pillar at the center of the cavern. The pillar was widest at its base and the diameter shrank as it rose tens of meters to the center of the domed ceiling. The dome seemed to glow with candlelight, and so did the walls. The wall with the gate to the outer passage was solid-faced, but Harper saw coves cut into the five other walls. Equal in size and shape, perfectly arranged. Four coves per wall, eight rows, equally spaced from floor to ceiling. He bent down, held his candle into one of the coves. Five chalk outlines of headless forms. *French copper scribble, for sure,* Harper thought. It was the same in the next cove and the next. Harper looked back at Gilles Lambert.

"The way these markings are drawn, it's exactly how you found the bodies, yeah?"

"*Oui, mon père.* There were one hundred of them in the first row of coves. When I was interviewed a few days later by the police, they told me the rest of the coves were empty. Only the first row contained bodies."

Harper backed out of the cove, looked up at the next row, and the next.

"Empty," he mumbled.

He stepped back and took in a wide view of the pillar, happy to bet another round of drinks at GG's that the pillar was 2.5 meters in circumference at its base and stood 25 meters high, to the bloody picometer. His eyes followed the shrinking diameter of the thing till it reached a perfect point almost touching the exact center of the glowing dome.

"What is it, *mon père?*"

"It's not a supporting pillar at all."

Lambert could see it, too.

"Then why is it here?"

"Good question. What's above us?"

"I don't know, why?"

"Because the pillar is pointing to somewhere up there."

"Oh. Do you know what is up there, *mon père?*"

"No idea."

Harper watched Astruc and the kid approach and circle the pillar, examining it by candlelight. The big man hadn't even bothered to look at the coves, the ones that contained all that evil he was so concerned about back at Les Deux Magots. Instead, Astruc was walking to the pillar, sidekick in tow. The two of them stopped at the far side of the pillar, seeing something. Harper whispered to Gilles Lambert.

"I want you to stay here, Gilles."

"Is something wrong, *mon père?*"

"I'm about to find out."

Harper marched toward the pillar. Goose saw him coming, took three steps back. Astruc looked at Harper.

"Ah, Father, I was just about to ask you to join us."

Astruc held his candle close to the pillar.

"I wonder if you might have a look at this and tell me what you make of it?"

Harper looked at the pillar. There was a relief set in the stone, the size of a book. And like a book, there were letters carved in the stone. Some of the lettering was ancient, some of it wasn't. Harper scanned it once, then twice . . . *Bloody hell.* Then he saw Goose from the corner of his eye, reaching into the pouch of his hoodie.

Harper looked at Astruc. "What about it?"

"As I said, I wonder if you might tell me what you make of it?"

"In my capacity as a professor of ancient languages at Lausanne University, along with my job advising the Pope, you mean."

Astruc stared at Harper. "Yes, as you mention it."

Harper nodded, raised his candle to the pillar, read the words on the tablet again.

"It's interesting."

"How so?"

"Three things. One: The writing is a variation of the Ge'ez script developed in Ethiopia in the ninth century BC. It tells the story of this cavern. Strangely enough it doesn't say anything about this being a place of evil. Quite the opposite, actually. Two: Something was added to the tablet in the Middle Ages. That bit is in Latin, the lingua franca of the day. This was written in the mid-thirteenth century. June 24, 1244, to be precise."

"You know this how?"

"Roman numerals, there."

"Could you translate it, please?"

"Sure. It says, 'The chosen of the fallen ones may recover what is hidden here by placing his hands on the tablet and reciting the sacred words.' Those sacred words are carved into the pillar itself, here; carved by the same hand. And they're in French. Strangely enough, the French words are an exact translation of the last sentence of the tablet, which, as I said, was written in the Ge'ez script. Meaning whoever wrote this in the thirteenth century knew a dead language from a part of Africa he couldn't have known about. It's the third thing that's the most interesting, though."

Harper sensed Astruc coil like a serpent.

"Which is what?"

"You know all this already, and it's the reason you brought me down here."

Astruc looked at Harper.

"An interesting syllogism, Father Harper. Though I believe it suffers from the faulty logic of the undistributed middle."

Harper saw the kid's shadow reflect in the opaque lens of Astruc's glasses, his hands and shoulders making a move, pulling something from his sweatshirt.

"In that case, call it a fucking hunch."

Harper tossed his candle at Astruc and spun around. He kicked and caught Goose's legs, dropped him to the floor. He pulled a Glock 17 from the kid's hands. He whipped around, targeted Astruc's head. Astruc was holding his candle in his left hand, a Mini UZI submachine gun in his right. Fully auto, thirty-two-round clip, effective range of a hundred meters. It was pointed at Harper.

"You may wish to consider your next move very carefully, Father Harper."

Harper shrugged. "What's to consider? You cut me in half, I put a bullet in your skull. Amen."

"This really would have been much easier had you just put your hands on the tablet."

"I have a bad habit of avoiding easy."

Gilles Lambert yelped.

"*Mon père*, what are you doing?"

Harper kept his eyes locked on the kill spot above Astruc's eyes.

157

"Gilles, listen to my voice," Harper said. "I want you to leave, now. Get the hell out of here."

"For the sake of your immortal soul, Gilles, stay where you are," Astruc commanded.

Gilles Lambert's eyes darted frantically between the two of them, settled on Harper.

"But *mon père*, you were sent by the Pope, you're a priest."

"Sorry, mate, I'm not a priest."

"Quoi?"

Harper nodded to Astruc. "He's the priest."

Gilles Lambert sank to his knees, the candle shaking in his hand.

"C'est de la folie . . . madness."

Astruc smiled, bowed slightly to Harper.

"Bravo. May I ask how you knew?"

"The way you prayed the Notre Père."

"It is a prayer of comfort in a world of evil."

"Glad to hear it. Though given the circs, I'd say your faith in the comforting power of prayer needs a bloody tune-up. What happened, Padre? Get a little too friendly with your favorite altar boy and they took away your collar?"

Goose flew from the floor, lunged at Harper. Harper turned just as fast, had the barrel pressed against the kid's forehead.

"What do you know, your ears work. I bet you're a right talker, too."

The kid's glassy eyes dripped with hate. He didn't speak.

"No matter. You just stand there while Father Astruc and I sort this out, yeah?"

Harper angled around till the barrel was at Goose's temple.

"Now, where were we, Padre?"

"It would be easier if you put down the gun," Astruc said.

"I thought we already covered me and easy. Besides, I've got a two-for-one shot. Bullet travels through the softest part of your altar boy's skull and into your head."

"But you will not pull the trigger."

"Why not?"

"Because you're the angel who saved Paris."

"You shouldn't believe what you read in the newspapers, Padre."

Astruc whipped his Mini UZI to the right, lit up the laser targeting. A red bead of light shot across the cavern, landed directly over Gilles Lambert's heart. Astruc shrugged.

"What I believe isn't important. What I will do for what I believe is."

Harper stared at him. *Sod it.* He released his grip on the Glock. It rolled and dangled from his trigger finger. Goose took the gun, rammed it into Harper's back, shoved him toward the pillar.

"Good," Astruc said. "Now, place your hands on the tablet and say the words."

Harper touched the stone and whispered, *"C'est le guet. Il a sonné l'heure. Il a sonné l'heure."* He wondered what the hell would happen next. There were long seconds of nothing till . . . *clunk, clunk.* A section of stone opened at the base of the pillar. Harper looked at his hands.

"Huh."

Astruc stepped closer.

"Now, step away and join Gilles Lambert on the floor."

Harper walked across the cavern, sat down against the wall next to Gilles. Goose stood over the two of them. He kept the barrel of his Glock pointed at Harper's head. Message loud and clear: *You move, you die first, then Lambert.* Harper smiled.

"Just should've put a bullet through your skull when I had the chance."

Goose signed *fuck off.*

Gilles Lambert looked at Harper.

"What is all this?"

"Don't ask, Gilles, and don't speak."

"But what will happen to us?"

Harper didn't answer. He kept his eyes on Astruc, watching him tuck the UZI into its holster inside his windbreaker, gather the candles spread about the floor. Relighting them and standing them near the pillar. Getting on his knees and reaching into the pillar. Slowly, carefully, removing a small wooden chest and resting it on the floor near the candles. The chest was old. Ninth or tenth century, maybe. Half a meter long, a quarter meter high, half a meter deep, with rounded corners. Looked like a single section of oak that'd been hollowed out instead of joined together. Wrought iron straps and hinges held the lid in place, and a plate lock mechanism was secured by a padlock of forged iron.

The more Harper looked at it, the more it looked familiar. Like a reliquary box he'd seen on the History Channel. He watched Astruc's hands tremble as he pulled at a chain hanging around his neck. A skeleton key was attached to the chain. Astruc eased the key into the lock . . . *click*. He raised the lid, looked inside. He looked at Harper.

"Praise to the Pure God, it is here."

"Swell. And what the hell is it?"

Astruc reached into the box, unwrapped layers of leather sheets, and lifted a six-inch telescope mounted on a triangle-shaped frame. The metal housing of the telescope and the frame glowed in the candlelight. Two lengths of the triangle were equally straight and joined a sixty-degree arc at the base. Mirrors and filters for the telescope, an index lever, and calibration dials fitted at the arc.

"You must be joking me," Harper said.

Gilles Lambert was fit to burst. "What is it?"

"It looks like a sextant," Harper said.

"A what?"

"A triangulating device to locate your position at sea."

"Down here, hundreds of meters under Paris? I don't understand."

"Welcome to the club, mate."

Astruc returned the object to the reliquary box, lifted it in one arm, and picked up a candle from the floor. He walked across the cavern, lay the box near Harper. He opened the lid and held the candle close.

"Perhaps you would care for a closer inspection."

Harper looked at it. The triangle-shaped frame and telescope were made of copper, had to be copper. And the thing was old, much older than the reliquary box. Candlelight reflected in the metal and Harper could see an elaborate design engraved into the legs of the triangle. The mirrors and lenses attached to the frame looked to be ground with a precision too exact for its age. The mirrors captured the dim glow of the candle and reshaped it into a brilliant needlelike thread of light, feeding it into the telescope. And instead of numbers along the arc, there were groupings of tiny strikes in the copper. The calibration dial was marked with fourteen astrological symbols. *Bloody hell,* Harper thought, *it is a sextant.* Though from everything Harper could recall from the History Channel, the one in Astruc's hands appeared to have been made thousands of years before a British mathematician named John Campbell invented the first sextant in 1757.

"You do not recognize it still?" Astruc said.

"Like I said, should I?"

"Because it was you who brought this sacred treasure to this place."

"Me?" Harper looked at the sextant again, laughed. "I'm sure you know what you're talking about, but trust me, I'm as clueless as a rock."

Astruc nodded, returned the sextant to the reliquary box, wrapping it carefully. He closed the lid, looked at Harper.

"You let them build a world void of truth to blind the souls of men from the stars. This is your original sin, and it must be cleansed."

"And how do you plan to do that?"

"Confess unto me, and I will give you absolution."

"Get stuffed."

Astruc ripped the Petzl lamps from Harper and Lambert's heads.

"So be it."

He dropped the lamps on the stone floor, crushed them underfoot. Gilles Lambert panicked.

"*Les lumières! Non!* We'll be blind without light!"

Astruc kicked Gilles Lambert against the wall, bent down, rammed an auto-injector into the man's thigh.

"Receive this, Gilles, receive your portion of the divine sacrament."

Lambert jumped as the needle punched through his jeans and into his leg. He screamed.

"*Non!* What are you doing to me?"

Astruc bowed his head.

"Holy Father, welcome thy servant in thy justice, and send upon him thy grace and thy holy spirit."

At the same moment, Harper felt a sting as Goose pressed an injector into his leg. Harper didn't jump. He waited for whatever it was in the needle to enter his bloodstream. Coming on fast. He checked Lambert. Already under.

"Will it kill him?" Harper said.

"What?"

"Your divine whatsit? Will it kill him?"

"You're the killer, I am the protector of men's souls."

A sensation of separating from his flesh began to rush through Harper's form . . . falling. He shook his head, trying to stay clear.

"That's right . . . you and your bloody hobby. Caring for immortal souls of men. Inspiring, really . . ."

The cavern was beginning to spin. *Bloody swell, boyo, every time you come to this bloody town, you end up dead.*

"Bloody inspiring."

He watched Goose pull a set of night vision goggles from his backpack. Watched him pull off his headlamp, mount the goggles to his oddly shaped head. Watched him pull out a second pair of night vision goggles, hand them to Astruc. Watched a few small plastic tubes slip from the backpack and tumble onto the stone floor, next to Astruc's knee. *Familiar-looking kit,* Harper thought, or Captain Jay Michael Harper thought. It was getting hard to tell who was who with the divine whatsit rushing through his blood. He put it together: The goggles captured undetectable levels of near-infrared light, amplified them to the visible spectrum, and it was bright, as if the world were lit by a green sun. The tubes were Cyalume ChemLights in the near-infrared range, eight-hour duration, only visible with night vision. Easy peasy.

"How 'bout that?"

Astruc regarded him with a quizzical look.

"Your pal with the ears. Goose, yeah? He's been dropping ChemLights. That's why he was at the rear. Dropping ChemLights to mark a trail so you two can find your way back with the night gogs."

"How clever of you to notice."

"Me? You kidding, I'm off my fucking head. I'm still trying to get my head around the whole gun-toting priest and his merry altar boy motif. Not to mention . . . the rest of it . . . whatever it was. Something about me, no, wasn't me . . . was the dead guy in my head. Pull up some floor, I'll tell you all about him. By the way, Father Fucking Astruc, him and me, or me and him, the both of us think you're a bloody loon."

Astruc leaned close to Harper, studying his eyes.

"Looking for something in particular, Padre, or is watching the light go out in someone's eyes the way you get your kicks?"

Astruc leaned closer. Harper caught the scent of something malodorous and ancient as Astruc whispered in Harper's ear.

"The reign of the Dark Ones is finished. Now is the time of salvation of all men."

"That's what this is about? The Dark Ones? And here I was thinking you were just a fucking lunatic."

Astruc slammed his fat fist into Harper's face, knocked him flat.

Harper rolled over slowly. He watched Astruc grab Gilles Lambert's backpack from the floor, toss it over his shoulder. Goose circled the cavern collecting the candles, blowing them out, and dropping them in his own backpack. As he held the last candle, he looked at Astruc and signed, *Are you ready, Father?* Astruc nodded. The two of them pulled their night goggles down over their eyes and switched them on. Goose blew at the flame and presto. It was more than dark, it was the complete absence of light. Harper couldn't help but chuckle.

"So, Father Astruc, it's been a swell evening. What happens next?"

"Next? Next is easy. Next we leave and you stay."

Harper listened to the priest's sepulchral voice, wrapped in a French accent, echo and rise through the cavern. Then came the sound of boots walking away. Then the rustle of bodies and gear as Astruc and the kid ducked under the lintel and into the passageway. Then the sound of steps climbing the passage to the real world. Then nothing.

BOOK TWO

WATCHMAN, WHAT OF THE
NIGHT? WATCHMAN, WHAT
OF THE NIGHT?

TEN

THE EIGHTEEN-WHEELER TURNED OFF THE ROAD AT THE CARSON lumberyards. They'd been following the slow-moving truck since leaving the house. Katherine watched the giant timbers sway and strain at the chains with every bend in the road, often wondering aloud what they'd do if the chains broke and the timbers spilled onto the road.

"We'd stop," Officer Jannsen said.

"No shit, we'd stop."

"Relax, Kat. Look, there isn't a cloud in the sky. Enjoy the drive."

Katherine turned to Max, strapped to his car seat like an astronaut, planted between his mother and Officer Jannsen in the backseat of the Ford Explorer.

"How about you, buster, you enjoying the drive?"

Max, too, had been watching the timbers atop the flatbed sway, tipping his head whichever direction they shifted as if expecting them to fall over any second. He turned to Katherine and spoke droolingly through the pacifier in his mouth.

"Goog."

Katherine rubbed the hair on Max's head.

"You bet."

They passed through Carson and joined Route 14 West, two lanes of asphalt that ran along the Columbia River. Officer Jannsen was right. It was a cloudless sky, and just now, the sun was breaking over the high forest and sparks of golden light skipped off the river and into Katherine's eyes.

Two Swiss Guards sat up front. One at the wheel, one with a Brügger & Thomet machine gun on his lap. "Riding shotgun," Katherine called it a long time ago. The Swiss Guards liked the sound of it, and the title stuck. The dashboard between the guards had been customized, the driver had explained to Katherine after she'd commented, "Looks like the deck of the *Starship Enterprise* up there." Katherine went on to note that she was talking about the Captain Picard version of *Star Trek*, not Captain Kirk. "You know, the episode where Picard gets kidnapped by the Borg?"

Officer Jannsen looked at Katherine.

"The Borg?"

"Yeah, 'We are the Borg. Resistance is futile, prepare to be assimilated.'"

The guard riding shotgun looked back at Katherine and said, "Yes, I like this program very much. I have all the episodes on DVD. The Klingon security officer, Lieutenant Worf, is my favorite."

"Woof!" Max added.

Katherine reached over, tapped Officer Jannsen's shoulder, pointed to the guard with the machine gun on his lap.

"See? Everybody loves *Star Trek*."

Officer Jannsen smiled. One of those smiles that caused Katherine's tummy to flip and flop. She turned her attention to Max.

"What about you, bud, what do you think of those stinky Borg guys?"

The whole trip Max had been carrying his rubber hammer in his right hand in the event a round of Whac-A-Mole might be called for. But without a mole in sight, the sound of the word *Borg* seemed to fire the same synapses in his brain, and he gave the air a firm bashing.

"Boog!"

"Yeah. Who needs the Swiss Guard when we've got you and your hammer? Hey, you want some applesauce?"

Max ceased to bash the Borg and looked at Katherine, licking his lips. "Aposoose."

"Yeah, I thought so."

Katherine opened the tote bag at her feet, removed a baby bib (the one with the blue bunnies and faded stains of assorted meals past on it), and tied it around Max's neck. She dug out the plastic container and spoon.

"Mmmmmm, applesauce," she said. "Max's favorite." She opened the container, dipped the spoon into the applesauce, and held it to Max's mouth. "Okay, beam up the good stuff."

Max opened his mouth and in went the spoon. He smiled with delight as rivulets of applesauce dribbled down his chin.

"Can't take you anywhere, can I?"

"Goo . . ." Max said, not even finishing his favorite word to experience the sensation of applesauce bubbles forming on his lips.

"See what happens when you talk with your mouth full, buster? You get bubble mouth. Not a good look on anyone."

Max remained very still as Katherine rounded up the drops and dribbles on his face and herded them back into his mouth. He wasn't that hungry, and after a drink of water from his sippy cup, and after Katherine washed his face with a damp washcloth, he offered a hearty burp that made the Swiss Guard with the machine gun on his lap turn around to make sure all was well in the backseat.

"*Guten appetit, Kapitän Picard,*" he said.

Max looked at him, smiled. "Woof!"

"No, he's not Worf, he's your buddy Luc. He always goes with us when we drive to Portland."

Max pointed his hammer at the back of the driver's head. "Woof!"

"No, that's . . . Sorry, what's your name again, besides Corporal?"

"I am Corporal Sebastianus Fassnacht, madame."

"That's it, and how could I forget? Mind if we make it Seb?"

"It would be my honor, Madame Taylor."

Katherine looked at Max.

"There you go, you can call him Seb."

"Woof."

Katherine curled her brow.

"Are you teasing Mommy?"

Max giggled at the tone of Katherine's voice.

"That's what I thought. Here, have a drink."

Max latched on to the sippy cup and promptly fell asleep. The fingers of his right hand slowly loosened around his Borg-bashing hammer. Katherine took the toy from his hand and tucked it next to him in the car seat. She pulled a blanket from the tote bag and wrapped it around him. She brushed back his black hair, kissed his forehead.

"My big, brave Max."

They slowed approaching Stevenson, drove along the main street past the barbershop, the Big River Grill, and Granny's Gedunk Ice Cream Parlor. They'd hit Granny's on the way back for a chocolate milk shake. That was the routine on Max-and/or-Katherine-go-to-the-doctor days. Played this way: Drive to Portland, Max gets a checkup or Katherine drops in to see the shrink, grab a milk shake on the way home. These days, Katherine considered Granny's Gedunk the highlight of the social season. She leaned across the seat, tapped the window next to Officer Jannsen, pointing toward the ice cream parlor.

"Promise?"

Officer Jannsen was looking through the messages on her mobile, smiling.

"Yes, Kat, I promise."

Kat lingered to enjoy the scent of Chanel emanating from the pulse points of Officer Jannsen's neck. Officer Jannsen looked up from her mobile.

"What is it?"

"Nothing. How long to Portland?"

"ETA is 09:45."

"Are you going to talk like a cop till we get home?"

"Just doing my job, Kat."

"Okeydoke, and out."

The Explorer sped up leaving Stevenson and quickly traversed the causeway at Rock Cove, passing Ashes Lake and Little Ashes Lake, then slowing again to let another timber-laden truck pass before turning south onto the narrow cantilevered bridge stretching half a mile across the Columbia River. Katherine leaned ahead for a better view.

"Wow," she said. "I never noticed that sign before."

"What sign?"

"The blue one, over the entrance ramp. 'Bridge of the Gods.'"

"Because you usually manage to sleep the whole way."

"At my age I need all the beauty sleep I can get."

"You're not even thirty."

"Never too early to start."

They passed under the sign, and the steel bridge rose one hundred forty feet above the river. And as another sign read 15 MPH, Katherine had time to enjoy the view. A daylight moon hanging in the blue sky, green mountains, flashes of light in water. It was pretty.

"Funny name for a bridge, isn't it?"

Officer Jannsen put away her mobile, looked out the window.

"It's named after a natural land bridge that crossed above the river," she said. "It fell into the water a thousand years ago. The Native Americans who settled here called it the Bridge of the Gods."

"And you know it how?"

"I read about it, before we moved here from Switzerland."

They reached the Oregon side of the river and looped around Cascade Locks and joined up with I–84. Katherine looked out the rear window and watched the Bridge of the Gods disappear. Just then, Max stretched his arms and woke up. Katherine found the sippy cup of water and set it to Max's lips.

"So what did you read about it? The bridge back there."

"You really want to know?"

"Yeah, why not? How about you, Max, you want to hear about the bridge?"

"Zug," he said.

"Yeah, yeah, but wait a sec."

Katherine handed Max his toy hammer. And with that, he smiled and kicked his legs and turned his eyes to Officer Jannsen.

"See? Max wants to hear it, too. Shoot."

Officer Jannsen looked up front. "How's our time, Corporal?"

"Still on track."

"And the road?"

"Normal. Drawbridge will be down when we reach it, lights are synchronized. No waiting time."

"Good."

She turned to Katherine and Max.

"All right, long ago, the Great Spirit traveled to this place from the ice world of the north. He brought his two sons, Klickitat and Wyeast. And they thought it the most beautiful place they had ever seen and wished to settle here. The sons couldn't decide where they would live, so the Great Spirit shot two arrows into the air; one to the north and one to the south. Klickitat followed the arrow to the north, Wyeast followed the arrow to the south. They were separated by the river, so the Great Spirit built a bridge of stone they could use to cross and visit each other. All the natives used the bridge as well, and as thanks, they called it . . ."

". . . the Bridge of the Gods."

"Yes."

"What else?"

"What else what?"

"Is that it?"

"Kat, settle back. I'm telling it to you."

"Okay."

"Everything was fine in the world until the sons both fell in love with a beautiful maiden named Loowit."

Kat sighed. "Yeah, yeah; there's always a woman. And she's always beautiful, and she's always a maiden. This is what's wrong with the world. I mean, look at the fashion mags. Overflowing with beautiful, coke-snorting maidens, not a real-looking banana in the bunch. What do you think, Max?"

Max waved his hammer, excited at the sound of his favorite fruit.

"Nanas!"

Officer Jannsen continued: "So, a war broke out between the brothers. Klickitat and Wyeast began to spew fire and throw gigantic rocks at each other till the earth shook so much that the Bridge of the Gods collapsed into the river. This made the Great Spirit angry, and he turned the three lovers into mountains. Today those same mountains are known as Mount Hood, Mount Evans, and Mount St. Helens."

Katherine stared at Officer Jannsen, waiting for more.

"It's creation mythology, Kat."

"Creation what?"

"Stories prehistoric peoples developed to explain how the world came into existence. The tribes of the Pacific Northwest were isolated, so their mythology remained localized. Other creation mythologies spread along trade routes, like the Silk Road from China to the Middle East. Many of those stories form the basis of most present-day religions."

"No kidding."

"No kidding."

"Anne?"

"Yes?"

"Sometimes you totally freak me out."

"Is that a compliment?"

"Yeah, it is."

"Then *merci, madame.*"

Max pointed his hammer toward the window.

"Choo, choo!"

Katherine saw a commuter train speeding at the side of the road.

"That's right, Max, it's a choo-choo train."

Katherine looked around. The land of rivers and trees where mountains were born had become a flatland of urban sprawl with a six-lane expressway running through it.

"Gee," Katherine mumbled to herself, "the Bridge of the Gods ain't got nothin' on the highway of men."

They cruised with the traffic, following the signs for downtown Portland. The sprawl gave way to suburban neighborhoods that gave way to perfectly squared city blocks of office and apartment buildings. The expressway reached the banks of the Willamette River, and the Explorer followed the traffic south, exiting for Morrison Bridge and the skyscrapers of downtown West Portland on the far bank.

"Look, Max, it's another river, and you can see all the boats and all the other bridges."

"Choo, choo!"

"Nope, these are boats. Boats go *toot, toot!*"

They looped off the expressway and drove south again with the river to their left. A cruise ship was tied up along the bank.

"And look at that big boat, Max. That's what we're going to do one day, we're going to take a ride on a big boat up the river. Would you like that?"

"Choo, choo!"

The Explorer's dashboard beeped and blinked to life. A 3-D map popped up on a small screen, and a voice sounded over the speakers.

"Right on Taylor Street, six blocks to Sixth Avenue, right again."

"Roger."

Katherine pointed out the window.

"Look at all the people and the cars, Max. And look, there's real-life shopping. The expensive kind."

"Left on Morrison Street."

"Roger."

"Toot, toot!"

Max was pointing to the trolley car clanging its way down along the tree-lined road.

"Nope, that's a train. That one goes *choo, choo.*"

"Toot, toot!" Max insisted.

"Left onto Broadway."

174

"Roger."

On the left there was a redbrick urban park the size of a city block. Katherine didn't know the name of the park, but it caught her eye each time they passed it on Max-and/or-Katherine-go-to-the-doctor days. And just now, with the bright autumn sun rising above the skyscrapers and flickering off the red leaves of the sycamore trees, it looked like a nice place. The Explorer eased across the next intersection and into the shadows and pulled into a parking space directly in front of the Jackson Tower, a twelve-storied, beaux arts, wedding cake of a building with a clock tower on top.

Max waved his hammer excitedly.

"Boo!"

Katherine looked out the window, saw the bas-relief lion's head above the arched entrance.

"That's right, there's Monsieur Booty. Isn't he a very funny cat? He's always here before we get here. And then he always gets home before we do. Isn't that funny?"

She threw her tote bag over her shoulder, unhooked Max from his car seat.

"Okay, buster, let's go see Dr. Supin. And if you're very lucky, Bonnie the Nurse will give you a lollipop. And if I'm lucky, I'll get one, too."

Officer Jannsen got out her side and rounded the Explorer. She quickly scanned the street before opening the left passenger door. Katherine stepped out, reached back inside the truck, and lifted out Max. And as they went into the building, Max watched the lion above the door.

"Boo," he whispered through his pacifier.

An hour later, Katherine was watching Max through the open doorway to the reception area. He was sitting on the sofa with Bonnie the Nurse, and she was reading Max a story about blue bunny rabbits who liked to eat purple carrots. Max sat attentively, chewing on his hammer, his eyelids growing heavy. He was happy as could be. Katherine turned her eyes back to Dr. Supin. A genuine *Marcus Welby, M.D.*, sort of guy, always gentle with Max, Katherine thought. And Max was always happy to see him, even managing to almost get his name right. *Soupy*, Max called him. But just now, good old Dr. Supin, sitting behind his desk, was the most terrifying man Katherine had ever met.

"What the hell do you mean, Max needs an MRI?"

Officer Jannsen was in the room, leaning against the wall behind Katherine.

"Kat, let the doctor finish."

Katherine spun around to face her.

"Did you know about this?"

"Kat—"

"Answer me."

Officer Jannsen nodded. "Yes, Kat, I knew there would be a test."

"Why didn't you tell me?"

Officer Jannsen tipped her head toward Max.

"Because of him, and because I know you. You would have displayed the same fear you're displaying now. Max would've picked it up. By the time he got here, he would have been in a state of severe stress."

Katherine stared at her a long moment.

"Hey, Anne, remember when I said you freaking me out was a compliment? Fuck you. I'm Max's mother, not you."

Officer Jannsen stepped across the room and sat in the empty chair next to Katherine.

"I understand that's how you feel right now. But do you think I'd allow anyone to do anything to hurt Max?"

Katherine combed her hand through her hair, remembering.

"I took my mother to have an MRI. It scared her to death, and I don't blame her. It's like a tomb, and the noise was deafening . . ."

She closed her eyes a second, let her memory fade. She gave a hard stare to both Officer Jannsen and the doctor.

"And you two want me to put Max into one of those fucking things?"

Officer Jannsen looked at Dr. Supin, biting her lip, trying to remind herself she was following orders. She threw the doctor an unmistakable look: *Help me make this right, or I'll beat the crap out of you.*

The doctor picked up the hint.

"Ms. Taylor, I felt a small growth in Max's abdomen on his last visit. It's still there. Now, I'm not that concerned, really I'm not. It hasn't grown, and as you report, Max isn't having problems with constipation or abdominal pain. I suspect it's no more than a benign cyst. But I'd like to have a better look to be sure."

"So take a fucking X-ray."

"That would require restraining Max or giving him a powerful sedative. Both those options would still subject Max to invasive radiation."

"What? You telling me an MRI isn't any of the above?"

"The MRI unit we'll be using is not the same as the one you're familiar with. It isn't as claustral, there are no vibrations or loud noises. Most importantly, there is no invasive radiation. I assure you, it is a harmless procedure."

"How harmless?"

"Well, it is difficult to explain in laymen's terms."

"Try me," Katherine said.

Dr. Supin cleared his throat. "Forgive me, I didn't mean to appear condescending. In fact, this particular MRI scanner is an entirely new technology."

"Hold it right there. I'm not letting you use Max as a lab rat for some new friggin' technology."

"I mean to say it's new to the States, Ms. Taylor. The fact is, it's an incredibly expensive technology developed in Europe."

"And you think I can afford it? I don't even have health insurance, do I?" she said, looking at Officer Jannsen.

"Kat, you don't have to worry about it."

"What do you mean, I don't have to worry about it? You heard him, it's incredibly expensive."

"Kat, all your bills are covered."

"How?"

Officer Jannsen held up her left hand, wiggled her ring finger. Katherine saw the gold band.

"You and Max are on my Swiss health insurance. No limit, no exclusions for preexisting conditions, worldwide cover."

"Really?"

"Of course. We're married, aren't we?"

Katherine looked at her own hand, saw her own ring.

"Okay. So what happens? How's it work?"

"The scanner passes various spectrums of light over the subject, and extremely sensitive optical sensors measure reflected luminance levels. Those measurements will yield the most accurate picture possible of Max's condition."

"What condition?"

"The state of his being."

"His what?"

"His health, I mean to say. Which, in all honesty, I have no reason to suspect is anything but perfect. And, if I might add, Ms. Taylor, I've come to know your son through his visits to Portland. I've tended hundreds of children in my career, but never a child like Max. He's just the most remarkable little fellow I've ever met."

Katherine felt a lump in her throat.

"Yeah, he is, isn't he?"

"That's why I want you to trust me on this, Ms. Taylor. I'm the same as Officer Jannsen, I wouldn't do a thing to hurt Max. But I recommend we go ahead with the test. Knowing everything we can about Max means we're doing everything we can to take care of him."

"And this machine won't hurt him, scare him?"

"Not at all. Max sits in a room and plays with a few toys—"

"Can I be with him?"

"I was about to ask if you would like to be with him."

"Yeah, I would."

"Well, then. Why don't we get started?"

"Now, like, now now? Where do we go?"

"One floor down. Forty-five minutes and we're done."

"That's it?" Katherine said.

The doctor smiled, nodded to the open door.

"Well, look at him, Ms. Taylor. I mean, he's just not that big."

Katherine looked out into the reception area. Max was leaning against Bonnie the Nurse, sound asleep, little hammer on his lap. She laughed to herself.

"No, I guess he isn't."

✢

ELEVEN

OFFICER JANNSEN PUSHED OPEN THE DOOR, AND KATHERINE stepped through and onto the street. Max was in her arms, and he immediately tipped back his head to see the stone lion's head above the entrance. He waved his hammer.

"Boo!"

"Yup, Boo's still up there."

Officer Jannsen crossed the sidewalk and opened the passenger door to the Explorer. Katherine took three steps toward it, then stopped. She looked up and down the street.

"What is it, Kat?"

"The sun."

"Yes?"

"It's everywhere. It's nice. How often does that happen?"

"Every day?"

"Ha, ha. You're so funny."

Katherine turned to the open square across Yamhill Street.

"You know what, I'm going to take Max over to that park, and we're going to sit in the sun and suck on our lollipops."

"Kat—"

"Don't *Kat* me. You didn't tell me what was happening today, so you're on our poo list."

"Your what?"

Katherine looked at Max.

"Tell her, buster. She's on our poo list."

Max giggled. "Poo!"

"That's right, a big stinky poo list."

"Poo!"

Officer Jannsen stared at the both of them staring at her.

"Come on, Kat. Max is fine. He played through the entire test."

"Doesn't matter. The only thing that's going to get *you* off our poo list is if *we* get to sit in the sun and have our lollipops. Right, Max?"

"Toot, toot!" Max cried as a trolley car banged its way across the intersection of Yamhill and Broadway. Katherine shrugged.

"Well, he would've voted for poo if he hadn't been distracted by the trolley. But no matter, we're heading for the park. You coming or not?"

"Why do you have this sudden urge to sit in the park?"

"Because the sun is shining and it's warm, and I've just had the crap scared out of me by Marcus Welby, MD."

"Who?"

"Doesn't matter. Point is, I'll give you a choice. You can go back into the lobby of the Jackson Tower and make a quick left into Margulis Jewelers and buy me something outrageously expensive to kiss and make up, or you can watch me and Max suck our lollipops in the park. Take your pick."

Officer Jannsen smiled.

"All right, stand by."

"For what?"

"So I can look at a map and reset the protection detail."

Officer Jannsen took her mobile from her coat, tapped the screen, studied it. She tapped the driver's window, and it lowered a crack. She told the driver the change in plans. She dropped the phone in her pocket, stepped to Katherine.

"*Allez*, Kat, let's go to the park and sit in the sun."

Katherine furrowed her brow.

"*Merde*, now what?" Officer Jannsen said.

"I was hoping for jewelry."

"Next time."

They waited for another trolley car to roll by. Max stared at it like it was magic. When it passed, they crossed the redbrick street to the redbrick park. The center of the square stepped down into an amphitheater. A few people were scattered about, sitting on the steps to take in the sun or read a book. Others had taken off their shoes and socks to set their feet in the pool of water at the bottom of a terraced fountain, and a long line of people were gathered at the Starbucks kiosk offering coffee and snacks. There were tables under the trees where people played chess, and from somewhere, a lone saxophone crooned.

"Would you reach in my bag and get Max's hat for me? Don't want him to get sunburned."

Officer Jannsen moved close behind Katherine, unzipped the tote bag, and dug through it. She pulled out a pint-size safari hat, reached her arms around Katherine, and set the hat on Max's head, pulling the chin strap snug. Katherine took that moment to ease back into Officer Jannsen's arms. For long seconds, Katherine noticed Officer Jannsen didn't push her away. Katherine turned around, looked Officer Jannsen in the eyes.

"Thanks."

"For what?"

"For being with me and Max. For everything."

"Kat, you have to understand that, sometimes, the things I have to do are tough."

"I do understand. That's why I'm thanking you."

"Does that mean I'm off the poo list?"

"What do you think, Max? Do we be nice to Anne now?"

Max reached up and tapped Officer Jannsen on the head with his hammer.

"Nnnn."

Officer Jannsen poked Max's tummy with her finger.

"Careful with that hammer, young man. Don't you realize I carry a gun?"

"Yeah," Katherine said, poking Max, too, "don't you know she can fill you full of lead?"

Max giggled, thoroughly enjoying the poke-me-in-the-tummy game, till a flock of sparrows flew low overhead and settled in the trees above the chess tables and the full force of Max's attention chased after them. He pointed his hammer in the general direction of the trees and hopped up and down in Katherine's arms.

"Birzies!"

"You want to see the birds, Max?"

"Birzies."

Katherine looked over Officer Jannsen's shoulder.

"I got an idea. Why don't you go over to Starbucks and get us a couple of lattes while I grab a table under the trees."

Officer Jannsen sighed, dug out her mobile, hit speed dial, connected to the Explorer.

"Circle the block and drive onto Morrison, Corporal. Wait on the north side of the park. You stay with the truck, have Luc get out and tag Swan Lake and Blue Marble."

She hung up.

"Can I ask you something?" Katherine said.

"What?"

"I know you guys talk in code. But who on Earth came up with calling Max 'Blue Marble' and me 'Swan Lake'?"

"Inspector Gobet."

"No way."

"Why do you ask?"

"Just wondering. Never knew he had a sense of humor."

"Humor?"

"Sure. *Swan Lake*'s a ballet about a beautiful young virgin who gets it in the end, and not in a fun way."

"You like ballet, Kat?"

"I saw *Swan Lake* in Los Angeles once, with a girlfriend. I cried like a baby. And I'll have a double shot in my latte, by the way."

Officer Jannsen held up a sachet of Midday Buzz tea.

"I'll have coffee, and you'll have this."

"Where did that come from?"

"I took it out of your tote bag when I got Max's hat. I'd already decided you were right about bringing Max to the park. We should hang out for a while."

"Hang out?"

"You don't want to hang out with me?"

"Yeah. It's just I never heard you say 'hang out' before."

Officer Jannsen looked past Katherine, saw the Explorer on Morrison Street, saw one of the Swiss Guards taking a position under the trees near the chess tables.

"The boys are here. I'll meet you by the chess tables. And stay in their sight."

Katherine watched Officer Jannsen walk away.

"Max, I think your mommy just got asked out on a date. What do you think?"

Max drooled.

"Yeah, me too. C'mon, let's go see the birds."

"See birzies!"

She walked toward the trees with the warm sun on her back. Max leaned from her arms.

"You want to walk awhile? Good, because you're as heavy as a bag of bowling balls."

She took the hammer from Max's hands and lowered him to the ground. When his feet settled on the red bricks, he bounced on his legs and tested the earth for support.

"You doing okay down there?"

Max looked up at his mother and smiled. She held out her hands, and he held on to her fingers and looked ahead, not sure which way to advance. A few more bounces and he kicked forward with his left foot, then his right, then he marched ahead. The Swiss Guard tailing her kept a distance of three meters; far enough to let Katherine and Max enjoy a moment of normalcy, close enough to throw them to the ground and cover them if need be. Max turned around and saw the guard, recognized him as the one he called *Woof*. He bounced on his little legs, forgetting for a moment what it was he was walking toward. He looked around the square, trying to remember, then marched ahead again. But as he walked, Katherine noticed Max was leaning to the right, away from the birds and toward the man playing the saxophone in the shadows of the trees. He was black and wore a long overcoat, and his foot was slowly tapping the bricks next to a small cardboard box bearing the sign *Support your local artists*.

"You want to go see the man with the saxophone, Max?"

"Zug!"

"No, it's not a toy, it's a saxophone."

"Ssfnnmnn birzies."

"Close enough. Let's go."

As Max pulled his mother closer to the music, Katherine noticed how the sounds circled around the amphitheater and floated in the air. Then she noticed the song the man was playing: "South City Midnight Lady," slowed way down, like blues. Max stopped at the cardboard box near the saxophoneman's tapping foot and he stood very still, watching the man's bristled cheeks swell and deflate with air and his long fingers press and release the keys. And when the man finished the tune, there was applause from the people sitting on the steps of the amphitheater. The tall black man bowed his head to the crowd, and he looked down at the little boy at his feet.

"Hello, little dude. You like the music?"

Max bounced up and down. "Ssfnnmnnzug."

"That so?" the saxophoneman said. "Well, about as fine a compliment as I ever heard, little dude. What about you, young lady, you like the music?"

Katherine smiled.

185

"Yeah, I did. I didn't recognize it at first, but it's one of my favorite songs."

He balanced his saxophone on a small metal stand. "Well, I'm glad you liked it. But perhaps you might consider dropping some coins in the box."

"Oh, yeah. Hang on."

There was a chess table next to her, the pieces and game clock set out for a match. She sat on the wooden bench on one side of the table, balanced Max between her legs, and dug through her tote bag. The saxophoneman sat across from her.

"Oh crap, I didn't bring my wallet," Katherine said, lifting Max onto her lap. "But my friend is coming in just a sec."

"That's fine. While we're waiting, maybe the little dude would like to take me on in a game of chess."

"Max?"

"Max. Now isn't that a fine name? So what do you say, Max, care for a game of chess?"

"I think Max's style of chess would be to toss all the pieces into the next county. He's got a great pitching arm."

"No problem, I've played all kinds. Played an English fellow a long time ago, when I was working the streets of Cambridge. Fellow's name was J. E. Littlewood. A quiet man, awful good with numbers. Once told me when the numbers get big enough, then miracles can happen. Smoked a pipe while he played chess. Said there were only ten to the power of ten, to the power of fifty, possible moves in chess. Wrote down a long mathematical equation proving his point. Maybe Max's style of play is telling the rest of us he knows all the moves already."

The saxophoneman picked up the game clock at the side of the table.

"But tell you what I think he'd really like to play with, is this."

He set the game clock before Max. Max stared at the thing: two clock faces, two buttons on top. The saxophoneman hit one of the buttons to start the counting of seconds on one of the clocks, then he hit the second button. The sweep hand stopped on the one clock and began to tick away on the second clock. Then he hit the first button again, stopping the second clock and setting the first sweep hand back in motion. Then back and forth, back and forth.

"What do you think of that, little dude?"

Max hammered his fists onto the buttons, watching the clocks stop and start.

"Take it easy, buster, or you'll break it," Katherine said.

"No, he's fine. Go ahead, little dude. See if you can stop that old dog time in its tracks."

"Zug." *Bang.* "Zug." *Bang.*

"I think you've released the inner Max," Katherine said. "He likes to bang things. His favorite toy is this rubber hammer. He'll make a great carpenter."

"That's good work, being a carpenter. I've done some carpentry now and again, here and there."

Katherine looked in the saxophoneman's eyes.

"You sound like you've been around," she said.

"Suppose I have. Me and my horn tend to blow with the wind."

"What brings you to Portland?"

The saxophoneman pointed to the large silver orb atop a tall black pole standing next to the trees. There was the figure of a smiling sun poking from the orb.

"Come to see the weather teller."

"Yeah, what's it do?" Katherine said.

"Come noon, it'll tell us what's coming."

He was a little odd, Katherine thought, but funny. He reminded her of some of the street people in Santa Monica. Most of them gentle and kind, all of them living in their own worlds.

"Any idea what it'll say?"

"Couldn't say, young lady. That's what the weather teller's for."

Just then, Max stopped banging at the chess clock; he stared at it. Katherine leaned down to him. "Give up, buster?"

Max didn't respond to her voice; he continued to stare at the clock. Then, slowly, he reached out both hands and gently pressed both buttons at the same time. Both clocks stopped.

"Well, how about that?" the saxophoneman said. "He figured it out. Caught time by the tail and stopped it in its tracks. Good on you, little dude."

Max looked at the man and giggled, then quickly turned his attention to the chess board. Scattering the pawns, moving a rook, knocking over a bishop, picking up the knight and attempting to stick it up Katherine's nose.

"Horsey," he said.

"Yup, that's a horse," Katherine said, taking the knight from his hand and setting it back on the table. "And Mister Horsey wants to be down here with all his friends and not up Mommy's nose."

Max knocked a few more chess pieces over and picked up the knight again. "Arp," he said, pointing *that way* with the chess piece.

Katherine saw what Max was pointing at: the T-shirt under the saxophoneman's coat. At first it looked like some hip airbrush job, a collection of grays and blacks on white. Then she saw the silhouette of a form descending through the sky. Words under the picture: *Older Than Dreams*. She stared at it. Slowly, it came to her.

"Paris."

"Excuse me, young lady?"

"The picture on your shirt. I've seen it before, or something like it. Yeah, on television. There was a guy falling from a bridge during a terrorist attack in Paris. I only saw it for a second. That's weird."

"That's what it is. The angel who saved Paris."

"No way."

"Really funny thing is, people are seeing him everywhere."

"Yeah, like where?"

The saxophoneman panned his eyes over the square.

"All you have to do, young lady, is look around."

Katherine looked at the crowd. *Holy cow,* she thought. "They're all wearing the same shirt. What the heck's going on?"

"Hard to say what goes through people's minds when it comes to angels. Maybe these folks know they're in a world of hurt."

"Who's hurting?"

"Angels, little lady."

Katherine laughed, and her mind carried her back to Lausanne.

"You know, I knew someone who believed in angels. He thought they were hiding in a cathedral because they had no other place in the world. He thought he needed to protect them."

"What about you?"

"What about me?" Katherine said.

"You believe in angels?"

Katherine stared at him. Dark brown skin, grizzled face, pale-colored eyes . . . almost blue, almost green. Bit of a mad look in the eyes, like the gentle street people in Santa Monica. If they didn't see angels, they saw aliens. If not aliens, they saw things only they could see. And like the man sitting across the chess table, they always made for pleasant conversation.

"Doesn't everyone?" she said.

"Not yet. But time's coming when they will."

"That would be nice. I hope they get here soon."

The saxophoneman moved a pawn two places, then a bishop, then a queen, then a knight, and set them to the east, north, west, and south.

"Oh, they're already here, young lady. They're here to protect the one who's gonna save this sorry world from itself. See, Mr. Littlewood had it right. The numbers got bigger than anyone ever imagined, and the miracle is happening right here, right now, right under our noses."

Katherine nodded politely, remembering that as pleasant as the conversation could be with the street people in Santa Monica, there was always the point where it made a turn toward gibberish. It was their way of saying good-bye. Katherine looked down at Max. He was busy setting up the pieces on the board and knocking them over, one by one. Katherine grabbed Max's hands.

"C'mon, buster, I think you've done enough damage. It's way past your nap time. We need to find out what happened to Anne." She looked at the saxophoneman. "It was really nice talking to you, but we have to go. Sorry about not having any money for the box."

"Next time."

189

Katherine shifted Max from lap to arms and stood.

"Can you say good-bye to the nice man, Max?"

"Goobye."

Katherine's jaw dropped.

"Wow, you actually got a *good-bye* out of him, kind of. Major break-through. Well, good-bye, thanks for being so nice."

"Be seeing you," the saxophoneman said.

Katherine looked at the scattered pieces over the board.

"Sorry about the mess."

"No problem. Anything you'd like to hear for the road? On the house, seeing as you got no money."

"Yeah. 'Someone to Watch Over Me.' Seeing as everyone here's got angels on the brain."

"Fine choice, young lady, mighty fine."

He set the reed to his lips and he blew slow, soulful sounds.

Katherine turned and walked away. She saw Officer Jannsen at the head of the Starbucks line, waiting to collect her order. Katherine waved to her, and Officer Jannsen waved back. Just then, trumpets blared through the square. A cloud of mist shot from the silver orb atop the weather teller, and it opened and the smiling sun sank into the orb. The figure of a blue heron appeared for a moment, to be replaced by a dragon, then the sun again.

Katherine bounced Max in her arms excitedly.

"Yeah, you see that? It's the weather teller. Isn't that fun?"

Max's eyes were locked on the orb, and he giggled.

The trumpets sounded and the mist sprayed again and the dragon reappeared, rising into the sky. Max stared at it. He stopped giggling and began to shrink into Katherine's arms. He felt suddenly warm.

"Max?"

Max's face contorted into a frightened mask, and he began to cry.

"Honey, it's all right, it's only a silly old dragon."

His hands formed into fists, and he pounded at Katherine's shoulder.

"Max, honey, what is it?"

She tried to move away, but the mob was closing in to watch the weather teller, all of them wearing the image of the angel falling through the Paris sky.

"Excuse me, let me through, please," Katherine shouted.

She found herself in the arms of the Swiss Guard.

"Stay calm, stay calm," he said.

Katherine held on to Max, let herself be guided through the crushing mob. The mob faded away near Starbucks. Officer Jannsen was there, paper cups in her hands; she saw Max crying.

"Kat, are you all right?"

"Yeah, Max got upset. I need to calm him down."

She sat on a nearby bench, set Max on her knee, took off his hat. His hair was wet and matted, and he continued to cry.

"What happened?" Officer Jannsen said.

"Oh, too much excitement. First the guy with the saxophone, then all the noise with the clock and the dragon coming out of the weather teller thing, then the mob. I should've known better. He's not used to it."

Officer Jannsen shot a glance toward the Swiss Guard; he shook his head no. Katherine caught a flicker of concern in Officer Jannsen's eyes. She looked back at the guard; his face was like a blank wall.

"Luc? Didn't you see him?"

He didn't answer. Katherine turned to Officer Jannsen.

"What's . . . what's going on?"

Officer Jannsen sat next to Katherine.

"Where did you see him, exactly?"

"By the chess tables, under the trees. Right over . . ."

The mob was still scattered about the stone steps, laughing and talking among themselves . . . but the saxophoneman was gone, the chess table empty of pieces.

Katherine looked at Officer Jannsen.

"He was here, Anne, I saw him."

"All right, all right. Let's just leave and get back to the house."

"No, we're supposed to hang out. What's going on?"

Officer Jannsen set the cups on the bench, pulled Max from Katherine's arms and stood. "Let's go."

"Where are you going?"

"Away from here."

Katherine jumped after her.

"Hey!"

The Swiss Guard wrapped his arms around Katherine, half lifting her from the ground, following after Officer Jannsen.

"Luc, what the fuck are you doing?"

She felt herself carried through the crowd, felt the eyes of strangers watching her. Out of the park and across the street. The Explorer's engine was already running, the rear door open. Officer Jannsen turned, handed Max to Katherine.

"Get in, Kat. Get Max into his seat."

Katherine stopped, looked back at the park. All the people in the T-shirts, still watching.

"Jesus, what the fuck is this?"

"Get in."

Katherine climbed in, and Officer Jannsen closed the door. Katherine strapped Max into his car seat, and he fussed and twisted and banged his fists in the air. Katherine dug through her tote bag, found a water bottle, and poured some onto her hand. She patted the back of his neck and wrists to cool him down. He settled.

"There you go, all better now?"

"Boo?" he said.

"You want Monsieur Booty?"

"Mnsoor Boo."

"He's home, honey. That's where we're going now. He's waiting for you, and when we get home you can pull Monsieur Booty's tail and pretend it is that silly old dragon, how about that?"

Max thought that a fine idea and kicked his little legs in approval.

Katherine opened a small bottle of juice and poured it in a sippy cup.

"And look what I got. Some of Molly's homemade apple juice, just for you. Yum, yum."

"Mowy's juuz. Yum."

She held the cup to Max's mouth. He puckered his lips and drank.

Officer Jannsen climbed in her side of the truck. The Swiss Guard closed the door behind her. He jumped in on the shotgun side up front, and the driver pulled away. Katherine heard the *clackclack* of a machine gun made ready up front. She jumped at the sound, looked at Max. Not even a flinch. For Max, a guy feeding bullets into the firing chamber of a machine gun was normal. She wondered at the absurdity of "normal" in Max's life. Riding in a bulletproof truck, protected by three Swiss Guards carrying enough firepower to take over a small country and a mother who had the habit of going loopy at the drop of a hat. And here Max was, sipping at his apple juice, staring through the bucket seats, watching the 3-D screen on the dashboard light up. Transfixed by the little dot moving through the grid of avenues and streets as it tracked their position. He turned his head to study it from this angle and that angle till his eyes grew heavy. By the time they reached the west bank of the Willamette River, he was fighting to keep his eyes open. Katherine combed his black hair. There was one curl that refused to cooperate and kept popping up each time Katherine pressed it down . . . all the while replaying the scene from the park in her mind. When she reconnected to being in the back of the Explorer, she noticed they were heading a different way, crossing streets and bridges she didn't recognize.

"Where are we?"

"We're taking side streets out of Portland."

"I thought you were in a big hurry to get me home. Why aren't we taking the highway? It's faster," Katherine said.

"Sometimes we like to mix up our itinerary."

"Especially after I start going loopy and strangers are staring at me, you mean."

Officer Jannsen looked at her.

"You get noticed in a crowd, we change our plans. But don't read too much into it. It's only standard procedure."

"Standard procedure, my butt. Crazy mom on the loose in downtown Portland. Did you see the way those people were looking at me?

This kind of stuff was supposed to stop. For crying out loud, between the medications and the teas, I'm supposed to be . . . friggin' fuckin' normal."

Officer Jannsen sat back in her seat.

"Kat, give yourself a break. You had a rough morning, and you're on edge. Your imagination got the better of you, that's all. I really don't think it's anything to worry about."

"It's not me I'm worried about, it's Max."

Katherine looked out the window. They were crossing Fremont Bridge now. The Willamette River rolled beneath the steel girders. The Cascade Mountains reached for the sky on the horizon.

"What if I'm contagious?"

Officer Jannsen reached across the backseat and took Katherine's hand. She gave it an easy shake.

"He's fine, Kat. But he's very sensitive to your moods. You know that. He feels what you feel."

"You say that all the time, like a broken record."

"Because you need to be reminded that there's nothing wrong with you, or him."

"Okay, so tell me again."

"Max is fine, you're fine."

Katherine turned, looked at Max. There was a dribble of drool on his cheek, and she wiped it away.

"Max saw him, too."

"What?"

"The guy with the sax, the guy with the drawing of an angel on his shirt."

"He had the same shirt as the people in the crowd?"

"I didn't tell you?" Katherine said.

"No."

"It was the same shirt the crowd was wearing."

"Maybe you got it wrong. Maybe you only thought it was the same."

Katherine scratched her head. She saw herself sitting at the chess table.

"No. It was the same. It looked like the angel jumping off the bridge in Paris. The one I saw on the news, before you pulled the plug. It wasn't the exact same picture, it was a drawing, but it looked almost the same. And there were words under the drawing: *Older Than Dreams*."

"Why do you call it an angel?"

"What?"

"You called it a drawing of an angel. Why?"

"Because that's what he called it . . . the angel who saved Paris. Then he said the angels were coming to protect the one who'd save the world. It was gibberish, Anne. And yeah, it's the kinda thing I could imagine, I admit it. But I know it happened, because Max saw it first."

"What did Max see?"

"The shirt. He pointed to it, that's when I saw it."

"You sure he wasn't just reacting to you?"

Katherine thought about it, then she rolled her eyes and waved her hands in front of her face and laughed.

"Yeah, you're right." And she started singing a long-ago Motown tune: *"Just my imagination . . . runnin' away with me, now."*

Officer Jannsen looked at Max, stared at him.

Katherine stopped singing.

"Attention, loopy mom on medication going for laughs here. Don't you want to sing along?"

Officer Jannsen didn't answer. Katherine tapped her shoulder.

"Okay, let's try this one: *Ground Control to Major Anne.* C'mon, Seb and Luc, everybody sing."

No response.

"My singing can't be that bad."

Officer Jannsen touched Katherine's arm.

"Tell me what happened again, Kat. Tell me exactly as you imagined it."

Katherine did.

Officer Jannsen listened.

It wasn't until they crossed over the Bridge of the Gods, back into

Washington State, that Katherine finished the story. Officer Jannsen pulled out a small black notebook and started writing.

"What are you doing, Anne?"

"Making notes of your description of the man with the saxophone."

"Standard procedure?"

"Yes."

"You know, the more you say 'standard procedure,' the more I think something's way out of whack."

Officer Jannsen stopped writing, looked at her.

"Listen, Kat, you had a conversation with someone, and I just need to make sure he's not a threat."

"How can he be a threat? He didn't come after me, I walked to him."

"Why?"

"Why what?"

"Why did you walk to him?"

Katherine thought about it.

"Because me and Max were waiting for you and we heard music. He was playing the Doobie Brothers, come to think of it. Just caught my ear. And then Max did one of his pointy things, and we walked over. And why are you asking me the same questions, Anne? You're making me dizzy."

"I'm trying to confirm whether or not Max experienced a sighting, too."

"'A sighting?' Jeez, the guy was a little out-there, but he wasn't a friggin' little green man just off a UFO."

"Sorry, my English was turned around. I meant to say, Max saw him the same time that you did."

"No. Max saw him before me."

"Did he interact with Max?"

"I told you already, remember?"

"How? What happened? Did they talk, did he touch Max?"

"Oh for cripes sake, now the guy's supposed to be a perv?"

"Kat, I'm just asking questions."

Katherine stared at her.

"And your questions sound like you're saying I was imagining the guy, or that you don't trust me to be on my own with my son in public."

Katherine looked up front to the Swiss Guard riding shotgun. He had his own set of rearview mirrors, and she watched his eyes dart from the 3-D display to the road ahead.

"Hey, Lieutenant Worf—I mean Luc—you saw me talking to him, didn't you?"

She watched Luc's eyes connect to Officer Jannsen for two seconds, then back to her.

"*Oui, Madame Taylor.* I saw him."

Katherine smiled at Officer Jannsen.

"There you go. Lieutenant Luc Worf, chief security officer of the *Starship Enterprise*, confirms the sighting of one saxophone-playing alien in downtown Portland, Oregon."

"I'm not saying you didn't see him, or that I don't trust you."

"Then what are you saying?"

Katherine stared at her, waiting for a response. She watched Officer Jannsen smile with that knee-weakening look of hers.

"I am saying I need to know everything that happened, and what was said, between you and Max and the little green man with the saxophone, just off a UFO."

Katherine's jaw dropped, then she laughed.

"Wow, Anne, not bad. In the funny bone department, I mean."

Katherine looked at Max. His head was tipped to the side and his mouth was open and he was making that little puffing sound with his lips that he always did when he was sleeping in the car. Katherine lifted his blanket from the seat and tucked it around his legs, adjusted the headrest of his car seat to make him more comfortable. She looked at Officer Jannsen, saw she was looking at Max. And she saw the *way* Officer Jannsen was looking at Max, as if knowing that he was completely defenseless, and in the blink of an eye . . .

Katherine shuddered. "Okay. Ask away," she said.

They went through it three more times. And each time, Katherine repeated the saxophoneman's words about angels being in a whole lot of hurt just now. But it was Katherine remembering the saxophoneman talking about a miracle happening, right here, right now, that caused Officer Jannsen to write feverishly in her little black book.

"Anne?"

"Yes?"

"It's really okay—all us fruitcakes see angels."

"What do you mean?"

"I mean, I'm joking. And you're making me dizzy because I'm still telling you the same thing over and over again. And we're in Stevenson and Granny's Gedunk Ice Cream Parlor is up ahead. And you promised me a chocolate milk shake on the way back."

Officer Jannsen checked the road, then made eye contact with the guards up front.

"All clear?"

The guards scanned their toys on the dashboard.

"Looks fine, *Chef*."

"Pull up in front. Notify Control we're stopping."

As the truck pulled up to the curb, Max woke up and looked out the window, instantly recognizing where he was.

"Gnnny!"

"That's right, buster, it's Granny's. And that means ice cream."

"Skeem!"

"You bet. I scream, you scream, we all scream for ice cream."

"Skeemskeem!"

Katherine undid the shoulder straps and lifted him from the car seat. Officer Jannsen got out, walked around the truck, and opened Katherine's door. If Max could fly, he would've taken off out the door.

"Hold on, buster," Katherine said. "You don't have your wings yet."

Officer Jannsen reached Max. "Here, I'll take him."

Max kicked his little legs and waved his arms as he was passed over. Katherine climbed out and they went into the shop. Granny herself was behind the counter and saw them coming.

"Well, land's sakes, look who's here!"

"Gnnny!"

"Hello, there, Max. You just keep getting bigger. And how are you girls?"

"Doing just fine, Granny."

Officer Jannsen clucked her tongue.

"One moment, you need to take Max. I must go back to the truck."

Max kicked his legs and waved his arms on the way back to Katherine.

"What's up?" Katherine said.

"I forgot to see what the protection detail would like. Order me a double dark chocolate."

"You're actually trusting me to order the milk shakes? All by myself?"

"See, I do trust you on your own."

Officer Jannsen walked to the Explorer, her back to the shop. The guard riding shotgun saw her coming, opened the door. Officer Jannsen handed over her notebook.

"Good pickup telling Madame Taylor you saw him, Luc. I want you to get on to Berne, give them a readout of my notes. Advise them Madame Taylor and the boy have experienced a sighting. Also, ask them to run a search of mobile activity in Pioneer Courthouse Square during the time Madame Taylor was there. I want confirmation about the crowd. And while you're waiting for an answer, Google a description of the T-shirt with the message on it. The message is in my notes."

"We already ran it, *Chef*."

"What did you get on the crowd?"

"It was a flash mob."

"A what?"

"Texts go out to mobile phones. 'Everyone meet here, or there at this time.' The phone logs confirm it."

"What about the shirt?"

Luc nodded to the 3-D display. There was an image of a poster. The picture of "the angel" falling through the fog in Paris two weeks ago, psychedelic lettering across the top and bottom: *Older Than Dreams Tour . . . Locomotora . . . Aladdin Theater, Portland.*

"A rock concert?"

"They're from Finland, and they're using the image from the Paris operation to promote their concert."

"What kind of music?"

"Post-rock. No lyrics, just instruments, harmonics, and drones, very loud. According to Google, Locomotora is on the cutting edge with a very eclectic following. People travel the world to attend their concerts. That's who made up the flash mob. Thing is, Locomotora rarely have concerts."

"So we have a flash mob following a rock band, Madame Taylor and her son, and the saxophoneman all coming together at the same moment. Not to mention the picture from the Paris operation."

Officer Jannsen looked back at the shop, saw Katherine through the windows. She was holding Max while Granny gave him a taste of this and that. *He really does love his skeem,* Officer Jannsen thought. She turned to the guards.

"There must be a line of causality running through it somewhere."

She watched the guards look at each other.

"What is it, gentlemen?"

"*Es gibt einen,*" Corporal Fassnacht said.

"You saw it as it happened?"

"No, *Chef,* but we know what it is. We were only waiting for the proper moment to discuss it with you."

Officer Jannsen noted they didn't say "report to you." Meaning they were coming very close to disclosing confidential information they had been ordered not to discuss with anyone.

"What can you tell me?"

"Marc Rochat was the last person to see the saxophoneman."

"Are you sure of this?"

The guards nodded.

"That's why we went ahead and ran a search," Luc said.

"Go on."

"After Marc Rochat began to awaken to his duality, the two of us were assigned to tail him, keep an eye on him. Before he died, he made a trip to Vevey."

"The medics?"

Luc nodded.

"On the way back, at the train station in Lausanne, we noted Rochat talking to someone who wasn't there. HQ matched our report with a meeting he had with Monsieur Gübeli a few days later. Marc Rochat told him he talked to the saxophoneman."

"What did they talk about?"

"Angels being in trouble," the corporal said.

Officer Jannsen nodded, taking it in. Either she was being set up in some field test to check the manner of her thinking, or the guards were telling her something they shouldn't. She checked the street, coming and going cars.

"That's the thing about lines of causality, gentlemen. Find one, there's always another. That's always been my experience."

"Yes, *Chef.*"

"From the looks on your faces, you know what the next line is."

"Yes, *Chef.*"

"Did you know this information before today?"

The guards didn't answer. Confirmed they were talking out of school and that was all she was going to get.

"Show me," she said.

"You may not believe it."

"If I had a problem with working in the realm of the unbelievable, I wouldn't be in this line of work, gentlemen."

Luc swiped the screen, another poster from the band: *Older Than Dreams Tour . . . Locomotora . . . Le Jazz Café, Lausanne.* Written in the same trippy script, above and below a picture of Lausanne Cathedral, lit up against a dark and stormy night.

"When was this concert?"

"Three nights before the battle at Lausanne Cathedral."

Officer Jannsen felt herself wobble a bit.

"I'll be damned."

"Chef?"

"Ich vill verdammt sein. But for the moment, gentlemen, the sentiment seems more appropriate in English."

Flash Traffic
tdc: +p441-01sbc+
Ex: Blue4/GrovMil

Eyes Only: Dragon6/SUTF
Subject: Portland

Please review notes re: SAXMAN sighting/flash mob.
Request brief and guidance.
<file: XRB.201>

Flash Traffic
tdc: +k995-97cfr+
Ex: Dragon6/SUTF

Eyes Only: Blue4/GrovMil
Subject: Portland

Sighting: SAXMAN apparition confirmed by HQ.
Purpose:
1) Identity confirmation re: BLUEMARBLE/SWANLAKE
as part of light scan test; 2) Warning of impending
intersecting lines of causality re: death. Flash mob
identified as protective cover surrounding SAXMAN
by deep asset MAGIC BUS
Guidance: <file: XRB202>

Flash Traffic
mml: +p003-46twt+
Ex: Magic Bus

Eyes Only: Dragon6/SUTF
Subject: Dream Catcher

Vision ex: DREAM CATCHER
Subject: Impending Lines of Causality re: Gospel of
Matthew 2:10/Deep Asset, Paris Operation
<file: XRB.009>

TWELVE

"MONSIEUR, ARE YOU AWAKE NOW?"

The voice had been calling from the far beyond, then coming closer, then pulling back the veil of unconsciousness. Harper opened his eyes. Nothing but the absolute dark and an unfolding notion of *Where the fuck am I?*

"Monsieur? Are you awake?"

"Who are you?"

"It's me, Gilles Lambert."

The name sounded familiar, just.

"Is there anyone else?"

"*Non*, monsieur. Only you and me."

Harper skimmed back through his timeline. Was something of a blur. Again.

"So . . . where are we?" Harper said.

"In a cavern, under Paris."

"A cavern. Under Paris."

"*Oui.*"

Silence.

"Gilles?"

"*Oui?*"

"I'm having a bit of trouble seeing things."

"Because there's nothing to see, monsieur, there's no light down here."

"Yes, well, that too. Look, I need to ask a rather stupid question."

"*D'accord.*"

"What the hell am I doing in a cavern under Paris?"

"You don't remember?"

"Like I said, I'm having trouble seeing . . . remembering, I mean."

"Because they drugged us."

"They? Who are they?"

"The priest and the other one."

An auto-injector slamming into his thigh, then something warm rushing into his blood. He could see the two of them, the priest with the cut-up face and the other one with the oddly shaped head. He could hear the priest's voice . . . *receive your portion of the divine sacrament . . . Holy Father, welcome thy servant in thy justice . . .* Harper ran the words. He'd heard them, some of them, somewhere. Wasn't from the Catholic Mass, wasn't from any Catholic prayer he knew.

"Bloody dreaming it, maybe."

He tried to move his arms and legs. They felt like lead.

"*Qu'avez-vous dit?*"

"What?"

"You said something."

"No, I didn't say anything. Just the way our voices are echoing in this place."

"Oh."

Harper struggled to sit up. He rested his back against the stone wall.

"Dark place this, isn't it?" he said.

"*Oui*"

"Any idea what the time is?"

"I don't know. I have a watch, but I can't see it."

Harper checked his own watch. The phosphorescent paint on the sweep hands had faded completely.

"Same here. Means four to six hours, at least."

"I don't know, monsieur, I really don't know."

. . . really don't know, don't know, don't know . . .

Silence.

"I hate to ask another stupid question, Gilles, but what happened to the bloody lights?"

"There are no lights in the tunnels. We had lamps, but the priest took them from us and smashed them."

"Right. And who was this bloody priest?"

"His name was Astruc. You cannot remember what happened, *mon père?*"

Harper raced through the blurred images on his timeline. The images were there. But with no ambient light to fuse with, the radiance in his blood was breaking down into inert matter. He was badly in need of a hit. He patted the pockets of his windbreaker and trousers looking for his smokes, for a second wondering what he was doing in a windbreaker, and where the hell was his coat? He felt some spare change, no fags or sparks.

"Look, Gilles, I need some light, any light. You don't happen to have— Hang on, what did you just call me?"

"Mon père."

"I thought what's-his-name, Astruc, I thought he was the priest."

"Oui, but earlier, he said you were the priest, before we came down here. He said you were an expert in ancient languages from Lausanne University."

"What?"

"He said you were sent by the Holy Father in Rome to investigate what I found in the tunnels, and to protect me from evil. That's what he said. I believed him, I believed you."

"So what happened?"

"Pardon?"

"If I was supposed to protect you from evil, how did we end up like this?"

"They had guns."

"The priest had a gun?"

"And the other one. Goose was his name. You tried to stop them, but they threatened to kill me, so you surrendered. It was very confusing, I can't quite remember it."

Harper flashed an image of the odd-looking kid, Goose. Then a standoff . . . *Notre Père* and drop the fucking gun. Something close to it, anyway.

"Right. Any rate, got a match?"

"I did, in my backpack. And some spare candles. But I can't find it, not in this dark."

Harper flashed Goose and Astruc cleaning out the cavern before they took off.

"No, they took it. I saw them take it. Your backpack and all the candles."

"You did?"

"Just before I went out."

"Oh. I was hoping, perhaps, it would still be here."

"No. It's gone."

. . . it's gone, it's gone, it's gone . . .

Silence.

"Tell me, Gilles, is anyone coming to get us?"

"*Non.*"

"Why not?"

"No one knows we're down here."

"Of course not. Look, you'd be doing me a huge favor if you ran a few things by me, just till I get a grip of the picture."

"*Je compris.* It took me time to remember things, too. What do you wish me to tell you, *mon père?*"

"Whatever comes to your mind. And stop calling me *mon père.* It's confusing the hell out of me."

"*Oui,* mon . . . sieur. What should I tell you?"

"Freeform it, that's the best way. Remind me who you are, for starters."

"I'm a file clerk in the mayor's office of the fourteenth arrondissement. I guided you, all of you, to this place."

Harper flashed back again, saw himself with Gilles Lambert, Astruc, and the other one named Goose entering the cavern. Small headlamps strapped to their heads, four beams of lamplight reflecting off the black glasslike stone. Then Goose, setting candles about the floor, Gilles Lambert telling them to turn off their lamps. Harper saw the immense cavern with the rows of coves cut into the walls. He stopped, jumped further back in time. The big man with the blue lenses over his eyes, telling Harper that Gilles Lambert was the best cataphile in Paris, knew the tunnels like the back of his hand.

"That's right. You discovered the cavern a few weeks ago."

"You remember it now?"

"Let's just say it sounds familiar. We came here to see something, a crime scene of some kind, yeah? Mutilated bodies."

"*Oui*, they were here when I found this place weeks ago. Their heads were gone, and their skin had been sliced off. It was terrible to see."

"The bodies weren't here, though," Harper said. "They'd been taken away. The cavern was empty."

"*C'est vrai ça.*"

"Right. Got it. So at the risk of sounding like a complete dolt, what are we doing here?"

"Because . . . because of you."

"Me?"

"There was a pillar in the center of the cavern . . ."

Harper saw it. Looked like a supporting pillar, but it was only an illusion. The cavern was supported by the walls, and the pillar rose to a perfect point almost touching the center of the dome, as if pointing somewhere *up there*. Harper snapped back to nowtimes. Gilles Lambert's voice still echoed through the dark, telling the tale.

"The priest told you to put your hands on the pillar. That's when you fought with them and took a gun from the little one, Goose. And that's when the priest threatened to kill me, unless you surrendered and put your hands to the tablet drawn on the pillar. I've never seen such a thing, monsieur. You touched the tablet and you said 'This is the watcher, it is the hour,' but you said it in French. And a door opened in the base of the pillar. And there was a wooden chest inside, very old. The priest re-moved something from the chest."

The something flashed through Harper's eyes . . . one or two frames . . . then it was gone.

"What was it, can you remember?"

"A sextant. That's what you called it. And you said it was for finding your position at sea. It's all so very strange."

Harper rubbed the back of his neck.

"Listen, Gilles. Give me time to recover. We'll figure something out, we'll get out of here."

. . . out of here, out of here, out of here . . .

Silence.

"Monsieur?"

"Yes?"

"Who are you?"

"Me?"

"If you are not a priest, who are you?"

Those bits on his timeline fell into place.

"My name is Harper, Jay Harper. I do security work for Guardian Services Limited out of Switzerland. I was asked to check up on this Astruc character."

"You're a detective?"

"More or less."

"So you knew about all this before. You knew what would happen to me last night."

"No, I was flying blind on this job."

"What does that mean?"

"It means . . . it means I knew fuck-all. It's the way my agency works sometimes. It's a sort of disguise."

"Oh, I see."

. . . I see, I see, I see . . .

"Are you going to kill me, monsieur?"

"Am I going to what?"

"At first, after I woke up, I thought you were dead. You weren't breathing, not at all. But suddenly you mumbled something about killing them, killing all of them. It sounded like you were talking in your sleep. Then it sounded like you were having a nightmare. I was afraid you might wake up and kill me."

Harper laughed a little, thinking, *Our kind do not sleep, our kind don't dream . . . But it seems we do babble whilst mightily drugged.*

"What did you say, monsieur?"

"Sorry?"

"You said something, just now."

"No, I didn't say anything, I was thinking."

"Oh. I thought I heard something."

"No, I told you, it's just the way our voices are echoing in this place."

. . . echoing in this place, in this place, this place . . .

Silence.

"So, you're not going to kill me?"

Harper laughed again, this time thinking how his laughter must sound to a frightened man sitting somewhere in the absolute dark. Right up there with ghoulies and ghosties and other long-legged wackos that kill in the night.

"Be a stupid thing for me to do, wouldn't it? So far, you're the only one who really knows what's happened down here."

"But I don't," Gilles Lambert said. "I don't know anything. I'm terribly confused. I was betrayed by my confessor, the man I trusted with my soul. I believed you were a priest, sent to protect me. I was tricked. And then, I saw such strange things . . ."

"Gilles."

". . . and I saw you open the pillar by touching it, as if your hands were keys. And that thing, that sextant thing . . . what was it doing down here? I've been sitting here thinking none of this could have happened, but I saw it with my own eyes. Please, tell me, what is happening?"

Harper thought about it. In the absolute dark, the man was losing his grasp on reality. Didn't mean Harper could help him. Not yet. Maybe it would come to that, but not yet.

"It's a complicated case. I don't really understand some of it myself. Even if I did, I couldn't tell you what I know."

"But . . . but why not?"

"Because that's the way it is in my job."

"But you must tell me!"

"Mate, you need to stay calm."

"Calm? I've been left to die in this evil place. Why this torture? Why didn't they just kill me?"

. . . why didn't they just kill me, kill me, kill me . . .

Harper listened to the man's voice, the way it echoed in the dark. And he asked himself the same damn thing. Couldn't come up with an answer that made sense. Then again, since when did murdering wackos make sense? Maybe these murdering wackos thought their victims would find this mise-en-scène a more entertaining way to die. Wake up in the absolute dark, think you're dead, find out you're still alive. Now the pain begins. Harper had to admit, it was as creative a method of murder as it was twisted. But he kept the thought to himself and sat quietly. After five minutes—could've been fifty—Harper heard the sound of human tears.

"Gilles?"

"Please, monsieur, I don't want to die like this."

Harper listened to the man's voice again, counting the cycles of slow, dense, reverberating sound. He'd heard the same fearful sound a billion times through the ages, in thousands of languages—*I don't want to die like this*—and through the ages, Harper watched them die.

He listened to the voice again.

It wasn't echoing off the walls. It was drifting like some disembodied thing. Then, like a ton of bricks . . . *wham*, Harper knew. He lowered his head and whispered: *"Cum tacent clamant."*

The words passed his lips and rose through the cavern, chasing after Gilles Lambert's voice.

. . . cum tacent clamant, cum tacent clamant . . .

"Who's there?"

"It's just me, Gilles."

"What . . . what were those words? It sounds like Latin."

"That's right."

"What does it mean?"

"It means: 'When they are silent, they cry out.'"

"Such strange words."

Harper concentrated, trying to find the man's voice. There—no—over there.

"Gilles?"

"*Oui?*"

"Where are you just now?"

"The other side of the cavern."

"How did you get there?"

"*Quoi?*"

"You were next to me when they . . . when they drugged us. How did you get to the other side of the cavern?"

"Oh, that."

Harper could tell the man didn't want to say it.

"Tell me, Gilles."

"When you started talking to yourself about killing people, I thought you might wake up and kill me. I was so terrified, I soiled myself. So I just crawled away."

"Why didn't you just keep going?"

"How?"

"You're the best cataphile in Paris, aren't you? You know these tunnels like the back of your hand, remember? You could've tried to find your way using your hands."

"*Oui*, I remember. And I remember wanting to try. But I thought it best to sit here and wait."

"For what?"

"I don't know. But that's what I thought. And then I felt I would never leave this place. It was an odd feeling. I've spent so much time down here, and now I would be here forever. Then I thought about my Laguiole pocket knife. It was a gift from my father; I always carry it. I thought

I might carve my name into the wall with the knife, in case someone found me."

. . . someone found me, found me, found me . . .

Silence.

"What were we talking about, monsieur?"

"We were talking about how you got to the other side of the cavern. Which reminds me, which way did you go?"

"Pardon?"

"Clockwise, counterclockwise?"

"Clockwise. *Non*, the other way. Why?"

Harper struggled to his feet, touched the black stone wall with the fingers of his right hand. "Because I'm coming over to you."

"Pourqoui?"

. . . pourquoi, pourquoi, pourquoi . . .

Harper stepped through the absolute dark, following the echoing sound, slowly, as if expecting to step into a bottomless pit any second.

"For one, it'll take less effort to talk to each other if we're closer."

"But it isn't an effort, monsieur, really it's not. I'm fine where I am. Please don't come near me."

Harper stopped. *His soul knows; his mind can't accept it.*

"Be not afraid, Gilles."

There was that delay in response that always came when human beings heard those words from one of Harper's kind. The words echoed and drifted till they found Lambert.

"I don't understand what that means, monsieur. I hear the words, but I don't know what they mean."

The man's voice had settled. Harper stepped softly, not wanting to chase it away. He squeezed his eyes closed, reaching for shreds of radiance. He saw the tablet—just for a microsecond, but it was enough.

"Just listen to my voice. This isn't a place of evil, Gilles, it never was. The bodies you found here were those of warriors, slain in battle."

Silence.

"What battle? When?"

"Good guys, bad guys. A hundred and thirty thousand years ago. The battle took place directly above us, wherever the pillar of the cavern is pointing. The good guys lost, and the ones that were captured were slaughtered. The good guys that survived returned at night and collected the bodies. They covered them in oils to preserve them and laid them in these coves."

"How do you know this?"

"It was written on the tablet, the one on the pillar. The whole story."

"You remember it?"

"I can see it now."

"So . . . so this place is a burial chamber?"

"That's right."

"And the thing they found? The sextant? The priest called it a sacred treasure, he said you brought it here. But it was ancient, it looked—"

"Thousands of years old."

"*Oui.* How could you have brought it here? How could you have known about this place already?"

"I think Astruc's got the wrong . . . the wrong guy. I think he only needed one of my kind to pull it off."

"One of your kind?"

"That's right."

Silence.

"Monsieur?"

"Yes?"

"What you are telling me, none of it is possible."

"Trust me, mate, spend enough time watching the world go by and you learn just because something isn't possible, doesn't mean it can't happen."

"But there were no people here a hundred thirty thousand years ago, monsieur. The first human settlements didn't appear in France until 5000 BC. No one lived in the region of Paris until 15 BC."

"You know your history."

"I was very good in history, monsieur."

"Well, all I can tell you is these warriors weren't from here. They were from another place."

"Another country?"

"Bit farther. A lot farther, actually."

"I don't understand."

"You don't need to understand, Gilles. You only need to listen to my voice and trust me. There's nothing to fear about this place."

Harper was next to Gilles Lambert now. He pressed his back into the wall and eased down next to the man. The man didn't move.

"I'm very sorry for the smell, monsieur."

"Don't be. I've been in a few trenches. It happens. I'm sure it's happened to me more than once."

"You were a soldier? You have been in war?"

"Many times."

"Have you . . . Have you killed in war, monsieur?"

"Yes."

"Many times?"

"Yes."

Silence.

"You're one of them, aren't you, monsieur?"

"Sorry?"

"Those warriors from another place. You are one of them, and that's how you know about this place. It was the battle between good and evil as told in the Holy Bible. I understand now. You were one of the survivors, you helped bury the dead. They were the angels of God."

"Gilles . . ."

"That's why the priest called you the angel who saved Paris. He knew. And . . . and that's why the pillar opened when you placed the palms of your hands to the clay tablet. It was . . . it was a miracle, because . . . because you are an angel of God."

Harper whispered, "Gilles, it wasn't a miracle."

"*Non?* Then what was it?"

215

"Manipulations of frequencies based on mathematical equations that affect the behavior of observed matter."

"*Quoi?*"

"Quantum mechanics, Gilles. That's all it was. That's all miracles have ever been."

"I don't understand."

"Miracles, gods, angels. Those are just names, Gilles. You need to let go of them. They're not important anymore."

"*Pourquoi il-faut pas d'importance?*"

"Because names are things of the living."

. . . of the living, the living, the living . . .

Silence.

"Am I dead?"

"You're hanging on, but yeah, this is the time of your death."

"The priest, he killed me?"

"Yes."

"But he couldn't kill you, because of what you are."

Good point, Harper thought. *What the hell am I still doing here?* Then he recalled his undefined metaphysical condition. You die in your form, boyo, but your form keeps coming back. Sounds swell, except for the fact there wasn't enough radiance in paradise to keep him going. Soon enough, the very form keeping him alive would crush and extinguish the last trace of light trapped inside. A wave of nausea washed over Harper, and he fought for breath . . . *Christ, the weight.*

"No, Gilles, I'm dying, too. It's just different for me."

"How can you be dying? No one can kill an angel."

"Trust me."

Silence.

"But I cannot be dead, monsieur. I'm talking to you."

"You are, and you aren't," Harper said.

"I really don't understand."

"You don't need to. You just need to know you're not alone. I'm here just now, and I'm going to help you."

"How?"

"All you have to do is look into my eyes."

"But I can't. There isn't any light."

Harper scraped at the last of the radiance in his blood, drew it to his eyes.

"There will be, then all will be well, I promise."

Gilles Lambert's voice flared with panic: "But, monsieur, I can't see anything. I can't move."

"It's all right. Hang on. I'll find you, don't worry."

He reached through the dark, found Gilles Lambert's head, pulled him closer.

"I'm right next to you, Gilles. Just look into my eyes."

"There's nothing. Oh, monsieur, there's nothing!"

"It must be, it has to be. Keep looking, Gilles, don't stop."

Silence.

"Gilles?"

Harper heard the man's final breath escaping from his lungs, brushing by his face like something lost.

"No, Gilles, not yet."

Harper let the weight of his form crush down on his eternal being. His blood pumped faster and he pulled Gilles Lambert's face close again.

"Look into my eyes, Gilles. I can make it work."

Harper's eyes were running on empty.

"Fuck. Hold on, Gilles. Keep looking."

The man's last breath was gone.

"No, Gilles, wait. Fucking wait."

Harper felt himself blacking out, slumping down, losing hold of the dead man.

They're dying . . . They're all fucking dying . . .

"God dammit, no!"

Harper threw his fist through the dark, hit the stone wall, felt the bones snap and pain burn firelike through his body.

"Fuck! C'mon, fucking do it!"

He felt a spark of light in his eyes. He reached for Gilles Lambert in the absolute dark but couldn't find him.

"Gilles, where the fuck are you?"

Harper crawled over the floor, slapping the stone, the light in his eyes fading. He found the dead man curled on the floor.

"It's in my blood, Gilles, I just can't hold it in my eyes. But it's in my blood, it's . . ."

He heard Gilles Lambert's voice, still drifting through the dark.

I thought about my Laguiole pocket knife . . . a gift from my father . . .

Harper dug frantically through the dead man's pockets, found the knife, opened it. The blade was razor sharp. He made a slice across the palm of his broken right hand, set the knife between his teeth, raised the palm of his left hand to the blade and sliced across it. The blade cut deep, and Harper spit out the knife. "Christ!" He rolled the dead man onto his back, pressed his bleeding palms down onto Gilles Lambert's eyes.

"Listen to my voice, Gilles. *C'est le guet. Il a sonné l'heure. Il a sonné—*"

Something rushed through the dark, grabbed Harper's arms, and pulled him from the dead man. Then a muffled voice: *"Lachêr de lui, il est mort."*

"No! Not yet! I can save him!"

Two sets of unseen hands dragged Harper over the stone floor, shoved him hard against the wall, then a muffled voice: *"Bougez plus. Il est mort."*

Harper twisted to break free.

"He's not dead, not yet, there's fucking time!"

"C'est plus trop."

"Let go of me!"

Harper's feet were kicked out from under him and he fell. The unseen hands caught him, lowered him to a sitting position, pinned him down. Harper pushed back.

"Get your fucking hands off me!"

He felt something cover his nose and mouth.

Sissshhhh.

The muffled voice again: *"Respirz."*

Harper swung his arms, caught something with his broken hand.

"No, let go of me!"

Then a voice: *"Bougez plus et respirz."*

"Sod off!"

A fist slammed into Harper's guts, and air exploded from his lungs. He felt himself yanked upright, his nose and mouth covered again. Then another voice, English with a French accent.

"Breathe, Mr. Harper, just breathe."

An autonomic response in his brain flashed; he sucked in the gas. Cool, pure—every muscle in his form relaxed.

"I'm giving you a mixture of pure oxygen and radiance."

Harper felt it seeping into his blood.

"Light," he mumbled. "I need light."

"If we hit you with the full spectrum, the radiance in your blood will fry your optic nerves. You need to take it slow. We're going to turn on a small lamp in the UV range at three hundred nanometers. It's outside the range of human perception, but under the gas your mind will register it as dark blue. You can't look directly at it for more than ten seconds. When I tell you to close your eyes, do it. Keep them closed and continue to breathe. Nod if you understand what I'm telling you."

Harper nodded.

"On y va."

A pinprick of blue appeared in the absolute dark. *In the beginning,* he thought, *there was . . . no bloody idea.*

"Close your eyes. Continue to breathe."

Remnants of blue light still excited the receptors of Harper's optical nerves, and he saw the light as long threads stretching from the other side of the universe. He felt radiance sparkle in his blood, and a burst of pure light pumped through his form and into his eyes. He settled back against the stone wall, inhaled deeply. The voice coached him along.

"That's it. Now, keep breathing as you open your eyes, but don't look directly at the lamp. Do you understand?"

Harper nodded.

"Good. Open your eyes."

A blue-tinted glow swelled throughout the cavern and gave it shape. High dome, coves cut into the walls. He was in the middle of the cavern, his back against the central pillar. No sign of Astruc or his pal, no sign of the reliquary box.

Two men kneeling in front of him.

Both of them wearing night vision goggles fitted with infrared illuminators; both of them with gas masks over their noses and mouths. One of the men was setting a pressure bandage to the palm of Harper's left hand and wrapping it in gauze. He had a Belgian SCAR submachine gun hanging from his shoulder. The other one held a respirator over Harper's nose and mouth. He was looking at his watch, counting seconds. He was the one speaking English.

"We can't give you morphine with the gas, but we need to stop the bleeding. This will hurt."

Harper nodded.

The medic lifted Harper's forearm, rested it on his leg, and ripped apart a pressure bandage. He stuffed the cotton pad into Harper's right palm, wrapped the gauze strips around the crumpled fingers. And it did hurt like hell. Harper gritted his teeth, sucked hard at the gas. Didn't stop the pain, but with radiance saturating his blood, he couldn't have cared less.

Harper saw a third man crouching at the entrance of the cavern. Night vision gear over his eyes, MAC-10 submachine gun in his hands, targeting up the passageway. Harper's eyes focused on a fourth man, a Micro UZI hanging at his side. He was the one holding the small blue light. Harper saw their rough, dirty clothes. The kind that hadn't been washed in a week, maybe never. Harper mumbled through the respirator.

"The tramps from under the bridge."

They didn't answer.

Harper shot another glance at the mismatched weapons. They weren't French police.

"Who are you people?"

The one holding the respirator over Harper's mouth, the one speaking English, said, "You don't need to know who they are. I'm the only one you need to know. Continue to breathe."

Harper looked at him. SIG strapped to his side, killing knife hooked to his belt.

"Who the hell are you?"

"Sergeant Gauer. Special Unit Task Force of the Swiss Police."

Took a second to click. The man behind the wheel of Inspector Gobet's Merc during the Lausanne job. Ex–Swiss Guard, the one who made a head shot from a kilometer and a half with a sniper's rifle.

"Inspector Gobet's driver?"

"I've been tracking you since l'Église de Saint-Germain-des-Prés."

Harper looked at Sergeant Gauer's clothes again, analyzed his voice.

"You were the tramp on the steps. The one reading from *Purgatorio*. You thanked me for dropping a coin in your hat."

"Affirmative."

"What the hell are you doing in Paris?"

"What's it look like? Saving your ass. Now shut the fuck up and breathe."

Harper rested his head against the pillar, took another deep breath. Images began to flash through his eyes. He turned his head, saw the curled form on the cavern floor. Lambert . . . *Jesus*. Harper reached for him. "Gilles."

Both men held Harper down. Sergeant Gauer checked his watch.

"Sixty more seconds of gas."

"It's enough, I can fire up my eyes now. His soul needs to see my eyes."

The tramp slammed Harper into the pillar.

"*J'ai vous dit. C'est trop tard.*"

"Let go of me, there's still time."

Gauer slapped Harper's face. Harper took a sharp breath.

"Continue to breathe, and listen. It's too late, his soul has separated from his body. It's too late."

"What?"

"Astruc set off an explosive charge at the top of the corridor. A ten-meter section collapsed. It took us three days to tunnel through. Gilles Lambert has been dead that long."

Harper worked the timeline of human death. Four hours: skin turns purple, waxy. Twelve hours: full rigor mortis as the body tries to hold on to the soul. Twenty-four hours: body temperature equals surroundings, cell death complete. Thirty-six hours: rigor mortis fades, soul abandons form, dust to dust.

"Can't be. I was just talking to him. He'd just taken his last breath."

Fifteen seconds ticked by. Sergeant Gauer closed the valve on the gas tank, removed the respirator from Harper's face. The cavern reeked of rotting meat. Harper gagged and spit.

"What the hell?"

The tramp across the cavern, the one holding the small blue light, moved close to Gilles Lambert's body and rolled it over. Harper saw the swollen limbs and distended stomach, the discolored skin.

"I don't get it."

"What's to get? You were talking to an empty corpse."

Harper saw the smears of fresh blood over Gilles Lambert's dead eyes. He looked down at his own bandaged hands. He flashed the scene through his eyes. Like something out of a horror flick.

"Christ, what the hell was I doing?"

Gauer looked at the dead man, then Harper.

"From the looks of it, I'd say you were reaching way above your pay grade."

❧

THIRTEEN

I

KATHERINE HAD BEEN SITTING WITH MAX FOR THE LAST HOUR. He was in his crib, on his back, his blue-green eyes watching shadows moving over the walls and ceiling of his bedroom. He'd always been a sound sleeper. Give him a bath, dress him in his jammies (Shaun the Sheep jammies tonight, the ones he wanted), and lay him down with a bottle at seven. Ten minutes later, he was down for the count. Not a peep for twelve hours. But since Portland, three days ago, he would lie in his crib for hours before sleeping.

Not like he was upset.

Not like he was anything.

He'd just stare at the never-the-same shadows, babbling to himself now and again. And not baby kind of babbling, Katherine thought. No, this was more like the little guy was talking to the shadows. And damn if there weren't a few times when it seemed Max would tip his head as if hearing the shadows talk back.

Earlier in the day, Katherine called the doctor in Portland to talk about it.

"What kind of shadows are they?" the doctor said.

"What do you fucking mean, 'What kind of shadows are they?'" Katherine replied.

"Where do the shadows come from, Ms. Taylor? How are they made?"

"Security lamps in the back garden, bleeding through the evergreen trees outside the window," Katherine explained.

"So have the lamps and trees and shadows always been there?"

"Yes, but they never kept him awake at night. And now he's talking to them."

The doctor told her not to worry. Just exploring his imagination, he said. Perfectly normal. Important thing is not to show any distress, but to let him think it's a game.

Katherine was relieved and spooked at the same time. Relieved that Max was "normal," spooked to think that if Max's imagination was anything like hers lately (especially the part where she imagined Max was communicating with shadows), then therapy and/or medication might be in order.

She expressed that concern to Officer Jannsen.

Officer Jannsen rattled off a thesis-length description of Jean Piaget's theory of cognitive development in children. Something about young children's brains constantly being rewired to organize and interpret sensory data into schemata, aiding in the cognitive representation of self. Katherine had no fucking idea what Officer Jannsen was talking about. But the lecture did end with, "So relax, Kat."

Katherine was telling herself those very words when she remembered: *teasing shadows.* It was what Marc Rochat called the shadows in the high corners of Lausanne Cathedral. And she remembered Marc in the belfry of Lausanne Cathedral, greeting the shadows in passing, or scolding them for their teasing ways. For a moment, she saw him. Long black overcoat, black floppy hat on his head, lantern in his hand, pointing to the wiggly, dark, high-above things and telling her, "Because they're the teasing kind of shadows. They like to play in the cathedral.

224

Sometimes they leave the door to the tower open and sometimes they chase after echoes. They're very friendly shadows."

He faded from her eyes.

She looked up at the ceiling, saw the shadows in Max's bedroom. She laughed to herself. They really did look like the teasing kind of shadows. She looked at Max.

"Is that what you're doing, honey? Playing with the teasing shadows?"

Max didn't answer. His eyes stayed locked on the ceiling.

Katherine tickled his belly. "Don't you dare ignore Mommy Dearest . . ."

Max squealed with delight.

". . . or she might have to tickle you forever."

Max kicked his legs and laughed. She bent down and kissed his forehead.

"You know, I knew someone once. He talked to shadows, too, and he had lots of imaginary friends. They all lived in a cathedral. And some of his friends were lost angels."

Max stared at her, as if hypnotized by the sound of her voice, not even blinking.

She remembered the first time he looked at her that way. He must have been two months old, and it totally freaked her out. She called Officer Jannsen, thinking something was seriously wrong with him. Officer Jannsen told Katherine that Max had lived inside her body for nine months, and that from twenty-four weeks, he not only heard her voice, but *felt* her voice vibrating around him, especially the sound of vowels. And that outside the womb, now, certain sounds in Katherine's voice created a harmonic wave that resonated in the thalamus region of Max's brain, like a tonic note of a musical score.

"Your voice is like no other voice in the world to Max, it always will be," Officer Jannsen said. "Of course he's going to stare at you sometimes. He's looking to you to guide him through his imagination. You should tell him stories."

"I read him stories all the time."

"No. I mean stories from your own imagination. Tell him those stories."

"Me?"

"Yes."

"What about?"

"Doesn't matter. It's more about the sound of your voice. It's magical, it's mysterious to him."

Katherine raised an eyebrow.

"This time you're making it up."

"What?"

"The whole harmonic vibration thingy."

"Actually, research on the impact of sound on fetuses is well documented. The rest of it, the part about the harmonic resonance of your voice impacting the thalamus region of Max's brain, that's my own theory."

"You're kidding."

Officer Jannsen wasn't kidding. And staring at Max just now, Katherine thought Anne Jannsen was not only pretty damn smart (and pretty enough to make Katherine melt just thinking about her), but right. The expression on Max's face said he was hanging on the very sound of Katherine's voice.

"So what do you think? You want me to tell you a story about the angels hiding in the cathedral?"

"Angeh."

"Yeah, angels."

"Angeh."

"Come on, you can say it: angels."

"Angeh."

"I know, that *L* sound is kinda tough when it gets stuck in the back of your throat. Let's try it in French. *Les anges.*"

"Weezangeh."

"Weezangeh? What the heck is a weezangeh? Come on, say it properly and I'll tell you the story of the lost angels in the cathedral."

Max kicked his legs and giggled. "Weezangeh."

"Okay, okay. What was I thinking that French would be easier? It's French, for cripes sake."

"Fensh."

"Exactly. We'll stick to English. Ready?"

"Goog."

"Okay. Here we go. Once upon a time . . ."

She stopped, had a thought.

"Wait a sec, wait right here. I'm going to get something so I can really tell you the story about the lost angels. Okay?"

"Fensh."

Katherine tickled Max's tummy, and he giggled and kicked again.

"Whatever. I'll be right back."

She walked through the adjoining doors into her own bedroom. On the dressing table, near the window, was an old lantern and a black floppy hat. Some of the things left to her in Marc Rochat's will, and presented to her in two large cardboard boxes by Monsieur Gübeli at the end of his visit to Grover's Mill. She remembered Gübeli's driver slowly opening the trunk of the limousine to reveal the cardboard boxes as if they were lost treasure. And she remembered before he left, Monsieur Gübeli said, "I trust these simple things will serve to remind you of the goodness and kindness that was Master Rochat's nature, madame."

Katherine got the boxes home and, not knowing what to do with them, she took them to her bedroom. She stared at the boxes a long time before opening them. And when she did, there was a musty smell that sent her flying back to the little room between the bells high above Lausanne, higher than the Alps on the far shore, higher than the whole world. She found Rochat's sketchbooks and one hundred candles in one box . . . his hat and lantern in the other. When she picked up his hat, tears welled in her eyes. She pressed the hat to her breasts.

"Jesus," she said.

Then she lifted the lantern from the box. There was the stub of a candle inside, topped with a blackened wick. Katherine trembled. It would have been the last candle Marc Rochat had set alight, she thought. And staring at it, she remembered how he'd died horribly and painfully to save her. She had always thought he did it because the brain-damaged and crooked little man had believed she was a lost angel. But in the end, before he died, he knew the truth. That she wasn't an angel; she was a hooker on the run. And now, holding his lantern in her hands, something he treasured, she knew the real reason he died to protect her: The crooked little man loved her. She cried her eyes out that night. And when she stopped, she lay his hat on the dressing table and set the lantern next to it. She tried to look at the sketchbooks, but she couldn't. It was too much, too soon. They'd have to wait till another day.

Katherine blinked, wobbled a bit with déjà vu.

She was still standing at the adjoining doors between the bedrooms. She looked back at Max in his crib. He was sitting up now, his hand reaching through the bars of the crib and holding on to Monsieur Booty's tail. The cat had emerged from one of his hiding places to jump on the stool next to the crib for another round of manhandling by Max. Sometimes Katherine imagined the cat didn't hide at all. She was sure the beast simply materialized from nothingness at will. And if that turned out to be the case, she wouldn't be surprised. Not one bit.

"Boo," Max said.

"Sorry, I got a little distracted. You guys wait there, I'll be right back. Then we'll do the story."

There was a knock on her bedroom door.

"Kat, it's Anne. Can I come in?"

"It's open."

Officer Jannsen opened the door and poked in her head. "All's well?"

"Yeah."

"What are you up to?"

"Um, nothing. I'm hanging out with Max. Why?"

"I was going to ask you down for a cup of tea."

"That time already?"

"Afraid so."

"I'd like to stay with Max till he goes to sleep."

"Kat, he's okay. You can monitor him from downstairs."

"I know, but I'd rather stay. Why don't you make a cup of tea for yourself and me and come back? We'll both hang out with Max. I was going to tell him a story."

"What kind of story?"

"About lost angels. Hiding in a cathedral."

Officer Jannsen gave an expression somewhere between pleasant surprise and *holy fucking shit*. Katherine put her hand on her hip.

"What, you don't think I can tell my own kid a story I made up myself?"

"Kat—"

"Lemme tell you something: I'm sure I can tell a better story than your story about gods from the Great White North who get all pissed off with each other and turn into volcanoes."

"That's not what—"

"And lemme tell you something else: You wouldn't believe the stories I had to tell to make guys think I wasn't just loving it, but *really* loving it. Actually, forget that part. Point is, I'm going to tell my son a story. You can chaperone if you want. Make sure I don't scare the crap out of him."

"You don't need me to chaperone, Kat. And I was only thinking it sounds like fun. And I'd like to hear this story myself."

"Really?"

"*Oui*, really."

"Okay. Go get the tea, then."

Officer Jannsen ducked out the door . . .

"Anne?"

. . . and back in again.

"What?"

"Does Control monitor Max's room when I'm up here?"

"*Pardon?*"

"You know. Do they keep an eye on me with him?"

229

Officer Jannsen stepped into Katherine's bedroom, closed the door behind her.

"Where is that question coming from, Kat?"

"My mind. What's left of it."

Officer Jannsen crossed the room, stood close to Katherine.

"Video and audio is only operational when he's alone in his room."

"You sure?"

"Yes. Why do you ask?"

"No reason. Just asking."

Officer Jannsen reached up and combed her fingers through Katherine's hair.

"We keep an eye on things, you know that. We can check every room in the house if we have to. But never when you're in one of the rooms, and never when you're alone with your son."

"Okay."

"I'll brew the tea."

"Okay."

Officer Jannsen left the room.

Katherine looked back through the doorway. Max was still holding on to Monsieur Booty's tail. They were both looking at her, waiting.

"Weezangeh."

Mew.

"Yeah, yeah. Just had to tell Obergruppenführer what I was up to. Where was I with you guys? Never mind, I remember. I'll be back."

She walked to the dressing table, sat down in front of the mirror. She picked up Rochat's floppy black hat and set it on her head, tucking her long blond hair up into it. It was a perfect fit.

"Matches, I need matches."

She found some in the drawer. She opened the glass door of the lantern, struck a match, lit the candle. The wick sparked and flashed. She lifted the lantern, watched the flame rise and fall as it breathed. She looked at herself in the mirror. Hat on head, lantern in hand. She laughed to herself. If Max thought his ex-hooker of a mother was cuckoo for Cocoa Puffs before . . . "Wait'll he gets a load of Mommy now."

She turned off the lights in her room, walked through the dark in a pool of soft, yellow light. She reached the adjoining doors, stood in the opening. She raised the lantern, brightening her face. The light of the lantern spilled into Max's room, and Katherine saw the light sparkle in his blue-green eyes. At first, he didn't know who it was in the doorway. Then he recognized his mother's face. He smiled and giggled and shook Monsieur Booty's tail. "Weezangeh." The cat, too, was transfixed by the vision in the doorway and didn't object to having his tail shaken so excitedly. Then, as if spotting something undetectable to human eyes, the beast hunched into a crouch and clawed at the chair, and the fur on its back stood up.

Mrrrrrewww.

"Oh relax, fuzzface."

The beast heard Katherine's voice and calmed down.

"That's better. How about you, Max? You ready for story time with crazy Mommy?"

"Goog."

"Okay. Here we go."

Katherine walked slowly toward the crib.

"Once upon a time—"

There was a knock on Katherine's door again. She spun around.

"What?"

"Open up, Kat, I've got the tea."

Katherine turned to her attentive audience, all two of them.

"One second, I'll be right back."

She walked to the door and cracked it open.

Officer Jannsen was in the hall, two steaming mugs in her hands. Night Clouds tea for Katherine, green tea for her. She looked at Katherine, saw the hat, lantern, and fire.

"*Mon Dieu*, Kat, you're really going for it in the imagination department."

"C'mon, get in here. I'll have to do my whole entrance again. But it's okay. I think I was holding back a little. I know I can do better."

They stared at each other through the doorway.

"Kat?"

"Yeah?"

"If I'm going to see the show, you must first let me in."

"Oh yeah, oh yeah."

Katherine opened the door wide.

Officer Jannsen hurried through, steaming mugs in her hands, fully loaded Glock semiautomatic on her hip, and crossed into Max's room. There were sounds of furniture being rearranged as Officer Jannsen moved a chest and dragged a chair across the room to set next to Max's crib. Then it was quiet. Katherine waited a second.

"Are we finally ready in there, boys and girl?"

"Weezangeh."

Mew.

"*Oui.*"

Katherine took a step . . . stopped. She saw her black cloak on the bed. She set the lantern on the floor, put on the cloak. She picked up the lantern and checked herself in the mirror.

"First rule of making a killer entrance, girl. Give 'em their money's worth."

She walked slowly to the doorway.

She raised the lantern, filled the room with firelight.

Three pairs of waiting eyes were hers for the taking.

"Once upon a time, in a faraway land . . ."

II

THE ARCHAEOLOGICAL FORM TOOK A HAUNTING SHAPE AS HE cleared the forest. It was a volcanic pluton, all that was left of a fire-breathing shaper of Earth. Millions of years ago, the volcano cooled and lava gushing from the magna reservoir slowed. The vent and crater sealed, and the still-boiling lava caught in the conduit solidified into solid black rock. The sides of the volcano wore away, leaving a massive limestone dome rising three hundred meters from the surrounding ground.

Astruc stopped to look at it. He could just make out the last of the sun reflecting off the south wall of the fortress atop the dome. It would be a steep walk from here, and soon the light would fade. But they had to wait till the handful of tourists and guardians of the site had left. He checked the nearby road. The parking area was empty. All was well.

He removed the goatskin from his shoulder and took a drink of water. He heard a rustle in the trees. He looked back, saw Goose coming into the clearing. Goose raised his head to see the high-above fortress from under the cowl of his hoodie. His glassy eyes tried to focus. It was impossible for him to see clearly beyond two hundred meters. The very potion that gave him a measure of vision was eating away at the retinas of his eyes. But he could see the haunting shape rising from the ground, and he could just make out the squared shapes of rocks silhouetted against the sky that could have only been cut by human hands. Astruc laid his hand on Goose's shoulder.

"We're close now. An hour more and we'll be there. Would you like to rest? The way is difficult."

Goose shifted the weight of his heavy backpack. It was stuffed with technical kit, ammunition, and weapons. Astruc carried a backpack, too. Sleeping bags, clothes and food, the reliquary box he'd taken from the black stone cavern beneath Paris.

When they left the cavern, the priest and his charge followed the infrared ChemLights through the tunnels back to the surface. It was three thirty a.m. They hurried along the abandoned railway and climbed to the street. The rain had fallen still, and the streets were empty and dark. They were unnoticed by anyone. They climbed in their van, changed into clean, dry clothes. They drove to the 16th arrondissement and parked on Rue Pergolèse. They walked to Avenue de la Grande Armée, caught a passing taxi to Gare de Lyon. They took the 04:30 train from Paris to the Mediterranean city of Montpellier. A connecting train carried them south along the coast to Perpignan, very near the Spanish border. It was the long way around to Montségur. It would have been easier and quicker to travel by way of Toulouse. But they were hunted by the Dark Ones, so they laid a false trail to the east.

On the TGV from Paris, Goose opened his laptop. An Apple laptop, but it was only the shell. Goose had ripped out the circuits and motherboard and replaced them with those of his own making. The laptop was much faster, much more powerful. He connected the laptop to a 4G USB device. He hacked into the French Customs and Immigration database in seven minutes, listed himself and Astruc as passengers aboard an Egyptian freighter, the *Arabian Crescent*, bound for Alexandria that night from Perpignan. Under assumed names, of course, but the hunters searching the Internet would see their faces on two virtual Spanish passports. Goose slapped the passports together in five minutes with a bit of simple copy and paste. When he uploaded the data into the French servers, he ejected the USB, walked to the baggage compartment, and slipped it in the pouch of someone's suitcase. Didn't matter who, Goose thought. People being what they are meant someone would find the USB, slip it in their own computer, discover it had no security lock. The someone would use it from wherever they were, sending out a second false trail on the Internet. The Dark Ones would turn their gazes for as long as Astruc and Goose needed to execute the second phase of their mission. After that, they would be exposed, and it would be a race to Heaven's Gate and Spain, where they would execute the third and final stage of their holy mission.

They arrived at Perpignan just after dawn. Exiting the station, they spotted a man wearing a suit in the parking lot. He was removing a valise from the trunk of a Peugeot 307. A traveling man on an overnight trip. Goose waited for the man to enter the station, then hurried to the car. It took him sixty seconds to silently break into the car and hotwire the starter. Astruc climbed in and they drove northwest to Saint-Estève. They left the highway and drove west along a country lane. The crowded flatlands of the Mediterranean coast became the hills of Languedoc. The hills leveled to become vineyards, then rose again. Two

kilometers short of the village of Estagel, in a lonely part of the countryside, they pulled onto a dirt track. It led to a dilapidated barn set behind a copse of tall willow trees. The barn was open, and they drove in
and stopped the motor. They knew this place. They'd set out for Paris
from this place just forty-eight hours ago. They knew no one would find
them here.

They slept till two in the afternoon, when the residents of Estagel
closed their shutters for siesta. Goose rose, found Astruc's backpack and
the rest of their supplies they'd hidden in a stall of the barn. Under the
supplies, wrapped in waterproof tarp, were two shepherd's crooks and
a sealed plastic bag containing two long necklaces of old, braided
leather. A scallop shell hung from each of the necklaces. They tied them
around their necks, let them hang outside their coats. Astruc opened the
side pouch of his backpack, found an auto-injector, and handed it to
Goose.

"In the name of the martyrs," Astruc said.

Goose signed *Amen*, took the injector, and slammed it into his own
thigh. The needle broke through his jeans, found muscle, and the potion flooded into his body. Goose closed his eyes, prayed a moment. He
opened his eyes. Astruc was watching him.

"Are you well enough, now?"

Yes, Father.

"Good."

They lifted their backpacks onto their shoulders. Astruc took one of
the shepherd's crooks, gave the other to Goose.

"May the Pure God protect our spirits from evil."

They left the barn, walked to the lane toward Estagel. The village was
quiet, wooden shutters all closed against the afternoon sun. They
walked slowly, keeping their eyes to the ground, and crossed the river to
the D117. It was a country road of two lanes bound by rocky hills and
autumn-colored trees. The air was cool, the sun was warm. There was a
walking path next to the road and they followed it west, walking in the
shadows of trees. To anyone driving by, to anyone giving them a casual

glance, they appeared as religious pilgrims. To anyone driving by, to anyone giving them a casual glance, they appeared as religious pilgrims making their way across the south of France toward Saint-Jean-Pied-de-Port. There, they'd cross into Spain and join Le Chemin de Saint-Jacques de Compostelle—the Way of Saint James.

They looked a little strange, perhaps. The big man in the long brown overcoat and blue-lensed glasses, followed by a smaller man who hid his face under the cowl of a hooded sweatshirt. But it was this strangeness that gave them a cloak of invisibility. That and the thousand-year-old Christian tradition of believing pilgrims who wore a scallop shell and walked the Way of Saint James with wooden staffs were making penance for their sins. They were not to be harmed or bothered in any manner. And perhaps their strangeness helped in another way: They did not look like the run-of-the-mill happy tourists who made the long trek in the summer months. No, the big man looked hard, and the small one hid from the world. Perhaps they truly were doing penance for their sins.

They skirted the towns of Saint-Paul-de-Fenouillet and Quillan. At Bélesta they followed the D9 south through Fougax-et-Barrineuf. The road was isolated, and it wound through farmlands bordered by thick forests. At night, they made rough camp in the forests. They ate high-protein biscuits, cleaned their bodies with antibacterial wet-wipes. They did not build a fire, they did not use flashlights. When needed, they moved through the night wearing night vision goggles. They buried their trash, they brushed the flattened grass where they'd slept; they left no sign of having been there.

Three days from Perpignan now, they arrived at the foot of the volcanic pluton called Montségur. Goose pulled his cowl from his head. He let his backpack slip from his shoulders and sat on the ground. Astruc leaned his back into the trunk of a dead, limbless tree. He offered the goatskin to Goose. The kid took it, drank deeply. Astruc looked up at the darkening, cloudless sky. The summer triangle of Deneb, Vega, and Altair were already visible to the southwest.

"It is a good night. A good night for watchers of the sky."

Goose scanned the sky with his glassy eyes. To him it was nothing more than looking into the underside of a dark blue umbrella. But he could feel the wind on his face. It felt clear, dustless. He handed back the goatskin and signed, *Will we see it, Father? Will it really come tonight?*

Astruc took the goatskin, slung it over his shoulder.

"If there is to be any hope for the eternal soul of mankind, it must be tonight."

Goose smiled and signed, *If this is your belief, Father, then it will be so.*

"It isn't what I believe, it's what was foretold to the pure of faith."

Goose pointed down the hill to the clearing, where a stile stood atop a stone altar.

Is that the field, Father?

Astruc turned and saw the stile, saw the field of grass beyond bound by a simple wooden fence. The stile was too far away to see the cross and inscription carved into the stone, but Astruc didn't need to see those things. The day was seared into his memory.

EN CE LIEU LE 16 MARS 1244

PLUS DE 200 PERSONNES ONT ÉTÉ BRULÉES

ELLES N'AVAIENT PAS VOULU RENIER LEUR FOI

In the fading light, the stile was backlit like something forever sacred. And he saw shreds of mist rise from the field and into the light as if the souls of the burned had never left this place.

"Yes, that's the Field of the Burned. We'll stop there to say the Lord's Prayer before we leave. Come now, the light is fading."

Goose lifted his backpack to his shoulders and followed Astruc along the path. A deer watched them pass from the cover of the forest. They walked quietly. Quietly enough to hear the wind pass through the branches of autumn-colored trees. The taller trees bowed to the east; the wind was coming from the west. Astruc checked the horizon. Still not a cloud in the darkening sky.

III

"CAN I TOSS IN A PRINCESS?"

"A what?"

"A princess."

"Why do you need a princess in the story?"

Katherine tipped her head toward Max without looking at him.

"Because I don't want to say the *H* word in front of you-know-who."

Officer Jannsen, at first captivated by the story so far, was lost. "The *H* word?"

Katherine rolled her eyes, her mouth slowly forming the word *hooker*.

"Ah, I'm with you now. In that case, I think a princess would be fine."

"Great."

Katherine tried to remember where she'd left off with her story. She'd set the stage. Once upon a time, in a faraway land, a strange and wonderful young man lived in the belfry of a cathedral and watched over the land through the night. He watched for fires and invaders and bad shadows. And he wore a black hat and black cloak and he carried a very old lantern.

"And I'll tell you a secret. It was this very same lantern."

Max's eyes widened, watching the fire at the tip of the lantern's candle.

"And you know what else?"

Max looked at his mother. She moved slowly toward him, and she smiled.

"The strange young man had a cat. A big, fat, furry cat. And the cat's name was Monsieur Booty."

Max looked at the furry beast sitting on the stool just outside the bars of the crib, the beast Max had by the tail.

"Boo!" he said.

"That's right, Boo is in the story, too! Isn't that funny?"

Max giggled, certifying that the coincidence was very funny, indeed.

"Okay, so. One night, this strange young man—"

"Excuse me, Kat?"

Katherine put her hand on her hip and regarded Officer Jannsen with mock horror.

"Oh, what now?"

"Shouldn't he have a name?"

"Who?"

"The strange young man in the belfry."

Katherine thought about it.

"Okay. Anything else?"

"*Non.*"

"You sure? Because you're really throwing me off my method."

"Your what?"

"My method. It's an acting school thing."

"You were in acting school?"

"Took a couple classes at UCLA before I dropped out and became a you-know-what."

Officer Jannsen smiled that half smile of hers.

"*Je comprend.*"

"Good. Can I go on now? I'd like to finish the story before Max hits puberty."

"*Excusez-moi, mon petit canard.*"

"Okay. So, once upon a time, faraway land, strange young man, and his name was . . . What did you just say?"

"I said, 'Excuse me.'"

"No, after that."

"I don't remember."

"Anne, you just called me your little duck."

"*Comme ça?*"

Katherine saw Officer Jannsen's pale white skin flush with color. *Mon petit canard* did mean *my little duck*. Katherine also knew it was a term of affection among the French, who had a habit of referring to loved ones as cats, pigs, chickens, eggs, and/or fleas. And the more *petit* any of them was, the deeper the affection. Katherine realized why Officer Jannsen was blushing and, realizing it, she felt her own stomach do flip-flops again.

She quickly looked at Max. He and Monsieur Booty had been going back and forth between the two women as if watching a game of tennis. Not knowing the rules or how the game was played, but knowing a game of some sort was being played, and it was most entertaining to watch. Just now, Max and Monsieur Booty were focused on Officer Jannsen, as she'd made the last play with *Comme ça?*

Katherine took a breath, tapped the glass of the lantern.

"Hey, Max and Fuzzface, stay with me, I'm working here."

Max and Monsieur Booty turned to Katherine. Almost too frightened to look at Officer Jannsen, Katherine stepped closer to her, feeling the Swiss cop's eyes watching.

"Okay. So, the strange young man's name was Marc Rochat, and he watched over this faraway land, yadda, yadda, yadda. See, there was a sadness in the land, as bad shadows began to rule the world and the angels had nowhere to hide. Rochat kept his lantern shining in the belfry so they could find their way to safety in the cathedral to hide from the bad shadows. Then, one dark and stormy night, Marc Rochat saw the most beautiful hooker in the world . . . shit, princess, I mean . . . the most beautiful *princess* in the world."

IV

THE SUN HAD SET DURING THEIR CLIMB, AND THEY HAD TO STOP to put on their night vision goggles to make their way through the dark, close-in forest lining the trail. Even so, the switchback trail was tricky to negotiate. The black stones of the trail were worn smooth by tourists and pilgrims, and it was easy to slip. Fifty-eight minutes later they were standing at the south wall of the fortress. A breeze circled the walls from the west. Astruc looked at the sky again. It was a new moon tonight; a thousand stars would be visible to the naked eye. But with the night vision goggles, even stars unseen by the naked eye became bright things, and the sky above Montségur was aglow with sparkling light. And the spiral galaxy of the Milky Way stretched two hundred thousand kilometers across the horizon like a churning fog.

Goose stood next to Astruc and signed, *It looks alive, Father, as if it's breathing.*

"It is, Goose. It's been breathing for fourteen billion years."

He found the Big Dipper formation within Ursa Major. Then the pointer stars of the dipper, Merak and Dubhe. His eyes traced an imaginary line across the sky to the huddle of five stars four hundred thirty-four light-years from Earth. From this distance they were the stuff of visual illusion, appearing as one star. Men called it lodestar, guiding star, Polaris. Astruc found the two inner stars of the Big Dipper's cup, Phecda and Megrez . . . then Alioth, Mizar, and Alkaid in the handle, traced two imaginary lines across space into the NQ3 quadrant till they intersected amid the fourteen stars at a right ascension of 17 hours and declination +65°. This was the constellation Draco. And at the point of intersection was a rare white giant, a massive dying star, listed according to its Bayer designation as Alpha Draconis. The pharaohs of Egypt called it Thuban, the snake. Three hundred times brighter than the sun, but at three million light-years from Earth, Thuban appeared no more than an insignificant smudge of light. But six thousand years ago in the time of the pharaohs, before the axial precession of Earth tipped the planet twenty-six degrees on its axis, Thuban was the lodestar, the guiding star of men. And tonight, Astruc thought, it would be again.

"Come, let us make things ready."

They walked under the south wall, climbed the wooden staircase rising five meters to an open arch. They stepped inside, dropped their backpacks on the ground. The fortress interior was shaped as an irregular pentagon, the five corners giving a sum of 540 degrees. It was an odd shape designed to maximize the limited space atop the pluton. At the west end stood the squared tower of the keep. Astruc saw the archer's slit in the stone of the tower's east wall. There had been a matching slit on the west wall before the wall collapsed hundreds of years ago. The arrow slits led to a legend about the keep. On the dawn of the summer solstice, the first rays of the sun were said to pass unbroken through the keep like some holy thread of light. It led to legends of the fortress being a place where the Cathars held secret rituals to worship the sun. Astruc smiled. It was nothing but a legend; even so, the truth of the Cathars was more strange than any legend men could have imagined.

"Et auran liurat."

Goose looked at Astruc. *Father?*

"I was thinking of the innocent men and women who were sacrificed in this place to lead us to this moment."

Goose couldn't see the eyes behind the goggles, but he sensed another vision about Montségur had passed through the priest's mind. But it didn't take hold of him, not this time.

Do you wish to rest a little before we begin, Father?

He watched the priest shake himself. "No, not now. There will be time for rest."

Goose opened his backpack, sorted pieces of his gear. His laptop, a small external hard drive, a Krypton laser pointer with remote trigger, a transceiver, panels for a portable satellite dish, cables, and spare batteries. He arranged the gear across the open arch of the north gate, connected it together to make a base station. He assembled the sat dish, connected it to the transceiver by long cables. He carried the dish to the wooden platform at the south gate. He used his iPhone to figure azimuth and elevation of a communications satellite parked forty-two thousand miles above Earth. Next was the laser pointer. He circled around the outside of the fortress along the narrow cliff till he reached the northwest corner of the tower. The ruins of the terraced village lay twenty meters below the plateau. He climbed down, looked for a clear line of sight. He anchored the laser pointer to fire at a latitude of 1°50'00.80" E. He activated the remote trigger once and adjusted the intensity of light. It was perfectly set, making a thin green line of light directly beneath the north gate of Montségur before dead-ending into an outcrop of rock. From here, the beam would be visible from above, but hidden from anyone below the mountain. He crawled back up the cliff, walked to the north gate, stepped over the base station and into the fortress. He switched on the gear, tested the satellite link.

Everything is set, Father.

"Very good."

They took off their night vision goggles, let their eyes adjust to the dark. Goose had fixed a red filter over his computer screen and set the luminance to its lowest level. It preserved the rhodopsin in their eyes and did not blind them from seeing the constellation Draco, Thuban, and all the stars of the heavens.

"We should have our evening meal now," Astruc said, sitting down on the wall. "It will be a long night."

Goose opened his backpack and dug out a box of high-protein biscuits. He gave two biscuits to Astruc, one for himself. Astruc lowered his head to offer thanks for the gifts they were about to receive. Goose bowed his head, too. There were no words, only a meditative silence that continued as they ate. When they finished their meal, they used water from their goatskins to wash their faces and hands.

"Let us begin."

Goose opened the laptop, connected to the Internet through a spiderweb of encrypted proxies that circled the planet nine times before finding its target. He had already hacked the target's security codes and created his own access name. Now it was a simple matter of feeding the data from his external hard drive to the target.

We're in, Father. It will take three hours to upload the program into their computer. You should rest a little, Father. There is nothing to do until it happens.

"Yes, all right. A little rest, then."

Astruc opened the reliquary box, lifted the sextant into his hands. There was a large rock protruding from the brown grass of the courtyard. He sat on the grass and rested his back against the rock. He touched the grass, the dirt, the stones.

"Et auran liurat," he whispered.

A cool breeze drifted down from the Pyrenees and through the south gate. Astruc closed his eyes and breathed deeply. It was pure, it was life-giving. He opened his eyes, and in that moment, the gate was like a tunnel, and just beyond the entire expanse of the universe was moving, rolling like the crest of a mighty wave come to wash over the Earth and make it clean.

V

W ELL?"

    "C'est magnifique, Kat."

When Katherine finished her story about the strange young man named Marc Rochat who saved the angels hiding in Lausanne Cathedral because they had nowhere else in the world to go, *and* the hooker princess who was being chased by the bad shadows, she stood very still, lantern in her hands, the fire of the candle flickering in her eyes. She stared at her audience: Max sitting in his crib, Monsieur Booty sitting on the nearby stool, and Officer Jannsen sitting in a chair pulled up and parked next to the crib. The three of them had formed a captive front row for Katherine's performance. And after she'd finished the last act, there wasn't a squeak. It was as if they were frozen in a moment of time. Max still had hold of Monsieur Booty's fluffy tail, and Officer Jannsen had yet to take a sip of tea from the mug in her hands. The three of them stared at Katherine with the widest eyes. Katherine waited a full thirty seconds for a round of applause. There was none, just the continued gaga gaze of the peanut gallery. Katherine lowered the lantern and set her hand on her hip.

"Well?" she said.

Officer Jannsen said, *"C'est magnifique, Kat."*

"You think?"

"I've never heard anything like it."

"Really?"

"Oui. It was so full of imagination, I feel like I was taken to another place. A really special place."

"Really? Wow."

244

Katherine looked at Monsieur Booty.

"How about you, fuzzface?"

Mrrrrrewww.

"I'll take that as a thumbs-up—or claws-up, in your case."

She looked at Max.

"What about you, buster? Did you like the story?"

Max didn't speak or babble. He just stared at his mother as if she were a thing of magic and wonder. Even better than Whac-A-Mole. Then he lay down his head and slept.

FOURTEEN

THERE WAS A SMALL STONE ALCOVE TO THE RIGHT OF THE DOOR. Inside the alcove, a cross was mounted into the stone. It looked old, made of two thin strips of metal. Harper stared at it. The cross had been painted once. Looked a well-faded gold or yellow. Sergeant Gauer reached behind the cross and pressed a button. He stood next to Harper, the both of them facing the door.

"Stand still, let them get a look at you," Gauer said.

"What's this place, then?"

"How would I know? I'm not here, neither are you."

The address was Number 4, Rue Visconti. It was tucked in an alleyway in the 6th arrondissement. It's where Sergeant Gauer brought Harper after coming up from the cavern. In the same bloody cab with the same bloody driver that picked Harper up at Gare de Lyon three bloody days ago.

"I thought he was working with Astruc," Harper said, recognizing the cabbie.

"So did Astruc," Sergeant Gauer answered.

Harper blinked, saw the spyhole in the door, and thought, *If I saw the likes of two blokes just up from* les carrières, *filthy and rough, I wouldn't open up.*

But ten seconds later, *click* . . . the door opened.

Into a vestibule and down a hall. Could've passed for an abandoned house, this place. The green wallpaper, imprinted with some arabesque pattern, was tattered and peeling in places. The wooden flooring not only creaked but was so worn that iron nails poked from slats. The bare neon lamp hanging from the cracked plaster ceiling was a nice touch. Gave the place a nauseating glow—or maybe that was just the way Harper felt. There wasn't anyone about, but there were security cameras in the high corners of the hall. Harper followed Sergeant Gauer to a metal door with seven slots for seven keys. It was open a crack, and there was a light beyond. Harper looked at the door. Steel, six inches thick. It'd been forced open. Sergeant Gauer heaved the door aside and stepped in. Harper stopped at the threshold. A large rectangular-shaped room. Antique floor-to-ceiling bookcases with beveled glass doors lining the walls, patterned carpet on the floor.

"Well, well, what have we here?"

Another step and he saw a hand-carved walnut table stretching the length of the room. It was swell. Matched the bookcases. There was a line of brass lamps with green glass shades down the center of the table, and they filled the room with contemplative light, perfectly balanced at 3200 degrees Kelvin. Chesterfield chairs of aged, brown leather were placed around the table. As he stepped clear of the door, Harper saw Inspector Gobet sitting in one of the chairs. Not at the head of the table, but at the immediate place to the right. *La place d'honneur,* Harper thought. Made him wonder who got the big chair. The inspector's muscle, Mutt and Jeff, stood behind the inspector. They paid Harper no notice. They were too busy leaning up against the bookcases, scribbling in moleskin notebooks. The inspector, too, was otherwise engaged with the file that lay open before him. It looked familiar, and it made Harper feel sicker than he already did. He shook it off.

"Good evening, sir."

"Sit down, Mr. Harper, we'll begin the debrief in a moment," the inspector said without looking up.

Sergeant Gauer eyeballed the empty chair across from the inspector. Harper took the hint and sat down. In the chair next to him were his overcoat and sports coat. Neatly folded. Interesting, Harper thought, how he kept losing the bloody things and they always found their way back to him. Harper looked at Sergeant Gauer.

"Where did you find those?"

"In an abandoned van off Avenue de la Grande Armée."

"Astruc's?"

"Affirmative."

Meaning: *Not only have we been tracking you since Saint-Germain-des-Prés, Mr. Harper, but we knew what Astruc was up to and let you walk into a trap, anyway.*

"Right."

Harper sat down.

Sergeant Gauer took a position directly behind him, made like Mutt and Jeff with his own moleskin. Sitting comfortably, listening to the sound of pens on paper, Harper caught a whiff of something dead. Took him a second to realize it was coming from his own clothes. He recalled why, felt sick again. He looked at the inspector.

"Couldn't this wait till I get cleaned up?"

"It cannot. We're on something of a tight schedule."

"A schedule?"

Silence. Meaning: *Just sit there and wait to find out.*

Harper did . . . for twenty seconds. Shit.

"Whose place is this?"

The inspector looked up from the file.

"I beg your pardon?"

"Whose. Place. Is. This?"

The inspector didn't answer. He didn't have to. Just then an elderly gent in a rumpled tweed suit, briar pipe anchored between his teeth and leaving a trail of Bergerac tobacco smoke in his path, stepped through the open door. The gent looked familiar, like the file on the table. Ditto on that queasy feeling. For some reason, Harper looked at the man's shoes. Wingtips, scuffed, heel-worn. And at his well-worn heels came the three tramps who'd helped rescue Harper from the cavern. The elderly chap took the Chesterfield chair at the head of the table.

Harper noticed the tramps had swapped their submachine guns for more discreet lumps of heavy metal under their coats. They positioned themselves in a triangle around the elderly chap, each one standing with their hands belt-high, fingertips touching. Standard protocol for close protection. Made it easy to crouch into a firing stance, reach inside the coat to rip heavy metal from holsters and fill the room with lead, all within one-point-five seconds. At the same moment, Mutt, Jeff, and Sergeant Gauer closed their moleskins, slipped them into the pockets of their raincoats, and adopted the same stance.

Terrific, Harper thought. *Someone sneezes, everyone ends up dead.*

It was the elderly chap who broke the standoff.

"I hope you are feeling somewhat better, monsieur, after your ordeal in the cavern."

"Tip-top. Thanks for asking," Harper said. He turned to Inspector Gobet. "Who the hell is this?"

The inspector's tone was sharp: "Focus, Mr. Harper."

The elderly gent raised his hand to show no offense had been taken. *"Ça vous dérange si je lui pose quelques questions, Inspecteur?"*

The inspector nodded. *"Voluntiers."*

The elderly gent looked at Harper.

"I have been told by Inspector Gobet that if I speak my name to you, it will . . . *Comment dites-on, ça va provoquer une vision?"*

Harper looked at the inspector, caught the command: *Answer the bloody question, Mr. Harper.*

"An imagination in time," Harper said after long seconds.

"Oui, an imagination that carries you to the point in time where we met."

Harper scanned the gent's eyes, the eyes of the tramps. More than clean, they were human. He looked at the inspector again, this time wondering why the mechanics of imagination and flashing through

249

timelines were being revealed to *them*. The inspector glared: *Get on with it, Mr. Harper.*

Harper looked at the elderly gent.

"My name is Bruno Silvestre, special investigating judge for . . ."

Fragments of disordered time tumbled through Harper's eyes at the speed of light. The same elderly gent sitting at a desk in a sealed office, gold emblem on the wall. Scottish thistle, the words "Brigade Criminelle" curving above it. Got it.

"Bedroom slippers," Harper said.

"Pardonnez-moi?"

"You were wearing bedroom slippers when we first met. At the cop shop on Quai des Orfèvres, the night of the attack on Paris."

"Oui, c'est moi."

Harper leaned across the table.

"Then that makes you the fucking clown who sent me to La Santé Prison for enhanced interrogation, doesn't it?"

"Control yourself, Mr. Harper," the inspector said.

"That was done at the order of the French president," the judge said. "In fact, monsieur, I was doing all I could to help you and protect you from harm."

"Is that right?"

"Oui, monsieur."

"Well, cheers, gov, and fuck you very much."

"Mr. Harper!" the inspector said.

Harper kept at it. "You're the one they deleted from my timeline, but I know you're the fucker who planted the memory of a dead man in my head, aren't you?"

"C'est vrai, but—"

"Why? Why did you fucking do it?"

"Mr. Harper!"

"As I said, monsieur, it was the only way I could—"

Harper knocked aside a lamp, lunged at the judge. "Fucker!"

The tramps had their guns out and pointed at Harper. Only thing that kept lead from flying was Sergeant Gauer throwing a neck lock around Harper and pulling him back to his chair.

"Let go! Sod off, the lot of you!"

The inspector slammed his fist on the table: *bang.*

"Mr. Harper, that will be quite enough!"

The beveled glass doors of the bookcases rattled.

Quiet.

The inspector addressed Harper with the tone of a schoolmaster.

"Another outburst like that and I'll have you back in the tank so fast, you won't know up from down. And you can spend the rest of your days trying to claw your way out of your form, seeing as it worked so well for you the last time. Do you read me?"

Harper knew he was trapped in a bad joke, but he couldn't remember the bloody punch line. His eyes locked on the file on the table. The blue ribbon, the thin, yellowed paper with handwritten script. He flashed back to Brigade Criminelle, saw the judge reading from the same goddamn file: *Your name is Jay Michael Harper . . .* And he heard the dead man in his head: *Please, help me . . .* Then came a rush of icy panic.

"Oh fuck."

He backed away from the table, curled over, and vomited onto the carpet. He gasped, breathing the stench of death and vomit, retched again. He squeezed his arms against his sides to hold in his guts.

"Bloody hell."

"*Ici, monsieur.*"

It was Sergeant Gauer, portable oxygen tank and respirator in his hands.

"*Respirez quatre fois. Tu te sentiras mieux.*"

Harper wanted to tell him to bugger off, but there was a craving . . . a need for something, anything. He let Gauer set the respirator over his nose and mouth. He breathed four times, stared at patterns woven into the carpet. Seventeenth century, Ardistan from Kashkan province. *Strange,* he thought, *the things one flashes after two and a half million years of hiding among men.* Sergeant Gauer pulled away the respirator, handed a handkerchief to Harper. Harper took it, straightened up, wiped his face. Gauer dropped an upended wastebasket over the mess to kill the odor.

"Sorry about your carpet."

"It is not my carpet, monsieur. And this is not my place, monsieur," the judge said.

"Whose is it?"

"Christophe Astruc."

"Astruc."

"*Oui, monsieur.* This was his *cachette*, his hiding place for many years. We discovered it the night of the attack on Paris."

Harper scanned the bookcases. He didn't notice it coming in, but there were no books behind the beveled glass doors. Just files, like the one on the table. Thousands of them, all bound with blue ribbons.

"What the hell are these files?"

"The files are you, Mr. Harper," the inspector said. "Or rather, a search for you throughout history. Myths, legends, religious texts."

Harper pointed to the file on the table. "And that one?"

"This? This is the mother lode. Every apparition you have made for the last eight hundred years as compiled by one Christophe Astruc. It appears you were, for lack of a better phrase, his obsession."

Harper picked up something in the inspector's voice.

"What are you getting at, Inspector?"

"Mr. Harper, let me bring you up to speed. Monsieur Silvestre, the judge, is indeed a member of the French Police. He is also, secretly, the deputy leader of a partisan cell in support of our kind. A sleeper cell, as it were."

Harper looked at the judge, then the inspector. "So, the two of you are all old pals then."

"On the contrary, it was only since the Paris operation that I became aware of the judge, this cell, and the cavern."

Harper gave it five seconds.

"Bull. Every partisan cell in Europe is under your command."

"You may recall, Mr. Harper, I had no knowledge of the cavern beneath Lausanne Cathedral or what was down there until you found it and revealed it to us. Given your work in this case, I'd say you have a talent for such things."

Harper thought about it. Maybe he did have a talent for such things, just as the inspector had a talent for leading him down the garden path.

"Then how did you two meet?"

"When you did not emerge from the police cordon around the *Manon*, we assumed you had been arrested. Knowing you would never divulge your identity, I circulated an all-ports warning with the French Police for one Jay Harper, wanted on suspicion of felony burglary in Lausanne and suspected of hiding in Paris. If the APW wasn't answered, it would be logical to assume that you had gone to ground and were waiting for us to find you."

"But if someone responded?"

The inspector nodded. "I would know you were being held by some-one who not only knew who you were, but what you were. This was confirmed two days later when I was contacted by the judge. He was most forthcoming with your situation and offered guidance as to how we might accelerate the glacial process that is the French judicial sys-tem. Most helpfully, he provided us with the exact coordinates of where you were being held within the two-meter thick walls of La Santé Prison, making it possible for us to pull you out with just enough time left over for a cleanup crew to lay down the trail of rather mysterious escape. Well, you know how things are in police work; interesting cases are discussed, information is exchanged. In particular, the judge asked if I could offer assistance in checking out someone who had been spotted prowling around the tunnels and quarries under Paris, asking questions of cataphiles."

"Him . . . the priest, Astruc."

The inspector considered Harper's words.

"How did you know he was a priest?"

"He told me. No, I figured it out, after the cover you fed him blew up in my face."

"Your cover?"

"You told him I was a priest, associated with—"

"The Vatican?" the judge said.

Harper stared at the two of them.

"That's right. You built me up as being the personal representative of the Pope to investigate the cavern and to protect Gilles Lambert from evil. Tall order, gents, especially when the target was a priest in the first place. He saw me coming from a mile off."

The inspector shifted uncomfortably in his chair.

"In fact, your cover was that you were a professor of ancient languages from Lausanne University, nothing more."

"Sorry?"

The judge turned to one of the tramps. *"Le photo, s'il vous plaît."*

The tramp reached into his jacket, pulled out a three-by-five photo, handed it over. The judge lay it on the table. Harper looked at it. Group shot. Young men in two rows, standing in St. Peter's Square, all of them wearing black and white robes. A yellow circle had been drawn around one of the men in the back row.

"Who's this?" Harper said.

"Father Christophe Astruc, OP. On the day of his ordination at the age of twenty-four."

Harper looked at the photo again. The highlighted priest was tall. He was also blond, freshly scrubbed, and skinny.

"When was this taken?"

"Thirty-seven years ago. Is this the man you met at Saint-Germain-des-Prés?"

Harper gave the photo one more scan.

"Maybe, maybe not. The man I met was muscular, his face looked like it'd been through a meat grinder. And he couldn't be more than midforties. If you've got your dates right, Father Astruc would be in his sixties."

"Did you see a cross?"

"A cross?"

"Of any kind?"

Harper flashed through the night.

"No, but I wouldn't have expected to."

"Why not?"

"Because the priest I met had a bloody machine gun. And he handled it like someone who had knowledge of weapons and tactics. And I watched him kill an innocent man."

"But he told you his name was Astruc, and that he was a priest."

"He admitted it when I called him on it."

"Could he have been pretending to be a priest?" the judge said.

Harper flashed Astruc reciting the Our Father in French.

"No, he was telling me the truth."

"And you know this because?"

"Because I heard it in the sound of his voice."

"Pardon?"

"It's the way we do things, gov, like imagining our way through time."

The judge pointed to the photograph.

"This is the only surviving picture of Christophe Astruc. We know he was an orphan, raised by the Catholic Church, and later ordained into the Dominican Order. He was considered brilliant, and something of a protégé in the field of apocalyptic studies."

"End-times, you mean. Armageddon and the like."

"Non. His work was closer to the true definition of the word *apocalypsis."*

Harper ran the word: Greek, root words *apo* and *kalyptein.* Meaning: to uncover something that is hidden. Harper wondered if now would be a good time to mention the something hidden Father Astruc—or whoever the fuck he was—had uncovered in the cavern two hundred plus meters below Paris. *Not yet, boyo.*

"And?"

"Given his specialty, Father Astruc was assigned a research position within the Congregation for the Doctrine of the Faith at the Vatican."

"Hang on, Astruc told Lambert I did the same damn thing."

"Are you familiar with this office, monsieur?" the judge said.

Harper scanned the History Channel. Landed on an episode called *Inside the Vatican.*

"Enough to know it's responsible for safeguarding the faith and morals of the Church and that it reports directly to the Pope. Had a rough go of it lately when it was discovered the same office responsible for Catholic morality was covering up the sexual abuse of children by priests. Has something of an even worse past, though. It was first known as the Office of the Holy Inquisition. Famous for burning witches and heretics at the stake in the sixteenth century, but its work actually began in the mid-thirteenth century with the extinction of the Cathars of southern France."

The judge bowed his head a moment, his lips trembling. If Harper didn't know better he'd say the man was praying.

"Indeed, monsieur. It is one of the darkest passages in the history of the Catholic Church. More than five hundred thousand human beings were slaughtered in the most horrific and unimaginable ways, all in the name of Christ."

Harper stared at him, seeing the mournful look in the gent's eyes. Words ran through Harper's brain: *Oh, ever thus, from childhood's hour.* He wondered where he'd heard the line. No idea.

"What was Astruc doing for the Church, the last you know?" he said.

"He had been asked to research those events in preparation of a Statement of Responsibility to be delivered during the millennium year by Pope John Paul II. It was the wish of the Pope to ask forgiveness for the millions of innocents who suffered and died at the hands of the Church. He was given complete access to the Vatican Library as well as the *Archivum Secretum Vaticanum*, the private archives of the popes. His research led him to the Archdiocese of Toulouse, the seat of the Inquisition. He made many trips there, from his days as a seminarian."

Harper added it up.

"He was feeding me his own history. Why the hell would he do that?"

"Why, indeed," Inspector Gobet said.

Harper stared at the inspector, waiting for an answer. It didn't come.

"So what happened to him?"

"He was defrocked by Pope John Paul II sixteen years ago."

"Why?"

"Murder."

Harper thought about it.

"That's some career change. Why the hell is he still on the streets?"

The judge picked up the story.

"When the Toulouse police went to arrest Father Astruc, he had already disappeared. Two and a half years later, a man described as very large with wounds on his face and calling himself Father Christophe Astruc arrived at an orphanage outside Toulouse. He demanded that a certain twelve-year-old boy be released to him, as if the boy were a prisoner. When the staff refused, the man pulled a pistol and proceeded to kidnap the boy. There were no security cameras to record the kidnapping, and the police assumed the discrepancy in descriptions of the kidnapper to be related to the stress of the moment. It was also noted by the staff that the boy did not resist being taken and acted as if he recognized the man. He was heard addressing the man as 'Father.'"

Harper flashed the kid with Astruc.

"What did he look like, the one Astruc kidnapped?" Harper said.

There was a moment of silence.

"Why do you ask, Mr. Harper?"

"Because the Astruc I met at Saint-Germain-des-Prés had someone with him. Someone who'd match the timeline you laid out."

More silence.

Harper looked at the judge. "You telling me your boys didn't see the kid with Astruc?"

The judge ignored the question.

"What was the name of the boy with Astruc?" the inspector said.

"Goose."

"Describe him, Mr. Harper."

"Not tall, just over five feet. Light build. Astruc said the kid was twenty-six, but he could pass for much younger. Suffers from a form of paedomorphia. His head's too small for his body and neck, and it's misshapen. Small ears pinned back to the side of his head. Presents himself as deaf, but he hears well enough. He communicates through sign language. He's got an IQ of over two hundred according to Astruc. I tend to believe it. He's fanatically devoted to Astruc."

The inspector and the judge stared at him.

"I get something wrong, gents?" Harper said.

"The boy you have described is George Muret," the judge said.

Harper gave it five.

"If we're talking about the same kid, Astruc called him 'Goose.'"

The judge turned to the tramp standing behind him. The tramp handed over another photo, it ended up in front of Harper. Black-and-white shot of a small boy sitting on a man's lap. The man had cruel and bitter eyes; the misshapen boy on the man's lap was Goose at two or three years old. Like looking at an antique photograph of a ventriloquist holding a grotesque dummy.

"That's him. That's the kid," Harper said.

"Are you absolutely sure, Mr. Harper?"

Harper looked at the inspector.

"Yes. I'm sure."

"Did you get a read of his eyes?"

"No, there's a milky haze over his irises. I assumed it to be some sort of masking drug."

"Anything else that impressed you?"

Harper flashed back to the kid in the doorway next to Les Deux Magots.

"He knows how to hide in shadows, as well as you or me. But looking the way he does, I'm not surprised."

"Please explain your reasoning."

"What's to explain? The kid was tormented as a freak his entire life. Probably ran for every shadow he could find to avoid being seen."

"How do you know that?"

"Know what?"

"That he was tormented as a child."

"The priest, Astruc, he told me. At Les Deux Magots, before we went down into the tunnels."

Harper's explanation was greeted with silence. He looked at the photograph of Goose and the man again. Father and son, had to be. And in the father's cruel and bitter eyes, Harper saw one part undiluted hate, one part face-slapping truth. He looked up from the photograph, stared at the judge.

"This is Goose's father. He's the man Astruc killed, yeah?"

The judge nodded.

"What happened?"

The judge took a long puff from his pipe.

"George Muret was born in Toulouse. His mother died at birth. He appeared normal at first, but within the first three months it was obvious the boy was suffering, as you say, from a form of paedomorphosis. As he grew, his deformity became more pronounced and it was discovered he was deaf. Though in some unknown way, he displayed an ability to *feel* the meaning of words and sounds, as if hearing them. This ability was regarded as one more example of the boy's . . . strangeness."

Harper thought about it. Forget an IQ of over two hundred; how about completely off the bloody chart?

"What else to you know?"

The boy's father, Monsieur Pierre Muret, was a drunkard and suspected of sexually abusing his son. After spotting repeated bruising on the boy's arms and legs, a local doctor reported the situation to the police. The police investigated and, upon seeing the boy, were quick to accept Monsieur Muret's explanation that his son was clumsy and an idiot. Attitudes being what they were in that day, the matter was dropped. The boy was rarely allowed outside and had no real social interaction, but by order of the local council, he was enrolled in a school for the deaf near Toulouse Cathedral. The school was run by Dominican nuns. Father Astruc served as chaplain there and said Mass every Friday afternoon. It was at the school that Father Astruc met the boy and took an interest in him. He found the boy to be extremely bright and began to tutor him privately. Within months, the boy was reading with adult comprehension. He also demonstrated proficiency in math and languages, mastering calculus, German, and English by the age of nine. By now, Monsieur Muret was suffering from alcohol-induced paranoia.

Seeing such remarkable progress in his son, the man became unhinged. He was known to tell his neighbors that his boy was possessed by the devil, speaking in tongues. He withdrew him from the school. One night, while in a blind rage, Monsieur Muret attacked his son and pulled the boy's tongue from his mouth with a pair of pliers and cut it off with a carving knife. Monsieur Muret was found walking the streets with the boy's tongue in his hands, calling it the sign of the devil."

Harper filled in the rest. "Astruc finds out about it, kills the father, disappears. Shows up six months later—or someone calling himself Astruc shows up—kidnaps the boy."

The judge nodded.

Harper looked at Inspector Gobet.

"Interesting tale. But you still haven't explained how Astruc went from wholesome priest to the bruiser, whiskey-swilling fanatic I had the pleasure of meeting at bloody Saint-Germain-des-Prés."

The more Harper thought about it, the more interesting it got.

"And come to think of it, you have yet to ask me about what happened in the cavern, or what Astruc found down there."

Harper scanned the room. All eyes on him.

"Let me guess: You already know."

The inspector nodded.

Harper wanted to rub the back of his neck, gave it a pass with his hands in bandages.

"So what the hell are we doing here? What's the purpose of this debrief? As you already know what there is to know."

The judge leaned forward "Are you familiar, in any way, with Bernard de Saint-Martin?"

Harper ran the name. "Doesn't ring a bell."

"Are you sure of that, Mr. Harper?" the inspector said.

Second time the inspector has gone for the "Are you sure?" line in the name game, Harper thought.

"Bernard de Saint-Martin? Hard one to forget, even for the likes of me. Who is he?"

"He is the leader of this cell," the judge said.

"He gives you your orders, then?"

"Oui, monsieur."

Harper looked at the two of them. They'd morphed into police asking questions they already knew the answers to. Harper felt like he'd escaped from one trap, only to find himself being dumped into another.

"So where the hell is he? I'd like to meet him, ask him a few questions. Maybe he can enlighten me as to what the hell this is about. Because I'm telling you, at this rate, my manner of thinking is never going to find its way to whatever timeline it is you two are parked in."

The inspector and judge didn't respond.

"So, gentlemen, is Bernard de Saint-Martin making the bloody scene or not?"

The judge folded his hands, his index fingers touching and pointing up like the steeple of a very small church.

"Monsieur, when I say de Saint-Martin is the leader of this cell, I mean to say we are the latest disciples to carry out the mission laid out by him when he founded this cell nearly nine hundred years ago."

"Sorry?"

"Bernard de Saint-Martin appeared in Paris as a homeless beggar at the steps of l'Église de Saint-Germain-des-Prés in the year 1244. It was there that he revealed himself to the first disciples. He showed them the entrance to the cavern and told them the secrets of what had happened at this place in the beginning. He showed them a reliquary box and the ancient sextant inside. He told them it was a sacred treasure from the East, and that he would hide it in the cavern. He charged his disciples to assure the box be kept from the eyes of men, down through the generations, until he returned and was revealed to the world."

Bloody hell, Harper thought. He looked at Inspector Gobet. Not a hint of surprise. Harper turned to the judge.

"You know, human history is chockablock with legends and myths, gov. What's to say this isn't one more?"

"There have only been a handful of disciples at any one time, monsieur. Precisely to prevent the truth from becoming legend. And, of course, there is the undeniable fact that deep beneath l'Église Saint-Germain-des-Prés is the cavern."

There was that.

"All right. But I still don't get how I'm supposed to know him. Where's the connection?"

"That's what we are trying to determine," the inspector said.

Harper shot a look at him. "What's to determine? If I had come across him at any point in time, I'd see him when you said his name to me. That's the way it works for our kind."

Inspector Gobet looked down at the file, his thick fingers peeling through the pages in delicate moves: *shhhwip, shhhhwip.* He removed a photograph and laid it on the table for Harper to see. It was the photo of a winged form dropping through the backlit fog that had enveloped Pont des Arts.

"Mr. Harper, the man you met who claims to be Father Christophe Astruc took this photograph and put it on the Internet."

"How did you find that one out?"

"A tip was left with the judge's office regarding this address. Upon arriving, the judge's men found a video camera connected to a desktop computer. The still grab of you jumping from Pont des Arts had been uploaded onto the Internet not ten minutes earlier. Next to the computer was this particular file, the one the judge read to you when you were arrested."

Harper looked at the judge.

"The tip came from Astruc. He wanted you to find this place. He wanted you to know what I am?"

The judge shrugged. "I believe there is more to it."

"Such as?"

The inspector took over: "Such as the attack on Paris being engineered by Father Astruc in an attempt to confirm your identity."

"You're bloody joking."

The expression on the inspector's face said he was not joking.

"Our advance intel on the attack, including the last-minute shift of ground zero from Saint-Sulpice to the river Seine, was picked up in pieces. Pieces embedded in hundreds of messages left on certain chat rooms known to be used by the enemy. SX analysis confirms the computer found in this library was the source."

Harper thought about it. "Astruc chatted about the cavern online, what was down there. He picked up followers, the enemy. By tracking the followers, he hacked into the enemy grid and learned about their plans to attack Paris."

"That seems to be the timeline of events."

"So how did we get ahold of attack plans?"

"Father Astruc e-mailed them, anonymously, to my office in Berne. He was kind enough to include a link to an encrypted website where I was invited to log on for updates."

"You couldn't track him, find out where he was working from?"

The inspector smiled, approving of the manner of Harper's thinking . . . for the moment.

"SX discovered the site was protected by a unique intrusion detection program. Any attempt at tracking the transmission point would cause the site to disappear. We would be in the dark. Our first priority was to assure we were in the loop to intercept enemy operations. Indeed, it was by monitoring Father Astruc's site that we learned of the last-minute change of target zone."

Harper shook his head.

"Christ, the bloody priest really is insane."

"Why do you say that, Mr. Harper?"

"Tens of thousands would've died that night, millions more for the next thousand years. Adds up to barking in the first degree."

The inspector turned back through the pages of the file. He stopped, looked at one page. Harper could see it. It was a piece of old parchment, looked like a medieval drawing. The inspector held it delicately and laid it on the table.

"In fact, Mr. Harper, it would seem that in suspecting what you are, Father Astruc had the utmost confidence that you would manage to save the day."

Harper looked at the drawing. An angel descending from the heavens and through the clouds, basking in a celestial light. Below him a river in flames; above him, amid the stars, a comet streaking through the sky. He looked closer. Sword in his right hand, raised to strike. Half-hidden by the curl of a wing, the angel's left arm braced against his chest, holding the same damn reliquary box Harper had seen in the cavern. The lid was open; inside was the sextant.

"What the hell is this?" Harper said.

"It was drawn by one of Bernard de Saint-Martin's first disciples, a monk working in the scriptorium of the Abbey at Saint-Germain-des-Prés. It refers to a future event that the descendants of this cell were instructed to watch for: specifically, the reincarnation of Bernard de Saint-Martin in the form of an angel, who would save Paris from destruction."

Harper's eyes darted between the photo and the drawing. The similarity between the images was enough to make any set of eyes look twice. Harper gave it three.

"You're not actually suggesting this is me."

"Why not?" the inspector said.

"For starters, there's no way Astruc could know I'd end up jumping from Pont des Arts."

"Why not?"

"We flash back through time, not into the future."

"Because?"

"What do you mean, 'because'? Because the bloody future hasn't happened yet."

"That would leave coincidence."

"No such bloody thing. So what are you getting at?"

"Some rather curious intersecting lines of causality."

"What lines?"

"The counterattack tactical sent to you in Paris wasn't ours."

Harper added it up. Astruc cracked the enemy's computer grid, downloaded the attack profile, knew the attack would shift from Saint-

Sulpice to the river Seine. Left disclosing that bit of news to the last minute, so there'd be no choice but to jump onto the *Manon*.

"Astruc sent you the counterattack plan when he told you the target had shifted; you sent it to me."

"Oddly enough, it was the most logical of options. It also made it possible for Father Astruc to confirm the connection between you and Bernard de Saint-Martin."

"You're talking nonsense, inspector."

The inspector shoved the drawing closer to Harper. Harper gave the drawing another go.

Angel with sword. Burning river. Reliquary box and sextant. Comet amid the stars . . . streaks of fire in the comet's tail forming these words across the sky:

C'est le guet. Il a sonné l'heure.

He flashed back to Astruc lifting the ancient sextant from the box: *It was you who brought this sacred treasure to his place* . . . Harper blinked back to nowtimes. The tramps, Mutt and Jeff, Sergeant Gauer, the inspector and the judge: all eyes on him again.

He stared at Inspector Gobet. "'The chosen of the fallen ones.'"

"I beg your pardon?"

"Words carved into the tablet in the cavern. That's the only one who could open the pillar."

"Quite."

"And you're telling me I'm him?"

The inspector glanced around the room, pointed to the bookcases.

"We've only had sixty-seven hours to go through these files. But we've covered a lot of ground while waiting for you to emerge from the tunnels. From what we've managed to put together, you made an unauthorized apparition in the form of a beggar calling himself Bernard de Saint-Martin in 1244. And that you spent forty days in Paris, forming a cell and engaging in the events as described by the judge."

Harper thought about it.

"Our kind don't make unauthorized apparitions."

"No, we don't. HQ lists you as in stasis for most of the thirteenth century."

"Well?"

"I'm afraid, at present, I have no comment on the matter."

Meaning the cop in the cashmere coat knew the skinny, but wasn't saying. Harper looked at the judge.

"Who was he, this de Saint-Martin?"

"A knight from Languedoc, listed in the rolls of the Inquisition as burned as a heretic with the last of the Cathars at Montségur in March of 1244."

"Burned. As a heretic. At Montségur."

The judge nodded.

"Any witnesses?"

"Ten thousand of them, monsieur, not including the Archbishop of Toulouse and his entourage."

Harper smiled, shook his head.

"I really hate to rain on your parade, gov, but when we die in our forms, we're dead forever. We're not like you, we don't come back. When it ends for us, it bloody ends."

"Inspector Gobet has explained this to me. The inspector has also explained that, presently, you are suffering, as it were, from a certain condition that causes you to . . . not die in your form."

A wave of nausea burned through Harper's form, and he tasted bile in his throat. *Non mortem timemus, sed cogitationem mortis . . . We fear not death, but the thinking of it.* No idea who said the words, Harper thought, but they were bloody appropriate just now.

"Till quantum mechanics kicks in."

"Monsieur?"

Harper looked at the judge. "Punch line of a bad joke, gov. I just got it."

The judge bowed his head, his lips trembling again. He *was* praying, Harper realized. Silently, profoundly. When he finished, he said, "Monsieur, you are the chosen one of the fallen. You are the reincarnation of Bernard de Saint-Martin."

Harper read the judge's eyes, seeing the man believed his words to be holy truth. Harper felt another blast of nausea, and he rested his head in his hands. He saw the signet ring on the little finger of the judge's left hand. He flashed back to the night he met the judge at Brigade Crimi-nelle, seeing the same ring; this time, Harper could make out the insig-nia. A conical pillar pointing to a comet. Harper raised his head, looked at Inspector Gobet.

"Right. Any more surprises?"

FIFTEEN

TGV 9261, Paris to Lausanne: 07:44 hours.

COACH 17, LIKE THE REST OF THE TRAIN, WAS PACKED.
Harper sat next to a snoring Chinese gentleman who was busily sleeping off the Kung Pao Chicken takeout he'd carried on board and devoured within minutes of leaving Paris. No worries. Kept him from bumping into Harper's slinged-up arm. Across the table was a retired American couple from Boston, Massachusetts.

Taking a grand tour of the continent, the wife said. They'd done Paris and were now on their way to do Florence, then Venice. On the way they thought they'd take the waters at Leukerbad in the Alps. They'd be staying at l'Hôtel de la Source. Five stars, of course. Harper heard all about it after he'd made the mistake of saying yes when asked by the woman, "Would you happen to speak English?" The woman hadn't stopped talking since, often returning to the subject of Harper's unfortunate accident in Paris. ("Hit by a tour bus on the Champs-Élysées," Harper had told her.) And each time she returned to the subject, she was reminded of yet another relative or friend dispatched in similar fashion.

"I remember my aunt Dahlia. Charming woman, though somewhat

forgetful. She was walking across Madison Avenue in New York, when suddenly, last summer . . ."

Nice thing about a one-sided conversation, Harper thought, *one doesn't have to pay much attention.* And serious one-siders, of which the American woman was Olympic-class, didn't require any attention at all. Gave Harper an opportunity to take in the English-language newspapers behind which her husband hid. All the papers carried the same picture on the front page: a comet hanging in the night sky above Paris.

Herald Tribune: "Unknown Visitor Crosses Earth's Orbit"

The Guardian: "Celestial Wonder Over Europe"

Daily Mail: "What the Hell Was That?!"

Of the three, Harper thought the *Daily Mail* put it best. Fact was, the comet had come and gone in a most uncometlike fashion. He'd seen that one with his own eyes, back in Astruc's library on Rue Visconti. On top of it, rather. Just after he looked at Inspector Gobet and said, "Right. Any more surprises?"

That's when a section of the built-in bookcases creaked open and from behind it stepped a woman in black leather clothing and boots. Took Harper half a second to clock her as Corporal Mai from the vineyards in Grandvaux. She'd swapped her Swiss Guard camouflage for heavy metal biker gear. She wore it like she was born in it. Her jacket was open and there was a Heckler & Koch MP-5 slung from her neck. Meaning Corporal Mai was as comfortable with an up-close contact kill as she was with the long-range sniper variety. She glanced at Harper, and he almost smiled as he recognized the genetic trait of her half-breed eyes.

"*C'est l'heure moins quinze minutes, Inspecteur.*"

The inspector checked his watch, looked at the judge. The elderly gent was repacking his pipe with tobacco.

"Thank you, Corporal Mai. We need one minute."

"*Oui, Inspecteur.*"

The judge was packing his pipe with Bergerac tobacco, and when finished, he patted his pocket for a light. Inspector Gobet already had a match at the ready.

"My dear judge, allow me," the inspector said.

The judge drew the fire to his pipe.

As Harper watched the judge disappear into another cloud of head-swallowing smoke, he flashed through his timeline. All the times Inspector Gobet offered a light for one of his own fags, Harper had yet to see the Swiss copper light a bloody match. The fire was just always there, at the ready. *Our kind survive in a world of dual, and sometimes opposing, realities,* Harper thought, *the line between them often blurred.* And for a second Harper wondered which part of his own dual reality noticed the inspector's trick with the match. Was it that eternal being from another place, *knowing* all physical matter could be manipulated by a mastery of gravity? Or was the dead man in his head, Captain Jay Michael Harper, manipulating his imagination to *see* the world for what it truly was? *Doesn't matter a tinker's damn,* Harper thought, or Captain Jay Michael Harper thought, or maybe even Bernard de fucking Saint-Martin thought. The magically appearing flame was a swell trick.

The judge's head reappeared from the smoke.

"Thank you, Inspector. Shall we adjourn to the roof?" he said.

The two gents pushed away from the table and made a move for the exit. Harper didn't get up.

"Wait, are we done here?"

The inspector turned back, raised an eyebrow.

"Not in the least, Mr. Harper. But as I explained earlier, we're on something of a schedule this evening. We'll continue with the debrief later."

Harper stood, stepped toward him.

"Not bloody good enough, sir."

Mutt and Jeff jumped, grabbed Harper's shoulders at the brachial plexus, and squeezed. Harper froze, unable to move. The inspector coughed.

"Mr. Harper, we may be dealing with one more legend of our kind, or we may have been handed the key to all there is to know about our being here. I, for one, should like to know which it is. Come along, and do try to make yourself genuinely useful if called upon to do so."

The inspector turned and walked away. Mutt and Jeff released Harper and walked after the inspector, the two of them looking back at Sergeant Gauer.

"Grab his shit and bring him along."

"And keep an eye on him. He's the sort that'd get himself lost in a paper bag."

Sergeant Gauer dropped the respirator tank into a backpack, tossed it over his shoulder. He picked up Harper's sports coat and overcoat, tossed them over his left forearm. He pointed to the passage behind the bookcase.

"Let's go."

"So what are you, now, my guardian angel?"

"At the moment, I'm your fucking butler. Move it, *s'il vous plaît*."

Five floors up a creaky wooden stairwell and they were on the roof. It was one story higher than the surrounding buildings, and with a one-meter-tall hedge along the roof's perimeter they were hidden from the surrounding locals. Harper saw the Eiffel Tower above the rooftops to the southwest, just as it began to glitter madly with a billion flickering lights. Maybe not that many, but no matter, he thought. The flickering lights made it the top of whichever hour it was.

Three men on the roof already.

Harper made two of them as Inspector Gobet's boys. They had that too-smart-for-the-real-world look, and they wore the uniform. Black-framed eyeglasses, black suits, white shirts, skinny black ties under black overcoats. Same as the light mechanic who fitted Lausanne's old town with Arc 9 filters; the chap with a fascination for the terminal velocity of falling cats. These boys, the ones on the roof, sat at a makeshift table, banging away at Crypto Field Terminals. For a sec, Harper wondered how he knew what the machines were called. Wondered again how he knew they were top-secret, magnesium-shelled laptops for spooks. The dead British soldier in his head must have used them in Afghanistan, he thought.

The terminals were connected to four twenty-seven-inch monitors displaying numbers, graphs, elliptical patterns overlaying elliptical patterns, and a shitload of chemical analysis data. No clue what the information meant. Next to the table were two parabolic antennae units pointing to the southwest sky, right over the top of the Eiffel Tower. The dead soldier in Harper's head identified the gear as AEHF; Advanced Extremely High Frequency satellite uplinks and downlinks. Meaning whatever Inspector Gobet's computer geeks were up to, it couldn't be tracked, hacked, or jammed.

A third man stood behind the computer geeks. Midthirties, clean-shaven mug. He wore a Barbour coat over a cable-knit sweater and corduroy trousers; there was a pair of Steiner 10x50 binoculars hanging from his neck. He was bouncing on his heels, brown eyes wide, brown hair standing at perpendicular angles from his head. No way this chap was one of the inspector's boys, Harper told himself. This chap was jazzed to the gills. Like a plane spotter just receiving word Amelia Earhart's Lockheed Electra had been spotted after eighty years and was making its final approach at Le Bourget. Not even noticing the crowd of suits, muscle, and guns coming onto the roof to gather behind him. The man in the Barbour coat kept his eyes locked on the monitors, gasping at regular intervals, "Holy crap, holy fucking crap." His accent was British.

Harper checked the sky as the billion blinking lights on the Eiffel Tower switched off, meaning it was now five minutes after whichever hour it was. No sign of Amelia. Looked like the sky on any night, minus one moon. Given the light pollution of central Paris, it was a night sky minus most of the stars. The judge tapped the giddy man in the Barbour jacket on the shoulder. He turned around, shook his head with disbelief.

"I mean . . . holy fucking shit. How did you know this would happen?"

The judge took his pipe from his mouth.

"Know what, exactly, young man?"

The man pointed to the monitors. "That! If this is real and not a hoax, then we're on the verge of a celestial event of unimaginable proportions."

Inspector Gobet joined in the conversation. "May I ask why?"

The man looked at the cop in the cashmere coat.

"Who are you?"

"I am Inspector Jacques Gobet of the Swiss Police. I have provided the technical equipment and support staff for tonight's operation."

"You? You're the one hacking into Blue Brain?"

"My dear fellow . . . By the way, what is your name?"

"Leo."

"Leo what?"

"Mates, Dr. Leo Mates. But you can call me Leo."

"Unfortunately, my position requires me to keep things on a more formal level, Dr. Mates. But let me assure you, everything being done here is completely aboveboard. No one is hacking into Blue Brain. We are merely monitoring the activity of two individuals who are."

"Who are they?"

"Why do you ask?"

"Because they're brilliant, whoever they are."

"I'm afraid information as to their identities is classified. Suffice it to say, you are participating in a joint police operation between Brigade Criminelle of France and the Special Unit Task Force of the Swiss Police."

Given his clothes still reeked of death and vomit, Harper kept himself well in the shadows and downwind of the conversing men, but he could hear their words. As usual, when the cop in the cashmere coat was speaking, most of the words didn't make sense. Adding the pipe-puffing judge into the equation yielded a quotient of confusion-squared. Harper looked back at Sergeant Gauer.

"The inspector is talking about Astruc and the kid. They're the hackers, yeah?"

"Good guess."

Harper thought about it.

"So what the hell is Blue Brain?"

"Supercomputer at EPFL."

"The research center outside Lausanne."

273

"Affirmative."

"What's it used for?"

"Mapping a single synapse of the human brain. Something along the lines of mapping the human genome, only a billion times more complicated."

"One of the inspector's toys, is it?"

"Do pigs fly?"

"In the inspector's case, all the time."

"*Et voilà.*"

Harper thought about it some more.

"Sorry, but what does mapping the human synapse have to do with Paris?"

Sergeant Gauer looked at Harper.

"*Je ne sais pas.* I've been underground for three fucking days trying to dig out your sorry arse, haven't I?"

Harper returned his attention to the conversation on the other side of the roof where Dr. Leo Mates was laying out his CV for the benefit of Inspector Gobet. Astrophysicist from Oxford with three PhD's under his belt. Has his own television program on the BBC explaining the wonders of the universe to the great unwashed. World's leading expert on the composition of ice crystals in the Oort cloud (a theoretical spherical body parked a light-year from the sun, he explained; to which the inspector replied, "Fascinating"). In town to read his latest scientific paper at l'Académie des sciences tomorrow evening (revealing new mathematical models to prove beyond a doubt that the oceans of planet Earth were formed by a bombardment of frozen water comets and asteroids 4.5 billion years ago; to which the inspector replied, "Most impressive"). Arriving at Gare du Nord this evening, he was stopped by members of the French Police and advised his presence was requested by one Monsieur Bruno Silvestre, special investigating judge of Brigade Criminelle, to consult on a matter of great urgency. That being a comet that would appear in the constellation Draco at 03:05:00 hours for a period of sixty seconds exactly. Dr. Mates did have plans to have an early dinner with friends and then retire to his hotel, but considering he was presented with this predictive information at 19:15:17 hours, the eminent astrophysicist was intrigued. He'd spent all night on the roof with Inspector Gobet's computer geeks, taking in the numbers and graphs and ellipses and chemical analysis data. He'd worked himself into such a state, he made a kid waiting for Christmas look bored. Which explained the wild hair, Harper thought, watching Dr. Mates pull at it with disbelief.

"I mean holy crap!"

Raised a question in Harper's head: Why was Leo the Astrophysicist being let into a world locals were never meant to know of? Just then one of the geeks at the Crypto Field Terminals spoke up.

"*Pardonnez-moi, Inspecteur.* According to the data, we will have visibility emanating from constellation Ursa Major in three minutes, thirty seconds."

"*Merci,*" the inspector replied, continuing his conversation with Dr. Mates. "So, in fact, would you describe what we are about to witness as a comet?"

"If you're asking me if the data says that what's supposed to appear is made of ice and has a cone-shaped tail, then yes, it's a comet. But it isn't possible."

"For what reason?"

Dr. Mates pointed to the sky.

"Comets don't appear from thin air, they come from somewhere. I don't understand how the science community couldn't have picked this up, not with the array of radio telescopes we have around the world."

"Perhaps," the judge said, "no one had their telescope pointed in the right direction. And if I am not incorrect, the annual Draconid meteor shower has been known to offer a surprise now and again. Perhaps this is just a stray meteor."

Dr. Mates shook his head.

"No, no. The Draconids aren't due to begin for another two days. Besides, Earth is passing through the tail end of the Draconids this year. There'll be twenty sightings per minute tops, nothing special. And you're wrong about the telescopes. We've got the entire deep space

VLA grid in New Mexico pointed toward Draco right now, looking at a white dwarf binary called KL."

"A white what?" asked the inspector.

Dr. Mates waved his hand dismissively.

"It's very complicated stuff for laymen. Point is, it's impossible one of those telescopes wouldn't have picked up this kind of activity. It's just impossible."

The judge puffed at his pipe a moment.

"As you continually remind us, Doctor," he said. "But you must agree, a meteor shower is not like a Swiss watch."

The inspector enjoyed that line and chortled his approval. "I should say not."

Dr. Mates stared at the policeman with disbelief.

"For heaven's sake, the Draconids aren't the point!"

"No? Then what is the point?"

"Look, the Draconids are made up of Giacobini-Zinner."

There was a pause for Dr. Mates to consider no one knew what he was talking about, or at least pretended not to know. Harper would lay odds on the latter. He knew it to be a sure bet when he caught the tone in the inspector's next line.

"Could you elaborate, please, Dr. Mates? After all, I'm only a lowly Swiss policeman involved in a criminal investigation."

"Okay. Let me try to explain it. Giacobini-Zinner is the parental comet of the Draconids. But I'm telling you, the Draconids and *this* aren't connected."

"Again, why not?"

Dr. Mates pointed to the monitors. "For one, the data says this is a different comet from a different part of the galaxy. Two, it just can't happen. It's impossible."

The two police considered the doctor's argument with blank expressions.

"Nevertheless, the Draconids meteor shower is imminent," the judge said after four-point-two seconds.

"So fucking what?"

The inspector smiled.

"In police work, Dr. Mates, we never say 'so fucking what?' to the facts."

"No disrespect, gentlemen, but the fact is you keep missing the point. This comet has fuck-all to do with Giacobini-Zinner, or the Draconids."

"Are you quite sure?" the inspector said.

Dr. Mates pulled at his hair.

"Look, try and keep up with me on this. There are four thousand, one hundred, eighty-five known comets on record. Some of them are short-period comets, some are long-period; I'm talking about their orbits. All those have been recorded through history and are predictable. Giacobini-Zinner is one of those, so is Halley's Comet. Then there are single apparition comets, such as Caesar's Comet in 44 BC or Hale-Bopp in 1995. All recorded comets, whether predicted or single apparitions, were visible for days, weeks, months even. Hale-Bopp was visible to the naked eye for eighteen months. And all those comets appeared in graduating stages of luminance to a peak magnitude, then faded away."

"Again, your point?" the inspector said.

"The data being analyzed by Blue Brain says this never-before-known comet will suddenly appear for sixty seconds at a magnitude of negative seven-point-five. That makes it one of the brightest comets ever, one of the brightest things in the entire night sky, from nowhere? I'm telling you, it's impossible."

"But if I understand you correctly, unknown comets do appear now and again. Single apparitions, as you say."

"Appear, yes; predicting it will appear, absolutely not. No one can predict a single apparition comet. We learn about them as they are observed, not before. You want facts, I'll give you one: Astronomy is science. We don't pull bunnies from hats."

The policeman paused. He and the judge looked at each other to further consider the evidence. The judge spoke with his pipe clenched between his teeth.

"So what you're confirming to us is that what we are about to see is a comet, possibly emanating in the constellation Draco."

Dr. Mates couldn't believe what he was hearing. If his jaw stretched open any farther, it would have fallen from his face.

"Excuse me?"

The judge shrugged. "I said, you are telling us that we will be viewing—"

The astrophysicist was fit to burst.

"I'm not telling you that! No way am I telling you that!"

The inspector sighed with frustration. "Oh goodness gracious, Dr. Mates, what are you telling us, then?"

Harper wanted to laugh. They were beating up on Leo the Astrophysicist pretty good. It was taking effect. Dr. Mates was rattled.

"Look! Someone is predicting a never-before-seen celestial event, unlike anything that has ever happened in recorded history! Someone has discovered something that looks like a comet but is something completely . . ."

The policeman leaned toward Dr. Mates, awaiting the completion of his thought. When it wasn't forthcoming, the inspector leaned even farther. "You were saying, Dr. Mates?"

". . . different."

Just then, light flickered in Harper's eyes and shadows appeared on the floor of the roof. Instinctively he matched the shadows to the men. All good. He raised his eyes to the men's faces. All of them looking to the sky, all their faces aglow—except for Dr. Mates with his binoculars pressed to his eyes. His face was in shadow, but the front lenses of his binoculars looked like warning lights from the far beyond. Harper looked up.

"Blimey."

A great ball of silver light hovered and sparkled in the southeast quadrant of the sky, then a long shimmering tail took shape, curving across the night and stretching into the northwest, as if some lesser god had slashed open the firmament so the wondrous thing might be revealed. Harper mumbled to himself, "Something completely different. No shit."

Watching it, Harper realized Paris had fallen quiet and still. Must have been the same all over a big chunk of Europe. Millions of people stopping cars and trams, rushing to windows and opening doors, all eyes turning to the strange light in the sky. Speechless, drifting through a wrinkle in time where one moment coupled to the next without a sense of passage. Then came a voice. Harper was relieved to realize it was only one of the inspector's computer geeks and not one from on high.

"The comet should fade from vision in five, four, three, two, one . . . now."

And so it did.

Dr. Mates read the data now displayed on the monitors.

"Incredible," he said.

The inspector adopted his I'm-very-sure-I-have-no-idea tone. "Is there something of interest, Dr. Mates?"

"Well, yes. I'm not sure how he did it, he only had one minute. Your hacker tracked the comet on a line beginning at Alpha UMi—that's Polaris—to Cassiopeia. He's calculated forty degrees, or 31.28 parsecs, exactly. That's a distance of over a hundred light-years."

"Meaning what?"

"In and of itself, nothing. In astronomy, a hundred light-years is across the street. But it's exactly as he predicted it. And look at this: He's running a phenomenal number of triangulations from various points around the Earth, tens of thousands of them."

"Again, Dr. Mates, I'm only a Swiss policeman," Inspector Gobet said.

"He's plotting the exact distance from all these positions on Earth to the comet's transit."

"To what end, would you say, given your expertise?" the judge said.

The doctor studied the monitors a minute. "It looks like he's using Blue Brain to configure a 3-D model of planet Earth's exact position in the galaxy, based on the Cartesian coordinate system."

The last three words sent Harper ripping back through time. He saw the one-eyed priest, Astruc, at a side altar of l'Église de Saint-Germain-des-Prés. Entombed in the nearby wall was René Descartes. The great headless man who devised the Cartesian coordinate system. Harper blinked, called from the shadows.

"Why the fuck would he do that?"

Dr. Mates turned to the voice. "Excuse me?"

"The Cartesian coordinate system. Why?"

"Who's asking?"

Harper stepped into the glow of the monitors. "Me."

Maybe it was the tone in Harper's voice, maybe it was connecting the voice to a physical presence that looked as if it had stepped from the hard end of a battlefield. Combined with Harper's Brit accent, Dr. Mates was thrown off balance.

"Who . . . who are you?"

Harper nodded toward the inspector and the judge. "I'm with them."

"The police?"

"That's right, and answer the question."

Dr. Mates looked nervously at Inspector Gobet. "If you don't mind my asking," Mates said, "what sort of crime are these hackers involved in?"

The inspector cleared his throat. "At present, let's just say it would be best if we asked the questions and you did the answering."

The line was perfectly placed for maximum effect. The doctor surrendered. He looked at Harper.

"What was your question again?"

"What does the mathematical formula of a dead man from the seventeenth century have to do with building a 3-D model of planet Earth?"

The doctor swallowed, cleared his throat.

"It's how you build an algorithm that supports a digitized structure in three dimensions. All modern computer animation, 2-D or 3-D, is based on Descartes's mathematical formulae."

Harper thought about it. Made sense, maybe.

"You telling me he's trying to make a globe, or a map?"

"Yes. But if he is, he's wasting his time."

"Sorry?"

"There's nothing new in creating a 3-D image of Earth or the universe as we know it. We do this sort of imaging all the time. In fact, the whole process has gone Hollywood. James Cameron did it in *Avatar*."

"Who?"

"The American movie director. He created an entire planet, Pandora, using the Cartesian coordinate system. I was a consultant on the film, actually."

Harper looked at the inspector. The inspector's gaze read, *By all means, Mr. Harper, do make yourself useful and give him a nudge.* Harper walked straight toward Dr. Mates.

"Congrats on your brilliant career, Doc, but let me tell you what I think. The one who hacked into Blue Brain, the one running these calculations, kills people. So I doubt he's trying to make it big in Hollywood. What do you think?"

Dr. Mates got a whiff of the foul stink from Harper's filthy clothes. Harper checked the man's eyes, saw the most primitive part of the man's brain kick in. Reptilian brain it was. Millions of years old on the evolutionary chain, and just now it recognized the smell of death and was screaming "Run away!" back up the chain. Dr. Mates reversed slowly, bumped into the table. He surrendered again.

"All I can tell you is he's building an incredibly complex algorithm to figure Earth's exact position in the galaxy."

"Why?"

"I don't know."

"Sure you do, you're from bloody Oxford, three PhD's, got your own TV show on the bloody Beeb. Makes you a right genius."

Harper saw something go *boing* in the man's eyes.

"What?"

"It's a clock. He's using Descartes's formulae to make a clock."

"A clock?"

"It has to be. I mean, I know it sounds crazy, until you realize space and time are the same thing. Measuring the expansion of the universe and telling the time are both done by triangulating and calculating the relative distance between three or more separate points. A map and a clock serve the same purpose. They tell you where you are in the universe at any particular moment."

"Keep talking, Doc."

"Well . . . it's like the grandfather clock in the hallway of my house is only the triangulation of a big hand, little hand, and the seconds pendulum in relation to the clock face. That's what he's doing, it must be. All these reference points on the planet, those are the seconds. The minutes were the comet's path. Presto, it's a clock."

Harper flashed that before the cathedral job, he'd been in stasis since 1917. He took a second to ask himself how these creatures of free will had discovered time and space were the same thing in less than a hundred years. He blinked, snapped himself to nowtimes.

"What about the little hand, Doc?"

"What?"

"The hand marking the hour, where is it?"

"I don't know, but it must be somewhere on the Earth. A horizon of some kind, from wherever he's watching the sky."

Harper flashed the sextant from the cavern.

"Could he be using the sea?"

"No, he's measuring to the quintillionth of seconds, attoseconds. That's the time it takes for light to travel the length of three hydrogen atoms. I mean, an attosecond is to a second what a second is to nearly thirty-two billion years. That's why he's using Blue Brain to make the calculations. No, it can't be the sea. He needs a perfectly still horizon, not even a flat geographical plain would work. He needs an artificial horizon, probably a laser. Gads, that's it! He's feeding coordinates into Blue Brain, and Blue Brain is running with it! Blue Brain can see it! I'm telling you, it's one great bugger of a clock! Gads, this is the most remarkable thing I've ever seen. It's brilliant!"

Harper looked at Inspector Gobet and the judge, reading that the two of them already knew the score. They were testing Dr. Mates, seeing if an ordinary man could imagine it.

"So, Doc," Harper said.

"Yes?"

"What time is it?"

"Pardon me?"

"You said it's a clock. What time is it?"

"I don't know."

"Why not?"

Dr. Mates pulled at his hair, trying to reattach his own brain back to Earth.

"Look, imagine the grandfather clock again. Seconds, minutes, hours running around a clock face. Three independent elements circling above a common plane that mean absolutely nothing in and of themselves without a common zero point that makes it possible to *tell* the time."

"Which is what?"

"Both hands straight up. Twelve o'clock high."

"So what's their twelve o'clock high? The hackers, I mean."

"A star, most probably."

"Which star?"

"If he's doing it by the naked eye, then it could be any one of six thousand stars. If he's using a radio telescope, then it could be . . . any one of three billion . . . times a hundred billion. It's just . . . impossible."

The man's voice fizzled away to a place of disbelief. *That's it,* Harper thought, *Leo the Astrophysicist has reached the outer limit of his imagination.* Harper glanced back over his shoulder, saw the inspector chatting discreetly with the judge. Harper knew what was coming. He turned to Dr. Mates, spoke softly, and with a touch of kindness.

"That's a lot of stars, Doc."

Dr. Mates responded to the tone, laughed a little.

"Tell me about it. I just wish I knew how he was doing it. What tool he was using to make his initial calculations."

"What do you mean?"

"It can't be one of the radio telescopes or observation telescopes, I'd know about it. I know what any one of those is doing any day of the week."

Harper looked into the sky, too. There were only a handful of stars visible over Paris now.

"He's using a sextant."

Dr. Mate's eyes went from disbelief to childlike joy.

"Holy fucking . . . amazing . . . of course. But how do you know?"

"I've seen it."

The man was giddy. "No way, you've seen it, really?"

"Yes."

"Well . . . what kind of sextant is it?"

"An old one."

"How old?"

"Not sure, really. Only got a glimpse of it. Five thousand years; older, maybe. However bloody old it is, it was made to be used tonight."

Dr. Mates appeared dazed as the truth dropped into his head.

"My God, someone knew this would happen tonight. Someone thousands and thousands of years ago knew this would happen. That's . . . that's . . ." The doctor was finding it increasingly difficult to express himself.

"Impossible?" Harper said.

"Well, it is. Isn't it?"

Harper shrugged. A few hours ago, he was in a cavern deep beneath Paris, talking to a dead man who kept saying the same bloody word: *impossible, impossible*. Now, on a rooftop above the Left Bank, he was hearing the same word. *Not much difference between the living and the dead when exposed to a world they were never meant to be aware of,* Harper thought.

"I tell you what's impossible, Doc: a comet appearing out of thin air and hovering in the sky at a magnitude of negative seven-point-five as part of an intergalactic alarm clock."

Dr. Mates's mind was ready to explode and he laughed, slipping from his very Oxford tones into a native northerner's twang.

"Fookin' 'ell, I'm a bleedin' scientist, you know? But I tell you, I feel like I've been let in on some wonderful cosmic secret tonight. It changes . . ."

Harper gave the man a second.

"Changes what, Doc?"

Dr. Mates looked at Harper.

"Everything."

Harper looked down, saw a formidable shadow moving over the roof. The cop in the cashmere coat was coming their way. Harper smiled at Dr. Mates.

"Glad you enjoyed it, Doc. Too bad you won't remember it."

"Why not?"

Inspector Gobet stepped quickly between them and locked on to the man's eyes.

"Doctor, I'm afraid you must excuse Mr. Harper. He's had a rather distressing evening, as you can see. Hit by a tour bus on the Champs-Elysées this very evening. Sort of thing that happens when one doesn't bother to look both ways."

"An accident?"

"Yes, most upsetting to even hear about it, I agree," the inspector said, pointing to the stairs. "Shall we go down to the library, Doctor? I think a cup of tea would help calm the excitement of the evening."

"Tea?"

"Quite. I have some rather soothing herbal blends. Never leave home without them. I think you'll find one in particular most relaxing. Mixed with a bit of Japanese hand-rolled Sencha from a small plantation I know very well. Near Wazuka in the Kyoto Prefecture. Do you know it?"

"Japan?"

"Indeed. Lovely part of the world, I think. This way if you please, Dr. Mates."

Mutt and Jeff moved in on either side of Leo the Astrophysicist, practically lifting him off his feet and edging him to the door. He tried to protest.

"But . . . but there's so much to know yet! The hacker's not finished with building his clock!"

The inspector laughed politely.

"Yes, well, you know how it is with time, it goes on and on. Besides, I'd be very interested in hearing that theory of yours again."

285

"My theory?"

"Yes, regarding this evening's event being no more than a rogue piece of Giacobini-Zinner that burned up upon entry into Earth's atmosphere, thereby accounting for this evening's rather spectacular celestial vision."

"But I never said that."

"No? Why, I could swear you did. Well, you know how it is with policemen. Always needing to hear things again and again to get the facts through the thickest of skulls. I'm sure we can sort it all out with a nice cup of tea. This way, if you please."

Harper watched them disappear down the stairs. A couple cuppas from now, the man would be singing the inspector's tune and believing every word of it. So much so that Harper imagined tomorrow evening's lecture at l'Académie des sciences, where Dr. Mates would amend his prepared remarks regarding the oceans of planet Earth being formed by a bombardment of frozen water comets 4.5 billion years ago, to include his considered opinion on the previous night's celestial event (which he personally viewed whilst strolling along the Left Bank), and thereby set the record straight for mankind. *"Ab uno disce omnes,"* Harper mumbled.

It was quiet on the roof, the din of Paris still hushed in the wake of the celestial visitor. Inspector Gobet's computer geeks kept working at their Crypto laptops, numbers and equations now dripping down the monitors like rain. Off to the side was the judge, puffing on his pipe, staring at Harper. The three tramps spread around him in a protective arc, doing their own bit of staring. Clarity required. Harper looked back over his shoulder to Sergeant Gauer, held up his bandaged hands.

"Don't suppose you could get me a fag? They're in a cigarette case in the right pocket of my overcoat."

Sergeant Gauer found the case in the left pocket. He pulled a cigarette, set it between Harper's lips. Unlike the inspector, Sergeant Gauer actually had to strike a match and hold the flame to the tip of Harper's cigarette. Harper sucked in the smoke. As always, relief was just a drag away.

"Anything else, Mr. Harper? Need me to help you take a piss or anything?"

"Clever lip for a Swiss cop."

"*Merci*, but just so you know, if it comes to it, you'll be pissing your trousers."

Harper raised his left hand. His fingers poked through the bandages. He pulled the cigarette from his lips with his fingertips.

"I'll manage."

"*Bon.*"

"I'll be back."

"Where are you going?"

Harper nodded toward the judge. "For a walk."

"Is that a good idea, without the inspector being present?"

"No worries, I'll take the scenic route. Besides, knowing Inspector Gobet, this is the way he had it planned."

He walked over to the computer geeks, stood behind them. They sensed his presence but didn't turn to look at him.

"Was he right?" Harper said.

"Who?" the geek on the left said.

"Dr. Mates. Was he right about Blue Brain and the clock?"

"Yes, but he was trying to explain it to you in very basic terms. It's quite complex, actually," the geek on the right said.

"How so?"

"That depends."

"On what?"

The geek on the right looked at Harper.

"How much do you know about Minkowski's space-time theory?"

"Unless it's been on the History Channel, not a bloody thing."

The geeks looked at each other, then back to their Crypto Terminals. The one on the left said, "In that case, sir, find a chair and sit down. We can spend the next fifty years explaining it to you."

Nothing quite like a put-down at the hands of the very creatures you were sent to protect two and a half million years ago, Harper thought. Then again, with some of them knowing space and time were the same bloody thing, they were learning fast.

"Cheers."

He turned around, walked toward the judge. The tramps straightened up seeing Harper coming.

"At ease, lads. Just coming over for a chat."

He stopped before the judge, took a hit off his cigarette. Did his best imitation of the head-swallowing smoke trick.

"Mind if I ask a few questions?"

The judge prayerfully bowed his head a little. Or maybe Harper was imagining it. Hard to tell. The whole disciple thing was rather new.

"*Bien sûr, monsieur,*" the judge said.

"First. I take it the crime scene in the cavern was run by you to put pressure on Astruc, forcing him to make a move; seeing as you seem to run things at Brigade Criminelle."

The judge's silence meant yes.

"So you moved the bodies of the fallen to safety, to Base Aérienne 442. Same place you stashed the bomb from the Paris job, so you could send a dud to the generals, yeah? But nobody knew the truth, but for you and your gang."

Yes again.

"When are you putting the bodies back?"

"As soon as we remove the body of Gilles Lambert for burial."

"No. Leave him down there."

"*Pardon?*"

"If I am who you think I am, that'd mean you still take your orders from me, regardless of what form I'm in just now, right?"

The judge bowed his head. "*Oui, Monsieur de Saint—*"

"Stop right there, gov. I already have one dead man running loose in my head, I don't need another one. Call me Harper."

"*D'accord, Monsieur Harper.* As you wish."

He looked at the judge and his attending bums.

"Right then, here's the drill. I want you to lay Lambert in one of the coves, his hands across his chest. And I'd like you to leave a sanctuary candle burning in the cavern. Be a bitch of a job going down there every week to light a new one, but that's the way I want it."

The tramps fidgeted.

"I know he's dead, lads," Harper said. "I'm just not sure about the state of his soul. I'll sort it after I sort whatever the hell's going on just now. Also, somewhere down there you'll find a pocket knife, a Laguiole. I want you to carve his name into the stone above his cove, leave the knife next to his right hand. Like I said, sorry about the fuck-about factor in getting it done."

The judge cleared his throat.

"In fact, Monsieur Harper, there is a secret ladder from the surface to very near the passage leading to the cavern. Because of the damage caused by Father Astruc's explosives, we were unable to use it in rescuing you. But it will be repaired very soon."

"A ladder. You're kidding me."

"*Non.* It begins in l'Église de Saint-Germain-des-Prés."

Harper flashed his tour through the church.

"Let me guess. In Chapelle Saint-Benoît, behind Descartes's tomb."

The judge smiled.

"Actually in the priest's compartment of the confessional. May I ask, Monsieur Harper, why would you honor Gilles Lambert this way?"

"Because he bloody well deserves it."

The judge did a slight bow again. "Thy will be done."

Giving orders to disciples. Interesting concept, Harper thought. He nodded to the sky.

"Right, the comet, tonight. By chance, way back when, did I happen to mention what all this was supposed to mean, if and when it happened?"

"You said, 'By this sign you will know that the time of the prophecy is at hand.'"

"The time of the prophecy? I said those exact words?"

"Those were your exact words."

Harper thought about it.

Resurrection, reincarnation, thirteenth-century heretics burned at the stake, not to mention a strange light in the sky as the bearer of some prophecy come true . . . all in one night. Was making for a swell evening in paradise. Harper drew on his smoke again. Realized there was only one question.

"Just out of curiosity, gov, did anyone happen to jot down what this prophecy was, exactly?"

A voice called across the roof. "Actually, Mr. Harper, we were hoping you could tell us."

Harper turned around, saw the cop in the cashmere coat coming back.

"All's well with our eminent astrophysicist?" Harper said.

"Indeed. My men are serving him tea and showing him a short film we prepared earlier today. Something to better assist him in understanding this evening's events. More to the point, you say you have no idea what the prophecy is?"

Harper took a hit of radiance, scanned the men around him. One Swiss copper, one investigating magistrate from Brigade Criminelle, three bums with guns. They were staring him down again. Harper exhaled, shook his head.

"Sorry, gentleman. Haven't the foggiest. Seems more than my timeline's been scrambled on this one."

Inspector Gobet rocked on his heels.

"Then it would appear the only ones who know the meaning of the prophecy are one renegade priest with a penchant for murder and a misshapen young man suffering from paedomorphia. As of now, we have no idea where they are."

"Is there anything we do know?"

"We know the enemy is tracking Astruc and the boy with everything they've got. Which suggests something rather ominous."

Harper took a drag on his smoke. Sounded like marching orders about to drop.

"I'm listening."

"If the enemy doesn't know about the prophecy, they will very soon."

"You're telling me not one of our kind, not one of us knows what the hell this is about?"

The inspector didn't answer. Maybe he didn't have an answer, maybe he wasn't ready to let Harper know what he knew. Maybe the inspector's silence was saying, *When I want shit from you, Mr. Harper, I'll squeeze your head.*

"Right. So what do you want me to do in the meantime?"

The inspector looked at his watch.

"You'll be billeted here for the night, get cleaned up. The judge has kindly arranged for a doctor to tend to your hands and arm. I want you on the first TGV to Lausanne, it leaves in three and a half hours. I'll remain in Paris, see what I can find shifting through Father Astruc's library."

"Lausanne? What the hell am I supposed to do in Lausanne?"

"Oh, I'm sure you'll figure it out along the way. Good night, Mr. Harper."

BOOK THREE

AND THE WATCHMAN SAID:
THE MORNING COMETH,
AND ALSO THE NIGHT

❧

SIXTEEN

I

AFTER GOOSE UPLOADED THE FINAL TRIANGULATION INTO BLUE Brain, he shut down the satlink. He opened the intrusion detection program on his laptop. Nearly three hundred thousand attacks, not one intrusion. He looked out the north gate. The priest was standing at the edge of the cliff with the sextant in his hands, still staring at the sky. Goose hit the remote trigger for the laser gun, shut down the thread of light beneath the south gate of the fortress. It awakened the priest from his reverie, and he turned back to Goose. He saw the boy's face aglow in the light of the laptop's screen.

"All is well?"

Goose signed, *We're clear, Father. They tried to find us, but I think we got off the satellite in time.*

"Good," Astruc said.

He walked through the gate, stepped around the transmission gear. He lowered himself to one knee, carefully laid the sextant in the reliquary box, and closed the lid. He looked to the southern sky, saw Sirius floating between Orion and the dark shadows of the Pyrenees.

"We have an hour to the morning twilight."

Goose smiled, picked up the night vision goggles, handed a pair to the priest. *The way down will be easier than the way up.*

Astruc looked at the boy. It was good to see him smile. It was such a rare thing.

"I'm very proud of you, Goose."

Thank you, Father. Thank you for trusting me.

Goose shut off the laptop and it was very dark. They fixed their goggles over their eyes, switched them on, and were returned to a bright green world of near infrared light. Goose disconnected the laptop from the base station, walked across the courtyard to where a sharp rock poked from the ground. He smashed the laptop against the stone and broke it open. He pulled out the memory cards and CPU, dropped them in the pocket of his leather jacket. He left the broken laptop where it lay. He walked back to the base station, disconnected the external hard drive. He slipped it in the pouch of his sweatshirt.

Astruc was busy redistributing the weight of their backpacks. Ammunition, weapons, high-protein biscuits, cold weather and rain gear, sleeping bags. He wrapped the reliquary box in one of the sleeping bags, packed the roll into his backpack.

"Our burden is lighter now, Goose. If the weather holds, we'll reach the high country by nightfall and Heaven's Gate the next day."

God willing, Father.

They lifted their backpacks and adjusted the shoulder straps. Goose took up the walking staffs, handed one to Astruc. They walked toward the south gate. Astruc stopped, turned back to look through the open arch of the north gate. He didn't move.

Father?

Goose watched the priest step slowly toward the gate as if in a trance, dropping his staff and raising his eyes to the sky, opening his hands and lifting them to the heavens; and he cried out:

"*Notre Père!*"

Goose felt the powerful voice echo off the fortress stones. And for a moment, Goose sensed the earth quake. *Surely,* he thought, *his is the voice of the prophet.* Goose waited, watched the priest, hands still lifted to the heavens as if waiting for an answer to his cry. The priest slowly lowered his hands, then he lowered himself to his knees. Perhaps he was praying, Goose thought. After many minutes, and seeing Astruc was not moving, Goose moved closer to him. He heard the priest whispering again and again to himself.

"How is it that you did not burn?"

Goose had heard the words many times in the night, as the priest lay half awake, half asleep, bound in the place of a terrible dream that haunted him like a ghost. Goose bent down, signed before the priest's eyes, *We must go now, Father. The morning twilight is coming.*

Astruc raised his head. "What happened?"

You were dreaming of the man who did not burn. But it is finished, Father. You have defeated the Dark Ones. Soon, all the world will know of the prophecy, and you will be able to sleep.

Astruc looked around the fortress.

"Yes, yes. We're finished here. We must leave."

Goose helped Astruc to his feet, and they left the fortress and made their way down Montségur. The black stones on the trail were wet with dew now, and they used their walking staffs to keep from slipping from the cliffs. By the time they reached the Field of the Burned, the sky above the mountains had begun to brighten. They removed their night vision goggles and stowed them in their backpacks. They rested their staffs against the wooden fence surrounding the field and drank water from their goatskins. A haze lay over the field, and there was the chatter of swallows from the surrounding forest.

"Goose."

Yes, Father?

"Reach in my backpack, bring out the box."

Father?

"It should be buried here, in the Field of the Burned, to honor the souls who died here. We have no use of it now."

Do we have time?

"If you hurry, there will be time."

Goose rested his walking staff against the fence, stepped behind Astruc, and opened the priest's backpack. He dug through the sleeping bag and found the reliquary box. He picked up his walking staff, stepped into the field, stopped. He looked back at Astruc.

Is it all right to walk on this ground? Where they died?

"Only their ashes were left, Goose, and their ashes became part of the corruption of Earth. Their souls were lifted to the stars to be with the Pure God."

Goose looked back to the field as if searching for something, then said to the priest, *Where was it? Where did it happen?*

Astruc studied the field. There was a rise in the ground, hidden by newly harvested stalks of hay. He pointed to it.

"Over there. Where the ground rises."

Should I bury it there?

"No, it might be found when the farmers work the ground. Take it across the field and into the trees."

Goose nodded.

He pulled his hoodie over his head and walked ahead. Astruc watched the boy's feet move silently over the ground. The watching brought the dream to the priest's eyes. Two hundred fifteen men and women, ankles and wrists bound, walking into the field. They'd been dragged down Montségur by French Crusaders, condemned to death by the Inquisition. The palisade ahead of them looked large enough from the heights of the fortress, but as the frightened men and women approached it now, they saw it was half the size of the fortress itself, with timber walls almost four meters high. The Crusaders had formed a gauntlet from the edge of the field to the wooden gate of the palisade, and as the men and women passed through it the Crusaders slapped them, kicked them, spat upon them. The Crusaders saved their bitterest blows for the twenty-seven fighters who refused to surrender and instead became heretics themselves. Astruc could see some of their faces . . . especially the traitor, the Dark One in their midst. Dominican priests stood closest to the gate. Rosaries in hands, praying and weeping false tears; entreating the martyrs to turn to Holy Mother Church for forgiveness. Through the gate, the men and women climbed atop a great mound of wood, pitch, and hay. There were no stakes to be bound to, and they huddled together as the Crusaders closed the gate and dropped a cross brace to trap the last of the Cathars inside. Then came the fire . . . screams and forever pain . . .

"No!"

Father?

Astruc saw Goose standing before him.

Are you all right, Father?

Astruc straightened up.

"Yes, I'm fine. I was meditating on the martyrs."

The dream?

"Yes. Have you finished with the box?"

Yes, it is buried.

"How are your eyes, Goose? You must be tired from the night's work. Do you need a shot?"

No, Father. I will wait till the evening.

Astruc reached in his overcoat, found the leather-strung scallop, hung it around his neck. Goose found his own scallop, put it on.

And once again, we are pilgrims on the Way of Saint James, he signed.

"And may the Pure God keep us alive long enough to serve the prophecy."

He has led us this far, Father, he will not abandon us now.

They followed the road to the northwest. The road wound through a narrow valley bordered by steep cliffs, and they walked in morning shadows. Now and again they saw lights burning in the kitchens of farmhouses where women laid out coffee and bread for their husbands. The Great Pyrenees mountain dogs guarding the farms from wolves and bears picked up the scent of passing strangers and let out throaty howls: *I hear you! I smell you!* One farmer emerged from his kitchen, shotgun in his hand. But it was still too dark to see into the shadows, and the man scolded his dog to be quiet. The beast bowed its head, circled once, and slunk to the ground: *I heard them, I smelled them.* Soon after, a tractor hauling a load of hay approached from behind a bend. Astruc and Goose stepped from the road and into the trees so they would not be seen in the tractor's headlamps. It was not from fear of detection they avoided the farmer; it was to protect him. Dressed as they were, as pilgrims traveling the Way of Saint James, Astruc knew the farmer would offer them a lift, invite them to take breakfast in his home. It was the custom among the common people of the Pyrenees. But such an act of kindness would put the farmer and his family in the gravest danger. The Dark Ones would be searching, hunting.

When the farmer passed, they continued along the road till they were west of the peak of Saint-Barthélemy. They left the road and took a hiking trail through the forest. The trail rose at a gentle grade at first, then began to climb above the tree line, where they crossed over a rocky ridge then descended again into forest. It was crossing the first ridge that they stepped through the sharp rays of the rising sun, and crossing the second ridge they stopped to watch the light of the sun race over the land like an awakening thing.

By ten o'clock, they reached a small shelter next to an alpine lake above the tree line. The shallows at the bank had iced over during the night, but the ice was thin, like a hint of winter's approach. They dropped their backpacks, broke through the ice, and drank deeply. The water was pure and cold. They washed their faces and hands. Goose opened his backpack and found a pack of high-protein biscuits. They sat on the wooden bench and rested their backs against the already warm stone of the shelter. The sun beat down on their faces. As they ate, a small brown shuffle wing landed at their feet to collect any crumbs that might fall.

"And what are you doing here, with winter coming soon? You should be nesting farther down, near the trees. We have no food for you here."

The little brown bird hopped on its legs, back and forth before them.

"I believe he has us trapped, Goose. We must surrender."

Goose laughed. And this time he let an audible sound escape his mouth. He broke off a piece of the biscuit and tossed it to the ground. The shuffle wing quickly picked it up and flew away and down below the ridge. Goose looked to the west and north to check the sky. He signed, *The weather is good, and looks like it will hold.*

"So far we're lucky. If we reach Heaven's Gate before it turns, then we'll reveal the prophecy to the world."

II

K ATHERINE CLOSED HER CLOAK OVER HER FLANNEL PAJAMAS AND put on her fuzzy slippers. She opened the sliding glass doors of the sitting room, stepped quietly onto the patio. Officer Jannsen was still standing in the shadows of the back garden. Katherine spotted her from the bedroom window, drying herself after a long hot bath, and she thought it odd. The back garden lights were always burning at the perimeter, lighting up the trees from sundown to sunup. But just now, the lights were off. Maybe that's why Anne was out there, Katherine thought, seeing what's wrong. She was on the phone, talking to Control most likely and getting it fixed according to her usual "I want it done now!" Katherine laughed to herself thinking how *"Ich will es jetzt getan!"* sounded so much more kick-ass in German. Then again, everything in German sounded that way. Cripes sake, sometimes even a hearty *"Guten morgen, Fräulein!"* from one of the Swiss Guard boys sounded more like, "Attention, the sun has risen and you are ordered to have a nice day!"

She watched Officer Jannsen close her cell phone, snap it to her belt, stand there. The lights stayed off. That's when Katherine noticed Officer Jannsen wasn't looking at the trees, counting the seconds till the lights would kick on; she was looking at the stars. Stepping onto the lawn and moving quietly toward Officer Jannsen, Katherine caught the bodyguard's Chanel perfume six meters away. She reached out her hand to touch Officer Jannsen's shoulder . . . There was a blur, then the barrel of a Glock pointing at Katherine's right eye.

"Jesus!"

Officer Jannsen lowered the gun. "Kat . . . what are you doing down here?"

"What am I . . . What do you mean, what am I doing here? I live here. And how the hell did you do that?"

"Do what?"

"Move like that."

"Lots of training."

"That wasn't fucking training, girl, that was a special effect."

Officer Jannsen holstered her weapon.

"Is Max all right?"

"Sleeping like a . . . Jesus, why did you draw your weapon on me?"

Officer Jannsen smiled.

"I heard you coming."

"Walking on the grass. You heard me walking on the grass."

"It's harder to walk quietly on grass than bricks. That and the air pressure."

"What?"

"You were moving toward me, creating a wave of air ahead of you."

Katherine stared at her. "Are you all right?"

"Oui, pourquoi?"

"Because you're acting weird. The Swiss Guard boys, I understand; they were born that way, but you're supposed to be normal."

Officer Jannsen looked at her watch.

"It's almost eleven. Aren't you supposed to be in bed?"

"I was on my way, but I saw you from my window. Thought I'd come see what's up. By the way, what happened to the lights?"

"I've got one of the squads conducting night vision drills in the woods. I'm keeping the lights off for the night."

"Ah."

"Ah what?"

"Huh?"

"You're thinking something, Kat. What is it?"

"Nothing. It just looked like something else."

"Like what?"

"Like you looking at the stars and thinking."

Officer Jannsen smiled.

"I was, actually."

"So, what were you thinking?"

"Nothing."

Katherine looked at her, her eyes then sinking to the Glock on her hip. "You're kind of scary tonight."

"Why?"

"Because the first thing you thought of, after you were thinking about nothing, was killing."

"That's what happens when you sneak up on someone who's been trained to kill. I've told you before, don't do that sort of thing. Not to me, not to any member of the protection detail."

Katherine shrugged. "Okay. Sorry to bother you. Good night."

She turned, walked toward the house.

"Kat, wait."

Katherine turned back. "What?"

"Have you had your tea for the night?"

"Yup. But to be perfectly frank, I could use another blast after having a friggin' gun shoved in my face."

Officer Jannsen stepped close to Katherine.

"How would you like to try it again?"

"What do you have in mind?"

"Well, I will go inside and put on the kettle . . ."

". . . and I'll grab a couple of lounge chairs from the patio . . ."

". . . make us both a cup of tea . . ."

". . . and I'll get some blankets . . ."

". . . we'll meet back here in ten minutes."

"Deal."

And in ten minutes, they were tucked in blankets on the lounge chairs, sipping cups of tea.

"How long will the boys be out there?"

"All night."

"Poor them."

"It's their job. Besides, they're boys, they like to rough it up now and again."

Katherine snickered. "They're not the only ones."

"What?"

"Nothing, I was joking. Almost."

Katherine sat back in the chair, looked into the night sky.

"Wow, look at all the stars."

"It's a new moon tonight."

"You know, I never understood that one. Why do they call it a 'new moon' when there's *no* moon?"

"It marks the beginning of the lunar cycle when the moon is in the shadow of the Earth."

"That is such a Swiss cop answer. The facts, ma'am, just the facts. I know, why not call it a 'shadow moon'?"

Officer Jannsen sipped her tea.

"That's a good name, actually."

They sat quietly, watching the sky, only speaking when a shooting star crossed the sky; once, then again.

"Wow, look at that. It's a shooting star. The aliens are restless to-night."

"There's another one."

"Make a wish."

Katherine sipped her tea, curled on her side.

"Can I ask you something, Anne?"

"Of course."

"Do you think I should have Max baptized?"

"What?"

"You know, baptized. Have a priest splash him with water, make the sign of the cross over him, make him part of the club."

"Your family is Christian?"

"Oh yeah. And not just Christian, but Catholic. Big time. You?"

"My parents weren't believers."

"They were atheists?"

"No, they just didn't believe in the religions of men."

"So what did they believe in?"

Officer Jannsen looked back to the stars.

"All that."

"Outer space?"

Officer Jannsen started to giggle, then she laughed.

"What? What did I say?" Katherine said.

"'Outer space.' That is so American."

"What's wrong with American stuff? Where would the world be without hamburgers, Coca-Cola, and rock and roll?"

"I don't mean it in a bad way. It wasn't even an American who coined the expression 'outer space.' It was an English poet."

"Really?"

"Lady Emmeline Stuart-Wortley, 1841, in 'The Maiden of Moscow.'"

Katherine giggled. "Emmeline Stuart-Wortley. That's right up there with Corporal Sebastianus Fassnacht."

"But not quite as bad as Herr Alexander von Humboldt."

"Who?"

"A Prussian astronomer. He was the first one to use 'outer space' in a scientific context. And then, of course, it was H. G. Wells who made it really popular in 1901 with *The First Men in the Moon*."

Katherine shook her head.

"Jeez, the stuff you have crammed in your head would fill the Grand Canyon."

"*Merci, madame,* I think."

"No, really. It's something."

"I don't think I'm much different from you."

"Trust me, babe, you're *way* different from me."

Officer Jannsen looked at Katherine.

"You'd be surprised."

"Oh? You got a secret hooker past I don't know about?"

"No."

"Then what?"

"Well, to begin with, we're both madly in love with a boy named Max."

"This is true."

Officer Jannsen sipped her tea.

"That really was a wonderful story you told Max tonight, Kat."

"It was fun. And it helped."

"How?"

"*Olet tervetullut.* That means—"

"You're welcome."

"You speak Finnish?"

"Picked up a few words here and there."

She did her bead-flipping thing, recited her magic words to herself. Then, still staring at Harper, she stopped. She leaned across the table.

"*Tiedän kuka olet.* Do you know what that means?"

"Sure."

"What's it mean?"

"It means 'I know who you are.'"

She nodded approvingly. "Pretty good."

Maybe she was one of the sensitive ones, Harper thought, able to sense the presence of his kind on Earth. Or maybe she was just barking mad with a capital *B*. And so what? The two were not exclusive of each other and were often complementary. Didn't matter, really. What mattered was the odds of their lives crossing by chance were working out at 35 mill to 1.

"I know what you're thinking," she said.

"What's that?"

"You're thinking this isn't an accident. You and me on this train. Right here, right now. But you don't know what it is. That's what you're thinking."

"You don't say."

"There you go with that 'you don't say' stuff. Is that one of the rules for your gang? Never tell anyone who you are?"

Harper stared at her.

"Sorry, what's your name?"

"Karoliina. From Tampere. It was a sign, wasn't it?"

"Define 'it.'"

She leaned over the aisle and tapped her finger on the front page of the *Daily Mail*. The photo of the comet with the understated headline, "What the Hell Was That?!"

"You saw it, didn't you?" she said.

"So did a couple million other people."

"Because for the first time, I could see the good stuff about what happened to me in Lausanne. Hiding in the tower with Marc, becoming part of his imaginary world. It was a gift. And tonight, telling my story to Max, I felt . . . free . . . from fear. I mean, the fear's there, it always will be. But now I know there's something stronger than the fear. I don't know what it is, but I saw it in Max's eyes while telling him the story. It's like he understood, like he already knew."

"Knew what, Kat?"

Katherine bit her lip.

"What is it?"

"Well, after what happened in Portland, I'm a little scared to say."

"Go ahead."

"I was thinking, telling Max the story, that there really are angels . . . maybe. We just can't see them. That's what I thought in the cathedral, and here I am, passing the thought to him. It was kinda comforting."

Officer Jannsen smiled.

"I knew it," Katherine said. "You're going to call the shrink, get my medication adjusted."

"Not at all."

"Then why are you smiling? And tell me the truth, I've gotten very good at spotting your fibs."

"What are flibs?"

"Fibs, not flibs. It's lying, but not the kind you tell to hurt someone."

"*Eine Notlüge.*"

"What's that?"

"A white lie."

"That's it. And stop beating around the bush trying to come up with an answer."

"What answer?"

"To what you're smiling about. Spit it out, now."

Officer Jannsen laughed.

"Well, I was just thinking, *das ist es.*"

"That means *that is it.*"

"Bravo, Kat."

"Bull, and what do you mean, *das ist es*, Frau Blücher?"

"Who?"

"Dr. Frankenstein's girlfriend."

"There was no girlfriend in the book."

"I'm talking movie."

Officer Jannsen took a moment to remember.

"But there was no girlfriend in the movie."

"Not the movie with Boris Karloff, I'm talking the Gene Wilder version. *Young Frankenstein*."

"Are you sure about this, Kat?"

"Do not question me about movies. I'd clean up on *Jeopardy* in that category. We can rent it on Netflix if you want some proof that I'm not completely nuts. And you're still avoiding the answer to the question."

Officer Jannsen scratched her head.

"I can't remember the question."

Katherine leaned toward her, caught another blast of Chanel.

"Why? Were you? Smiling at me?"

"Ah. Because you said something that made me think how much alike we are."

"I did?"

"You did," Officer Jannsen said.

"What did I say?"

"That there are angels, maybe. We just can't see them. It's a nice thought, really."

Katherine stared at Officer Jannsen.

"So you're a sucker for fairy tales, too, huh?"

"Isn't everybody?"

Katherine's eyes lost focus for a half a second.

"Kat?"

Katherine shook her head, looked at Officer Jannsen.

"What did you say?"

"You said, 'You're a sucker for fairy tales'; I said, 'Isn't everybody?'"

"That's right. Must have had déjà vu. Always weird when that happens."

"What was it?"

"Someone, a guy. I was talking to him about fairy tales."

"Who?"

"I don't know. And you know how déjà vu is. Like playing hide-and-seek in the dark with your eyes closed. This guy's there, and not there . . ."

". . . at the same time."

Katherine's eyes lit up.

"Nail on the head. And it's always the same. Someone says something, or I think of something, and I can almost see him. If I could only remember his friggin' name, I'd see him. I'm sure of it."

"Is it happening a lot, the déjà vu?"

"Oh, God, please don't analyze me."

"I'm just asking."

"No such thing as 'just asking' for a cop."

"I'm off duty for the moment."

"You are?"

"Forwarded my phone over to Control for a few hours."

"You shut off your cell phone?"

"I told you. I wanted to look at the stars tonight."

"They allow you to do that?"

"Look at the stars?"

"No, shut off your phone. What if the big bad wolf shows up in search of fair maidens while they sleep."

"What?"

"I'm trying to keep with the whole fairy tale motif we've got going," Katherine said.

"In that case, the big bad wolf would find the house to be surrounded by a tactical unit of the Swiss Guard and end up with its testicles nailed to a tree."

"Ouch."

"*Genau.*"

"What's that?"

"German."

"For what?"

"Exactement."

"So why didn't you say so?"

"I was trying to keep up with you in the fairy tale department."

"Huh?"

"The Brothers Grimm were German."

"That's right, I remember. Had all the books when I was a girl . . . 'Rumpelstiltskin.'"

" '*Rumpelstilzchen.*' "

" 'The Frog Prince.' "

" '*Der Froschkönig.*' "

"Snow White."

" '*Schneewittchen.*' "

"What?"

" 'Snow White,' '*Schneewittchen.*' "

"No way."

"If it makes you feel any better, 'Cinderella' is '*Cinderella.*'"

"Oh, that's okay then."

"Ich danke ihen sehr."

They were quiet a moment.

"Anne?"

"Yes, Kat?"

"Can I kiss you?"

SEVENTEEN

"Kat, I'm not sure that would be a good idea."

"Why not? And remember, I'm nuts, so let me down gently."

"I'm not trying to let you down."

"That's what they all say."

"It's just I think I know what kind of kiss you're talking about, Kat."

"Well, duh."

"And that's why I don't think it would be a good idea."

Katherine stared at her. "Have you ever been with a girl?" she said.

"Only girls."

"Really?"

"Yes."

"So?"

"I've been celibate for a few years."

"Oh, God, you're a nun with a gun."

Officer Jannsen laughed.

"No, I've been celibate since joining Inspector Gobet's task force."

"Let me guess, he makes all his cops take a vow of chastity before they sign up."

"No. It's just when I realized what it was I wanted to do with my life, I decided to devote myself to it. Mind, soul, *and* body."

Katherine let her own eyes do a once-over of Officer Jannsen's body. *What a waste,* she thought.

"But it's not a rule or anything?"

"No, it's not a rule."

"Huh."

"Huh, what?"

"Well, it's just . . ."

"Say it, Kat."

"It's just I thought I was picking up some vibes from you."

"Vibes?"

"Yeah. A flirty look here, a boob flash there."

"A boob flash?"

"C'mon, you've got a great body, you know it. And you know I like looking at it. And I know you like looking at me."

"Celibate doesn't mean I'm dead, Kat."

"So you *have* been looking at me."

"Yes."

"And you like what you see."

"Very much."

Katherine let out a slow quiet sigh.

"What was that?" Officer Jannsen said.

"The closest thing I've had to an orgasm in years."

Officer Jannsen smiled.

"Good for you."

"Tell me about it."

She lay back on her side, looking at Officer Jannsen, who'd adopted the same position to look at her.

"So," Katherine said, "no sex."

"No sex."

"Not even letting your fingers do the walking?"

"My what?"

Katherine made slow flicking moves with the index and middle fingers of her right hand.

"Oh, *die selbstbefriedigung.*"

"*Die* what?"

"*Die selbstbefriedigung.* That's what it's called in German, if we're talking about the same thing."

"We can't be, not with a word like that. I mean, by the time you say it, you're finished."

"I'm sure we're talking about the same thing, Kat."

"So? Do you?"

"Of course, that's me being with me."

"Well, how about you and me . . ."

"Then that would be me being with you."

"How do you know what I was thinking?"

"Because I've thought about it, too."

"Really?"

"Yes."

"So when you're with yourself, do you ever think of me?"

"What?"

"Simple question," Katherine said.

"You don't expect me to answer it, do you?"

Katherine smiled. "You just did."

"Maybe we should change the subject, Kat."

"Okay, best girlfriend ever, but tell me once more why it's not a good idea, then I'll shut up about it."

Officer Jannsen looked up at the stars.

"I'm like you, Kat, I have emotions, too. But if something were to happen to you or Max because I let myself be distracted by those emotions, I would have failed you and everything I believe in."

"What do you believe in, besides all those stars you're looking at?"

Officer Jannsen spoke softly.

> *"Love's not Time's fool, though rosy lips and cheeks*
> *within his bending sickle's compass come:*

Love alters not with his brief hours and weeks,
but bears it out even to the edge of doom."

"Holy cow, I finally know something that you do. That's Shakespeare, from the sonnets. Number 116. *Let me not to the marriage of true minds.*"

"And now it's my turn to be impressed, Madame Taylor."

"Don't be, it's about the only thing I remember from high school. Only reason I do is I had this mad crush on a cheerleader at the same time I was reading the sonnets for English Lit."

"Sounds romantic."

"Sure, in the dime-store teen romance sort of way."

"What happened?"

"The cheerleader had her way with me, and then she broke my heart by switching to the quarterback. He was gorgeous, though, had him myself one night. Anyway, I had a little paperback of the sonnets and would cry myself to sleep reading them. Man, I was such a hopeless romantic. Still am, I guess."

Officer Jannsen smiled.

"See? I told you we weren't that much different."

Katherine stared at her, watched her begin to move away like floating in mist.

"Kat?"

"Huh?"

"You're crying."

"Am I?"

"Yes."

Katherine took a sharp breath.

"Go ahead, Kat, let it out."

"It's just . . . it's just I've been feeling things, sexual things, for the first time since . . . and they're nice things. And I felt them with you, and tonight . . . I mean, I didn't come down here to hit on you, it just happened."

"Don't feel embarrassed. It's good you feel these things again."

"I don't feel embarrassed, I feel like I've found part of me I've been

313

afraid of seeing. I'm just realizing how so very afraid I've been . . . I can see it."

"What is it, Kat?"

Katherine felt the tears burn. "Oh, God." Then she began to shudder and curl into a fetal position. She wept. Officer Jannsen let her alone a minute, then got up to sit next to her, put her hands on her shoulder.

"Kat?"

"Those men hurt me so much."

"But you're safe now. And I'm here for you, I'll protect you."

"I know, I know. Maybe that's why I got all . . . you know, hot on you."

"I know, and it's fine. And believe me, you're getting stronger by the day."

"You think?"

"I know it. That's what I see in you."

Katherine pulled the sleeve of her flannel pajamas from under her cloak and wiped her eyes and nose. Officer Jannsen started to get up.

"I'll get some tissues from the house."

"Don't leave me. Not now, not yet."

"All right," Officer Jannsen said, touching Katherine's hair and combing it with her fingers.

"It's very late, isn't it?"

"Yes, Kat, it's very late. You need to sleep."

"I know. Just one more shooting star, then I'll go to bed. It's been such a nice night. You, me, Max, telling a story. You, me, here, just now."

She looked up at the sky. *Must be a gazillion stars,* she thought, *and Anne Jannsen probably knows the name of each one.*

"Will they ever take you away from me, Anne?"

"Take me where?"

"Will they, you know, transfer you somewhere else?"

"Excuse me, Madame Taylor. I tell you I can't kiss you like a lover and you're already looking for my replacement?"

Katherine laughed.

"No. I just know how it works; they rotate the boys every four months. And you've been great to stay all the time, but I was wondering if you'll ever leave. You will tell me, won't you?"

"I told you once, Kat, there's no place I'd rather be than with you and Max."

"Yeah, I know. Just checking."

Katherine fell to sleep, and it was very quiet.

Officer Jannsen waited a few minutes to make sure Katherine was under, then she got up and tucked the blanket around Katherine's body. She leaned down, took a lock of Katherine's hair in her own hand, smelled it, kissed it.

"Yeah, me, too," Katherine murmured.

Officer Jannsen didn't move.

"Kat, are you awake?"

"No . . . just . . . hmmm."

Officer Jannsen listened to the rhythm of Katherine's breathing and knew she'd gotten it wrong. The Night Clouds tea had only induced Katherine into the theta wave stage of sleep, and only now was beginning to produce delta waves.

Then a voice: *"Je suis désolé de vous déranger, Chef."*

Officer Jannsen saw one of the Swiss Guards standing at the edge of the garden. She got up, walked toward him.

"What is it?"

"Flash traffic from Inspector Gobet. He wants you online, right now."

She pulled her mobile from her belt, switched it on. Two priority messages advising of flash traffic, one classified file. She sent the file to her decryption application, waited. The file opened. Officer Jannsen knew what it was, and her eyes dropped to the last series of numbers. She felt her heart pound. She closed the phone, hooked it to her belt. She looked at the Swiss Guard, nodded to Katherine.

"Carry Madame Taylor to her room, put her to bed. Then call in the squad from night maneuvers and light up the perimeter."

"Roger, *Chef.*"

She marched to Control.

The guard manning the Ops desk saw Officer Jannsen come through the door.

"We're on the bird and counting down," he said.

"How far back are we?"

"Six minutes, *Chef*. I'm adjusting the signal for lag time."

She walked through the room, toward a door marked SUPPLIES. She glanced at the security monitors from the house. Saw Katherine being carried up the stairs, saw Max asleep in his crib with Monsieur Booty curled up on the nearby stool. On the exterior cameras she saw the perimeter lights switch on and the night squad coming in from the woods. She stopped at the supply room door. She grabbed the door handle, tried to turn it. It wouldn't give. She remembered it wasn't that kind of door.

"*Öffnen sie die verdammte tür,*" she said.

The guard quickly entered a four-digit code on his computer keyboard, and the door popped open. Officer Jannsen stood still a moment, turned back.

"When you get an REM sleep registration from Madame Taylor, seal the door to the boy. Release enough masking potion to make her unsure about the last ninety minutes."

"*Chef?*"

"I want her to imagine the last ninety minutes as a dream, that she went to bed and didn't come out into the garden. And notify the pharmacy in Grover's Mill that her memory potions need to be adjusted again."

The guard tapped a couple keys, read something on his screen.

"Excuse me, *Chef*, there isn't any note of that on her medication log."

She shot a vicious look across the room.

"*Ich will es getan!*"

"*Natürlich, Chef.* Last ninety minutes to be redirected in Swan Lake's memory."

Officer Jannsen went inside the room, locked the door behind her. Barely a meter by two meters, just enough to fit a small desk and chair. There was a small blue light on the wall. A Crypto Field Terminal attached to a headset with a microphone. It was called the Quiet Room.

So quiet she could hear the sound of her own heart pounding. She sat down, put on the headset, adjusted the microphone. She watched the digital clock on the screen count down to real time, to the exact milli-second . . . *Love's not Time's fool,* she thought at the very moment the clock flipped to 00:00:00:00. Then a low-frequency hum vibrated through the room, and Inspector Gobet appeared onscreen.

"Good evening, Officer Jannsen."

"Inspector."

"I trust you've seen the news footage of the celestial event."

"Yes, sir. I was in the back garden watching the stars, trying to imag-ine it. How is spin control?"

"Proceeding as planned; though given the state of the world's media, we'll be awash in false prophets by the end of the day, I'm sure. We've arranged for a British astrophysicist to enter the conversation this eve-ning to calm the mood, as it were. And a statement from EPFL, which by curious timing was the only lab in Europe managing to gather any scientific data on the event, will lend gravitas to the spin. I should like to impress upon you that, given the events in Portland, Madame Taylor is not to be made aware of the comet in any way."

"I've already issued an order to all operatives through closed-circuit comms."

"Have you had time to review the data I have referred to HQ regard-ing the boy's light scan?"

"I just received it, sir."

"You saw the bottom line."

"Yes, sir."

"Your thoughts?"

"Confused, sir."

"Because?"

He was listening to her voice, analyzing her.

"Officer, I would appreciate it if you did not appraise the significance of your words before speaking. It only muddies the communication process between our species."

"Yes, sir. I'm having a hard time accepting the results."

"Please elaborate."

"It seems to confirm your suspicion that she wasn't impregnated by the enemy."

"Can you find room in the data for any margin of error?"

"None," she said.

"Indicating?"

"According to the results of the light scan, Madame Taylor's son is normal. He's an ordinary human being."

"And this is why you find it difficult to accept the results. You believe the boy to be special, unique."

"I know he is, sir."

"Would this be an emotional reaction because of what it would imply if he is an ordinary boy?"

She felt her throat constrict with anger.

"Yes, sir. And if I may say, cutting them loose would be . . ."

"Would be what, Officer?"

"Evil, sir."

"Walking away is the most terrible and necessary part of our job. Too often, most assuredly. I understand why, as a human being, you would find walking away from them to be evil. But that's the way it is in paradise."

"Not for me, sir."

"I beg your pardon, Officer?"

"I will not leave them. Not after Portland. Not after they saw him."

"The saxophoneman, you mean."

"Yes, sir."

"Officer, you are aware that our kind, including those bound by oath to us, are forbidden to interfere in the manner or time of anyone's death."

"Yes, sir, I'm very aware of it. I'm also aware that if the light scan is accurate, then HQ will pull all protection from Madame Taylor and Max."

"And you will choose to stay with them."

"Yes, sir."

"Knowing full well that we will wipe your memory of all knowledge of us, and the truth of existence in this place. You will be returned to one of them."

"Yes, sir."

Officer Jannsen watched Inspector Gobet watching her. One of those showdown moments wherein the inspector waited for the next word to be spoken to determine the manner of a subject's thinking. Waiting for it, Officer Jannsen had another thought.

"These aren't the real results. You've intercepted the real results and sent HQ a fake."

She watched the inspector light and inhale from one of his hand-rolled cigarettes with the gold filters. For a moment, she considered the oddity of working in the service of ancient beings from an unknown place; beings mankind called angels, and all of them exhibiting what humans would classify as a serious drug habit. She watched the inspector exhale.

"For the moment, let's say I seem to have mistyped a few numbers," he said.

Officer Jannsen remembered her conversation with Inspector Gobet ordering the light scan in Portland: *Our operations in protecting Madame Taylor and the child are based on the assumption she was raped and impregnated by the enemy . . . cannot go into details . . . need confirmation on the boy's status, one way or the other.* An ordinary boy, not conceived by the enemy, but not conceived by an ordinary man. That left one option.

"You discovered Max was conceived by one of your own kind," she said. "That's the confirmation you were looking for in the light scan."

"That was the primary possibility. But after reviewing the genuine results of the scan, and the case file of the Lausanne job, I'm ruling out that possibility as well."

"Sir, there are no other possibilities of conception. Not for the human beings."

"Outside the realm of the legends and myths of men, you mean."

"Sir?"

She watched Inspector Gobet draw deeply from his cigarette and allow himself a moment of pure radiance before continuing to speak.

"'Who, by procreation, is the primal father of truth? Who created the course of the sun and stars? Through whom does the moon wax and wane? These very things, and others, I wish to know.'"

She knew the words. From the Ushtavaiti Gatha of Zoroaster. She wondered at the connection. Religious mystic, prophet, priest from the Bronze Age. Born anywhere from Azerbaijan to Iran, lived anytime from the sixth to second millennium BCE. She'd studied him at university in Comparative Religions. Monotheist, dualist, articulated the concept of free will amid the creation. Good thoughts, good words, good deeds, would transform the material world into . . . paradise. And she remembered some required reading. John Malcolm's *History of Persia* in 1815. He had a line about Zoroaster. Born of an immaculate conception by a ray of the Divine Reason.

"With all due respect, sir, what are you saying?"

She listened as the inspector spent the next hour walking her through the real results of the light scan. She heard the words—*conceived of light, evolution, dream catcher, enemy knows, traitor in HQ, lockdown*—and when the inspector was finished with all his words, she signed off.

She sat very still for a few minutes, till she realized the guard manning the desk would know the inspector had already signed off the bird. And he'd remember the Quiet Room wasn't for being quiet, it was for receiving bad news. Officer Jannsen breathed calmly and hit the switch to open the door. She stepped out of the room.

"All members of the detail have returned to the compound and checked in?"

"Yes, *Chef*."

"What about in Grover's Mill?"

The guard tapped a few keys on his computer, took a few seconds to read the information on screen.

"Everyone is on site."

She took a calming breath.

"Pass the word: Stay put, it's going to be bumpy for a few seconds. They're amplifying the time warp to level one. Nobody gets in or out."

III

H ARPER BLINKED.
He was still in coach 17 of TGV 9261 to Lausanne. Crossing through the hills of Burgundy toward Dijon now. Passing farms, fields of cows, thick woods at three hundred kilometers per hour. Then it all went black as the train ducked into a long tunnel. Then there was a shudder and a ripping of light as another train passed in the opposite direction, heading to Paris. He felt his heart race, and he felt sick again.

"Easy, boyo, it's just the bloody train."

He pulled his eyes from the dark, took refuge in the glow of overhead reading lamps throughout the train car. The sleeping Chinese gentleman who'd been snoring next to him: gone. The American couple on their way to take the waters at Leukerbad: gone. The husband left his newspapers scattered over the table. Maybe he was being nice. Maybe, being a Yank, he expected someone else to toss them in the trash. Harper looked around the train car. Everybody else in place, with one new addition. A woman sitting across the aisle, facing him. Young, blond, wearing a dark brown hooded shearling sheepskin coat. There was a string of beads hanging from her right hand, and she was swinging it this way and that way, and the beads made tiny clacking sounds each time they wrapped around her index finger. There was a scent in the air, something familiar. Had to be coming from the beads, Harper thought. His eyes zoomed in. A string of 108 beads made of Tulasi wood. *Japa mala* they were called . . . Hindu prayer beads used in the recitations of mantras or in evoking the names of gods. Which might have been what the young woman was doing. Except as her lips rattled off silent words in rapid succession, she was staring straight at Harper.

At least it seemed she was; hard to tell. Her eyes were hidden behind a pair of tortoiseshell Ray-Bans. The train emerged from the tunnel and into the light. The young woman stopped chanting, stopped swinging her beads.

"Did I scare you?" she said.

Harper straightened up as a message kicked in from the depths of his own reptilian brain: *Must not die now.* He worked his options with bandaged hands and a right arm in a sling. Weren't many. Lunge ahead, ram his elbow into her throat, and break her windpipe topped the list.

"Depends," Harper said. "Where did everyone go?"

She nodded to where the Chinese man had been snoring.

"Him? He's in the café car drinking beer."

Harper nodded to where the American couple had been.

"What about them?"

She took off her Ray-Bans, clipped them to the collar of her T-shirt. Harper scanned her eyes; they were clean.

"The Americans? They're in the café car, too. They're drinking tea."

Harper relaxed, sat back in his seat. "Right."

"I'm Karoliina. I'm from Tampere. It's in Finland, in the middle bit. I'm on my way to Montreux to meditate. You?"

"I live in Lausanne."

"I got that. From the American lady. What I wanted to know was what you're going to do in Lausanne."

Harper analyzed her voice. She was telling the truth. She spoke English with a Scandinavian postal code. He tried to shift gears on the manner of her thinking.

"I didn't know the Paris to Lausanne train made a stop in Finland," Harper said.

"Ha, ha, you're funny. I just flew in from the States last night, got on the first train this way. There's an ashram close by there. It's in Les Avants."

"Is that where you're going?"

"Depends. Ever heard of Locomotora?"

"Interesting name for an ashram."

"It's not. It's a post-rock band from where I live in Tampere. There's a lot of post-rock bands there. But they're the best. They're the ones who know the real deal, the big scoop."

"You don't say."

"I just did."

She gave the beads another go this way, then that way. Her lips reciting whatever words they were in rapid-fire silence. Then:

"If you're wondering what I'm doing, I'm praying."

"For who?"

"For you."

"For me?"

"That's what I said. I was up in first class and got bored. I went to the café car to see if there was anyone interesting. I was told to look for someone interesting on the train. I got your story from the American lady. It sounded *really* interesting."

"My story?"

"About your accident in Paris. Hit by a bus, she said. She thought you were such a nice British gentleman. Very polite and reserved, didn't talk much. I've never met anyone hit by a bus before, so I came looking for you. I thought I'd pray for you. I do that a lot. I look for people I can pray for. I saw you and said to myself, *That guy needs my prayers.* You should check out Locomotora. The band, I mean."

"How did you know I was the interesting chap you were looking for?"

"How hard is it to find a guy who looks like he's been hit by a bus and is sitting in coach seventeen of the TGV 9261? You know, you're lucky."

"So the American lady kept telling me," Harper said.

"I don't mean the bus."

"No?"

"No. I mean I found you just in time. Your aura was surrounded by the Five Poisons."

"Sorry?"

"Ignorance, Pride, Attachment, Jealousy, Anger. They were all floating around you. I chased them away."

"Cheers."

"Billions, but I know what it really means."

"You do?"

"Tietysti, etkö?"

"Sure, I know what it means. It means a piece of a comet named Giacobini-Zinner burned up upon entering the Earth's atmosphere."

"Says who?"

"An eminent astrophysicist from Oxford. At least he will."

"When?"

"Tonight. He's giving a lecture at l'Académie des sciences in Paris. It'll be in all the papers tomorrow. Along with some impressive supporting data from EPFL."

"What's EPFL?"

"It's where the smart people live in Lausanne."

She tipped her head as if Harper were a curious thing.

"Why are you pretending?"

Harper smiled.

"Like you said, mademoiselle, those are the rules."

"So maybe I'm supposed to tell you what it means. That must be it, the reason we met."

"I'm listening."

She sat back in her seat, started flipping her beads.

"He. Is. Born."

Harper stared at her.

"Who's born?"

She smiled, leaned across the aisle, whispered, "A child conceived of light who will take us to the next level of evolution. He's already here. That's what it's all about. That's the real deal, the big scoop."

"And you know this how?"

She sat back in her chair, gave her beads a twirl.

"Everyone in my gang knows it. It's our job."

"At the ashram."

"No, in the band."

Karoliina from Tampere was mad, Harper thought, but nicely mad. The kind for whom life was a journey from one guru to the next and who jumbled all her life experiences into a place she called the ultimate truth of everything there is. And Harper had to admit, her take on the comet was entertaining. Had a kid's-Christmas-pageant feel about it. Matthew 2:2: *Saying, Where is he that is born King of the Jews? for we have seen his star in the east, and are come to worship him.* Adding to the imagination, a guitar sounded from on high. Strumming a progression of descending chords built around a tonic note. The sound hung in the air, then repeated. It was a mobile ringtone. The young woman dug through her overstuffed Prada bag. She found her phone, checked her messages. Harper chuckled to himself. Even the sensitive ones in search of universal truth need to be connected 24/7, it seemed.

The train slowed.

A recorded announcement played through the train car. *"Mesdames et messieurs . . ."* The train would be coming to a stop in Dijon. Next stop after Dijon, French-Swiss frontier. Harper waited for the announcement to run through French, German, Italian, and English. While it continued, the young woman closed her phone and dropped it in her bag. She started flipping beads again, staring at Harper the whole time. When the announcement finished, there was the *clackityclack* of the train running over steel rails and the rattle of the woman's beads, *andante moderato*. Harper gave it a few beats to see if the young woman would pick up with the he-is-born riff. She didn't.

The train eased to a stop at Dijon station. She pulled her Prada bag over her shoulder and stood up.

"Where are you going?" Harper said.

"I'm getting off."

"You said you were going to Montreux."

"I did, and I was. But the band is doing a gig in Toulouse. I have to be there."

"Toulouse is south, toward Spain."

"I know. I'll catch a train from Dijon. I'll be there in five and a half hours. It was all in the message."

"What?"

"This is how it works. The band announces a gig, sends you directions from wherever you are in the world. People drop what they're doing and get there. We get together, make a flash mob, do some stuff. Maybe you should come. Check it out."

Harper ran Matthew 2:10: *When they saw the star, they rejoiced with exceeding great joy.*

"Got it. But, if you don't mind, I'll say good-bye."

"There are no good-byes in the universe, only nice to see you again."

"If you say so, mademoiselle."

She reached to the overhead rack, grabbed a small suitcase. She pulled her Ray-Bans from the collar of her T-shirt. Her sheepskin coat opened making the move, and Harper saw the image on the shirt. A winged form, falling through the fog at Pont des Arts in Paris. Harper was looking at himself during the Paris job. He saw the words: *Older Than Dreams Tour . . . Locomotora . . . Aladdin Theater, Portland.*

"Hang on a sec."

"Yes?"

"Your shirt."

"What about it?" she said.

"Where did it come from?"

"From the band. Locomotora. Like it?"

"Sure. What does it mean?"

She slipped on her Ray-Bans, smiled.

"You're really funny."

She turned, walked away.

Harper looked out the window, watched her climb down the steps and walk along the platform and down the stairs. Then he watched the locals coming and going with their bags. He checked the billboard above the platform. He'd be in Lausanne in another two hours. Lausanne. He flashed Inspector Gobet coming back onto the rooftop in Paris, just after Bruno Silvestre of Brigade Criminelle dropped "the time of the prophecy is at hand." Unfortunately, no idea what the prophecy was, or meant. Inspector tells Harper to get on the next train to Lausanne . . .

Lausanne? What the hell am I supposed to do in Lausanne?

Oh, I'm sure you'll figure it out along the way, Mr. Harper.

Just then, Harper did.

"Not a damn thing."

Harper blinked, looked across to the next platform.

TGV 5001. Dijon–Toulouse. Departing in seven minutes.

"Bloody hell."

He got up, grabbed his coat, pulled it over his shoulders. He jumped off the train as the doors closed.

❖

EIGHTEEN

A T MONTPELLIER, THE ONE TGV STOP EN ROUTE TO TOULOUSE, Harper stepped off the train with the rest of the smokers desperate for a fag. A voice blared over the public address system, announcing it'd be a five-minute stop. Harper found a shadow to hide in. They'd redone his bandages in Paris as part of cleaning him up, and the wrappings were less clumsy. Still took him half a minute to pull a smoke from his cigarette case; ditto with lighting the bloody thing. He inhaled deeply, let the radiance seep into his blood. He scanned the crowd, especially the ones heading for the exits. Karoliina from Tampere was nowhere to be seen. He'd walked the length of the train, checking all the cars of the train, twice. Couldn't find her. And she wasn't on the platform now. He worked the odds that he'd been a right prat in changing his itinerary. They came up dead even. No worries, Harper thought; there was always the universal truth of everything regarding his job in paradise: No matter where Harper ran through time and space, trouble always had a way of being there when he arrived.

The trainman's whistle screeched, warning the TGV's doors were about to close. The locals all took last puffs and tossed ciggie butts onto the tracks. They climbed on board. Harper took a quick hit, dropped his fag on the platform, ground it into dust. Climbing onto the train, he kept his eyes drilled to the floor to avoid the notice of the locals. *Convenient trick,* he thought, settling into his seat. The art of being invisible in a crowd. Not the least for the fact he hadn't bothered to buy a ticket to Toulouse.

The train pulled out of Montpellier, and Harper kept his eyes focused out the windows now. Off to the left, the land flattened and there were towns built along a string of saltwater ponds. There was a horizon rising beyond the ponds to the southeast. Grayish blue, shimmering in the midday light. The Mediterranean Sea, it was. And it was the first time he'd seen it since taking the form of Jay Harper. It felt familiar, like some long-forgotten thing suddenly found . . . Then something in the hippocampus region of his brain kicked in and the thing was forgotten again.

Out the right windows, there were autumn-colored fields dotted with small villages, and farther on was the Massif Central. Bits of information connected in Harper's brain. One: The Massif covered eighty-six thousand square kilometers, making it twice as big as Switzerland. Two: The region was packed with mountains, canyons, high plateaus. There were nearly four hundred fifty volcanoes quietly simmering away, as they had for the last ten thousand years. Three: The Massif was made famous by one George Julius Poulett Scrope, nineteenth-century English geologist and economist who published *Memoir on the Geology of Central France, including the Volcanic Formations of Auvergne, the Velay, and the Vivarais* in 1827. Harper chuckled to himself, wondering where the hell, or who the hell, the info came from. Then he hit it on his timeline. Captain Jay Michael Harper. Studied geography at the University of St. Andrews. Before any more info bled through, the hippocampus region of Harper's brain did its thing and the not-so-dead captain went the way of the Med Sea.

"C'est la bloody *vie."*

The train slowed passing through Béziers. And slowly crossing the trestle over the river Orb, Harper saw a great gothic cathedral towering over the town on the far bank. Looked more like a castle than a cathedral, and whilst looking at it, his mind ran through another info thread he'd picked up somewhere in time. La Cathédrale Saint-Nazaire, completed in the sixteenth century. The cathedral on the hill had been built over the ruins of another one, destroyed in the thirteenth century. Then something flashed in Harper's eyes, so fast he nearly missed it. Coming into Montpellier, Harper had crossed into the Languedoc region of France. *Languedoc.* It meant "tongue of the Ocs"—the language of Occitania. Then came an episode of the History Channel: *In the Name of God: The Slaughter of the Cathars.* The episode ripped through Harper's eyes. It was here, Béziers, July 22, 1209, the French Crusaders drew first blood. The army surrounded the town, demanded the surrender of all Cathars. The Catholic citizens of Béziers refused to hand over their friends and neighbors who were Cathars. The Crusaders attacked. Thousands of innocents sought sanctuary in the old cathedral and the churches of Marie-Madeleine and Saint-Jude. The Crusaders surrounded the buildings; they hesitated. Inside were not just Cathars, but fellow Catholics. There was a man among the Crusaders, Arnaud Amaury, Abbot of Cîteaux, personal representative of His Holiness the Pope. He sensed the hesitation of the Crusaders. He climbed the cathedral steps, held up the cross of his rosary and commanded them . . .

"In the name of God, kill them! Kill them all! For He will know his own!"

So blessed, the Crusaders smashed through the doors of the churches and put to the sword more than twenty thousand innocents in a single afternoon. The flow of blood only fueled the slaughter, and the Crusaders ran amok through the town. Women were raped in their beds as their throats were cut open. Children were forced to run through the streets and used as target practice by archers. Hundreds had their noses cut off and eyes gouged out. They were banished to wander the earth like the living dead as a warning to any and all who would defy the infallibility of the Church. When the Crusaders had sated their lust, they sacked the town and burned it to the ground. And that was the end of the first Cathédrale Saint-Nazaire.

Harper blinked, focused back out the window. The cathedral and Béziers were well out of sight. And now, watching the land of vines and maquis scrub whip by, Harper flashed one more map from geography studies at St. Andrews, matched it to the History Channel. The train wasn't just carrying him to Toulouse on a wild hunch to check out some Finnish rock band; it was carrying him close to Bernard de Saint-Martin's last stand at Montségur in 1244. Odds there was a connection: 325,747,053 to 1.

"What have you got yourself into this time, boyo?"

No idea was his response to himself. But it was a long way there. He settled back in his seat, eased into hibernation mode. Slow breaths, still-ness, until the train stopped at Gare de Toulouse Matabiau. Harper snapped to, checked his watch: 15:00 hours on the nose. He followed the crowd through the station. Outside, on the square, he took in the view. Like any big-town train station. At least the ones he could recall, which would be Gare de Lyon in Paris, Simplon and Montreux in Swit-zerland. Cafés and two-star hotels across the boulevard, people in a state of perpetual motion. Except for those who stopped the world to have a smoke after being cooped up in a train for hours.

He pulled his cigarette case from his coat and lit up, considering the great unknown; *id est*, where does one go in Toulouse to find a merry band of Finnish rock-and-rollers? He puffed on his smoke, walking to the left; turning around and walking to the right to see if he could pick up a vibe in the air. Not that it was some wizardly technique at discover-ing the great unknown, but it's how he found Café du Grütli in the old quarter of Lausanne after his memory scrub a few days ago. This way, that way. Pace, pace, pace . . . An hour later, "Oh, yeah, it's that way."

While smoking and pacing, he dug through his pockets looking for his mobile. Found it. Took some effort to open the flip-top and push the buttons with his bandaged hands, but he managed. No messages, no missed calls.

"Fine then."

He closed his phone, dropped it in his pocket. Saw a drawing on the pavement. It'd been done with a stencil and blue chalk. He watched the locals passing by. None of them noticed it. It was the angel falling through the sky in Paris. Lettering under the form:

OTDT
21:00, ce soir
La Dynamo

Harper flashed lettering on the T-shirt of the woman on the train. *Locomotora. Older Than Dreams Tour.* La Dynamo had to be the venue. He looked for a taxi stand; it was ten meters away. He walked over, saw the same stencil drawing on the pavement outside each of the station exits. The taxis were parked in a long line with no takers at the moment. Harper approached the lead car, a Renault Vel Statis with a Capitole Taxi sign on top. The driver's window was down, and the man inside, North African–looking, was sleeping. Harper stood there, waited for the man to become aware of his presence. The man opened one eye.

"Qu'est-ce que vous voulez?"

"Excusez-moi. Connaissez-vous un club appelé La Dynamo?"

The driver sat up, rubbed his eyes, looked at Harper. Saw an English man speaking French with a very bad accent and looking much too old and dressed completely out of step with anyone wanting to know the way to such a place.

"You want to go to La Dynamo?"

"That's right."

The driver shrugged.

"It's in the Colombette Quarter of the city."

"And where might that be?"

The driver pointed through the windshield.

"Walk to the canal, by the trees over there. It runs down the middle of the boulevard. Cross over the canal, go left, and walk along the embankment. Keep walking till you come to the second bridge, go right. The next block, go left. That's Rue Amélie. There's no sign for it, but it's there. Number Six."

"Actually, I thought you might drive me there."

"You want me to drive you there?"

"That is the general idea of a taxi, isn't it?"

The driver returned to his sleeping position, waved Harper away.

"Lâchez-moi."

Harper saw the next taxi. The driver behind the wheel was sleeping, too, and the next one. Must be bloody siesta time at the taxi ranks in Toulouse.

"Cheers for the help."

The driver snored.

Harper followed the crosswalks through the boulevard till he got to the trees. He saw the canal hemmed in between stone embankments. It was like a small river. There was a barge going upstream, one going downstream. Harper had another shot of geography studies. Canal du Midi. Two hundred forty kilometers up and over the mountains and down to the Mediterranean Sea after working through ninety-one locks. Going the other way it hooked up with the Garonne River, and from there it was a winding trip to the Atlantic Ocean. Someone, somewhere, had called it one of the technical wonders of the world. That's all Harper could dig up about it. His eyes caught the graffiti job on the sign pointing to the footbridge. *Canal du Midi* had been squiggled out with yellow paint and replaced with *Canal de las Doas Mars*. Harper ran the words. Wasn't Spanish, wasn't French. It was Occitan, and it meant Canal of the Two Seas.

Not bad, Harper thought, questioning if it was himself knowing it or if he was getting a boost from Bernard de Saint-Martin, who probably roamed the town nine hundred years ago. He stopped on the bridge to finish his smoke, forgetting the question immediately. In its place he watched another barge coming up the canal. It was packed with Japanese tourists. All of them wearing the same colored hats and windbreakers. All of them with a camera of some sort in their hands. And as they passed under the footbridge, all of them looked up at Harper. Some of them connected with his eyes. Those ones waved. He waved back. Why not? He dropped his fag into the canal. It dissolved into nothing.

He walked to the embankment path, went left, as instructed by the cabbie. Ten minutes later he was making the turn onto Rue Amélie. It was a narrow street with the right side lined with flats, circa 1970s. Left side was what must have been a factory row from the nineteenth century. Solid-looking buildings made of brick. From somewhere, Harper recalled that was typical in Toulouse. Same sort of bricks were used all over the city back then. The local soil gave the bricks a tint of pink. The bricks gave the city its nickname, *La Ville Rose*. He stood a moment, taking note of the fact there was no one about noticing the bricks, or anything else that might happen at the moment.

He walked ahead, passing the doors of the factory row. He passed a joint called Le Rest'Ô Jazz. That was Number 8. At Number 6, no sign on or above the door. Harper heard a guitar. Strumming a progression of descending chords built around a tonic note. The sound hung in the air, then repeated. He flashed back to the train from Paris to Lausanne: Karoliina from Tampere, busily swinging her *japa mala* beads, her mobile rings. It was the same damn riff coming from behind the door. And as the guitar finished the riff, drums and bass kicked in with a slow 4/4 beat. Down on the pavement, another blue chalk stencil job of an angel falling from the sky. This time the words under the drawing read, *This must be the place.*

"Sure. But for what?" Harper said.

He checked his watch: 15:45 hours. Five hours, fifteen minutes to showtime. Maybe it was a matinee behind the doors. He pulled open the door, entered a small vestibule; the ticket window was closed. He walked ahead through a set of heavy curtains. There was a very large man standing there to greet him. Well over two hundred kilos. Black sneakers, black trousers, black shirt, black leather vest over the shirt. Badge on vest: Sécurité. The man had already seen Harper's eyes, so there was no getting around him without negotiating safe passage. Harper watched the man's lips move, which was about the best there was for communication, as the music nearly drowned the spoken word.

"May I help you?"

"Sure, where's the bar?"

"Apologies, monsieur, the bar does not open till eight."

"But the band is playing now."

"Sound and light check."

"What?"

"Sound. Light. Check."

Harper wasn't sure what it meant, but it sounded very much like *fuck off.*

"How about Karoliina?"

The man did a visual recon of Harper from head to toe and back again.

"*You* know Karoliina?"

"Sure."

"And *she's* expecting you?"

Harper waved the bandaged palm of his right hand before the man's eyes.

"Mate, can you think of another reason why I'd be here? And if you can't, you should just step aside and let me pass, then forget all about it."

The man stepped aside, and Harper squeezed by.

It was a huge, dimly lit space of old wooden floors and ceilings, supported by the original iron crossbeams and pillars. Far end of the space, five young men on a stage. Four with guitars, one on drums. They had their eyes to the floor as they played. All of them dressed in clothing off the racks of a Salvation Army thrift store. Their hair looking like it didn't know what a comb was. And there were a couple men in overalls walking around the open floor with tall stepladders. They parked the ladders under spotlights, climbed up, and adjusted the color filters and direction of light. *Seems the band likes the color blue,* Harper thought. Harper saw the bar to the right. He walked over. No bartender, and the bottles were locked up behind a cage.

He settled into the shadows, watched the band.

There wasn't a singer, just the instrumentalists playing the same riff over and over. The two guitarists at either end of the lineup were overlaying the progression of drums, bass, and rhythm guitar with riffs that sang and clashed and wailed. And all together the sound seemed to rise above the sum of its parts and into a slow hypnotic drone, circling the space and bouncing off the walls. Harper felt sound resonate in his chest. He knew it . . . from somewhere . . . a chant. Then it stopped cold. The guitarist moved around the stage, plucking notes or striking chords quietly. One of them passed a ciggie around and they all had a puff. Looked hand-rolled. The drummer yelled to someone.

"I still need more kick drum in the monitors!"

Harper made a mental note for future reference. Sound and light check. Got it.

Someone tapped Harper's shoulder from behind. That's when he realized how hypnotic the sound had been. For a moment, he'd lost concentration on the now. He turned around, saw Karoliina from Tampere. She was in her sheepskin coat and swinging her beads.

"Nice to see you again," she said.

"And you, too, I think."

"You saw the blue angel, didn't you?"

Harper flashed the chalk drawing on the pavement outside the train station.

"I did. There were a few of them."

"That's how it works. Most people are coming by train for this gig. Krinkle made the signs so people will know where to go."

"Krinkle?"

"The roadie for the band. You know, the guy who moves the amps and speakers and instruments, and the band, from one place to the other. Gets it all set up for the gig, then takes it down, takes it someplace else."

"Krinkle the roadie. Right. Tell me something, mademoiselle, can everyone see them?"

"See what?"

"The signs on the ground."

She smiled.

"Depends."

"On what?"

"On whether you're looking for them or not."

Harper looked at the band. The guitarists were still plucking softly at their strings, and the drummer was slamming at his kick drum whilst puffing on the hand-rolled ciggie.

"What are they smoking up there?"

"Some Toulouse homegrown. You want some?"

He looked at Karoliina.

"No thanks, I've got my own."

She gave her beads a happy twirl.

"What did you think of the music?"

"It's loud."

"Compared to what?" she said.

Only music he could flash up was from a program on the History Channel. *The Greatest Arias of Opera*. There was one song, "Nessun Dorma" from *Turandot*. Something about a man not being able to sleep. It gave Harper the chills.

"Compared to everything I know about music," Harper said.

He stared at her.

"Krinkle is backstage," she said. "He's the one you're looking for. He's waiting for you."

"Krinkle."

"Yeah."

"Is there more to his name, or is that it?"

"Yeah, some people call him Little Buddha, but Krinkle is what most people call him."

"And how do you know he's the one I'm looking for?"

"Because he told me."

"Sorry?"

"I was standing with him and we saw you come in. Krinkle said, 'Tell that guy with the bandages on his hands that I'm the one he's looking for, and I'll meet him backstage.'"

Harper checked the room. The stage was pressed up against a brick wall.

"Where's backstage?"

Karoliina pointed to the fire exit sign to the left of the stage.

"You go out that door, down the alley, and you'll see a big black bus. It's his. He's there."

Harper nodded, walked that way. He stopped, turned around. Karoliina was leaning against the bar, swinging her beads, watching him.

"You're not coming with me?"

"No. I need to be here when the band finishes the sound and light check. I restring and tune the guitars before every gig. That's what I do. That's why I had to be here."

Harper walked back to her.

"By the way, if it's not a trade secret, how the hell did you get here?"

"To Toulouse?"

"I checked the train, twice. You were nowhere to be seen."

"You were looking for me?"

"Yes."

She smiled, chuffed at the thought. Harper flashed the sentiment in Finnish: *Tyytyväinen.*

"No secret," she said. "I ran into a friend at the Dijon station. Turns out he was heading to Lausanne, too. He writes game programs for the Internet. Sells billions and billions of them, so he's loaded with billions. He had a private jet fly down from Paris, pick us up at Dijon airport, and fly us here."

Harper thought about it.

"You flew here."

"I told you, I had to be here to restring and tune the guitars."

"Right. That's what you do. Cheers."

"*Ei kestä.*"

Harper stared at her, working the words in his head: *My pleasure.* She reminded him of someone just then. She was a shadow on his timeline; she was in LP's Bar at the Palace Hotel. The hippocampus region of his brain snapped him back to now. He turned away, crossed the wooden floor, headed for the fire exit. He walked by the stage. The musicians watched him pass. The lot of them with that Karoliina-on-the-train gaze. *I know who you are.*

Out the door.

Down the alley.

Parked in the shade of a very old plane tree was a Mercedes-Benz Travego. It fit the bill. It was big, it was black. And a bit more stylish than the number 16 bus Harper rode often through the old quarter of

Lausanne. Looked like a custom job. The black metallic paint almost sparkled, the wheels were polished chrome, the windows running down the side were tinted to keep whomever was inside from prying eyes. Harper looked around. Nobody. He dug out his fags, lit up, giving someone a chance to show up. He checked the bus's license plate; it was registered in Germany. No other markings. Just then, a hydraulic pump went *shhhhh*, and the one door at the front of the bus opened. A set of stairs slid out and down to the ground. The stairs were chrome, like the wheels. And there were small blue lights along the edge of the steps.

Harper drew on his smoke.

"Must be my stop."

He walked over.

A disembodied voice said *"Please mind the gap"* in German, Spanish, Italian, English, and French. Harper dropped his smoke and climbed on the bus. He saw the driver's cockpit. Had a lot more bells and whistles than the number 16 in Lausanne. Thing looked like it could drive itself and explain Minkowski's space-time theory at the same time. Top of the steps there was a door to the passenger compartment. Harper looked at the empty driver's seat.

"Okay if I just go in?"

The steps retracted and the door of the bus closed.

"I'll take that as a yes."

Harper grabbed the latch, heard music from beyond the door.

Violins and a piano playing a progression of descending chords around a tonic note. Wasn't the same tune as the band in the club. It was soft, no percussion, floating. But it had the same feel—deep within the sound was that same droning chant. Harper opened the door, saw a well-appointed cabin of black leather sofas and chairs anchored to the red carpeted floor. A long desk lined one side of the cabin. It was topped with Apple laptops and monitors, a high-tech microphone. Huge speakers were mounted on either end of the desk. Between the speakers was a rack of DVD and CD units, reel-to-reel tape machines. There was a man sitting at the desk in a swivel chair. His back was to Harper. He had a shock of white hair, tied in a long ponytail. He wore denim overalls over a red-checked shirt. He didn't turn around as Harper entered the cabin, but he raised his left hand, index finger in the air, acknowledging his presence and telling him, *Hang on a second.*

Harper's eyes shifted to the green and red lights flashing down the line of equipment. The needles of meters on one reel-to-reel bounced up and down as the wheels turned and rolled tape at fifteen inches per second. *Must be the source of the music,* Harper thought. The man hit a switch on the desk and the music from the speakers cut. Same moment, a sign above the cabin door lit up red: ON AIR. The man leaned into the microphone, eased up one fader on the sound mixer.

"It's called A Symphony Pathétique from the neoclassicist drone collective known as A Winged Victory for the Sullen. Wherever you are in space and time, you're tuned to the last radio station on planet Earth, and yes, it's true: Locomotora is performing tonight in downtown Toulouse. But fear not if you can't make it, because we'll be presenting the gig live in about five hours. Spread the word. Meantime, we're winding back the clock with the Grateful Dead. Jamming at the Dream Bowl in Vallejo, California, back in 1969. February twenty-first, a soft winter's night. Hold on to your heads, brothers and sisters, it's 'Dark Star,' and I'm gonna let the concert run all the way to 'Morning Dew.' We'll talk on the other side."

The man's voice was laid-back and American as apple pie. He flipped the switch on the mixer, another reel-to-reel began to turn, and the cabin filled with music. More guitars and drums weaving around one another, looking for a place to connect, and when they did, the man at the desk eased down the fader on the mixer and the sound became a whisper. He pulled off his headphones, spun around in his swivel chair. He picked up a cup of tea and sipped.

Harper saw the man was tall, from the flip-flops on his feet to the long, unkempt beard that matched the color of his hair. Lines and creases etched in the man's face put him well into his sixties. But it was the shade of green in his eyes that gave away the man's true age. Two and a half million years.

"Hey there, brother," he said. "Long time, no see. We need to talk."

❧

NINETEEN

I

APPROACHING THE TOWN OF TARASCON-SUR-ARIÈGE, THE TWO men dressed as pilgrims making their way to Le Chemin de Saint-Jacques de Compostelle turned south into the Vicdessos Valley. They followed a two-lane road bound by hills thick with beech and silver fir. The sky was bright, but the direct light of the sun never found their steps. They kept a steady, quiet pace as they walked, and there were the sounds of a fast-running stream and woodpeckers hammering at trees. Nearing Vicdessos and Auzat, they climbed the north-facing slope of the valley to the top of the ridge, two hundred meters above the towns. Inhabitants of the region were welcoming. They would take notice of two pilgrims who had lost their way, surely.

"Messieurs, you should be going west to Aquitaine, to the crossing at Saint-Jean-Pied-de-Port," they'd say. "You can't cross the mountains without a guide, not here. It's very dangerous this time of year. The storms can come quickly now. If you become lost, no one will find your bodies till the spring melt."

Following the ridge, they stayed clear of Goulier and the castle ruins at Montréal de Sos. The sun warmed the hilltops, and at a clearing along the ridge, Astruc and Goose saw a handful of people walking the trail to the ruins.

What are they searching for, Father?

Astruc knew Montréal de Sos well. He'd combed the ruins and caves many years ago, searching for the same thing the tourists were looking for now.

"Hope. They're searching for hope."

Clear of the towns, they descended the ridge and joined a stretch of asphalt with no painted lines or passing traffic. A yellow sign, almost hidden in overgrown scrub, marked the road as the D8. It was quiet here; the road could pass for abandoned. They walked, leaning into their steps as the grade began to rise. By the time they reached the hamlet of Marc, seven kilometers south, they'd reached an altitude of eleven hundred meters. They'd also reached the place where all roads ended; there were only rugged tracks and mountain trails. From here, the land quickly climbed another two thousand meters to the crest of the Pyrenees.

The hamlet was very quiet. Most of the inhabitants had moved down to lower altitudes to escape the coming winter. Already, in the shadows where Astruc and Goose walked, a chilling cold seeped down from the peaks of Rouges de Bassiès, Montcalm, and d'Éstats.

Could we stop a moment, Father?

Astruc looked at the sky. The sun was sinking, but there was still an hour of good light. He pointed to a wooden bench outside one of the dwellings. Goose let his backpack slip from his shoulders. He pulled the hoodie from his head and slumped onto the bench.

"What is it, Goose?"

My eyes. I can't see clearly.

Astruc took off his backpack, opened it, and found an auto-injector. He undid the needle cap, set the injector on Goose's thigh, and hit the release. The potion acted quickly. Goose's vision returned.

It's better now, Father. Thank you.

"We waited much too long. I'll give you another shot before you sleep."

343

If the Dark Ones find us, they'll never believe I'm the savior of men.

Astruc knew Goose was making a joke, despite speaking the truth. He could see it in the boy's pale eyes.

"You carry the weight of the world on your shoulders, Goose, but it is your duty."

I know, Father.

Astruc rubbed the boy's head.

"You know what the Dark Ones will do to you if they find you."

Goose reached into his leather jacket, pulled a sharp dagger from its harness.

Yes, Father, but you trained me well. Even a savior of men must know how to kill.

Astruc looked at the boy's eyes, checking him for light. *So fragile,* Astruc thought. But then again, had not both of them, had not the entire world, been crippled in the never-ending war between darkness and light? A war that had done nothing but turn paradise into a wasteland of hungry ghosts?

"Tomorrow, we'll cross Heaven's Gate and reach the other side of the Pyrenees. Tomorrow we will complete our mission. Then we'll continue our trip to Le Chemin de Saint-Jacques de Compostelle."

Goose sheathed the dagger.

And then you will rest, won't you, Father? Then you'll be able to sleep.

"I'll sleep, Goose, when I am forgiven of my sins."

II

HANG ON, ARE YOU TELLING ME THE PRIEST IS ONE OF US?"
"That's exactly what I'm telling you," Krinkle said.
"Bullshit."
"I told you, he's fucked up."
"Define 'fucked up.'"
"As in the opposite of 'all is well.'"
"I watched him kill an innocent man."

"He's killed lots since he lost it. Mostly bad guys, trying to kill him or the kid. There's been some collateral damage."

"The man in Paris wasn't collateral damage. He was a bloody file clerk in the mayor's office of the fourteenth arrondissement."

"So I hear. Astruc thought he was working with you. He thought Gilles Lambert was one of the Dark Ones."

"The what?"

"We're all the same to him. Good guys, bad guys. He thinks you and I are as evil as the enemy. In his head, we've enslaved mankind with our war. You think about it, you think he may have a fucking point."

Harper flashed back to Astruc in the cavern beneath Saint-Germain-des-Prés. Saw the big man speak those very words: *the Dark Ones.* He thought about it. Wasn't easy. He was still trying to get his head around the fact that the hippie leftover from the 1960s, the one wearing the denim carpenter overalls and flip-flops and sitting on a decked-out bus in Toulouse, was one of his own kind. Then the real surprise dropped: So was Father Christophe Astruc, OP.

"What about the kid?"

"George Muret?"

"Astruc calls him Goose."

"That's what the locals called him in his neighborhood when he was growing up. He had it tough."

Harper stared at him.

"Mind if I smoke?"

"Mi casa es tu casa, hermano."

Harper fumbled in his coat for his cigarette case. By the time he had a cigarette to his lips, Krinkle had a flame at the ready.

"How the hell do you guys do that?"

"Do what?"

"The fire thing."

Krinkle opened the palm of his hand. He was holding a small gold-plated lighter.

"You think I was management?"

"Are you?" Harper said.

"Hell no, brother, we work for the same suit."

"Inspector Gobet of the Swiss Police?"

"Is that what you call him? Is that what he is to you, a Swiss cop?"

"You telling me he isn't?"

Krinkle scratched his head.

"I think management is what it needs to be, and I think it's never the same thing to any of us."

"So what's management to you?"

Krinkle formed his hand like a gun, aimed at the kill spot above Harper's right eye.

"Bang."

Message received: *I could tell you but . . .*

Harper drew on his fag.

"Just out of curiosity, how do we know we're talking about the same member of management?"

Krinkle reached in the pouch of his overalls, pulled out a pack of smokes. No brand, no logo. He flipped the top, gave the pack a jerk, caught a gold-filtered fag in his lips, and lit up. Krinkle inhaled deeply, held it a few seconds, nodded to Harper's smoke.

"We smoke the same brand, don't we?"

"Hand-rolled at a little shop behind the Ritz in Paris?"

"Check."

Harper looked around the bus.

"Mind if I ask what it is you do, exactly? The band, the music, drawing angels on sidewalks and T-shirts, this radio setup?"

Krinkle sipped his tea.

"Communications, inspiration. Taking the sounds of men and tossing them into the sky."

"Sorry?"

"Radio waves travel forever through time and space, brother."

"Does that mean there's something out there listening?"

Krinkle shrugged, had a swig of tea.

"Just doing what I'm told to do."

Harper took another hit of radiance.

"Right, so the kid, Goose, had it tough. What else can you tell me about him?"

"Haven't figured it out yet?"

"Sorry?"

"I heard you're pretty good with hunches."

Harper held up his bandaged hands. "You heard wrong. What do you know about the kid?"

"Same thing none of us did, until I paid a visit to the administration office of a certain school for the deaf in Toulouse. Today, on my lunch break. The school's near the cathedral."

The school Goose attended, where he met Astruc, Harper thought.

"What did they tell you?"

"Nothing."

"Sorry?"

"It was lunchtime, this is France, no one was there. That's why I went when I did. Let myself in, searched the office. Went to the file room in the cellar, dug around through the archives. Nothing on the kid."

"So how . . ."

"Because on the way out, I looked around. Figured the dimensions of the cellar to the floor space of the upper floor. Didn't look right. I found a false wall hiding a big fucking bank vault. A Mosler, with a forty-seven-thousand-pound door."

"Sounds big."

"Isn't about big, it's about solid. There were a few Moslers in Hiroshima when the Americans dropped the nuke. Every one of the vaults survived the blast."

"So cracking nuke-proof safes is a communication skill in your line of work?"

"Sometimes. Let me tell you, there's some nasty shit in there. Shit Holy Mother Church does not want the world to see."

"Like what?"

Krinkle smoked.

"The one you call Gobet said you'd ask that question, and I'm to tell you it's none of your concern in the greater scheme of things."

"And in the lesser scheme of things?"

"The kid's father isn't the kid's father."

Harper thought about it.

"The kid is a half-breed."

"Bingo, brother. Got a hunch on who the real father is?"

III

THEY FOLLOWED A CASCADING STREAM UP THE MOUNTAINSIDE AS the light began to fade. The rocks were wet with misty spray, and they climbed carefully. Three hundred meters up, they reached a clearing bordered by a rock-faced cliff on one side and a line of stunted silver fir on the other. Ten meters above, a gush of water spilled over a crag and crashed into a churning pool. A roe deer was drinking from the pool and didn't hear the approach of the men at first. Then its ears twitched and the animal looked up. Astruc and Goose stopped and watched the deer. Its coat was rust-colored, its face was gray, and there were erect antlers atop its head.

Goose signed, *Genus and species: Caprelous caprelous. It's a young male. Three to four years old.*

Astruc held his voice and signed, *How can you tell its age?*

Its antlers don't have branches yet. I think antlers are funny things. I liked reading about them and seeing the pictures. That's why I know.

Astruc nodded, marveling again at how Goose never forgot anything he'd seen or read.

"Then it must be true," Astruc said.

His voice carried through the clearing, and the deer heard it and darted into the pine trees. A small shelter stood a hundred meters away at the base of the cliff. Stone-walled, slate-roofed, simple wooden door. There were shelters like this all across the Pyrenees. They were marked on maps as *le refuge*. Once only known to smugglers, then to the Spanish Republicans fleeing Fascism, now they were used by tourists from around the world who came to trek across the rugged mountains during the summer months.

Astruc led the way to the shelter, found an official notice tacked to the door advising passersby that use of the shelter was *interdit* without an official permit from the commune authorities in Auzat. But it was autumn now, and the pass at Heaven's Gate was closed. There would be no tourists coming this way, or officials from the commune checking for permits.

They went inside.

It was dim, damp. The only light came through a small window on the south wall. Inside were two wood-framed bunk beds with straw mattresses, either side of the shelter, and a stone fireplace built into the north wall. Goose took off his backpack, pulled his hoodie from his head. He opened the backpack, found four candles, and anchored them in the slits of the roughly hewn floor. He lit the wicks, and the shelter glowed with warm light. He unrolled his sleeping bag and spread it over one of the lower bunks. Astruc took off his own backpack, unrolled his own sleeping bag on the opposite bunk. He sat down and sighed.

"It's been a long day, but a blessed day for the world. Oh, Goose, what have you done with the hard drive?"

Goose tapped the pouch of his sweatshirt.

I'm keeping it on me, in case we need to dump our backpacks and run across Heaven's Gate.

Astruc smiled. "And so the student has become the teacher."

Goose looked at Astruc.

I could gather wood and build a fire, Father. It would chase away the cold.

"We'd best not. Wood smoke travels far in these mountains. We'll endure the hardship for the night. But tomorrow, when we reach Lladorre, we'll have a good fire, and hot food, hot tea."

Goose nodded happily.

That was the plan, and so far it was going well. All they had to do was cross Heaven's Gate and reach the shelter on the Spanish side of the Pyrenees. If the weather conditions were accurate, a massive front would move in from the Atlantic and drop three meters of snow over three days in the higher elevations. The storm would cut them off from France, and the shelter in Spain was in an isolated spot; no one would find them there. They'd already provisioned the place with new clothes and boots, supplies and communications equipment. They'd stocked it themselves as part of the preparations for their mission. Now, as they rested for the first time in weeks, they knew their work was almost done. There was only reaching Lladorre, setting up the communications gear, announcing the prophecy to the world, and declaring the men and women of paradise free from the rule of the Dark Ones. Stage three of their holy mission would be complete.

And I will make spaghetti, Father. That will be our first meal in Spain.

"And I'll have a whiskey to go with it."

Goose smiled mischievously. Astruc thought again how good it was to see the boy smile.

"What is it, Goose? Why do you smile?"

I have a surprise for you, Father.

Goose opened the side pouch of his backpack, took out a small box, handed it to Astruc.

"What's this?"

A gift.

"But why?"

Because we've come this far.

Astruc opened the box. There was a silver flask inside. He removed it, saw the engraving: *in girum imus nocte et consumimur igni*. It was a palindrome, a puzzle, a sequence of letters that read the same from back to front as front to back. It meant "we go wandering in the night and are consumed by fire." It was thought to have been composed in ancient Rome. The sort of thing Romans found scrawled on the walls of the tunnels of amphitheaters to amuse the passing masses. The fact that it referred to the scientifically observed behavior of moths meant it was composed in the Middle Ages. But as Astruc looked at the inscription, rubbing his thumb over it, he was overwhelmed with its deeper meaning. Long ago, the man that was Father Christophe Astruc saw a pitiful, misshapen boy sitting in a classroom of twelve students. A Dominican nun was writing conjugations of the verb *vouloir* on a blackboard and signing the words:

Je veux, tu veux, il veut. Nous voulons, vous voulez, ils veulent.

The children in the class dutifully copied the words into notebooks, except for the misshapen boy, sitting at the back of the room as if in a daze. Perhaps it was the boy's deformity, perhaps it was the blank expression in his eyes, but Father Astruc watched him for long minutes. The bell for *récré* sounded, and though the children were deaf, they saw the flashing blue light next to the bell and dropped their pencils and raced to the school yard for fifteen minutes of play. The misshapen boy stayed in his seat, and it was then Father Astruc remembered seeing him before. During midday Friday Mass, that was it. The same boy sat in the shadows at the side of the chapel. Never praying, never coming to the altar to receive Holy Communion, never taking his eyes off the burning candles of the altar. Astruc entered the classroom. The nun saw the young priest, knew he was attached to the Archbishop's office. Doing research for the Vatican, she'd been told. All the nuns at the school were very excited to have someone so highly regarded to serve as school chaplain. She spoke with reverence:

"*Bonjour, mon père.*"

"*Bonjour, ma soeur.* Sister, why isn't this boy going to play with the others?"

"To be honest, Father, it's safer for him here."

"Safer?"

"Some of the children torment him because of his appearance. I'm afraid he really doesn't belong in this school. He belongs in an institution, where he can live with proper supervision. They can care for him there, and . . ."

"And what, Sister?"

"Well, I'm afraid it's even worse at home. His father is quite cruel to him. At an institution, he'd be removed from any danger of sin."

"Sin? What sin could a child like this be guilty of?"

"Well, I . . . You should talk to Sister Superior, Father."

351

"I will," Father Astruc said, looking at the boy. "Does he read lips and speak?"

"Oh, yes. Sometimes I think he knows more than he lets on, but I'm sure I'm only imagining it."

"Really? How is he in his lessons?"

"As I said, he needs to be in an institution where they can help him. He might learn something there. Here, he only scribbles and draws nonsense. If we try to take his notebook, he goes into a fit. We do our best, but there's no getting through to him. We've all but given up on the poor thing."

"Sister, this boy isn't a thing, he is a child of God."

The nun blushed.

"*Mon père*, I assure you, that's not what I meant."

"It's all right, I know you meant no harm. Why don't you go to the school yard, get some fresh air. I'd like to talk to the boy alone."

"Talk to him? About what?"

"I'm the chaplain of this school, *non?*"

"*Bien sûr, mon père.*"

The boy didn't hear the nun's steps as she left, and he didn't notice he was alone with the priest. Father Astruc walked toward the boy. The boy felt the steps through the floor, turned, saw the priest approaching. Astruc watched the boy cower and grin like some fearful animal that had been cruelly beaten, never knowing where the next kick was coming from.

"*Bonjour,*" Astruc said. "Don't be afraid. I've seen you before. At chapel, sitting in the shadows. I'm not going to hurt you."

The boy stared at him with the strangest eyes. There was a film floating over the irises, masking any trace of color. Father Astruc looked at the notebook on the boy's desk. The pages were full of circles and lines and wild scratches. Perhaps the sister was right; perhaps the boy belonged in an institution. Then, staring at the open pages, Father Astruc saw the boy had been writing the conjugations backward, mixing French and German letters. And along the margins were drawings of creatures and mountains and clouds. All of it hidden under wild, frantic scratches.

"May I see your work?"

Goose stared at him, resisting, continuing to read the priest's lips.

"It's all right. I can keep a secret."

Goose let the notebook slip from his fingers. Father Astruc turned it around and flipped slowly through the pages. All the same: wild scratches hiding grammar lessons, arithmetic. The numbers caught Astruc's eyes. The boy had gone beyond addition and subtraction. He was solving complicated division and fractions. Then, on another page, he saw a line of perfectly formed Latin script: *in girum imus nocte et consumimur igni.*

Father Astruc felt his hands tremble. He looked at the boy.

"Did you write this?"

The boy didn't answer, but Father Astruc could see a flicker of light in the boy's pale eyes.

"What is your name, my son?"

And now, all these years later, looking at Goose in the soft light of the candles set about the shelter, Astruc could almost see *her* face. Astruc lowered his eyes, looked at the flask, ran his thumb over the inscription again.

"How wonderful this is."

He unscrewed the cap and sniffed the contents. Single malt, twelve years old. He took a healthy swallow and closed the cap.

Do you like it, Father?

"Yes, very much. But the contents will go down much better with your excellent spaghetti, so I'll save the rest. We should organize ourselves for the night, have something to eat before we sleep. We'll be up with the dawn."

Yes, Father.

They unpacked fresh pairs of socks and thermal leggings. Then came the UZI machine pistols, the two Glocks, and clips of ammunition. They'd carry their weapons across Heaven's Gate. This time of year they should be the only ones there; anyone else would be hunting for them. They ate a few high-protein biscuits in silence. Astruc reached for his goatskin, but it was empty.

"Do you have any water, Goose?"

Goose found his own goatskin and shook it; it was nearly empty.

I'll fill them from the waterfall.

"No, let, me."

No, Father, you rest. I'll do it.

Goose grabbed the goatskin . . .

"No, no."

They both held on to it, pulling it back and forth in a teasing tug-of-war. Astruc surrendered and let it go. He glanced at the small window.

"It's gone dark, Goose. You'd best use night vision. I don't want to lose you down the mountain. It would be a very lonely trek through Heaven's Gate without you."

I can hardly wait. I've been dreaming of spaghetti, with lots and lots of to-mato sauce. Ever since Paris.

Goose tossed the goatskins over his shoulder, dug his goggles from his backpack. He walked to the door and opened it. A cold wind blew in the shelter. He stood in the doorway at the edge of the dark, fitted the goggles over his eyes, and switched them on. He glanced at Astruc. *I'll be back.* Astruc nodded, picked up his UZI, and loaded in a forty-round clip. He laid it on his bed, looked up. Goose was still there, waiting. It was his way to wait for a last word, Astruc thought, as if seeking a blessing.

"I'll be waiting, my son."

Goose pulled his hoodie over his head, stepped outside, and closed the door. There was the sliver of crescent moon, hanging low in the western sky. Invisible to the naked eye, but Goose could see it with his goggles. He looked at the ground and walked across the clearing, fol-lowing the rock face to the waterfall. He leaned against a protruding stone and held each of the goatskins into the cascade. It was cold and his fingers became numb quickly. When the goatskins were full, he tossed them over his shoulder, leaned close to the water. He drank deeply, never before having tasted something so pure and cold. He stood up, wiped his mouth, and stared at the waterfall. Watched it tumble over the rock face and splash into the pool. There, the water swirled and bubbled and formed into a stream running down the mountain. And as he stared at it, he wondered what such a thing must sound like. He walked back toward the shelter.

Something in the trees. He stopped, stared at the branches, looking for movement. A roe deer, he thought, or perhaps a fox. Seeing the light in the shelter maybe, waiting for wood smoke, hoping scraps of food would be left behind. Foxes were clever things, Goose thought. He imagined a fox coming to the shelter after they'd gone, jumping up and catching the latch of the door and letting himself in. He thought it would be a very good idea to leave behind a few high-protein biscuits.

Something raced into the open and behind him.

Goose spun around, saw a huge dog with a long, thick white coat. On its four legs, it was almost as tall as him. *Canis lupus familiaris,* he remembered, and he knew the common name of the breed. It was *le Patou.* The dogs grew to be fifty-five kilos. He'd seen pictures of them in books. He liked that they were called "gentle giants of the Pyrenees." They were working dogs. They traveled with shepherds, guided and protected the flocks during migration seasons. He remembered another word, *transhumance.* It was on page 1286, column two of the *American College Dictionary* he liked to read sometimes: *the seasonal movement of people with their animals.* He remembered it was a funny-looking word. Then he remembered something else: In the region of Heaven's Gate, the season of moving flocks to lower altitudes, the transhumance, had finished weeks ago. It was the reason Father Astruc had chosen to come this way.

Then from the far trees a second *Patou,* even larger than the first.

It walked across the clearing and stood itself between Goose and the shelter. Both dogs snarled and flared their teeth, black drool dripping from their mouths. Goose backed up slowly. The animals matched him step for step, and when he stopped, they stopped. One of the dogs tipped its head to see beyond Goose. Goose looked back over his shoulder. Two more *Patou* emerged from the trees. Goose felt his heart pound in his chest. He lowered his head to avoid direct eye contact with the beasts and made a slow circle, peeking out from under his hoodie. In the shimmering green light of night vision, the dogs appeared as monstrous things. As they crept closer, Goose saw their black, lifeless eyes.

Goose pulled his dagger from his leather jacket.

There was a blur as the dogs lunged, dragging him to the ground. He twisted, kicked, got to his knees, and swung his dagger, but the dogs' manes were too thick to draw blood. The bigger dog caught Goose's wrist in its jaws. Goose felt his bones crack in the beast's mouth. Goose flipped the dagger to his left hand, rammed his weight into the dog and lifted it up. He buried the dagger into the beast's soft belly. It didn't yelp, it didn't run. Claws tore at Goose's back, jaws clamped around his ankles. He fell to the ground again. He rolled onto his back, saw a flash of teeth coming for his throat.

IV

I T WAS A ONE-NIGHT STAND IN TOULOUSE AT THE BACK END OF A solo drinking binge. He was still in seminary, had yet to make his final vows. He met the woman in a bar; never saw her again, never knew he left her pregnant. Didn't know the boy he met years later at the school for the deaf was his only begotten son."

"Astruc wasn't awakened yet. Didn't know what he was," Harper said.

Krinkle nodded, finished his tea.

"They tried to awaken him in Toulouse. It didn't go well. He couldn't accept the duality of his being, especially when it came to the 'us against them' part. Not after what he'd found in the safe. It all got twisted. In his world, it was him and the kid against the Dark Ones. Like I said, I half understand Astruc's point of view. He's been on the run for years from the good, the bad, and all the fucked-up killers in between."

"Does the kid know Astruc is his father?"

"Unknown. But digging through the house in Paris, HQ says the kid isn't a victim. He's a player, he believes everything Astruc tells him."

Harper flashed back to the first time he saw Goose. Hiding in the shadows, his face half hidden by a hoodie. He saw the hatred dripping from the kid's glassy, colorless eyes. Sure, Harper thought, why wouldn't he? The kid considered Harper no different from the man who attacked him with pliers and cut out his tongue.

"HQ thought the kid was dead."

"He wasn't supposed to live beyond his mid-teens. That was the medical line. Of course, no one knew the kid was what he is. So his stamina is way above normal, even as small and frail as he is. Also, Astruc's been keeping the kid going with potions he cooked up in the kitchen sink. Same with himself. He's come up with his own radiance potion to ease the weight, also masks the light in both their eyes."

"So how fucked up can Astruc be if he's whipping up potions in a kitchen sink?"

Krinkle finished his tea, set the cup on the desk. He reached for a bottle. Single malt, half full. Two crystal tumblers were parked nearby. Krinkle poured a heavy hand, handed over one tumbler. Harper took it.

"Cheers."

"Astruc's half awake in nowtimes, half suspended in a war of his own making. Now his war is going to shit, and if we don't bail him out, he's taking what's left of our kind with him."

"How so?"

"The SX squad dug deeper into the desktop at Astruc's hideout in Paris. Seems he discovered a file hidden deep in the enemy's mainframe. Sucker was locked with a password that'd stretch from here to Berlin. Astruc cracked the password and downloaded the file to Paris. Care to know what was in it?"

"Sure."

"So would we. Astruc zapped it clean. Nothing left but a file name, *circa humana fabula miraculum nativitate*."

Harper ran the words.

"Regarding the Human Myth of Miracle Birth."

"Check."

"Meaning what?"

"Who knows? The only place that file exists is in Astruc's head. Point is, he knew we'd find his hideout in Paris and the computer. He knew we'd crack the computer; still, he left a clue of what he knew. And right now, the enemy's gone Code Red hunting him down."

"You suggesting I give him some slack?"

"I'm suggesting somewhere in Astruc's fucked-up head, he's trying to do the right thing. Besides, I would've thought you would know how messy an awakening can be."

Harper flashed back to the cathedral job. Saw himself kicking and screaming as they tried to shake him awake. He saw the trail of mutilated bodies strewn along the way. One of them was a lad with a lantern, bred by his own kind.

They sipped. Krinkle smacked his lips.

"Now that we got that out of the way, I'm supposed to communicate new orders to you from the one you call Gobet. Track Astruc, get him to Lausanne Cathedral by any means necessary."

"Why me?"

"There are two people who know what Astruc looks like these days. Astruc killed one of them, that leaves you. Advantage: Astruc thinks he killed you, too. His mind won't be tuned to look for you. Grab him, get him to the cathedral for a session with Gabriel. Astruc needs to be completely awakened."

Harper wound back his timeline till he saw a morphine-addicted tramp on the altar of Lausanne Cathedral, standing in the light passing through the giant stained glass window of the south transept . . . Monsieur Gabriel. Turned out that he was one of Harper's kind. Had the job of shaking stubborn sorts awake to the truth of their being. Was also the keeper of ancient secrets. Revealed them as required. Harper blinked himself back to the bus.

"What about the kid?"

"Grab Astruc, the kid will follow. Soon as the kid crosses into Switzerland, he'll be picked up, taken to the medic in Vevey."

"Why isn't the inspector issuing the orders himself?"

"Because, officially, he has no idea where you are."

Harper flashed back again. In the vineyards with the cop in the cashmere coat. Drinking tea, smoking radiance, watching the stars. Inspector tells Harper he's being sent back to Paris . . . *HQ doesn't know you're juicing me for a mission, do they?* Answer: no. Harper blinked, looked at Krinkle.

"So unofficially, Inspector Gobet told HQ fuck all about Astruc."

Krinkle made with the make-believe gun: *bang.*

"Got it. But if it comes to 'any means necessary,' what do I pull a trigger with? My teeth?"

"Come again?"

Harper held up his bandaged hands.

"Oh, yeah."

Krinkle kicked open the desk's lower drawer. Jars of ointments and clear liquids inside. Also a fully rigged kill kit, good to go.

"I've got some potions to fix up your hands. They'll still hurt like hell, but they'll be workable, sort of. The guns and knives are for you, too. And Gobet told me to remind you that while 'any means necessary' implies the use of violence, it also implies if violence isn't necessary, then it should not be used."

Harper had heard that one before. Somewhere.

"So if I need to shoot him, be nice about it."

"Check."

Harper took another sip of single malt.

"Any idea where I start looking?"

Krinkle grabbed an iPad from the desk. He tapped and swiped the screen a few times, handed it to Harper. Onscreen: one mangled laptop computer, one something else looking like a stereo amplifier, one two-meter sat dish.

"A transmission rig?"

"Most probably the gear used to hack into Blue Brain last night. A local found it at dawn. He called the local gendarmerie. This happens, that happens, then the rig is in Berne within three hours. The laptop is customized, the uplink gear better than current military specs in anyone's army. Protocol acceleration and encryption, data transfer speeds at nearly four hundred gigs per second; all crammed into a unit the size of a bread box. There was a cable connected to the laptop, probably to an external hard drive. The drive is missing. HQ suspects the kid made the gear himself. His room in Paris was filled with electronic gizmos and microchips. Get this: The kid worked by candlelight."

Harper thought about it. The kid from Toulouse, the lad from Lausanne Cathedral; the two of them with a thing for candles . . . *Bloody hell*. He looked at the iPad again, saw a small black tube next to what was left of the laptop.

"What's this?"

"A thousand-watt laser pointer. The beam can be seen from outer space. It was found planted on the side of the mountain, pointing east. Would've laid a line on a west-to-east horizon, perpendicular to the line of sight from the north gate, where they found the rig."

Harper replayed Leo the Astrophysicist and his theory about the great cosmic clock: *He needs a perfectly still horizon, probably a laser.*

"It's Astruc, no doubt about it. Where did they find all this?"

"One hundred twenty klicks south of my bus."

Harper stared at him.

"I give up."

Krinkle sipped his drink, reached over, swiped the screen. Harper saw a photograph of a giant rock shooting out of the ground and into the sky. The next photos were different angles of the fortress ruins atop the rock. Medieval, thirteenth century. Took Harper three seconds to make it from the History Channel's program on the Cathars. *Fancy that*, Harper thought.

"Montségur, in the Pyrenees."

"That's right, brother. Trippy, isn't it? That place . . . us."

"Us?"

"You, Astruc, me. The reason we're talking."

"I thought we were talking so you could pass along new orders."

"That too."

Harper flipped back and forth between the photos. Flashed last night's scene with Inspector Gobet and the judge. Drilling him about one Bernard de Saint-Martin, dispossessed knight from Languedoc, burned to death as a heretic at the end of the Montségur siege in 1244. In front of ten thousand bloody witnesses, but manages to show up in Paris a year later with an ancient sextant in a reliquary box. Gathers a few disciples, hides the sextant, tells the lads to keep up the good work, vanishes. Fast-forward to nowtimes: Astruc, half awakened, half mad, atop Montségur with the same damn sextant, predicting a celestial event to the bloody second that announces the time of the prophecy is at hand. Harper wasn't sure what Krinkle meant by *trippy*, but it sounded spot-on.

"So what's your connection to Montségur? And why are we talking about it?"

Krinkle reached over, flipped the photos till he landed on a wide shot of the fortress atop the pluton.

"The three of us were there, brother."

Harper stared at him.

"Inspector Gobet told you this?"

"Put it this way: The one you call Gobet's seen to it that my timeline is flipped wide open, for one night only."

Harper looked at the teacup Krinkle had been drinking from.

"Doctor's orders?"

Krinkle nodded.

"Drink the tea and talk to the one called Harper about old times. Then broadcast tunes through the night, call me in the morning."

"Lucky you."

"Book's still out. We'll see how it goes."

Harper sipped whiskey and smoked his fag, realized that he'd been standing since he came on board. He looked back, reached over to grab a chair. It wouldn't budge.

"It's a bus, brother," Krinkle said. "The chairs are anchored to the floor."

"Right."

Harper sat down, ran through his meeting with the judge and Inspector Gobet in Paris.

"Inspector Gobet says I made an unauthorized apparition in 1244," Harper said.

"Wrong. You were assigned to Montségur from 1243–1244, the three of us were. It's your trip to Paris, after the fire, where you went AWOL. And just because you're listed as AWOL doesn't mean it's legit. Because, I'm telling you, the shit I'm seeing in my eyes is mind-blowing."

From trippy to mind-blowing in sixty seconds. He did look wide-eyed, Harper thought.

"What can you see?"

Krinkle settled back in his swivel chair.

"Astruc and me, inside Montségur with the fighters. Him as Jean de Combel, me as Raymond de Marseillan. We both fought alongside Bernard de Saint-Martin—the man, I mean. He was one tough bastard. Led a few hard battles, massacred ten Inquisitors at Avignonet. I'm not surprised you slipped into his form. After the fighting, I mean. Of course he was dying from a crossbow wound, so that helped."

"Mate."

"Yeah?"

"Focus. Was I in the form of Bernard de Saint-Martin at Montségur or not?"

"Not till the fighting was over. All through the siege you were form-jumping, picking up whatever was lying around. You worked in the shadows of the pluton and down on the plain; you were tracking the Crusaders, hunting bad guys in the ranks. And when you found one, you mutilated him, left him in pieces with a killing knife buried in his chest. Scared the Crusaders shitless. They had a name for you: *le chevalier fantôme*."

Harper smoked deeply.

"What was our mission, exactly?"

"To keep the treasure of the Cathars from falling into the hands of the bad guys. What else?"

Harper stared blankly. "What treasure?"

"You playing me for a sap, brother?"

"Let's say I'm checking how the tea's working."

"Coming on strong. And let's call 'the treasure' that thing you took from Montségur and hid in Paris when you went AWOL. The thing Astruc got his hands on a few days ago. The thing he brought back to Montségur to make his big splash with the comet."

Harper flashed the sextant.

"And since you were there in 1244, you know what that thing is," he said to Krinkle.

"Didn't know then, don't know now."

"No?"

"The one you call Gobet didn't tell me, and for the likes of you and me, that means 'don't fucking ask about it.' And so what? During the siege, none of us did."

Harper glanced at the teacup, then Krinkle.

"Mate, what did they put in your tea? Because you're not making sense."

"No idea, brother. Package arrived by messenger. Open it up and there's the jars, your kill kit, and a tea bag with a note: *Drink me.* Maybe you're not supposed to mix the tea with alcohol. Whatever, I'm all over my timeline now, but there you go. What I'm telling you is, back then none of us—you, me, Astruc—knew what the real treasure of the Cathars was. All we knew was there were hundreds of bad guys hiding in the Crusaders' ranks, and we were ordered to keep them off Montségur. I Googled the place as the tea was coming on to see if I could kick-start my timeline. Down there, all across the Pyrenees near Montségur, legends and myths grow like weeds. Biggest one says Mary Magdalene came from Jerusalem and brought the Holy Grail of Jesus Christ with her. People think there was a pagan temple up there where people worshipped the sun. Some people think the Cathars were up to the same thing. Another legend says the Cathars had the Holy Grail and they were hiding it in the fortress. And that four Cathars escaped with it before the rest of them were burned to death."

Harper gave it a few beats.

"You asking me if the treasure was the Holy Grail? Because if you are, you're wasting your time."

"At the moment, I ain't asking shit. At the moment, I'm babbling like a speed freak trying to get to the point. Look, the Grail didn't hold significance for the Cathars. It was a thing of the physical world with no real connection to their faith. They didn't have a sacrament of communion, even, and they didn't believe that Christ was the Son of God. For the Cathars, Christ was an angel in human form, like all human souls. Hey, I remember where I was going . . . Astruc and me, in the forms of de Combel and de Marseillan, saw the real treasure before it was smuggled away. Gold, silver, writings on their faith, that's it. No Holy Grail, no anything the bad guys would be interested in, and nothing our kind would be interested in. Astruc reported the intel to HQ, HQ advised the three of us were being pulled out."

"Turn around and walk away," Harper said.

"*Tempus fugit, aeternitas manet,* brother. HQ said the bad guys had it wrong, there was nothing hidden at Montségur. HQ didn't want to take a chance of us being killed in our forms for nothing more than a bad guy mass killing. You were ordered to Toulouse to take out an enemy chief hiding in the Office of the Inquisition. Astruc and me were kept at Montségur till the end, just in case something popped hot on the treasure front. But like I said, there was nothing."

The filter of Harper's smoke was singed, Krinkle's, too. Krinkle grabbed his teacup, offered it to Harper. Harper dropped in his fag, Krinkle gave his a toss. *Phhht, phhht.* Krinkle set the cup on the desk, looked at Harper.

"You want my two cents, seeing as I'm the only one on this bus drinking the tea?"

"Sure."

"I think in the last days before the fire, while you were carving up bad guys, one of the goons under the knife let slip the truth. There was *something* hidden at Montségur. I think you reported that intel through a back channel and you were given new orders; orders you were told *not* to share with Astruc and me."

"Don't go to Toulouse," Harper said. "Take a form in the fortress, find what the bad guys were after."

Krinkle drank his whiskey. "And that's when it all went belly-up. Because by then, looking at my timeline, there was only one way of getting off Montségur without tipping off the bad guys."

"The fire."

"Amen."

"Can you see it?"

Krinkle's eyes lost focus for long seconds, then he blinked.

"The three of us are dragged down the mountain with the Cathars. Our ankles shackled with ropes. Astruc and me still clueless that you've taken the form of Bernard de Saint-Martin, so we stay separate from you and from everyone as much as we can."

"So the time mechanics could get a fix on you."

"Yup."

"And then?"

"There's an open field at the foot of the rock. The Crusaders build a palisade there and cram us inside. Two hundred twelve terrified souls, knowing they're about to die a horrible death. Men, women. Nobody can move, everyone's pressing up next to one another, everyone's standing on a thick floor of straw and pitch. Plan is, fire starts, smoke rises under the hay, a time warp drops over Astruc and me, and we're pulled from our forms."

"You sure you had no idea I'd jumped into de Saint-Martin? You're sure it actually happened?"

Krinkle looked straight into Harper's eyes.

"The Crusaders torch the corners of the palisade, the fire goes up fast, runs around the outer walls. Looking at the fire, I can tell something's not right. The fire isn't spreading, it's hunting. The Cathars at the outer edge of the pack get it first. The fire curls around legs, crawls up chests, wraps around faces. People start crushing to the center, then fire begins to burn up through the hay. It's all happening too fast. Then bodies start going up like matchsticks, but the fire's playing with them, torturing them. And the heat, man, the heat. Stuff I read on Google said the fire was so hot, the Crusaders were chased kilometers away. Burned into the night. Next day, when the Crusaders came back, the ash was still smoldering, stayed that way for days."

"The enemy spiked the pitch with fire potions."

Krinkle nodded.

"The heat caused the time warp to flutter. The mechanics couldn't stabilize a signal. You know how it is getting sucked into a warp; one microsecond feels like forever. They got a lock on me, I was suspended in time and safe . . . but Astruc caught fire, totally fucking the warp signal again. He was suspended in time, trapped in his burning flesh, and he suffered badly. He had this terrible look in his eyes. First I was thinking it was the pain, but in those microseconds, I realized he was experiencing a vision in the flames. Then I saw it, too."

"What vision?"

"You."

Harper stared at him. Wide-eyed or not, he knew Krinkle was spilling absolute truth.

"Keep talking, mate."

"You're walking through the fire, giving the Cathars comfort . . . and, brother, you don't burn. Fucking flames part for you like the Red Sea before the Israelites. You see us, suspended in time. You see him burning, suffering beyond imagination."

"Astruc."

"No, Jean de Combel—I mean, yes, Astruc . . . they're the fucking same. He recognized you for what you really were. He cried to you, 'Brother, brother, help me!' He begged you to stop the flames. You couldn't, but you were talking to him. And as if trying to comfort him, too, you told him everything. The treasure of the Cathars, what it's for and what it means, your orders."

"And then?"

"Nothing. That's where my timeline stops. That's when the mechanics must have stabilized the warp and pulled me out. Astruc . . . I don't know how long it took for him."

Harper looked at the whiskey in his own glass; nothing. He looked at Krinkle.

"Why can't I see it? If it happened and you're telling me the names, Jean de Combel and Raymond de Marseillan, I should see it."

Krinkle sighed, glanced at the reel-to-reel reaching the end of its roll. "Just a sec."

He turned to the desk, put on his headphones, flipped switches. One reel-to-reel stopped, another one began to roll. Krinkle leaned into the microphone.

"So goes the Grateful Dead at the Dream Bowl many moons ago. Coming back to nowtimes with a band of shoegazers from Sweden, Immanu El, and their epic track, 'Under Your Wings I'll Hide.'"

Krinkle hit a switch, and the bus filled with an ethereal sound, hanging in the air like flight. Then guitars softly playing against each other in descending progressions, then a voice like something from a forgotten dream:

"Fire haunts us, holds us now . . ."

Krinkle lowered the fader, took off his headphones, turned to Harper.

"I'll tell you why you can't see it. It's because you're fucked up, too. And come tomorrow, when this tea wears off and everything I've just told you gets wiped from my timeline and I'm staring at nothing but a black fucking hole, I'll probably have the same look in my eyes as you do right now. All of us that are left are fucked up, brother . . . We're tired. That's my two cents."

Flash Traffic
tdc: y032-77zfd
Ex: Dragon6/SUTF

Eyes Only: Blue4/GrovMil
Subject: Threat Level: 8

re: SX INTEL
attachments:
<file: XRB.395>
<file: XRB.466>

Summary:

Item 1: SX reports enemy strike detected 19:58 GMT. 42°42'35.18" N, 1°24' 19.54" E. Intel places last known location of offline asset suspected of bearing critical data <re: Swan Lake, Blue Marble> 50 kilometers NNE. 42°52'33.00" N, 1°49'59.48" E. Status of offline asset: Unknown.

Item 2: SX reports encoded enemy thread on Internet discussing "prophecy." Intel reveals discussion not in relation to critical data but advanced, detailed knowledge. file://localhost/<file/XRB.395>

Item 3: Advise proceed "attack drill" scenario next 72 hours. Advise Swan Lake renew weapons ready status: 9 Mil, Glock 19.

Item 4: Engage exfil from GrovMil upon direct order from Dragon 6. Exfil codes listed: file://localhost/<file/XRB.466>.

Item 5: Priority exfil: Blue Marble. Secondary exfil: Swan Lake (abandon if necessary). RNDVS: 45°31'06.28" N, 122°40'47.32" E.

❧

TWENTY

I

"OH, OH, BUSTER. WE NEED TO DO SOMETHING ABOUT YOUR face."

Max stared at his mother, dribbles of oatmeal spilling from the corners of his mouth as he smiled. He recognized the words *your face, buster,* and *oh, oh.* And he recognized his mother's body language. Her head was tilted to the side, her face scrunched up, eyes smiling. All together, Max knew something very funny was happening. He kicked his feet and banged his spoon on the tray.

"Goog."

Bits of wet oatmeal splashed onto Katherine's face.

"Yo, when I want a homemade exfoliating facial, I'll do it myself."

She wiped his mouth and chin, handed him his sippy cup of apple juice.

"Here, knock yourself out with the good stuff."

She picked up his bowl of oatmeal and carried it to the counter. She left the spoon, as Max's hammer was upstairs. She turned on the water pump, opened the tap, washed the bowl. Out the window above the sink, it was a nice autumn day. There was a patch of big leaf maple amid the pine, and just now, the sun sparkled on gold-colored leaves.

"Wow, don't get days like this very often, not this time of year; do we, Max?"

She looked back at him. He was slouched in his high chair, making smacking noises with his mouth as he drank the juice. His little feet, still wrapped in his jammies, wiggled in agreement to whatever it was she'd said. Katherine saw Monsieur Booty had taken her chair as soon as she'd turned her back. Max had the beast by the tail, and both beast and boy were watching her.

"We should go out today, take a walk in the woods. Maybe we'll see Bambi."

Max's eyes lit up hearing that word. It meant animals that sometimes came into the garden. They had very long legs and snouts and ears. They hopped through the garden and disappeared into the trees. He could see them in his eyes.

"Mmmmbies," he said, while continuing to sip his apple juice.

"Yeah, or maybe Bugs Bunny."

"Bnnnybugs."

"Him too."

Katherine filled the kettle and switched it on. She opened her box of teas and chose a sachet of Morning Light. She dropped it in a mug, looked out the window again.

"Yup, that's what we're going to do. Won't open the shop today. We're going to take . . ."

She saw one of the Swiss Guards beyond the tree line. Then two of them. She hadn't seen them because of the trees at first, and it was only when they moved that she noticed them at all. They were setting stakes in the ground at regular intervals. But it wasn't what they were doing she noticed; she'd given up trying to keep up with all the toys the boys had surrounding the house, in the house, under the house. Wouldn't surprise her to learn there was a ray gun hidden in the roof to hold out against a Martian invasion. No, it wasn't what they were doing, it was what they were wearing. Weirdly patterned overalls. And when they stopped moving, the two men almost disappeared into the background.

The kettle boiled and clicked off. She filled her cup, dropped in one of the Morning Light tea bags, and got that first blast of steam in her face that always said, *Good morning, and aren't we feeling good today?* Just then the guards stepped from the trees and crossed the garden, heading for Control. She saw the Brügger & Thomet submachine guns across their chests, Glock 19s strapped to their right thighs. "Loaded for bear," the locals of Grover's Mill called that particular look during hunting season. They stopped to look back toward the trees, and damn if they didn't seem to blend into the green of the lawn. She picked up her tea, closed her bathrobe. She walked to the kitchen door, opened it, and called across the garden.

"What the heck's going on, fellas?"

The two guards stopped.

"*Bonjour, Madame Taylor. Ça va?*"

"*Bonjour*, yourselves. Have the Martians invaded?"

"*Quoi?*"

"Little green men. Spaceships. Nanu nanu."

The guards looked at each other.

"*Pardon*, Madame Taylor, we do not understand what you mean."

Then a voice.

"They're setting motion detectors along the tree line, Kat."

She turned around. Officer Jannsen was in the kitchen, standing next to Max.

"Nnnn." Max grinned, always happy to see her, this time with apple juice trickling from the sides of his mouth.

"*Guten tag, Max.*"

He smiled at her, wagged Monsieur Booty's tail, turned to his mother.

"Motion detectors. Okay, if you say so. But what's with the uniforms? Those are really weird. It's like the boys are invisible."

"It's camouflage."

"Camouflage is Arnold Schwarzenegger in *Commando*. That out there, in the back garden, is the invisible monster in the trees from *Predator*, times two."

"What monster?"

"Hid in trees, ate people. Never mind. How's it work?"

"The cloth is imprinted with irregular-shaped pixels that absorb surrounding colors. It creates an optical illusion. Your eyes see the forms of the two men, but the uniform interferes with how your mind registers the information. It can't distinguish the human form against the immediate background."

"Made in Switzerland, I bet."

"It's a prototype."

"Cool. Can I get one?" Katherine said.

Officer Jannsen smiled.

"What would you do with it?"

"Rob a bank. Run away to a tropical island. Live happily ever after. You, me, Max. You'd like to live on a tropical island, wouldn't you, Max?"

"Goog!" *Wham.*

She looked at Monsieur Booty.

"How about you, you miserable beast?"

Mew.

Katherine looked at Officer Jannsen.

"There you go. Three to one. We're dressing up in camouflage and robbing the bank in Grover's Mill and heading to St. Barts, today."

"Grover's Mill doesn't have a bank."

Katherine thought about it.

"That's right, it doesn't."

Officer Jannsen rubbed Max's head, walked to Katherine. She called through the door to the guards.

"Est du périmètre de sécurité?"

"Oui, Chef."

"Bon. Nous commençons à quinze cent heures."

The guards continued to Control.

Katherine looked at Officer Jannsen.

"What happens at three o'clock?"

"We're running a lockdown drill."

"Oh, God, not again."

"The last time we ran a drill was two months ago."

Katherine shrugged like a frustrated kid.

"Ah, Mom, I was planning to take Max for a walk in the woods, look for Bambi."

"Not today, not for the next three days."

"Three days? The whole thing? Safe room drills?"

"*Mais oui.*"

Kat rolled her eyes.

"I hate the safe room."

"We need to be able to get you in there within ninety seconds from any location in the house."

"We had it down to eighty-two seconds the last time."

"This time you'll be taking Max with you."

"Max? We've always used a doll."

"I want him to get used to it. Make him think it's a game."

"What kind of game?"

"One where he has confidence that you're in charge, that he'll be okay. I'm also getting you on the firing range this afternoon while Max is having his nap. And the next three days."

"You mean I get to shoot stuff again?"

"If you mean will you be at the target range, requalifying with a Glock 19, yes."

"Oh, then. That's cool. But when do I get to shoot a machine gun?"

Katherine sipped her tea, watched the way Officer Jannsen looked away, seeing red in the corner of her eye.

"Anne? Have you been crying?"

"No, I haven't been to bed yet."

"How come?"

Officer Jannsen shrugged. "I was preparing for the lockdown drill. Kat, why is there oatmeal on your face?"

Katherine wiped her face, saw the grains on her hand.

"Max got a little excited at something or other. And you're lying."

"No, I'm not."

"Yes, you are. Come on, out with it."

Officer Jannsen almost spoke, then stopped. And just now, Katherine was very sure she saw Officer Jannsen's eyes water.

"Anne, what's wrong?"

Officer Jannsen took a slow breath.

"Last night, I learned something. Something I don't know how to tell you. Something I'm not allowed to say."

Katherine sipped her tea.

"It's okay. I know what it is."

"You do? How?"

"I dreamed about it."

"What sort of dream?"

"A lucid dream."

Officer Jannsen stared at Katherine.

"How do you know about lucid dreams?"

"Hold your horses. I'm getting there."

Officer Jannsen leaned against the kitchen counter. "All right."

"Good girl. I dreamed we were in the garden last night, watching the stars and talking the night away. And in the dream, I see myself fall asleep, and you kiss my hair. Then I feel like I'm waking up, but I tell myself I want to keep dreaming it again, and it happens again. It's always the same. I'm lying there, drifting off, you lean down. My eyes are closed, but I smell your perfume. Then you take my hair in your hands and you kiss it. I must have relived it a dozen times. Kiss, rewind, kiss, rewind. Then I went into this really deep and wonderful sleep. This morning, I woke up in my bed, and Max was still asleep. I went on Google and looked up dreams. I found a wiki page on lucid dreams, sounded like what was going on. It said human beings usually have at least one lucid dream in their lifetime, others have more, and a few can train themselves to participate in their dreams as a regular practice."

Officer Jannsen nodded.

"Yes, that's what it means. But, Kat, it doesn't have anything to do with—"

"It was your perfume, Anne."

"My perfume?"

"Sight and sound are the dominant senses in dreams, not the sense of smell. Surrounding smells can affect a dream, but people don't really have a sense of smell *in* their dreams."

Officer Jannsen didn't speak.

"I wasn't dreaming, was I, Anne? I was remembering what really happened. You kissed me when you thought I was asleep, and you were hoping I wouldn't remember. That's what you want to tell me, isn't it?"

Officer Jannsen looked down at the floor.

"Yes. That's what I wanted to tell you."

Katherine laughed.

"And you know what? I read this thing about Dream Yoga. I found a place in Portland where they teach it. I was thinking maybe I could go see what it's about. Maybe I could get really good at it, if I try."

Officer Jannsen remained quiet. Katherine reached over, raised her face.

"I know there's a red line between us. And I know why. No matter what you feel, you have a sense of duty to protect Max and me. I get it. You're not just a cop, you're a Swiss cop. But last night, you made it okay for me to feel something I'd been afraid of feeling for a long time. And today, right now, I'm happy. Not from what I can get from the world, but from somewhere within myself. And don't worry, I promise not to chase after you like a lovesick puppy."

Officer Jannsen nodded. "That's good. I wouldn't want the detail to get the wrong idea. If it was reported up the chain, it could make things difficult."

"It's our secret. But I'm putting you on notice, Ms. Jannsen. Day comes this whole hideout thing is over, you, me, and Max are robbing a bank, somewhere, and running away to the Caribbean. And we're going to live happily ever after. With the cat, too, of course. I don't think I could separate Max and Monsieur Booty with a crowbar."

Officer Jannsen looked at Max, holding on to Monsieur Booty's tail. She turned to Katherine, looked into her eyes, remembering the flash traffic from Berne . . .

Item 5: Priority exfil: Blue Marble. Secondary exfil: Swan Lake (abandon if necessary).

"I'll be back after lunch, Kat."

"Okeydoke."

Katherine picked up Max, grabbed her tea, and went upstairs. She changed his diaper and washed him, dressed him in blue jeans and a sweatshirt from Baby Gap, finished him off with a pair of Converse All Stars.

"Never too young to make a fashion statement. Especially when it comes to shoes."

"Shooz."

"That's right. One day you're going to have to try an entire sentence, just to humor me that you're normal."

She handed him his hammer and carried him and her tea to the bathroom. She sat Max on the floor. He happily banged away at no-see-ums while she jumped in the shower. She kept an eye on Max through the glass door: *wham, whamwham, wham.* Stepping out and drying off, she saw sunlight come through the window.

"Know what we're going to do? We're going down in the garden to sit in the sunshine. Soak up some vitamin D. How's that for an idea?"

She saw Max watching where the light met shadows on the floor. He pulled himself to his feet, unsteadily walked a few steps into the light, plopped down. He reached out with his left hand and touched the floor where light met shadow, watched the sunlight move over his hand.

"What are you doing, Max?"

He looked up at her and smiled as the light crawled up his body and brightened his face. He looked up, stared at it, pointed to it.

"*Sol.*"

"Yeah, *sol*, sun. And who's teaching you Spanish?"

"Solsnnn."

"*Sol* or sun, buster, take your pick. Saying them together makes you sound like you've been hitting the sauce instead of Molly's apple juice."

"Solsnnn."

"Hey, you, this is your mommy dearest speaking, one or the other."

Max saw the same funny look on his mother's face, and heard the same funny tone in her voice.

"Solsnnn, *maman!*"

"Yeah, yeah, yeah. Come here."

Katherine picked Max up from the floor, tickled him and kissed his cheek. She carried him into her bedroom and set him on the floor. Her bedroom faced southwest, away from the direct light of the early sun. Max seemed to study the layout of the room . . . floor, windows, angles. He giggled to himself, got to his hands and knees, hammer in his hand, and crawled in ever wider circles around the room.

"What are you looking for, Max?"

He kept crawling and giggling till he landed in the corner of the room. He spun around and sat with his back to the wall and stared at the floor. The sun crossed the bedroom window and a beam of light parted shadow and found Max in the corner. Katherine felt something stir, like a long-forgotten memory. Watching a light move over a dark stone floor, somewhere, finding her. And there were colors, brilliant colors, because the sun was passing through a great round window of leaded glass, high in a gray stone wall. She could see it. And the sun was warm, and she felt the warmth deep in her body, and there was a voice: *to purify the light before it touches the life within you.* Then the voice was gone, the colors were gone, and there was just Max sitting on the floor, now holding his hand into the beam of light coming through the bedroom window.

"Max?"

He looked at her.

The light has crossed his face, brushed his eyes.

She dropped her towel, put on her bathrobe. She slid her wet feet into her slippers, walked to Max, picked him up, and carried him to the bathroom. She carried him to the mirror above the sink, but it was fogged with steam and the light was coming from the wrong direction. She lifted Max to her right hip, carried him to his own bedroom. The sun was hitting the mirror above Max's dressing table and reflecting into the room. She stepped close to the mirror, into the light. Katherine studied

Max's face, his eyes. Then, she saw it. The color of Max's almond-shaped eyes had shifted from baby blue to match Katherine's own hazel color, and just now in the light, both their eyes sparkled with flares of emerald green. Max could see it, too; raised his right hand, pointed to Katherine's face in the looking glass.

"*Sol.*"

"No kidding."

She carried Max into the bathroom. Her Morning Light tea was sitting next to the sink. She poured it down the drain.

II

S HE SET THE BLACK CIRCLE BETWEEN THE REAR SIGHTS, RAISED the barrel of the Glock till the front sights lined up on the target, twenty meters downrange. She held her breath, squeezed the trigger, fired six shots in double taps. The Glock's slide snapped back. She pressed the magazine release behind the trigger, pulled the clip from the grip. She checked it: empty. She stuffed it into the clip pouch on her belt. She checked the firing chamber of the Glock: empty. She lay the weapon on the table, took off her ear protection and blast goggles.

"Well done, Kat," Officer Jannsen said, pointing to the screen of the electronic scorekeeper. "Looks like your first two shots went just wide of the circle, but the next four were in the second ring. Last four fired off in two and a half seconds. That's really good."

"Yeah, well, you know what they say about bicycles."

"No, what do they say?"

"Once you learn to ride it, you own it. Reload?"

"Go ahead."

"How many rounds?"

"How many do you feel comfortable with?"

"Fourteen, full clip."

"Go ahead."

Boxes of ammunition lay on the table. *RUAG Ammotec, AG. 9x19mm parabellum* the lettering on the lids read. Katherine pulled the magazine from her belt, loaded a round against the spring mechanism, pressed down with her thumb, then another.

"The bullets are like the water in this place," Katherine said.

"Pardon?"

"The bullets. RUAG Ammotec, AG. The AG means they're made in Switzerland, doesn't it?"

Officer Jannsen smiled.

"Yes. Why do you ask?"

"Nothing. Just that the bullets in this place are like the water we use in the house. They're imported."

"They're very common rounds, Kat. RUAG has factories all over the world."

"Is that right? So why don't we buy our bullets from Big Dick's Guns and Ammo down the road in Carson?"

"Who?"

"A gun shop next door to the lumberyards. It's set back from the road, so if you blink, you miss it. But the sign grabbed my attention on one of our trips to Portland to see Max's doctor, or my shrink, or my ob-gyn, or my dentist. I can't remember, have I ever been to a dentist since we've been here?"

Officer Jannsen crossed her arms under her breasts, still smiling.

"Yes, five months ago."

"Really?"

"Why do you ask?"

"Because I can't remember it happening. By the way, what's *parabellum* mean?"

"Parabellum?"

"It's on the box. Latin, isn't it?"

Officer Jannsen was wearing yellow-tinted blast goggles. She pulled her ear protection from her ears and let it hang around her neck.

"Did you have your tea this morning, and after lunch?"

"You were there, in the kitchen, you saw me make it, remember? So what's *parabellum* mean?"

"It means 'prepare for war.' From *si vis pacem, para bellum.*"

Katherine continued to load the magazine.

"*Pacem.* Now, I know that one from my one year at college. It means peace. So I'm guessing altogether it means 'you want peace, get ready for war.'" *Click.* "Fourteen rounds, ready to fire."

Katherine lay the loaded magazine on the table, put on her ear and eye protection. She grabbed the magazine, grabbed the Glock. Jannsen's hand slammed down and pinned Katherine's firing hand, smashing her knuckles into the wooden table.

"What the fuck are you doing, Anne?"

Officer Jannsen spoke calmly but firmly: "You're not concentrating."

"Who says I'm not concentrating?"

"Me. You put eleven rounds in the magazine, not fourteen. You lost count."

"So you smashed my hand on the table because I lost count?"

"No, because you're being sloppy with a weapon designed to kill."

"It wasn't loaded."

"It would have taken you two seconds to load the magazine into the grip and pull the slide with your left hand."

"So fucking what?"

"The index finger of your right hand is inside the trigger guard, Kat, that's fucking what. Rule number one: Your finger never goes inside the trigger guard until the moment you're ready to fire."

Katherine looked down at the Glock. Saw her finger wrapped around the trigger, heard Officer Jannsen's voice.

"You would have pulled the slide, loaded a round in the chamber. The jolt could've caused your finger to override the trigger safety mechanism and misfire. You're on a live fire range, there's no room for sloppy. Sloppy means dead."

"Can I have my fucking hand back, Officer Jannsen?"

"Of course, Madame Taylor. As soon as you lay down the magazine."

Katherine dropped the loaded clip with a thud. Officer Jannsen let go of Katherine's hand; the knuckles were bleeding.

"Step away from the table, Kat."

Katherine didn't move.

"I said, step away from the table."

"Is that a command?"

"Take it any way you want, but you will step away from the table or I will take you down so hard, you'll feel it for a week."

"Gee, that might fuck up your lockdown drill, won't it? Won't look good on your résumé."

"Do it!"

Katherine jumped, backed away. Officer Jannsen pulled a handkerchief from her coat, handed it to Katherine.

"Here, wrap this around your knuckles. Stop the bleeding."

"It's fine."

"ABC, Kat. Airway, breathing, circulation. Learn it, know it, do it. A cut you don't attend to becomes an infection. An infection means your firing hand is useless."

Katherine had heard the ABC's of survival before. All part of life in Grover's Mill. The heavy-duty physical workouts with the Swiss Guard boys, battlefield first aid, hostile environment recognition, weapons training. All things she thought she wanted to learn to protect herself. All things she'd been herded toward like a good little girl. She took the handkerchief, wrapped it around her hand.

"Thanks."

Officer Jannsen slid the Glock from Katherine's reach.

"Now, do you want to tell me what this is about?"

"If I looked up this house on Google Earth, would I see it? Would I find it on a map?"

"What on earth are you thinking?"

"What I'm thinking is none of *this* shit is real," Katherine said. "I mean, I'm here all right, but this place doesn't exist, does it?"

"Where is this coming from?"

"I did a little experiment. One of the boys came into the kitchen while I was making lunch. He was adjusting the CCTV camera. I asked to use his iPhone, to play solitaire on it. He did everything right before he gave it to me: disabled the Internet and the phone—but not the GPS.

I looked up the coordinates of the house. I jotted them down like I was making a grocery list. He left, and I logged on to my laptop, the one you let me use to keep an eye on me. I logged on to Google Earth. There's nothing at those coordinates but a forest. How come?"

"That's easy. Google Earth isn't up-to-date in this area."

"No?"

Officer Jannsen moved close to her, looked into her eyes.

"You didn't drink your tea this morning, did you?"

"I dumped it down the drain. Same way I dumped the midday tea, and the same way I'll dump the rest of it. I'm fucking tired of being a zombie for the cause."

"What cause?"

"Whatever fucking cause it is you and the rest of you are pretending is worth keeping me and my son as your prisoners. That's what we are, isn't it?"

"Listen to me, you're not yourself right now."

"No. This *is* me, and I feel fine."

"All right. Tell me what set this off."

"I told you, I dumped your fucking teas down the drain. Good-bye, Swiss mindfuck."

"Why?"

"Because I remembered something looking at Max."

"What is it you remember?"

"The color of Marc Rochat's eyes. Something happened to me at the cathedral, didn't it? Something that affected me while I was pregnant. Not that I give a fuck, but it means something happened to Max, too. Something you're hiding from me."

"What am I hiding from you?"

"It isn't me the bad guys want, it's Max."

Officer Jannsen stared at Katherine for ten silent seconds, then she whipped around in a blur, pulled her own Glock from her hip, and let off fourteen rounds downrange. Rapid-fire, spent casings flying. The slide popped, and in one quick move she dropped the empty magazine from the grip, slammed in a fresh one, ripped off fourteen more rounds in double taps till *blamblam, blamblam, click*. The gun was dry. Katherine looked at the screen display of the target. Twenty-eight shots in less than nine seconds, every one of them dead center. Officer Jannsen slowly pulled another clip from her belt, eased it into the Glock, reset the slide, and holstered her weapon.

"It's time you learn to speed reload, Kat."

III

AFTER THE VILLAGE OF VILLENEUVE-D'OLMES, THE TAXI WAS THE only car on the narrow road. At Montferrier, the taxi took a left and started to climb through a series of switchback turns. The headlights panned across trees and farms like searchlights. Coming around one turn onto a straightaway, the taxi was speeding up when a gray-faced deer jumped across the road. The driver hit the brakes, but it was too late. There was a sickening thud, and the taxi shuddered and skidded off the road. The driver turned right and left avoiding trees and stopped the taxi at the edge of a ditch. He shut off the engine, looked over his shoulder.

"*Êtes-vous blessé, monsieur?*"

Harper peeled himself from the back of the front seat.

"*Ça va,*" he said.

The taxi had done a three-sixty turn, and beyond the windshield, in the glare of the headlights, Harper saw the deer in the middle of the road. It was clawing at the asphalt with its front legs, trying to pull itself into the cover of the trees.

"It's still alive," Harper said.

The driver looked ahead.

"*Merde.*"

They got out of the taxi. The driver rushed to the front end to check the damage. The left headlight was out and the fender smashed.

"How bad is it?" Harper said.

"*Merde, oh merde.* The undercarriage and wheels are all right. I will get you to Montségur. We must see to the animal."

They walked toward the deer. They saw blood on the left hindquarters where the animal had been hit. Sensing them coming, the deer panicked, tried to climb to all four legs, but its rear legs would not stand, and the animal collapsed on the road. It struggled for a few seconds, then settled.

"Its back is broken," Harper said.

"Or its legs. Either way, there is nothing to do but put it out of its misery. I'll get something from the taxi."

The driver walked off.

Harper stared at the deer. Saw its wide, dark-colored eyes staring at him. He stepped ahead, slowly. The deer fidgeted but didn't panic this time. Harper knelt next to it, listened to the sound of its breathing. Quick, shallow. Harper sensed the deer was bewildered, unable to comprehend why its legs had given way, why it could not dash away into the woods. Harper lay his hand on the deer's chest, felt the warmth of its body, felt its racing heart.

"*Animus facit nobilem,*" he whispered.

Harper felt the deer's heart calm a little.

The driver returned with a folded tarp and a tire iron.

"What the hell is that for?" Harper said.

The driver waved the tire iron like a hammer. "To put it out of its misery."

"By beating it to death?"

"You think it better if I drive over it a few times? A few blows to the head and it will be unconscious. A few more blows, it will be dead."

The driver dropped the tarp on the road.

"And what's that for?"

"To wrap it up and put it in the trunk of my taxi."

"Sorry?"

"I have a cousin not far from Montségur, in Auzat. He's been out of work for a year. This deer will get him and his family through half the winter. You might have to help me lift it into the trunk, though."

The driver stood over the deer's head, raised the tire iron.

"Stop," Harper said.

"*Quoi?*"

Harper opened his coat, pulled his SIG from its holster. He pulled the slide, loaded a round into the chamber. The driver gasped.

"You're carrying a gun? In my taxi? A foreigner? What is this?"

"Yes, I'm carrying a gun in your taxi. And you're getting triple the meter for the ride because it was the only way I could bribe you to move your arse off the taxi rank. Now step aside. Let's get this over with."

The driver eased out of the way.

Harper walked to the deer, leaned down, pressed the muzzle to the deer's head. He put his finger inside the trigger guard. He let out a slow breath. He looked at the deer's gray face, saw a wounded piece of life begging to be comforted. *Not yet, not now.* Harper's hand began to shake; he felt something wet burn in his eyes. He pulled away the gun, stood up.

"Shit."

"What's wrong?" the driver said.

Harper looked at him. "Do you know how to shoot?"

"I was in the army."

Harper held out the SIG. "Here, you do it."

"Me? Why me?"

"Because I can't."

"*Pourquoi pas?*"

"Does it bloody matter?"

The driver stepped forward, traded his tire iron for the SIG. Harper bent down, gently laid the tire iron on the tarp. He knelt near the deer's head. The driver knelt next to Harper.

"I'm going to distract it," Harper said. "When I tell you, set the muzzle to the back of its head, fire away from us. Do it quick. Understand?"

"*Oui.*"

Harper knelt near the deer, looked in its eyes. He touched the beast's chest, waited to feel its heart calm again.

"Fire."

The shot echoed off the road and into the forest. There was a fluttering of birds and scattering of animals hiding in the nearby trees. The driver stood up. Harper waited with his hand on the deer, feeling its heartbeat fade.

"*C'est le guet. Il a sonné l'heure.*"

He stood up, took the gun from the driver. He pulled the slide, ejected the next round. The round fell and rang out as it hit the asphalt. Harper picked it up, dropped it in the pocket of his coat.

"What did you say to the animal, monsieur?" the driver said.

"I told it I was the watcher, and that this was the hour of its death."

"You said that? To a dead deer?"

"It wasn't dead when I said it."

The driver shook his head.

"Well, that's a very strange business. A foreigner pays me a fortune to take him to the least populated region of France and he's carrying a gun. I should call the gendarmerie."

Harper held the palm of his right hand before the driver's eyes.

"*Et memento hoc solum.*"

The driver stared blankly as Harper spoke.

"Listen to the sound of my voice. Tonight, you were asked by the chief of police in Toulouse to drive me to Montségur in relation to a case involving national security. You were told nothing about me and instructed to ask no questions. You were told not to discuss this trip, or me, with anyone. It was made very clear to you that if you did, you'd be paid a visit by the Central Directorate of Interior Intelligence. Twenty minutes ago, coming around the last turn, you hit a deer and broke its back. I shot it, finished it off. You said you wanted to take the carcass to your cousin so he'd have some meat for the winter. Just now you're a little shaken because of the accident, and the gunshot startled you. If you think about it, I'm very sure you'll realize this is what happened."

Harper lowered his hand.

"You all right?" Harper said.

The driver blinked, looked at his taxi, the deer, his taxi again. He watched Harper holster the SIG.

"*Oui, ça va.* The gunshot. It startled me, I think."

"It happens."

The driver nodded, took a deep breath.

"*Allors*, I must get the animal into the trunk. I am sorry for the delay, monsieur."

"No worries."

The driver spread open the tarp. He grabbed the deer's front legs and tugged. He couldn't move it. He looked at Harper.

"Could you help me, monsieur?"

"Sure."

Harper grabbed the back legs, and they dragged the deer onto the tarp. The driver wiped his brow.

"My cousin will eat for half the winter with this animal. You know, I feel terrible about the accident, but some good has come of it, *non*? Life is strange sometimes. I will bring my taxi closer. It will be difficult getting it into the trunk."

The driver walked away.

Harper knelt down, covered the deer's haunches with the tarp. Before covering its head, he looked into its eyes again. All light was gone.

❧

TWENTY-ONE

I

FIFTEEN MINUTES LATER, THE TAXI ENTERED THE VILLAGE OF Montségur. Harper looked at his watch: straight up on the witching hour. The driver pulled over, shut down the motor. There was a narrow lane ahead with oddly shaped houses on either side. Like a collection of mismatched stone boxes. No lights in the windows, no streetlamps along the lane.

"We are here, monsieur."

Harper looked out his window. There were two stone basins below an iron spout. A trickle of water poured from the spout into the basins. Looked the sort of place women came to do their laundry in the Middle Ages. Given the look of the buildings on the lane, maybe they still did, Harper thought.

"You sure?" Harper said.

The driver nodded to the fountain.

"That is la fontaine d'Orgeat. That means we are at the entrance of the village."

"Is there a hotel around?"

"There are rooms in people's homes that are rented. Where they are, I do not know, or if they are even open this time of year. I'm afraid you must see for yourself. I must get the deer to my cousin before it begins to rot."

"Right."

Harper opened his door. The driver turned quickly back to him.

"One thing, monsieur."

"What's that?"

"Seeing as the chief of police in Toulouse told me to say nothing about you, how do I explain to my cousin about the bullet in the deer's head?"

Harper replayed the night. Left the bus in the back of La Dynamo after nine. The building was vibrating with a droning sound. Nobody in the neighborhood seemed to notice. He walked back to the train station. Ticket clerk got a right laugh when Harper asked for a ticket to Montségur. There was a bigger laugh when Harper asked about any trains in the morning. Seems there were no trains to Montségur, any time of the day. But there was a train to Foix. Seven and a half hours, then a thirty-three kilometer walk.

He went outside to the taxi rank. Presented himself to the driver on point as a British tourist who wanted to see the fortress atop Montségur by dawn's early light. The driver was as excited about driving anywhere as the one Harper had met that afternoon. Thus, three times the meter. Driver said, *"D'accord."* Harper got in. Driver went twenty meters and stopped. Went into a *tabac* for an espresso and a smoke. Harper waited in the taxi twenty minutes. Finally, as his watch flipped to ten fifteen, they were on their way. No worries. Then the deer. Harper didn't want to think about it. He blinked himself back to nowtimes, looked at the driver.

"You'll come up with something."

"But, monsieur, I don't want a visit from the Central Directorate of Internal Intelligence. I haven't filed my taxes properly for fifteen years."

Harper shrugged. "Use your imagination."

Harper alighted from the taxi. The driver turned over the motor, made a three-point turn, drove away. Harper closed his coat and reached for his cigarette case. Easier now without the bandages on his hands, but the scar tissue on his palms was sore as hell. May take a day or two for the healing potion to fill in the cracks of the proximal phalanges, Krinkle told him. Suggested Harper try to avoid hitting any stone walls, or tough jaws for that matter.

Harper pulled a cigarette from his case and lit up. He looked up at the sky, saw a sea of stars floating between dark shores. The dark shores created by the shadowed forms of the Pyrenees. He turned slowly around. Somewhere out there, he thought, was a chunk of rock called Montségur. Radiance flooded into his blood, and the rhodopsin in his eyes became nine times more sensitive. His brain began to see the outline of jagged peaks. Then, above the narrow road and row houses, at 18° north by northeast, he saw it. Not a mountain looking like it'd been shaped over millions of years by fire and rain; more like it had been carved by a knowing hand. He saw the granite cliffs leading to the top of the pluton. There, against the north quadrant of the sky, he saw the fortress. At the far end of the fortress was the tower, standing like one more shadow in the night. His eyes drew a line from the tower to the sky. Directly above Montségur, Harper saw the constellation Draco.

"Swell, now what?"

He stepped to the fountain, saw a school of red-and-white-colored fish drifting in the water. *Caraccius auratus,* Harper thought, Sarasa comet goldfish. There was a sign on the stone wall above the fountain: s'il vous plaît, ne déranger pas nemo. Harper looked at the fish.

"Mind if I take a drink?"

Nemo, whichever one he was, didn't object.

Harper leaned over and drank from the spout. It was cold, and he drank deeply. He straightened up, wiped his mouth. Took another hit of radiance, watched the fish. He looked around. Place looked deserted. Thought about giving up on the hotel and just heading out for the fortress atop the pluton. Complications arose when he realized he didn't even know the way, and it was bloody dark.

"Like I was saying, now what?"

He saw a small hand-painted sign on a fence post. It looked old, almost buried in the weeds. The kind of sign no one would see unless they were looking for it. Top of the sign was an arrow pointing *that way* down the dark lane. Beneath the arrow were the words:

La Barraca. Chambre dans ma maison à louer. Pas de réservation nécessaire. "Guess that answers that."

Harper walked ahead, checked the buildings. They seemed to lean weirdly to the side. Pull one out, the whole bloody street would fall down. He scanned the windows . . . all the shutters drawn. There was a rise in the lane, and coming to a crest, a slash of light cut through the dark. It fell across a garden of wild grass and settled on the gate of a picket fence stretching across the road.

Harper stopped, looked back over his shoulder; nobody.

He looked ahead, took a long draw from his smoke, dropped it on the ground, and crushed it into dust. He walked ahead, saw the house beyond the gate. Simple place. Three floors, brown shutters, empty flower boxes in the windows. Coming closer he saw the open door of a shed next to the house. That's where the light was coming from, then came a hammer-on-steel clanging sound. The clanging stopped, then there were bursts of blue light and sparks of fire and acrid smoke. Had to be a welder with an oxyacetylene torch, or a coven of witches at play maybe . . . *Clang, clang, clang.* Either way, someone was up late, Harper thought.

He reached the gate, stood there, was only half surprised to see the sign on the gate: *La Barraca.* He waited for the clanging to stop. He sensed movement in the dark of the garden, then a bloody big dog— long white hair, huge paws, a head the size of a bowling ball—stepped from dark into light and stopped at the gate. It stared at Harper with black eyes. White slobber dribbled from its mouth. The clanging from inside the shed stopped.

"Shiva, de qué te nhaca? Qu'es aquò?"

Harper ran the words. *Shiva:* the destroyer, or transformer of the Hindu trinity of gods. The rest of it was Occitan, the indigenous language of the Pyrenees. The language of Bernard de Saint-Martin. The voice was asking, *Shiva, what's biting you? What is it?*

"And isn't it funny how you know that one, boyo?"

391

Just then, the light from the door was eclipsed by a human form. Harper saw the shadow of a large man in dirty blue overalls and a welder's apron. He wore thick leather gloves on his hands, and his face was hidden behind a safety mask. The man raised the mask.

"*Bonvengut.*"

The radiance spiked in Harper's blood, and though the man was no more than a shadow, Harper saw the man's eyes were clean.

"*Bon vèspre,*" Harper said.

"*Bon vèspre* would be more appropriate for the late afternoon, not the middle of the night. But I appreciate the attempt to speak my language."

"What should I have said?"

"*Adieussiatz* would do it. Works as hello or good-bye, any time of day."

"*Adieussiatz.* I'll keep it in mind. How did you know I speak English?"

"I guessed."

Harper gave it a few beats.

"I saw your advert by the fountain. The one for a room."

"And?"

"I could use a place to stay for the night, or I could use directions to the fortress."

The man in the shadow didn't respond.

"By the way, my name is—"

"Don't tell me your name," the man said.

Harper nodded. "If you say so."

"But I am Serge Gasca. *Dintratz*, come in."

Harper looked at the huge dog on the other side of the gate. It hadn't moved. Not even a twitch.

"What about the dog?"

"*Qu'ei tranquille.*"

Harper reached for the gate latch, stopped.

"How did you know I was standing out here?"

"The dog."

"The dog didn't bark."

"He moved from his place in the garden, the place he sleeps. He only

392

moves when there is something interesting to see. And in this place, a man appearing from nowhere in the middle of the night asking for a place to stay, or directions to the fortress, is most interesting. *Dintratz.*"

"I didn't appear from nowhere."

"No?"

"No. I took a cab."

Harper pushed open the gate. It creaked. He stepped into the garden. The dog took one step forward; Harper stopped and held out his right hand. The dog sniffed at it, bumped it with his furry forehead, then turned and walked slowly toward the shed. Harper followed. The man in the doorway, the man who called himself Serge, came into focus. Dark hair, dark eyes, a face looking like it'd been cut from stone. He held up his soot-covered gloves.

"Don't think me rude if I don't shake your hand. I am in the middle of something."

"No worries."

Serge went into the shed, and the dog lay on the grass to the side of the door with a distinct *thump.* Harper stepped through the doorway. There were traces of iron oxide fumes and smoke, and an exhaust fan fitted in a side window was doing its best to clear the air. A single lamp was fixed in the middle of the ceiling, and it dropped a dome of light over the man's work space. There was a sculpture standing in the light. Bent and twisted iron rods in the outline of a human form. Head bowed, hands across its chest. Harper looked closer, saw something else: wings draped from its shoulders like mournful things.

"It's an angel," Harper said.

"Yes, an angel," the man said, picking up the oxyacetylene torch and spark lighter. "You should look away. I must finish this joint or its wings will fall off. Do you smoke?"

"Yes."

"Don't."

The man lowered his safety mask, opened the gas valves, struck the spark lighter. A knifelike jet of blue fire shot from the nozzle. He adjusted the regulator till the flame was three inches long. The intensity of the flame hurt Harper's eyes and he turned away, looked about the shed. As Serge worked the weld, there were bursts of blue light that lit up the shed. The corners were filled with scrap iron and junk, and along the back wall were more angels. Dozens of them standing in close order formation like some silent army, all in the same mournful pose. Harper considered crunching the odds of his showing up, finding no room in the town but for a place where a guy seemed to be waiting up in the middle of the night, making iron angels in a shed . . . He gave up. Serge shut down the torch, closed the gas. He took off his mask and gloves, lay them on a worktable. He inspected the weld joint.

"That should do it, my noble lord," he said.

Noble lord, Harper thought. *That's one I haven't heard before.* Then, running it through his mind again, he knew he had. Somewhere.

"You're an artist?" Harper said.

The man shook his head.

"No, I'm unemployed. I used to work in a textile factory up the road in Laroque-d'Olmes, till it closed fifteen years ago. This whole region used to be big in textiles, this village, too. We had a thousand residents once."

"It looked empty, the village."

"There are only one hundred of us left. It was ninety-nine, but we had a new arrival in 2009, a baby girl. The village was drunk for a week. But we have hikers and tourists in the summer. They come for a day or two, climb the trail to the fortress, then they leave. Now and again one of them buys one of my angels. Between this and that, my wife and I survive."

"'That' being renting a room in your house to people who show up in the middle of the night."

"Yes."

Harper nodded. "That's good, then."

Serge looked at Harper.

"You'll be wanting to go to the fortress?"

"Yes."

The man walked to the pile of scrap iron and junk, found a staff of knotted oak with a brass tip.

"You'll need this. Not so much to get up, but for coming down. Lots of bending and tricky steps."

He held it out to Harper. Harper stepped in the shed, took it.

"Cheers. Happen to have a flashlight?"

"You wish to go now?"

"Why not?"

"It's dark, that means it's dangerous. One slip, you fall; you fall, you're dead. It would be better if you waited for morning."

"I'd just rather go it alone, not run into anyone."

"This time of year the trail opens at ten. If you leave at dawn, you'll be up and down before you are noticed, if that is what you want."

"That's what I want. How do I get there, back toward the fountain and out of the village?"

"You can't go that way. The villagers will have their shutters open by then. There is a gate at the back of my garden. It cuts through the forest and leads to the field. You cross the field, and there is the trail. None of the villagers will notice you if you go that way. Shiva will show you."

Harper followed the man's line of sight to the open doorway. The huge white dog was sitting there, watching them.

"The dog?"

"He knows the way, you don't. You will become lost without him. He won't climb the trail, but he'll stay in the field and wait for you. When you descend the mountain, he'll show you the way back, through the same gate. Come, I'll take you to the house."

Serge took off his apron, lay it on the worktable, walked toward the door. Shiva sat up to greet him.

"Mind if I ask you something?" Harper said.

Serge stopped. "What is it?"

"Why angels?"

Serge looked at the angel sculpture standing in the light, then at Harper.

"Because an angel passed this way once, stayed under this roof. At least that's the story in my family."

Harper shoved his hands in the pockets of his coat. "Is that so?"

Serge stared at Harper a moment.

"You do not believe me."

"Try me."

Serge cleared his throat.

"My family was one of the first families to settle this place, before there was a village, back in the late eighth century. They were nomadic shepherds from near Sant Pau de Segúries in Spain. They came here and became farmers. This house used to be nothing but a stone hut then."

"Cathars?"

"Yes, but my family renounced the faith before the Inquisition to escape being burned with the others."

"Right. Sorry for asking."

"It isn't penance, making angels, if that is what you think."

"I wasn't thinking anything. I was curious, that's all."

"About what?"

"Angels."

"Are you?"

"Yes. Especially one who might've stayed under your family's roof."

The man looked down at the dog, scratched the animal behind the ears.

"The story goes that after the Crusaders murdered the Cathars, they ransacked the fortress and the huts built on the cliffs outside the north gate, searching for treasure. When they found nothing, they leveled the fortress. Then the rains came, then the cold, then the Crusaders went home. My ancestors went to the field to bury the bones of the Cathars, but there were no bones to be found. There was only a great pile of sodden ash. It was terrible work. The ash had turned to mud, and you could easily sink deep into it and become trapped. It was growing dark, and my family gave up. Leaving the field, they found an angel buried in the ash. He was delirious, raving, weeping, his face blackened and singed. My family brought him to the hut and tended to him. Weeks, months. Then one day, he was gone."

"How did they know he was an angel?"

Serge shrugged, looked at Harper.

"Because in his delirium, he told them this. He told them he had tried to comfort the souls of the Cathars as they burned to death. He told them he was overcome with their suffering. Who knows? Perhaps he was a Frenchman, someone with the Crusaders who stayed behind and was digging through the ash looking for bits of gold or silver. Perhaps he became trapped and, fearing revenge when he was rescued, he told my family he was an angel to save himself."

"What do you think?"

"I think, back then, people had strange ideas about the world."

"But here you are, nearly nine hundred years later, making angels from scraps of iron."

Serge smiled again.

"I tried birds, horses. I tried avant-garde. Making angels is the only thing I'm good at. Come, I'll show you a place where you can sleep."

"Actually, I'm not tired. Do you have a computer with Internet?"

"Some do in the village, not me. Too much information for me."

"Do you have a TV?"

"In the kitchen. My wife likes to watch Spanish soap operas as she's jarring her vegetables and jams."

"Can I get the History Channel on it?"

"Yes."

He turned off the light. Harper stepped outside, and Serge closed the door.

"Shiva, move," he said.

The dog led the way through the dark. The garden was long and narrow. They passed the main door of the house, walked around the corner to a small stone patio. Serge pointed farther up the garden.

"The gate you need is back there. Shiva will be waiting for you."

Harper looked around for the dog. He'd wandered off to his spot under a tree with a view of anything coming or going.

"Right."

"Come, my wife always leaves food in the kitchen in case I'm hungry."

Serge walked across the patio, opened the door into the house. Harper rested the staff against the side of the house and went inside. There was a candle burning on a table. A plate of white cheeses, a baguette, a bottle of wine, and an empty glass.

"I hope you enjoy cheese. We're vegetarians in this house. But they're very good cheeses. Bethmale, Rogallais, Bamalous; all from the village, and the wine is from Corbières. My wife baked the bread."

"No, cheese is fine. I've been thinking I should become a vegetarian myself."

Serge looked at Harper, nodded.

"So should every person in the world."

There was a box-shaped television on a metal stand next to the kitchen table. Serge turned it on, found the History Channel.

"I don't need the sound up," Harper said.

"No?"

"I'm fine with the picture. I've seen most of the episodes before. Watching the pictures helps me pass the time."

"I understand. Are you sure you will not need a room to rest?"

"No, I'm fine."

Serge nodded.

"I understand. I will leave you to your peace and join my wife in bed. The stars will fade in four hours. You can set out then, Shiva will lead you. By the time you reach the trail to the fortress, it will be safe enough to climb. *Vos pregui slitz com a casa.*"

Harper ran the words: *Make yourself at home.*

"Cheers."

Serge walked through the small sitting room and up a set of creaking stairs. Harper poured a glass of wine, had a long swallow. He cut a slice of Bamalous, ate it with a piece of bread. It was good.

II

Once upon a time, there was a giant caterpillar who was very clever and wore a silly hat on his head. And his name was Pompidou, and he lived on snowflakes. Big ones, fat ones. And he flew around the world and beyond the moon."

Max pointed at the drawing of the moon in the notebook. *"La lune."*

"That's right, honey, that's the moon. See the loon in the *lune*. There are his eyes and his nose and his mouth. And see funny old Pompidou with his funny hat. It's just like the hat on Mommy's head, isn't it?"

Max looked up at his mother, saw the hat on her head, and touched the brim.

"Lune, moon."

"No, that's my hat, the *lune* moon's down here, in the book."

They were sitting on the floor of Max's room. Katherine on a blanket, Max on her lap, the two of them surrounded by pillows like a fort. The lantern was on a nearby stool and it cast light on their faces. Monsieur Booty lay at her feet like the Sphinx. All-knowing, all-seeing, waiting for the moment when there'd be a break in the proceedings for food.

They'd been in the garden earlier, where Katherine was trying to calm down from the firing range fiasco. She'd stormed off the range, telling Officer Jannsen to go fuck herself with a two-by-four from the Carson lumberyard. The sun in the garden calmed her down, and she laughed watching Max walk in circles, arms out from his sides to find his balance, before falling on his butt and giggling with delight because, for some reason, he found the idea of falling on his butt amusing.

Molly came by with some of her tofu pizza at lunchtime. It was the special at the diner that day, and she knew Max loved it. Molly also heard the house was running low on her homemade apple juice and she brought a jug of the fresh stuff. Max was very happy to see her, and the pizza, and the apple juice. He quickly made a mess of his face and hands. Molly couldn't stay, had to get back to the diner and work on dinner. She gave Max a big hug.

"Why, you're just the cutest little bug in the yard," she said.

"Boogy bug, Mowy."

"You betcha."

On the way out, Molly saw Katherine looking unlike her chipper self. Told her to come to town for some huckleberry pie. Picked the berries herself, Molly said.

Katherine smiled.

"Thanks, Molly. That sounds really good."

"Good? Girl, I make the best huckleberry pie in the American Northwest. Good ain't got nothing on me."

"Yeah, well, if Anne ever lets me out of prison, I'll do that."

"Now what are you talking about? Trouble on the home front?"

"That's a nice way of putting it."

"Oh c'mon, sweetie. There isn't a couple on the planet that doesn't have its ups and downs. And don't forget, Annie-girl loves you to bits."

"You think?"

"I know so, girl. I'll be seeing you."

Molly left, and Katherine sat in the back garden with Max. She watched him crawl over the grass as if searching for four-leaf clovers. Knowing Max, he probably was.

Clouds rolled in, then the rain.

Katherine picked up Max.

"Nap time for you, buster. And I think I just might join you. I'm beat."

She carried him into the house and up the stairs. She laid him on the changing table, changed his diaper. She carried him into the bathroom, parked him on the floor, ran a washcloth in warm water, and washed his face and hands.

"Stay put a sec. I need to clean my teeth."

No sooner had she started brushing than Max made a break for it and crawled into her bedroom. She called after him with her mouth full of toothpaste.

"Come back here, you. Don't you know we're in a lockdown drill?"

She finished brushing her teeth, splashed water on her face, grabbed a hand towel. She stood in the doorway of her bedroom patting her face with the towel. She watched Max crawl straight for the cardboard boxes of things left to her by Marc Rochat. He reached up, grabbed hold of the rim of the nearest box, and pulled himself to his feet. He looked at his mother, bounced up and down on his bowed legs.

"What's on your mind, Max?"

"Goog."

Monsieur Booty appeared from nowhere, walked to where Max was standing. The beast stood on its rear legs, front legs on the rim, looked inside the box, and sniffed.

Mew.

"So it's the both of you up to no good, huh?"

Katherine tossed the towel back to the bathroom sink. She walked across the room, looked down into the box. Marc Rochat's sketchbooks lay atop boxes of candles. She saw the lettering on the cover of the top book:

piratz
Une histoire drôle de Marc Rochat
pour Mademoiselle Katherine Taylor

She looked at the two of them.

"You two are starting to scare the crap out of me. You know that?" She looked at the book. "Or maybe I'm just scaring the crap out of myself. You, fuzzface . . ."

Mew.

". . . you were there in the cathedral. So you I give a lot of room to be nutty."

She looked at Max, remembering she was already pregnant while hiding in the cathedral.

"Come to think of it, so were you, Max."

She looked out the window. It was raining hard now.

"And it feels like none of us ever left."

She walked into Max's bedroom, spread a blanket and pillow on the floor. Max and Monsieur Booty watched her through the connecting door. She came back into her own room, put on the black floppy hat and lit the lantern. She headed back to Max's room, lantern in hand, bending down to grab *piratz* from the cardboard box along the way.

"C'mon, gang, let's take a spin through beforetimes. See what happens."

She stood the lantern on the stool, sat on the blanket, and made herself comfy. She rested the sketchbook on her lap, looked back through the connecting door. Max and Monsieur Booty were still standing with paws on the rim of the cardboard box, looking at her, looking at each other.

"Well, c'mon," Katherine said. "Beforetimes waits for nobody."

Max dropped on his butt, rolled to his hands and knees, and charged. Monsieur Booty brought up the rear, taking swipes at the fuzzy slippers on Max's feet. Max climbed onto Katherine's lap, shoved his hand in her mouth.

"Oh, thank you very much. Here, turn around and sit. Here's some apple juice."

She handed Max his sippy cup and he went at it. Monsieur Booty looked for space on Katherine's lap, found none, and made like the Sphinx at her feet. The more she read from *piratz*, the more Katherine felt as if she were back in the little room between the bells.

"And an evil wizard named Screechy lived in an ice castle and wore a pointy hat with a rooster on top and stole a big diamond that was a future-teller. And there was a band of funny pirates with wooden swords and paper hats, riding on Pompidou's back and flying just above the waves of the Boiling Seas of Doom on their way to the land of Saskatoon where—"

A red lamp in the high corner of the room flashed in threes.

"Shit."

She lifted Max from her lap, set him on her shoulder as she jumped to her feet. The book tumbled to the floor. Max pointed to it.

"*Lune* moon."

"Not now, honey, we have to go somewhere, but don't worry. It'll be here when we get back. Here, be a big boy, hold your sippy cup."

She hurried to her bedroom and the door to the hall. Max tried to jump from her arms, reaching back for the book.

"*Lune!* Moon!"

"Crap, you want moon, we'll take moon."

Katherine ran back, grabbed the book, ran for the door.

"Boo!"

"Oh, Jesus."

She ran back to Max's room, reached for the cat. He darted away.

"Goddammit!"

The door to Katherine's room opened. Officer Jannsen in the doorway, stopwatch hanging around her neck, along with a small machine gun. She spoke calmly, but seriously.

"Now, Kat."

"He wants the cat."

"Forget the cat."

"I can't—"

Officer Jannsen dashed into the room, pulled Max from Katherine's arms, and headed for the door.

"Jesus, what are you doing?"

Officer Jannsen was already down the hall and down the stairs. She heard Max crying.

"Hey, hey!"

Katherine ran for the door, dropped the sketchbook, flew down the stairs. She got to the kitchen, saw Officer Jannsen going out the door.

"Dammit! Come back here!"

In the garden she saw four of the Swiss Guards running into the trees, their Brügger & Thomets raised, firing . . . *blamblam, blam!*

"Fuck! Max!"

She ran for Control, two guards were inside with headsets, one watching the monitors as black shapes moved through the trees, approaching the house.

"Intruders 220 and 146 degrees. Two squad, engage and destroy 146 degrees. Repeat, engage and destroy at 146. Three squad, intruders have you on the flank from 220. Reposition firing line."

Katherine yelled, "What the fuck is happening?"

The Swiss Guard at the monitors saw her.

"Downstairs, Madame Taylor, now!"

Katherine ran down the hall. The false wall at the end of the hall had been slid open. She jumped through it and down a narrow stairwell. Something under her feet, tripping, grabbing the handrail.

"Max!"

She heard him shriek. She ran through a series of connecting passages. She went left, then right, turned right again. She stopped; she'd come to a dead end. Heard Max's voice again.

"Fuck it! Anne, you fucking bitch!"

She ran back to where she'd started. Ran through the drill in her head.

"Left, right, left, and left," she mumbled to herself.

She ran, found another set of steep stairs going down. She jumped, hitting the concrete floor hard. She looked ahead. Officer Jannsen was inside the safe room and the vault door was closing. There was no stopping it once it started to close.

"No! Max!"

She ran ahead.

Officer Jannsen jumped from the room, handed Max to Katherine. Max twisted and screamed. His face was contorted with panic.

"Jesus, is this real?"

"Get in."

"They're fucking shooting!"

"Get in!"

Katherine ducked in the safe room, the massive vault door sealed, and hydraulic bolts slammed into sockets like bullets: *BLAM! BLAM! BLAM!* Max jumped, was rendered silent for a second, but there was a terrified look in his eyes.

"It's okay, honey, it's okay. You're with Mommy, it's okay."

A fearful cry gushed from his mouth, and he swung his fists. His sippy cup was still in his right hand, and it caught Katherine on the side of the head.

"Shit!"

Katherine sat on the small bed, sat him on her lap, pulled at his hands, took the sippy cup.

"No, honey, it's okay. It's only a game, it's okay. Please, Max, it's okay."

Max thrashed about in her arms. She wrapped her arms tight around him.

"Jesus, please stop, Max. Stop. Listen to me, stop."

He shrieked, his whole body trembling.

"Max, please . . . please . . . please . . ." she whispered again and again.

Max shuddered, gasped for air, caught his breath. Katherine wrapped the sleeve of her sweatshirt around her hand, wiped Max's eye and nose.

"Shhhh, honey, there you go. See, it's all okay now."

Max looked around the room.

"Yeah, you've never been here before, have you? *Maman* always had to carry that dumb old doll. You want to see where we are?"

Max took a breath. He was settling. Katherine picked him up and stood in the center of the room. She felt her own body trembling.

"See, there's *Maman's* bed. Isn't that a funny bed? It's so tiny. And there's a computer and a TV where we can watch 'Shaun the Sheep.' And over there is a little bed for you to go night-night."

"Nnnnnight."

"That's right. And here's a box of toys over here, and over here there's a little table where we can eat, and here's our little tiny kitchen. All the things we need. And behind the door is our little bathroom. See, there's a shower and a potty and a—"

"Boo!" Max said.

She looked at Max; he was looking toward Katherine's bed. Under the bed was Monsieur Booty, cowering with his tail curled around him. Katherine saw herself coming down the stairs, tripping . . . It was Monsieur Booty. Of course, from the other drills the cat learned to chase after Katherine into the safe room. Seeing him under the bed, and the smile on Max's face, tears rushed to her eyes.

"Yes, see? It's that silly old Monsieur Booty."

She walked close to the bed, sat Max on the floor. The cat emerged from his hiding place, sniffed Max's nose, rubbed his head against his belly. Max giggled. Katherine sat on the bed, put her face in her hands, bit her lip to keep from crying. She looked up at the ceiling. Concrete. Like the walls, like the floor. Reinforced with iron bars and surrounded by sections of six-inch steel. Not a window, and only one way out; through the vault door. She heard the sound of an exhaust fan and felt a stream of fresh air. "Fresh" wasn't quite it, she remembered. There was a supply of breathable air, figured on their body weight. That's what she was told. It was the same system used on submarines trapped under the sea. The air was reoxygenated and scrubbers removed traces of carbon dioxide. The more she looked around the safe room, the more she felt as if she were on a submarine, trapped, deep beneath the sea.

She looked at Max and Monsieur Booty. They'd been watching her, sensing her panic.

"I know, let's sing something."

Max tipped his head.

"Well, we're down here, let's have some fun."

"Fnnnn."

"Yeah. Tell you what, let's sing Max's favorite song." She took her son's small hands in her own, clapped them softly together, and sang.

> *"In the town where I was born,*
> *Lived a man who sailed to sea."*

Katherine stopped, crinkled her forehead.

"What do you think, bustercakes?"

Max stared at his mother, listened to her voice. He knew the word *buster*, and he knew when his mother said it, she was talking to him. But *bustercakes* was a new word, and it sounded very funny. Even funnier when he realized it meant him, too. He shook his hands and giggled.

"Yeah, let's get to the really fun part."

She clapped his hands again.

"We all live in a yellow submarine."

Clunk, clunk, pshhhhhh.

Katherine looked at the vault door.

The hydraulic bolts were easing from their sockets.

". . . a yellow submarine."

The door opened on its hinges. Officer Jannsen came into the safe room.

"Nnnn," Max said.

"Bonjour, Max." She looked at Katherine. "That was about as sloppy as your performance on the firing range this morning."

"I was rattled. Max was upset, then the bullets."

"Blanks, Kat, we were firing blanks. It was an exercise."

"How the hell was I supposed to know?"

"That's not the point. The point is you panicked and screwed up."

Katherine took a second to think. She sighed.

"I know. I screwed up. I'm sorry."

"Don't be sorry. Just know that if it comes to it, I'll be in here with Max and you'll be on the outside with the killers."

Katherine combed Max's hair with her fingers.

"I understand."

"Bon. We're done upstairs. You can come out now."

Officer Jannsen turned to leave. Katherine had a feeling she was never coming back.

"Anne?"

"Yes?"

"Molly said she has homemade huckleberry pie at the diner. Maybe when the drills are over, you, me, and Max can go stuff ourselves."

Officer Jannsen folded her arms under her breasts, looked down to the floor.

"There are some things you should know, Kat. The killers have been looking for you all over the world. And you were right; it is Max they want. And you were right about this house. It can't be found on Google

Earth; it's in a security zone. It exists for one reason: to protect you and Max. And yes, we've been keeping your emotions and memories under control with the teas. But it's not for the reasons you think. You're not a prisoner here, and we're not trying to turn you into a zombie; we're trying to prevent you from falling back into madness. You want to leave this place, we can't stop you. You want to stop drinking the teas, go ahead. In two months, you'll be certifiably insane. On the way, you'll forget you have a son. But that would be for the best, because by then Max will be gone. But before you check out of here and lose your mind for real, remember what the killers did to you, remember what they did to Marc Rochat. Remember what they did all over Lausanne. Torturing people, flaying them alive, rape, beheadings, slaughter. Can you imagine it? Can you see it in beforetimes?"

Katherine nodded.

"Good. Now imagine what they'll do to Max if they get their hands on him."

Katherine looked at Max, combed his black hair with her fingers.

"Is he normal?"

"*Pardon?*"

"Are you giving him anything?"

"Outside the usual inoculations any child gets, no."

"Nothing in his apple juice?"

"Nothing but freshly pressed apples."

Katherine looked at Officer Jannsen.

"Then he's okay, yeah?"

"He's more than okay. Max is perfect."

Katherine felt her throat tighten; she bit her lip. She stood up, rested Max's butt on her hip, and gently bounced him up and down.

"I know, Max, let's go upstairs. You can help crazy Mommy make a cup of tea."

❦

TWENTY-TWO

I

HARPER REACHED THE TOP OF THE TRAIL AND STOPPED. THE SUN had cleared the Pyrenees, and the stone walls of the fortress glowed in the morning light. He looked down the steep cliffs. Far below, in the Field of the Burned, was the white dot of the dog who'd led him from the house. Two hours earlier, Harper had come out the kitchen door and seen stars fading from the sky. He'd turned to grab the walking staff he'd left by the door, and when he'd turned back, the slobbering Shiva was standing before him. Harper looked at the animal.

"Right. Lead the way."

And so the dog did, with a slow, flopping pace. First to the back gate hidden in the trees, where the dog waited for Harper to unhook the latch so they could pass through; then into the woods, where the cover of night had yet to be lifted. If Harper didn't know better, he'd swear the dog halted at irregular intervals to scan the forest for danger. Each time Harper waited for the dog to listen to sounds running through the woods or sniff scents in the wind, just in case that's what the dog was doing. Now, from the top of the pluton, Harper watched the dog sniff through the field till it found a patch of warm sun to sleep on.

"Good boy, stay," Harper said.

He felt a sudden rush of vertigo, felt sick. He backed away from the cliff, took a deep breath, steadied himself. When his head stopped spinning, he climbed the wooden stairs leading to the south gate and stepped into the courtyard. Empty, quiet. He looked around. From what he recalled from the History Channel, this wasn't the actual fortress of the Cathars. The Crusaders destroyed that one. But the Cathar fortress would have been built on the same exact ground, meter for meter. And looking at the layout, it was the smallness of the space that struck him first. He tried to imagine five hundred plus souls crammed together with no place to hide from the French catapults. He waited for something to flash through his eyes. Nothing.

He crossed the courtyard to the north gate, looked out over the valleys and flattening land. Tried to imagine ten thousand Crusaders coming up the valley. Tried to imagine two hundred fighters standing on the walls of the fortress, watching the invaders encircle the pluton. Tried to imagine him and two of his kind knowing there were hundreds of stone-cold bad guys hiding amid the Crusaders. Still came up with nothing. He stepped through the north gate, looked northwest down the side of the cliff. He saw the ruins of the stone huts that were the homes of the Cathar civilians. Down there's where they found the laser pointer, pointing west to east to make an artificial horizon . . . He looked back at the north gate. And that's where the kid set the transmission rig to hack into Blue Brain.

He looked back at the fortress.

The gate and laser may be perpendicular to each other, but they had nothing to do with each other. Coincidence? No such bloody thing. So where are the intersecting lines of causality on this one? He scanned the surrounding hills. Each of them had a clear shot at the northern quadrant of the sky and the constellation Draco where the comet appeared. Astruc and the kid could've done the job from any of the surrounding hilltops, and left the transmission gear undetected for a thousand years.

"So why here?"

Harper answered his own question.

"The priest was trying to make a point. So what the hell is it?"

He walked around the fortress, careful not to look down. Coming to the west rim of the pluton, the tower was a silhouette against a rising sun. Like a stone thumb lining up a point of perspective from here to the sun, ninety-three million miles away. He went back into the court-yard, walked in circles. He stopped at the foot of the stone steps leading to what was left of the ramparts. Something whipped through his eyes. Wasn't a flash of time; it was a feeling. The locals called it déjà vu, the closest thing they had to moving through time. Maybe it was Captain Jay Michael Harper, maybe it was Bernard de Saint-Martin, maybe it was a trace of every human form he'd occupied from the beginning . . . but just now he was getting a heavy rush of *been there, seen it*.

His eyes locked on the place where the tower met the ground.

There was a great slab of granite rising from the earth, half hidden under the tower. He walked closer to it, stared at it. Here, the rush was more intense. He lowered to one knee, touched the stone. Bits of time ripped through his eyes. Lausanne Cathedral . . . the junkie on the altar, the one his kind called Gabriel . . . standing in the midday sun pouring through the great stained glass window of the south transept, scratch-ing the crook of his arm, desperate for a fix, telling Harper, *The earth beneath these stones is sacred.*

Harper's eyes saw it.

Two and a half million years ago, eternal beings from another place had come to Earth bearing a spark of the first light of creation. They watched, waited, until a small band of humanoids crossed the plain. The humanoids scratched the grass and sniffed at the dirt, searching for signs of game. When night fell over the land, the humanoids took shel-ter in a cave and huddled together for warmth. The creatures from an-other place descended from the pluton and entered the cave, telling them to be not afraid. And they revealed the first light of creation. The humanoids stared at the flame, the light seeped into their eyes, and an eternal soul was ignited in the forms of men, so that mankind would one day know the truth—the universe and everything in it was part of one living being.

"Bloody hell," Harper mumbled.

He got to his feet, looked around the courtyard, then out through the north gate. His eyes flashed the rooftop in Paris, the comet, the triangulations downloading into Blue Brain. Thousands per second, all from the point of perspective of an imaginary line drawn from right to left across the sky . . . *This sacred earth* was Father fucking Astruc's point.

"First contact was here. It happened here."

From outside the south gate, the sound of a rock tumbling down the cliff.

Harper eased into the shadows under the south wall. He heard voices, American voices. Two minutes later, two young women stepped through the south gate and into the courtyard. They were dressed in blue jeans, hiking boots, fleeces. One of them had a camera around her neck. They looked about the courtyard.

"Wow," one of them said.

"I need to tweet this to Doug," the other one said.

That one pulled out a mobile and began to take pictures. It was when she turned to the southwest wall that she saw a man step from the shadows, wooden staff in hand.

"Holy fuck!" were the next words from her mouth.

"It's all right. Don't be afraid," Harper said.

The two women looked at each other, then him.

"Look, we know the fortress isn't open till ten. We just wanted to see it before the tourists got here."

Harper smiled.

"Actually, so did I."

"You're not a security guard?"

"No. I'm a tourist, like you. And I was just leaving."

The one who'd been taking pictures with her mobile said, "Do you know where the light comes?"

Harper looked at her.

"Sorry?"

"Where it comes through on the summer solstice? The Cathars were into that kind of stuff."

Harper thought about it.

"Today isn't the solstice. It was months ago," Harper said.

"We'd still like to see where it happens. Feel the energy. It never dies, you know."

Harper didn't have the heart to tell them this wasn't the real fortress of the Cathars. And he flashed something from the History Channel: There was a bit about people coming to see the light on the dawn of the summer solstice. Light came from the east, hit the fortress at a certain angle. He looked around the place, saw the arrow slits in what was left of the tower. Got it.

"Up there. Sun cuts directly through those slits in the stone, like clockwork."

The two women stared at the tower. Harper headed for the south gate and was almost through it when the one with the camera around her neck said, "Do you speak French?"

Harper stopped, looked back.

"What?"

"Do you speak French?"

"More or less."

"What does 'Montségur' mean? Is it 'safe mountain' or 'safe place,' or is it something else?"

Harper thought about it. He looked around the fortress . . . *this sacred earth*. He looked at the two women.

"Actually, Montségur is an Occitan word. The people that lived here before the French. It was the language of the Cathars."

"Really? So what's it mean?"

Harper smiled.

"It means 'Angel City.'"

Their jaws dropped, their eyes widened. One of them finally broke the silence: "That is so the coolest thing I have ever heard."

Harper looked up at the sky, saw heavy clouds drifting in from the west. He looked at the young women, passed the palm of his right hand before their eyes.

"*Divulgare verbum . . . Spread the word.* And don't stay up here too long, ladies. It's going to snow by afternoon."

He stared at them; they were motionless. It'd take them a few seconds to come around, and when they did, he'd be gone. But they'd have a memory of meeting someone . . . someone who appeared from the shadows and told them to be not afraid and showed them where the dawn of the summer solstice passed through the tower, told them *Montségur* was a word that meant "Angel City," and that they should spread the word . . . then he disappeared. The wildest part of their imagination would want to believe the man *was* an angel. Then they'd really have something to tweet about. Harper laughed to himself. He stepped out through the south gate, made his way down the trail.

He reached the Field of the Burned, followed his tracks across the grass in the direction of the house. He scanned the slope for his guide dog, Shiva. Spotted him sitting under a tree at the north edge of the field. Harper pointed southeast.

"I think the house is that way."

Shiva didn't budge.

Harper walked toward him, saw a patch of ground that had been turned over, like a small grave. Grass had been scattered over it in an attempt to hide it. Harper brushed away the grass with the tip of his staff. He saw boot marks in the dirt, as if someone wearing a size six and a half, maybe a seven, had stomped down on the mound. Harper knelt down, touched the dirt. It was moist, freshly turned. He poked at the dirt with his staff, began to dig. A meter down, he hit something solid. He laid his staff on the ground, scooped out dirt with his hands. A rectangular shape appeared in the earth. He outlined the edges with his fingers, brushed away a thin layer of dirt. It was the reliquary box from the cavern under Paris.

"You must be bloody joking me."

II

HARPER RESTED THE WALKING STAFF NEXT TO THE KITCHEN door. He kicked dirt from his boots, went inside. Serge was sitting at the table, drinking espresso from a shot glass. Clock on the wall read 08:25 hours.

"*Bono matin*. Will you take a coffee?"

"*Bono matin*. And I'd love a coffee."

Harper set the reliquary box on the table. Serge regarded it, didn't display surprise. He pushed himself from the table, walked to a coffee machine. He set another shot glass under the spout and pressed a button. The machine growled, and a stream of coffee drained into the glass. Serge carried the glass to Harper.

"There is sugar in the bowl."

"Cheers," Harper said, picking up the spoon on the table and dropping a healthy pile into his glass. He stirred, sipped, nodded toward the reliquary box.

"Look familiar?"

"No, but it sounds familiar."

"How's that work?"

"The angel who stayed under our roof carried a wooden box. A reliquary box. So goes the story."

"And in the story, did the angel tell your family what was inside it?"

"The story goes that the angel showed them what was inside it."

Harper finished his espresso. He opened the box, unwrapped the leather cover, pulled out the sextant, and laid it on the table.

"Is that what they saw?"

"From what has been told to me, it could be. Where did you find it?"

"In the Field of the Burned. It had been buried there two days ago."

"And you know it was buried there two days ago because . . ."

"Trust me."

Serge sat back in his chair.

"So it's true then."

"What's true?"

Serge nodded toward the sextant. "The story."

"Did the angel tell your family what it was for?"

"Not that I've ever heard. But the story only says it was revealed to us."

"Revealed."

"That's the word used in telling the story."

"Why?"

"I don't know. No one does."

"How was it described to you?"

Serge looked at the sextant.

"As it is. Old, copper, intricate drawings along the rim."

"It's script."

"Excusatz-me?"

"It's script. I got a good look at it in the sun. It's Avestan, from ancient Persia. The language of Zoroaster."

"You know this language?"

"I've come across it once or twice. The only surviving examples are in the *Yasna Haptanghaiti* and the Gathas."

"I do not know these writings."

"No, but you know about the Cathars."

"There is a connection?"

"Zoroaster was a religious mystic. And the first human to develop the concept of a duality in the universe. *Aša* was truth or light; *Druj* was untruth, darkness."

"Pure God, Evil God."

"That's right. It's all right here, in the script. And this down here, this is about a strange light in the sky that will announce that the time of the prophecy is at hand."

"You speak of the comet over the pluton two nights ago."

Harper thought about it. That's exactly how it would have appeared from the village.

"That's right."

Serge scratched his chin.

"So what is this prophecy?"

"No idea, do you?"

Serge laughed.

"Me? How would I know? My family were simple, superstitious shepherds. Their lives were full of myths and legends."

Harper listened to the man's voice. He was hiding something, but Harper couldn't sort it. He locked on to the man's last words: *myths and legends.* He sat back in his chair, watched the man study the calibration dials of the sextant. Waited.

"These symbols on these wheels, what are they?" Serge said.

"Constellations of stars in the north quadrant of the sky."

"Where the comet appeared."

"That's right."

"And these little hammer strikes along the arc, what are they?"

"No idea. How about you?"

"Why should I know this?"

"Because you're not a simple superstitious shepherd, you're a man with a shed packed with a small army of iron angels. Besides, those hammer strikes are the first things your eyes locked on when I showed you the sextant."

Serge looked at Harper.

"More coffee?"

"Sure."

"Make it yourself, I'll be right back."

Serge left the kitchen, rummaged through the bookshelves in the sitting room. Harper did the deed with the coffee machine, had a double shot this time. He sat back at the table. Serge lay a dusty old book next to the sextant. The book was open to a picture of a bone. Harper stared at it. There were sets of tiny scratches etched into the bone. He looked at the hammer strikes on the arc of the sextant. They matched those on the bone. Harper looked at the lettering under the photo. *Ishango Bone.* He looked at Serge.

"What the hell is an Ishango Bone?" Harper said.

"It's the fibula of a baboon. It was found in Africa by a Belgian archaeologist in 1960. His name isn't important. Look at these three sets of scratches, right here. Those carved to the left and right add up to sixty. The scratches in the middle make forty-eight. At first it was thought to be a lunar calendar or a counting tool of some kind. The bone was originally dated to be six thousand years old. Carbon testing found it was actually twenty thousand years old."

"Twenty thousand."

"At least."

"Somewhat early for a lunar calendar, or counting tool of some kind."

Serge pointed to the left column.

"Except for this. Nineteen marks, then sixteen, then thirteen and eleven."

"And?"

"Left to right, they're nothing but scratches on the fibula of a baboon. Right to left, they form a prime quadruplet with two pairs of twin primes and two overlapping prime triplets."

Harper looked at Serge.

"What did you say you did for a living fifteen years ago, before you started making angels?"

"Textiles."

"Doing what?"

"I was in charge of measurements. I'm also very good at mathematics. It's a hobby."

"A hobby. Right. So what is a prime quadruplet?"

There was a piece of paper on the table. Had a woman's writing on it, looked like a shopping list. Serge pulled it toward him, started scribbling under *les oeufs*. He turned the page around for Harper to see. Harper looked at it.

$\{p, p + 2, p + 6, p + 8\}$

"This is the formula of a prime quadruplet," Serge said, "where p represents the closest possible arrangement of prime numbers larger than the number 3. So, the first series of numbers is 5,7,11,13 . . . then 11,13,17,19 . . . then 101, 103, 107, 109. And on and on."

"What's the formula used for?"

"Like any mathematical formula, it's used as a proof."

"Of what?"

Serge closed the book.

"To date, the highest prime quadruplet formula is three thousand, twenty-four digits. Curiously, the formula shows no sign of resolving, suggesting a mathematical proof of twin prime conjecture."

"Which is what?"

"Infinity."

"Infinity."

Serge nodded. "And you know what they say about infinity."

"Actually, I don't."

"No?"

"No. How about a hint?"

"Infinity, as represented in twin prime conjecture, creates the mathematical possibility of specific supernatural occurrence."

Harper wasn't sure what that meant. Only that it had the same number of syllables as "undefined metaphysical condition." He slammed back his coffee, looked at Serge.

"Define 'specific supernatural occurrence.'"

"A miracle."

"A miracle, you say?"

"Yes. And if there is a mathematical possibility of one, then mathematically, there is the possibility of more. I have a book in the sitting room, *A Mathematician's Miscellany*. Perhaps you would like to read it."

Harper flashed the triangulations feeding into Blue Brain. Astruc was doing more than making a map of the world to build a cosmic alarm clock. He was looking for the confirmation of a miracle. Only there's no such thing in paradise. Or there's not supposed to be. Harper pointed to the sextant.

"Actually, what I'd like is to know if the angel who lived under the family roof mentioned where this thing came from?"

"Jerusalem," Serge said.

"Did the angel happen to say *who* it came from?"

Serge nodded.

"And who might that be, according to the story?" Harper said.

"It was handed down from Christ, brought here and hidden in a cave beneath Montségur during the Roman Occupation of Gaul. Which is what the world called Occitania before the French called it France."

Harper paused to render respect to the man's heritage. In fact, they had something in common with the land. This earth was sacred to both of them. He pushed the sextant closer to Serge.

"And how did this thing come to Christ?"

"It was a gift. Given to him a few years after he was born."

Harper flashed Matthew's Gospel.

Christ, born in a manger in Bethlehem. Shepherds in the fields and angels on high. Years later, three wise men arrive from the East with gifts of frankincense, gold, and myrrh . . . or so goes the legend. Legend called the wise men *magi*. Fact: *Magi* was the name of the followers of Zoroaster. Harper rubbed the back of his neck, flashed Karoliina and her Christmas pageant *he-is-born* fantasy on the train to Lausanne. Looking at Serge, Harper wondered if fantasy was contagious.

"Quite the family *histoire*," Harper said.

"It gave us something to talk about besides the weather. That is the old family joke."

Harper wrapped the sextant, laid it in the reliquary box. He looked at the box, noticing for the first time the wood was well preserved, but very old. Eighth century, maybe. And closing the lid, he noticed the box appeared deeper by half than the sextant. He stared at the box some more; closing the lid, opening the lid. After a bit of that, he removed the sextant and laid it on the table. He felt inside the box, tapped the bottom. There was a hollow sound. He pressed the inside corners. The bottom shifted. He pressed harder, heard a snap, and the bottom of the box separated from the frame. He lifted it from the box. Two little compartments: one squared, one rectangular. There was powder in the square compartment. Harper touched it with his index finger, rubbed the powder on the palm of his hand.

"It's clay."

"Is it?"

"Yes. Very old clay."

Harper replaced the false panel, then the sextant, then closed the lid.

"What else was in here, according to the superstitious shepherds in your family?"

Serge stared at Harper's eyes a moment.

"Come with me," he said.

Harper picked up the reliquary box.

"You can leave it here," Serge said.

"On the kitchen table? What if someone sees it?"

"They will think I made a very ugly bread box. Come."

Harper followed the man out the kitchen door and into the garden. Shiva joined in the small parade to the shed. Serge pushed open the door and went in. Harper saw the light turn on and spill from the door. That's when Harper noticed snow falling through the sky. He stopped, scanned the scene above the village rooftops. The Pyrenees had been swallowed by low-hanging clouds. Harper felt Shiva nudge at the back of his legs, coaxing Harper as if he were a lost sheep: *Move along, move along.*

Harper walked into the shed. Shiva sat outside the door, snapping at snowflakes.

Inside, Serge was at the worktable, clearing the surface. There were shelves built into the wall behind the table, loaded with cans, tins, toolboxes, junk. Harper watched him sort through the shelves and carefully remove a round tin. White, a small picture of a red-and-blue impatiens above the word *Sucre*. There was a muted rattle from inside the tin as Serge laid it on his workbench. He turned back to the shelf, pulled down a squared tin this time; green with pink roses and a smiling baby on the lid, *Biscuiterie Nantaise* printed along the side.

"Come and see."

Harper walked over, saw the tins were antiques.

"Very nice. What's inside?"

Serge opened the lid of the biscuit tin, reached in, and pulled out a wad of leather. Same type of leather that was wrapped around the sextant. He laid the wad on the table, unwrapped it. Whatever it was, it was broken.

"And this is a what?"

"One third of a burnished clay cup."

"A broken clay cup, at the bottom of a reliquary box. From Jerusalem, sometime during the Roman empire."

Serge nodded.

"Interesting. What's in the sugar tin?" Harper said.

Serge opened the lid, pulled out a leather scrap tied closed. He opened it, pulled out something wrapped in old linen. He laid it on the table and opened the linen. A carpenter nail, five inches long, iron. Harper stared at the linen, saw traces of blood splatter. He looked closer at the nail. Ancient blood on iron.

"That's interesting, too. Looks like it would fit in the rectangular compartment of the box."

"Yes, it does, doesn't it?"

Harper rubbed the back of his neck. "What else do you know?"

"Only what has been passed down through the family."

"Tell me."

"In the nineteenth century, a professor of antiquities from la Sorbonne came to Montségur to visit the fortress. He stayed in our house. He was shown what was left of the cup and the one nail. My family lied, told the professor the things were bought from an antiques dealer in Languedoc. The professor examined the clay fragment and said it was part of a cup, sort of thing people drank wine from. He said it was at least two thousand years old, from the Near East, brought by the Roman army, most likely. He said the nail was from the same period. Given there was blood on the nail, the professor suggested it had been used in a crucifixion."

"A crucifixion."

"So said the professor from la Sorbonne, passing through this place in the nineteenth century."

Harper felt a chill down his spine. *No bloody way.*

"The Romans crucified people all over the empire, Serge. It was their preferred method of dealing with troublesome locals. Or maybe this nail belonged to a carpenter who missed and hit his hand with a hammer. After all, it takes three nails to make a crucifixion."

Serge leaned down, studied the broken cup.

"As it would three matching pieces of clay to make this the Holy Grail."

Harper leaned down, stared at the cup. The lines of the break were clean, not ragged. It had been carefully sliced into three parts. He worked the odds there were two sets of the same sort, hidden somewhere in the world. Coming up 1,000,000,000 to 1, and it had the feel of a safe bet.

"So this angel, nine hundred years ago. He stays a few weeks in the family hut, gets his strength back, disappears with the sextant, but leaves a broken cup and a bloody nail with your family. Why would he do that?"

Serge shrugged, nodded at the nail and broken cup.

"Simple. The broken cup and the nail are the things of men, but the sextant was a thing of the Gods."

"Gods, not God?"

"Gods."

Pure God, Evil God . . .

Harper felt dizzy, rested his hands on the table.

Bloody hell.

Montségur wasn't just a place where lines of causality simply intersected; here they ran in circles at the speed of light, crashing into one another head-on, releasing enough energy to shake the fabric of time and space. Strangest of all, the two American girls at the fortress this morning weren't that far off; the Cathars *were* into that kind of stuff. A faint sound rang through the shed. Serge reached into his trouser pocket and pulled out a mobile, connected the line.

"*Bono matin.*"

Harper watched the man listen, then talk . . .

"*Conter vos recontrar, monsieur. Mercé. Adieussiatz.*"

. . . then hand over the phone.

"It's for you," he said.

Harper took it.

"Yes?"

"Get your roller skates on, brother, I got a lead on Astruc and the kid."

It was Krinkle. Harper could hear the same trippy sound in his voice, trippy music blaring in the background.

"Where?"

"A guy driving south of Auzat found him walking in the middle of the road last night. He was carrying the kid in his arms. The kid was mauled pretty bad. Looks like the bad guys got to them."

"What happened?"

"The driver stopped, thinking they'd been in a car accident. Astruc pulled a Micro UZI on the driver, told him to take them to the nearest hospital. Driver headed back to Auzat with Astruc raving about the kid being the light of the world and the Dark Ones finding them at Heaven's Gate."

"Heaven's what?"

"It's a pass across the Pyrenees. Astruc and the kid must've been trying to cross into Spain when the bad guys found them. Looking at a map, Astruc must've carried the kid all night to reach Auzat. He passed out in the backseat."

"Where are you getting this info?"

"I told you, I'm in the communications business; I was tuning in to what the French cops were communicating with one another. And let me tell you, it's mighty weird."

"What?"

"Cop sees a car speeding through the streets of Auzat, sees blood dripping from the trunk. Cop stops the car, realizes it's a taxi, finds Astruc passed out in the backseat with the kid in his arms and a Micro UZI machine gun hanging from his neck, both of them covered in blood. Cop opens the trunk, and there's a dead deer with a bullet in its head. I mean, the French like it surreal, but this was one step beyond."

"The cabbie, from Toulouse."

Took two seconds for that one to sink into Krinkle's head.

"Yeah, how did you know?"

"Long story. Where are Astruc and the kid now?"

"The kid was medevaced to a small hospital in Foix. Astruc tried to patch him up, but he's in critical condition."

"The kid is a half-breed; the doctors can't help him. They might kill him."

"Don't worry about the kid, I got him covered. You need to get Astruc."

"Where's he?"

"In a French jail."

"What?"

"You show up in the back of a taxi, machine gun hanging from your neck, bloody and passed out, with a half-dead kid in your arms, you'll probably get arrested in this country. He came to as they were locking him up, got rowdy. The police hit him with fentanyl, he went down. More fun: Cops in Foix ran Astruc's prints, ID'd him as the long-lost Christophe Astruc, OP. Toulouse is sending down a paddy wagon to pick him up on outstanding charges of murder and kidnapping."

"When are they picking him up?"

"ETA at twelve thirty. Which gives you enough time to get to Foix and nab Astruc before he's hooked and booked. Oh yeah, you've got clearance to touch the locals if you have to, but do no harm."

"What's that supposed to mean?"

"How should I know? Maybe scare the crap out of them, just don't kill anyone. Bottom line, get Astruc to Gare de Foix by twelve fifteen."

"There's a train to Lausanne?"

"Yeah, but don't take it, don't even go in the station. Just wait outside."

"Where outside?"

"At the bus stop, brother, where else?"

The line went dead.

Harper handed back the mobile to Serge.

"You wouldn't happen to have an automobile, would you?"

"Why do you need an automobile?"

"I need a lift. Have to make a couple stops in Foix."

"Where must you go in Foix?"

"The gendarmerie, then the train station. You know where they are?"

"The gendarmerie is on Allée de Villote, Gare de Foix is nearby on Rue Pierre Semard. But if you don't mind my asking, and seeing as you're asking me for transportation, what must you do at the gendarmerie?"

Harper tried to imagine a polite way of putting it. There wasn't one.

"I need to break someone out of jail."

Serge scratched his chin.

"I see."

He wrapped the broken cup and bloodied nail, replaced them in their proper tins, set the tins back on the shelves. He turned back to Harper.

"I do not have a car, but I can borrow a bread truck."

BOOK FOUR

FOR THE LORD GOD OF
ISRAEL HATH SPOKEN IT

TWENTY-THREE

I

IT WAS A BREAD TRUCK. A YELLOW, 1971 CITROËN H-TYPE. FOUR cylinders, forty-six-horsepower. A bloody antique. *Gasca Boulangerie & Pâtisserie, Avenue Alsace Lorraine* painted neatly along the sides. It belonged to Serge's cousin. He lived in Montségur, had a bakery in the next town. Worked nights, slept in the day. Rattling along at forty klicks per hour through the snow, it was slow going. The truck's interior smelled of freshly baked bread. Harper looked in the back. There were some croissants in a bin.

"Suppose your cousin would mind if I had a croissant?"

"They are leftovers from the morning, but help yourself. I'll have one, too."

Harper undid his seat belt, hunched down and walked into the back, grabbed two croissants. He got back in his seat, handed over one of the croissants.

"*Mercé,*" Serge said, biting into the bread.

Harper chomped his own.

They wound down the north slope of the Pyrenees and onto the plain. The storm followed close after them. Soon the snow came in fat flakes, quickly covering open patches of ground at the sides of the road.

Then came a farm where horses in a field quivered to shake the snow from their backs and withers. Serge flipped on the windshield wipers. The blades made squeaking sounds over the glass.

"It's a big storm," Serge said.

"Looks it."

And thinking about it, Harper imagined Astruc and the kid crossing the Pyrenees through a place Krinkle called . . .

"Heaven's Gate."

Serge was chewing.

"Excusatz-me?"

"There's a pass across the Pyrenees called Heaven's Gate. You know it?"

Serge nodded warily. "I know it. La Porta del Cel. It's a high mountain crossing from Spain to France. A very difficult crossing."

"Where is it from Montségur?"

"Southwest, about sixty kilometers as the crow flies."

"Could a hiker reach it in a day, two days?"

Serge glanced quickly at Harper, then back to the road.

"Yes, if they were fit. One day to reach the base of the pass, cross over the next day. Are you considering taking a hike? It is a popular trek for tourists. Very scenic. Though I would not recommend it in this weather. There would not be a lot to see, and you would most probably freeze to death."

Harper looked ahead. Snow drifted over the two-lane road.

"I'll keep it in mind. How did it get its name? Heaven's Gate?"

Serge shrugged.

"It's more than twenty-five-hundred meters high."

"Must be more to it than that."

Serge shrugged again.

"It was used by Catholics fleeing the conquest of Spain by the Saracens in the eighth century. It was used again by Republicans fleeing the Fascists during the Civil War."

"So that's how it got its name."

They passed through a small forest. It grew dark on the road; Serge switched on the headlights.

"I suppose so," he said.

Harper listened carefully to the sound of the man's voice. As if sensing Harper's attention, Serge shifted uncomfortably behind the steering wheel. There was a turnoff to the motorway. A long line of taillights in the direction of Foix said the motorway was jammed because of the weather.

"I'm afraid we must take the side roads, through Montgaillard. We will be at the gendarmerie in ninety minutes, and the train station is two minutes from there."

Harper checked his watch: 10:15 hours. Gave him a half hour to snatch Astruc and get to Gare de Foix by 12:15. *Swell,* he thought. *Running late, no backup or time warp for support. Have to get in and get out the old-fashioned way.* But running late gave him time to focus on Serge. Harper bit into his croissant again.

"Not bad," he said.

"My cousin is a very good baker."

"How is he at watching the shed when you're away?"

Serge kept his eyes on the road. "What do you mean?"

"Your family name is Gasca. It's a Catalan name, from the other side of the Pyrenees, yeah?"

"Yes, and what has this to do with my cousin the baker?"

"I'm just killing time on the way to Foix, filling in the rest of your family history, pre–Cathar era."

"I do not understand."

"You said your family was one of the first to settle under the pluton in the eighth century. From near Sant Pau de Segúries, yeah?"

"Yes? So?"

"You left something out. It was your family who brought the reliquary box to Occitania."

Serge had another bite from his own croissant, chewed thoughtfully.

"Why would you say this?"

"The History Channel."

"Compreni pas."

"I watch a lot of the History Channel."

"I know, on my wife's television last night."

"That's right. And last night, between looking at stars and smoking fags in the garden, there was a program about the Caliphate in Spain, 711 to 1492. Just now, driving through the snow in your cousin's bread truck, the penny dropped."

"You are very strange, I think."

"You're not the first man to mention it. Would you like me to tell you what I think?"

"Perqué pas?"

"After 720 AD, the Caliphate would have extended from Gibraltar to the Pyrenees, just south of Montségur."

"This is true. So?"

"I think one fine summer's day, in the eighth century, your family carried the reliquary box across Heaven's Gate and hid it in a cave beneath Montségur."

"Why would we do this?"

"Because you were told to, by someone like me."

"Someone like you."

"You know, like the one your family found in the ashes in the Field of the Burned."

"Are you saying it's the same person, this someone like you and the one my family found in the ashes, separated by five hundred years?"

"Maybe, maybe not."

"So are you saying someone like you commanded my family to carry the box from Spain to keep it from falling into the hands of the Caliphate?"

"The religions and flags of men mean nothing to me, or those like me. Religions and flags come under the heading of free will. We can't make those sorts of choices for men. It's a certain breed of evil hiding behind the religions and flags, the ones who sow fear and greed among men, that we're interested in. But I'm sure you've heard all about it from your father, as he heard it from his father."

"You give my family too much credit. We were superstitious shepherds."

"You also said they were nomads. Someone like me would look at such a family and think they'd be good cover."

"To do what?"

"To take the reliquary box, follow the constellation Draco north across a place described to them as Heaven's Gate, then travel to another place called Montségur. Hide the reliquary box and watch over it till someone like me returned to you again. Your family turned from nomads to farmers to do just that. Fast forward to 1244: This time evil is hiding behind a royal crest and a cross, and they're closing in. The rest brings us to nowtimes."

"What is nowtimes?"

"You and me in your cousin's bread truck at this very moment in space and time."

Serge finished his croissant, brushed crumbs from his coat.

"All this was on the History Channel last night?"

"No, most of it was me imagining."

"Imagining, you say."

"That's right. It's how the ones like me do things."

"I see."

They didn't speak for a long time.

The snow-covered countryside gave way to gas stations, used auto dealerships, and discount shopping outlets. Locals were at their doors with shovels and brooms, fighting a losing battle with the mounting snow. A road sign advised they were traveling the Route d'Espagne, and after turning left at a rotary, another sign advised they were now traveling the Avenue de Barcelone. There were old stone houses along this road. Harper saw children making a snowman in one front garden. He heard the thump of a snowball hitting the thin side panel of the bread truck, then the sound of young laughing voices. The clouds lifted a little here, but the snow kept falling. Harper saw a river running along the left side of the road, and above a clump of buildings beyond the river, a medieval castle on a low hill.

"This is Foix," Serge said. "There is an old city under that castle. If you were not in a hurry to break someone out of jail, you might enjoy visiting it."

"Something to look forward to the next time I pass this way."

Serge nodded, turned left at a rotary, and crossed a small bridge onto a tree-lined road. There was a parking area set between the opposing lanes of traffic.

"It was your eyes," Serge said.

"My eyes."

"We were always told about a light in the eyes of those who visited my family. The story was, we were given a gift to see that light. A gift that was passed down through the generations. When I saw you outside the shed last night, you were surrounded by darkness, but I saw a flame in your eyes."

Harper flashed back, saw it happen. He blinked.

"That's why you didn't want me to tell you my name, that's why you wouldn't shake my hand. You know we can't touch the locals."

"So I was told."

"You were expecting me last night?"

Serge shook his head.

"Not really. The Field of the Burned was nine hundred years ago. Family stories lose their hold on the soul with time. Then I saw the comet."

Harper thought about the impact on a disbelieving man to have a family secret, long thought to be no more than legend, to suddenly burst across the night sky in a revelation of brilliant light.

"You were told the comet would appear one day by the one your family found in the ashes. That it would be a sign that he would return to this place again, that it would mean the time of the prophecy was at hand."

"No, that's not what happened. The one my family found knew nothing more than there was a treasure beneath Montségur, and that he needed to remain alive for one hundred more days."

"You know what it means, don't you?"

"Of what do you speak?"

"The prophecy. Your family didn't just carry the reliquary box to Montségur, they carried the prophecy and passed it to the one they found in the ashes."

"That was what we were meant to do from the beginning. That was the mission given to us by someone like you thirteen hundred years ago."

Harper watched the road.

"What is the prophecy?"

"Do you command me to tell you?"

"Is that what it takes?"

"According to the story, yes."

"Then I command you to tell me about the prophecy."

Serge rounded a hairpin turn; the bread truck slid a little, but steadied and drove on.

"That when the comet appeared in the northern sky and was eclipsed by the pluton, it would mean a child, conceived of light, had been born. That he would lead mankind to the next stage of evolution."

Harper flashed back to Karoliina, the girl on the train. She was connected, but a local, and she'd said the same damn thing. *What the hell?*

"Has anyone in your family ever told anyone else about this?"

"Of course not, it was our sacred duty to say nothing. Why do you ask?"

Harper finished his croissant.

"No reason, just checking up on you. Making sure you were keeping to your sacred duty."

Serge smiled.

"I understand. By the way, what should I do with the sextant?"

Harper saw it, in the reliquary box, sitting on the kitchen table. Shit. Serge saw the expression on Harper's face.

"Do not worry," Serge said. "Shiva is a very good watch dog. The greatest danger is my wife opening the box and putting the sextant on the mantle above the fireplace. She likes to collect junk."

Harper chuckled imagining it.

"Keep the sextant in the box, hide it in the shed. Might as well put the broken cup and the nail in the box, too."

"As you command."

Harper looked at him.

"For the record, I'm not really in the business of giving commands."

"No?"

"No."

"Whose business is it to give commands then?"

"Well, there's a cop in a cashmere coat above me. Beyond that, no bloody idea."

"Interesting."

Serge came to the end of the road, looped to the opposing lane, and drove back toward the river. Halfway along the road he pulled into the parking area and shut down the motor. He looked at Harper.

"My family has been in the service of the noble lord for thirteen hundred years. Today, I am very proud to be a member of my family. Do you understand this?"

Harper flashed back to Serge's shed, watching the man weld bronze wings to an angel. *Nobel lord*, the man called the sorrow-laden thing.

"Sure."

Serge tipped his head toward the windshield.

"The gendarmerie is out there, across the road."

Through the falling snow Harper saw two gray buildings. Four floors, burnished red trim along the corners and windows. Black letters in relief on the building to the right: GENDARMERIE NATIONALE. The letters weren't quite straight for some reason. There was a green gate between the buildings; it was open.

"The building you want is the one with the sign."

Harper saw bars on the windows of the first floor.

"Jail's there, behind the bars?"

"That's just to keep young Occitans from throwing rocks through the window. The holding cells are in the basement. There's a door on the side of the building. You go in, there's a reception counter with a police-man. Behind the desk is a steel door. It's controlled by a button under the counter. Behind the door are stairs to the basement. At the bottom of the stairs is another policeman, and there is a guard locked inside a bulletproof office. The one in the office controls the cell doors. There are only four small cells."

"You sound like you know the setup."

"When I was young, I was a rock thrower for the glory of Occitania. I'm the reason they put up the bars. I caught a policeman on the head. I was only ten, so they let me go. After they locked me up for three days to teach me a lesson."

"Maybe they've added a few upgrades since you were a rock-throwing lad."

"Are you serious? This is the *département* of Ariège. Nothing changes here."

Harper looked at his watch: 11:54 hours.

"Just about lunchtime."

"Good timing. Most of the police in Foix will be heading to cafés for their meals. Except for the ones in the jail, of course. And the few hun-dred of them that live out the back."

"Sorry?"

"All those buildings in the back. Those are residences for police."

Harper looked through the gates. The place was more than a small-town cop shop; it was a compound.

"Oh, swell."

"Not to worry. With this weather, they'll be in their rooms playing with their guns, hopefully."

Harper looked at the back of the bread truck.

"Is the rear door open?"

"I'll unlock it."

"And how far to Gare de Foix? Two minutes, you said?"

Serge pointed out his side window.

"Back over the river and go left. The train station is very close. But it will take three or four minutes in this weather."

Harper looked out the window. The clouds had come down again and there was nothing but a blur of heavy snow.

"Right."

He removed the bandage from his right hand, stretched the fingers. He pulled his killing knives from their sheaths, then the SIG. He ejected the clip, checked the firing chamber was clear. Serge watched with interest.

"No bullets, no weapons. A most interesting method to break someone out of jail."

"Not here to harm anyone, just need to do a job."

"Is he someone like you?"

Harper looked at the man. "He is, but he doesn't know it."

"How can that be?"

"Comes to telling forests from trees, we're not that different from you sometimes."

Serge pointed to the little glass objects on Harper's weapons rig.

"What are those tiny jars? If you do not mind my asking."

Harper looked down at the vials of flash and fog on the straps of his weapons harness.

"Things to make us disappear."

Serge smiled. "This I would very much like to see."

Harper holstered his empty SIG.

"Maybe you will, and maybe you should keep the motor running."

"This is not a good idea."

"Why not?"

"We are almost out of gas."

Harper rubbed the back of his neck. He looked deep into Serge's eyes.

"I want you to listen to me. If it goes bad, you drive away. Don't look back, go home."

"As you command."

Harper opened the door, stepped out, pulled up the collar of his coat.

"By the way, you and your ancestors are the noble ones. Without your family, the ones like me would've been wiped from the Earth long ago."

Serge scratched his chin.

"I should like to ask you something about my family story, in the event I do not see you again."

"All right."

"Why would this someone like you see to it that the things of Christ were delivered to my family in the eighth century and command us to protect them, only to leave behind the broken cup and the bloodied nail, calling them 'the things of men'?"

"Sounds like a philosopher's riddle."

"One I have tried to answer all my life."

"Come up with anything?"

"A third of a cup, one of three nails. In pieces and separate, they are the things of men. Rejoined and together, they become things of the Gods again."

Harper thought about it.

"That's a damn good bit of imagining, Serge."

"*Mercé*. By the way, have you ever broken anyone out of jail before?"

"No idea. But I saw it on the History Channel once. It was a reenactment of a jailbreak in the Old West. Arizona, it was."

"Then you should do just fine."

II

HARPER CLOSED THE DOOR, WALKED ACROSS THE ROAD AND through the open gate. There were CCTV cameras mounted at the gate and above the door marked BUREAU. Harper looked down, watched his feet kick through the snow. He got to the office door, went in.

Fluorescent lights in the ceiling, greenish paint on the walls, brown linoleum floor. A poster board along the inner wall was stuffed with official notices, and there were red plastic chairs anchored to the floor underneath. Everything about it said *This is an official reception area of the Gendarmerie Nationale and you are not welcome.*

Harper looked out the barred windows. Saw the bread truck in the parking lot, saw Serge watching him. Far end of the room was a counter and one French policeman leaning over a newspaper. He couldn't be bothered to look up to see who came through the door. Harper walked over, saw a bank of video monitors under the counter. Surrounding grounds of the compound on monitor one, cells in the basement switching every two seconds on monitor two. He saw the form of a big man lying still on a cot in one of the cells; the other cells were empty. Monitor three was Harper himself standing in the reception area. He looked up, saw the small CCTV camera in the corner. *Getting better all the time,* he thought.

"Vous désirez, monsieur?" The policeman asked the question while checking the sports page.

"What I need for you to do is to stand up straight, look into my eyes, and listen to my voice."

"Je ne parle pas anglais."

Harper rested his hand over a picture of Lionel Messi scoring against PSG. The policeman looked up; Harper smiled, spoke slowly.

"Je veux que vous vous leviez, que vous me regardiez dans les yeux, et que vous m'écoutiez."

The policeman stood up, stared at Harper. *"Quoi?"*

"That's better."

Harper waved the palm of his right hand before the copper's eyes.

"Dulcis et alta quies, placidæque simillima morti."

The policeman slumped. Harper rounded the counter and caught him, set him in his chair. He pulled the policeman's gun, chucked it in a desk drawer. He found the door release and hit it, and the door popped open. Harper passed through, went down the stairs. He called back to the sleeping policeman, *"Merci, ah?"* giving it his best imitation of a hotshot French detective from Paris coming down to throw his weight around the provinces. The prison guard at the bottom of the stairs saw Harper coming, but hearing Harper's voice call back to the reception, he didn't react.

"*Bonjour,*" Harper said, reaching to shake the guard's hand.

The guard took the bait, Harper latched on tight.

"*Bonjour,*" he said. "*Vous êtes ici pour le prisonnier?*"

Harper nodded. "*Oui, c'est moi.*"

The guard looked back up the stairs, looking for the rest of the armed detail.

"*Où est l'escorte armé?*"

Harper explained the armed escort was late because of the snow. The guard was annoyed.

"*Merde,*" he grumbled. "*On voudrait bien aller déjeuner.*"

Harper switched to English.

"Sorry, lunch is canceled on account of snow."

"*Quoi?*"

Harper spun the guard around, twisting his arm and slamming him face-first into the bulletproof window. The guard inside the office jumped for the alarm. Before he touched it, Harper pulled his SIG, pressed the muzzle to his captive's head.

"*Vous touchez l'alarme et je tire.*"

The guard in the office froze.

"*Jetez votre arme par terre, ouvrez la porte, mettez vos mains sur la tête, et vous allez dans la salle.*"

There was a second where nothing happened. Harper hoped the guard was startled enough not to notice there wasn't a clip in his SIG, and that his threat to pull the trigger, while true, was complete and utter shit.

"Do it!"

The guard in the office pulled his sidearm and dropped it on the desk. He hit the button to open the outer cell door. The door buzzed open. The guard put his hands on his head, stepped out of the office and into the cell block. Harper nudged his captive forward.

"Mains sur la tête, lentement."

The guard raised his hands, slowly. Harper pulled the guard's side-arm, stuffed it in his coat.

"Move inside."

He herded the two men into the hall between the cells. Keeping his eyes on them, he reached in the office, grabbed the second gun, stuffed it in his belt.

"Ouvrez la porte du prisonnier," Harper said.

The guards looked fit to piss themselves. Obviously, a jailbreak was something new in these parts, Harper thought.

"Je ne peux pas."

"Pourquoi pas?"

"Le déverrouillage est à l'intérieur du bureau."

Harper glanced in the office, saw four buttons controlling access to the cell block. He checked the cells. Astruc was in number three; he was beginning to stir. Keeping his eyes on the police again, Harper reached in, hit the release to cells one and three: *bzzzz, clack, clack.*

"Les portables sur le sol, lentement."

The police unhooked their mobile phones, dropped them on the floor. Harper signaled the police to get inside cell one; they obeyed. Harper moved quickly, kicking closed the cell door, kicking the phones across the hall. He reached in his pocket, pulled out the guns, tossed them in an empty cell. He turned to the police.

"Je veux que vous me regardiez dans les yeux et que vous m'écoutiez."

The police obeyed again. Harper waved the palm of his right hand before their eyes: *"Dulcis et alta quies . . ."* The men slumped to the floor before he finished the rest of it. Harper looked at his watch: 12:06 hours. He turned to cell three. Astruc was sitting on the edge of his cot now, staring at Harper.

"Hello, Padre," Harper said.

Astruc rushed from the cot, pushed open the cell door, charged at Harper. Harper cut left, caught Astruc's ankles, dropped him to the floor. The sedatives made Astruc's reactions slow, but he swung his fist wildly and caught Harper's jaw. Harper fell back, came up with his foot and drilled Astruc in the balls. Astruc went down, had trouble getting to his feet. Harper knocked him back down, knelt next to him, pinned his head to the concrete floor.

"You're dead!" Astruc shouted. "I buried you!"

"And three days later I rose from the dead. It's been known to happen."

Astruc tried to pull away; Harper shoved the muzzle into his neck.

"Listen, Padre, we can do this the easy way or the hard way. Either way, you're going to Lausanne Cathedral."

"Why?"

Harper rolled him over, stood up, pointing the SIG at Astruc's head.

"Because you're as fucked up as I am. Get up."

Astruc wiped his face with the back of his hand.

"Goose?"

"Your son, you mean."

An expression of horror crossed Astruc's face.

"Relax, we all have our failings, Padre. Just now, all you need to know is he's still alive. You want to see him, you come with me."

"You are one of the Dark Ones. You live by deceit and betrayal."

"Maybe I am, maybe I'm not. Who cares? You want to see Goose, you come with me. Or you can stay here, because in a matter of minutes, a squad of police from Toulouse will come down those stairs to arrest you for a sixteen-year-old murder. If it was up to me, I'd let them take you. Choice is yours."

Astruc got up from the floor. They hadn't cleaned him up, and there was blood on his clothes and hands. He glanced at the guards in the cell.

"Are they dead?"

"Killing the innocent is more your line, padre, not mine."

"The innocent?"

"Gilles Lambert. He was just a man; a lonely, innocent man with a soul, and you killed him."

Astruc looked at Harper.

"That isn't possible. I looked into his eyes."

"Told you, you're fucked up. Move."

Astruc turned, headed up the stairs. Harper followed, thinking sooner or later, someone was going to figure out there weren't any bullets in his SIG. Top of the stairs, Astruc saw the copper sleeping in his chair.

"Out the door," Harper said. "Go left, walk across the road. Quick, but don't run. There's a bread truck directly ahead in the parking lot. Wait at the back. I'm right behind you. Take off, run away, you'll never see Goose again."

Astruc walked out the door. Harper gave it five seconds. He holstered his SIG, walked out the door, saw Astruc crossing the road, walking toward the back of the truck. Serge saw Astruc coming, turned over the motor. Then an alarm sounded from the gendarmerie. Harper didn't look back, kept walking at a steady pace. He got to the back of the truck, pulled open the door. Astruc threw up his arms.

"Demon!"

Harper slammed into the big man, shoved him into the back of the truck, jumped in.

"Drive!"

Serge put the truck in gear, pulled away with the back door still open. Astruc twisted and kicked, and Harper nailed him in the face. Astruc fell back, slammed into the side panel, practically knocked the truck over. Harper pressed the heel of his boot into Astruc's windpipe, pressed down to hold him in place.

"*Merde,*" Serge laughed. "It seems they have some improvements to the gendarmerie."

Harper glanced out the windshield. A small army of French coppers running from the compound, weapons drawn. Harper reached under his coat, pulled two vials of flash and fog. He threw them to the snow-covered street.

"*Et facta est lux.*"

A blue flash exploded and the world seemed to disappear. Astruc knocked away Harper's foot, jumped up and grabbed Harper by the throat, pulled him to the floor. Harper rammed back with all his weight. Astruc slammed into shelves, croissants flew. The bullet clip and killing knives flew. Harper rammed his elbow into Astruc's stomach, the big man let go, and Harper spun him around, hook-punched his sides. Astruc cocked his elbow, came up with his forearm. Harper flew across the compartment, slammed into the side wall, and the truck almost went over on it's side again. Astruc kicked under Harper's feet, dropped him. He grabbed a knife from the floor, jabbed. Harper rolled, but the blade cut through his shirt, sliced along his flesh.

"Shit!"

Astruc raised the knife, held it over Harper's throat.

"He is not my son, he is the light of the world!"

Serge caught the action in the rearview mirror and pounded down on the brakes. Astruc flew forward, smashed his head into the back of the driver's seat. He was out cold and missing the fun of a Citroën H-Type bread truck spinning around the traffic circle and heading for the river. The truck went up on its right wheels. Serge steered into the skid, and the truck came down on all fours. Serge cut the wheels back, steadied it, headed for the train station.

"Are you all right back there?" Serge said.

Harper sat up, checked his chest. The blade had slashed his left side over the heart, and it was oozing blood. The wounds on his palms were bleeding, too.

"I'll live."

"We are coming to the train station."

"Is there a bus stop out front?"

"Yes."

"Anyone there?"

"No."

"Pull over."

Fifteen seconds later, the bread truck stopped. Harper picked up his SIG, the clip. He reloaded the gun, holstered it. He picked up the killing knives, slipped them in their sheaths. He kicked open the back door, slid out.

"C'mon, Padre."

He reached in and grabbed Astruc's ankles, dragged him half out the back. He looked at Serge.

"I'll be back."

"Or someone like you."

Harper slipped his right arm under Astruc's arms, lifted, balanced the big man against his chest. He reached in the truck, grabbed a croissant from the floor, held it up.

"One for the road?"

"Help yourself."

He stuffed it in his mouth, stepped away, and kicked closed the door. The bread truck drove away into the storm. When it was ten meters away, Harper lost sight of it in the snow. He hauled Astruc to the bus stop, dropped him on the bench.

"Now stay there."

He looked both ways. Nothing either way, and dead ahead, the train station was barely visible.

"Bloody arctic adventure this is."

He sat next to Astruc, kept him from falling over. There were two sparrows sitting at the other end of the bench.

"Greetings, Earthlings."

Harper took a bite of the croissant, saw the shell hanging by a leather string around Astruc's neck. He yanked it off, looked at it, stuffed it in a pocket of his coat.

He checked his watch: 12:15 on the nose.

He looked up, saw halogen lights cutting through the snow, coming his way. Then yellow side lights, then blue lights running along the chassis, then a black bus emerging from the storm and pulling to a stop in front of the bus stop. A hydraulic pump went *shhhhh*, and the door opened. Blue lights on the steps and Karoliina from Tampere in the driver's seat, flipping her *japa mala* beads.

"Fancy that, I was just thinking about you," Harper said.

"Nice to see you again, too. There's blood on your croissant."

Harper looked at it, dropped it on the snowy ground for the birds. They flew down and shredded the croissant with their beaks.

"*Bon appétit,*" Harper said.

The birds chirped their thanks.

Harper lifted Astruc, carried him over the snow and onto the bus. Karoliina closed the door behind them, put the bus in gear, drove ahead. Krinkle was at his audio control panel, headphones on his bopping head. Harper dropped Astruc on the floor. Astruc began to stir. Harper tapped Krinkle on the shoulder, and Krinkle looked back at him. Harper heard music blasting from the headphones.

"We're live, and I'm in the middle of a serious segue," Krinkle said.

"Swell, but Father Astruc is a raving lunatic and he's about to wake up."

Krinkle kicked open a lower drawer. Harper saw a dozen auto-injectors all in a row, each one a different color.

"Use the green one. No, wait, the police gave him fentanyl—use the blue one."

Harper grabbed the blue one, pulled off the cap, leaned over Astruc. Astruc's eyes were open and he saw the injector in Harper's hand. He tried to get up.

"No!"

Harper slammed him into the floor, rammed the injector into Astruc's thigh, and hit the release. The needle popped and the potion rushed in. Astruc grabbed the lapels of Harper's coat, but his grip was weakening.

"Have you killed me?" he said.

"No."

"Why not?"

"Orders."

Astruc's pupils dilated, his eyes lost focus, his hands fell from Harper's coat. Harper stared at him; he was deeply asleep. Harper picked up Astruc's hands, crossed the arms, and rested them over the chest.

"Qui dormit non peccat."

Harper got up, saw Krinkle fast at work on one of his laptops. All of the screens were streaming code like mad, the reel-to-reels along the shelves all rolling at once. Harper walked to the front of the bus, sat in the seat behind Karoliina, looked out the windshield. The bus was heading out of Foix and winding through a forest. Even though it was midday, darkness was coming down, and no matter which direction the bus turned, the snow seemed to be coming straight at them. Karoliina had one hand on the steering wheel, one hand still flipping her beads.

"Bit of a light touch on the wheel, isn't it? Considering we're in the middle of a blizzard," Harper said.

"Krinkle's bus practically drives itself. All I have to do is nudge it to where we want to go. *Prochain arrêt, Lausanne.*"

"What happened to the boys in the band?"

"In the back, sleeping. We had a long night last night."

"The concert."

"After the concert. That's when we do our real work."

Harper turned around, saw the door to the back. A sign read Do Not Disturb.

"Which is what?" Harper said, turning back to Karoliina.

"You're funny," she said, giggling.

Harper watched Krinkle work his laptops, watched Astruc out on the floor. He heard droning sounds, felt harmonic vibrations. At first Harper thought it was coming from Krinkle's headphones, but it was rising from underneath the bus.

"What's that sound?"

"The motor," Karoliina said.

"What sort of motor goes *ommm*?"

"Soon as we find a straight patch of road going east, you'll find out. There are battlefield med kits under your seat."

"What?"

"Your hands are bleeding."

Harper looked at them. Wasn't bad, but bad enough. He reached down, pulled open a compartment. Inside were two black boxes. One marked *Us*, the other *Them*.

"Which one?"

"You and Krinkle are *Us*. The other one is for civilians."

Harper opened a bag; it was jammed with saline solutions, auto-injectors, potions, and bandages. He pulled out two field bandages, one patch bandage. He opened his shirt, set the patch over the slice on his chest.

"Which one would you be?" he said.

She kept her eyes on the road.

"You mean am I human or a half-kind?"

"Sorry?"

She glanced at Harper in the rearview mirror.

"Half-breed is a vile term when talking about children born on this side of the light. I mean, they're as much one of the club as you, aren't they?"

Harper opened the field bandages, set the cotton wads in his palms, wrapped the tails around his hands.

"Maybe. Doesn't answer the question, though. Which one are you?"

"You looked in my eyes on the train to Lausanne, you know what I am."

"You're human."

"*Oikein hyvä.*"

"How did you know about the prophecy, then?"

Karoliina made a wide turn, eased down a snowy slope of a road.

She smiled at him again in the rearview mirror.

"You still don't get it, do you?"

"Get what?"

"She dreamed it, brother."

Harper looked back. Krinkle had spun around in his swivel chair. Headphones down around his neck. He was pouring boiling water from a kettle into two cups.

"What do you mean, she dreamed it? When, where?"

"In Portland, Oregon, before the comet appeared above Paris."

Harper got up, walked back, sat in the chair across from Krinkle. Astruc between them on the floor.

"What were you doing in Portland?"

"A concert. How was the jail?"

"Everything but the horses."

"Whatever that means, sounds cool."

"Where's the kid?"

"I put him on another bus. One with an operating room for our kind."

"You've got more than one bus?"

Krinkle replaced the kettle on the heater, kept talking as if not hearing the question.

"Blood traces from the attackers were found in the kid's wounds."

"Dead black?"

"Yup. Looks like the bad guys tried to tear him to shreds. There was one bullet wound in the kid's left calf. HQ traced the blood to the kill site. Nothing but a pack of dead mountain dogs. Big white fuckers."

"I just saw one of those dogs. He was friendly and smart as hell."

"Your dog was a dog, not a transmuted monster bred to kill. All of them had been shot to hell. Adds up to Astruc getting to the kid after the attack started. Astruc emptied nine clips into the dogs. Can't believe he only shot his son once. Then again, he was damn good with a crossbow. Weird thing is the kid had a scallop shell around his neck. His hands were closed around it, like he was protecting it more than himself."

Harper reached in his coat, pulled out the shell he'd pulled from Astruc.

"Like this?"

Krinkle looked at it, nodded. "Like that."

"What is it?" Harper said.

"Pilgrims wear them walking the Way of Saint James across northern Spain. It's an act of penance for one's sins. The walk, I mean. The scallop is letting the world know you're a sinner."

Harper flashed it from somewhere: Le Chemin de Saint-Jacques de Compostelle. Site of the buried remains of James the Apostle, carried there by boat from Jerusalem in 40 AD. *Bloody hell, that's how it happened; that's how the sextant, the broken cup, the one nail got to Spain.* Harper bounced the scallop shell in his hand, then he shoved it back in his pocket.

"We're on the highway," Karoliina called from the front. "Satellite shows a twenty-kilometer stretch going north in sixteen seconds."

"We hit it, you punch it, sister."

"Roger that."

Krinkle picked up the two steaming cups, offered one to Harper. Harper didn't take it; he nodded toward Karoliina.

"How could she dream something our kind didn't know about? And dream it before it happened?"

"You mean how can she see the future?"

"If that's what you call it."

Krinkle shrugged. "It's what she does, along with being a very good guitar tech. All her dreams have been reported to HQ since she was six years old. Girl's a dream catcher, first one in four hundred years. You've been turning up a lot in her dreams, then you show up on the front page of every newspaper in the world."

"Bingo. I'm shanghaied south to Toulouse."

"Dig it, brother, you're the prophecy man."

Harper shook his head.

"I didn't know shit about the prophecy till twenty minutes ago."

"You forget, you *did* know about the treasure hidden under Montsé-gur. And you told Astruc, the day of the fire, trying to comfort him. Seems he figured the rest of it out by himself, long before the rest of us did."

Harper looked down at Astruc. "He says it's the kid, Goose."

"Astruc said Goose was the child of the prophecy?"

"Back at the jail. He said Goose wasn't his son, said the kid was the light of the world."

Krinkle looked at Astruc. "Man, he *is* fucked up."

The words ran through Harper head.

"You mean the prophecy isn't true?" he said.

"It's true, all right. But Astruc's got the wrong kid. Mind taking your tea? My arms are getting tired."

Harper took it by his fingertips, tried not to spill it on his lap.

"Who is it? The child?"

"A boy between a year and a year and a half old."

"How do you know?"

"I've seen him."

"Where?"

"In Portland, before the concert. That's why we had the concert there. Had to get Karoliina in position to get a look at the child; see if he matched the child in her dreams. By the way, that's the dream that got you shanghaied to Toulouse."

Harper reached in his coat, pulled out a smoke, and lit up.

"The child in Portland, does he have a name?"

Krinkle pointed his trigger finger at the kill spot between Harper's eyes: *Bang.*

"Right."

The bus jumped like it had hit a patch of ice. Then the drone of the motor grew louder, vibrating up through the floor. Harper looked ahead. The headlights had been switched off and there was only a world of blinding snow coming in rapid bursts of blue light.

"Fear not, you're on the magic bus," Krinkle said.

"No such thing as a magic bus, not even for the Zoroaster's magi."

"But Zoroaster's gang knew a few good tricks."

"Such as?"

"Inverted time warp."

"Never heard of it."

"We're disconnected from the gravitational pull of the Earth at the forty-fourth latitude of the planet. It's spinning under our wheels at 1279.1 kilometers per hour. We'll shimmy north to the forty-sixth latitude, reconnect at an out-of-the-way spot near Lausanne, and cruise on in. By the way . . ." He called to Karoliina. "Sister K, you need to flip the license plates to Switzerland, Canton de Vaud. You know, the one with the little green-and-white flag?"

"Already done," she said.

Krinkle looked at Harper.

"Anyway, the bus gets us wherever we need to be in the world, in one quarter the time."

Harper thought about it.

"If the planet is spinning at twelve hundred plus klicks, why's it take so long to get there?"

"Sideways is easy; it's the up-and-down part that's hard."

Harper thought about it. "Second philosopher's riddle I've heard in one day."

"Drink your tea," Krinkle said.

Harper smelled the steam rising from his cup. Mint, ginger, a scent of shut-up-and-enjoy-the-ride.

"More doctor's orders?"

"Nah, just something Karoliina whipped up to take off the edge when we reconnect. Sit back and enjoy the ride. Standing orders are if a warrior like you hitches a ride, he's put under with the green auto-injector before he gets on."

Harper looked at the door to the back of the bus: Do Not Disturb.

"Like the band?"

Krinkle smiled.

"You're catching on."

Harper sipped his tea, thinking about an apostle's bones coming to Spain not long after Christ disappeared, shepherds in the fields near the Pyrenees twelve hundred years ago, and Finnish rock bands on a magic bus in nowtimes. Funny old world.

"So if orders are to put me under when I get on, what am I doing sitting up straight? How come I'm not with the band?"

Krinkle pulled a gold-filtered smoke, lit up.

"Word on the street is you've only got a few weeks till lights out."

It had been a while since the notion crossed Harper's mind.

"That's right, and so what?"

"You and me have been through some shit together. You may not see it, given you're completely fucked, but I do. Some of it still burns in my eyes. So let's just put this down to me forgetting the rules and regs so you can experience one of the cooler imaginations of all time."

Harper felt something. Gratitude maybe.

"And what might that be?"

Krinkle slipped his headphones onto his head.

"Sometimes, brother, like the angels of men, we fly."

"Sorry?"

Krinkle spun around in his swivel chair, raised a fader on his control panel, leaned into the microphone.

"That was a band of shoegazers from Denmark called Mew with their mighty tune, 'Comforting Sounds.' Wherever you are in time and space, you're tuned to the last radio station on planet Earth. Just now, we're opening a chapter from *Numinosum*, the LP of revelations. Brothers and sisters, come, fly with me and bear witness to the Ascension of the Watchers."

Krinkle flipped a switch, cranked up the sound. A man's voice echoed through the bus.

"I didn't know how empty was my soul, until it was filled."

Then a slow backbeat and a thumping bass resonated through the floor, guitars floating and a harmonic drone breathing, rising . . . *ommmm* . . . then a voice singing, as if chanting to the architect of the unremembered beginning:

> *"Je vois les yeux de Dieu,*
> *Je vois les yeux de Dieu,*
> *Dans la neige qui tombe,*
> *Dans la neige qui tombe."*

Harper looked out the windshield.

Passing through the storm, lost in the clouds.

Flash Traffic

tdc: +k556-34fcc+
Ex: Station Hong Kong

Read Status: Operations Desk/SUTF
Subject: Frequency Fluctuations M-Band Time Warp

Ten-second drop in power status in time warp over protected zone "Blue Zone 3."
No intrusion detected.
Residents: status normal.
Utility Scan detects no software or operational glitch.
Possible external hack. Threat level: Unknown
Request Guidance.
<file: XRB.885>

Flash Traffic

tdc: +q709-24nrp+
Ex: Operations Desk/SUTF

Eyes Only: Station Hong Kong
Subject: M-Band Time Warp

SX Analysis detects no external hack threat.
Conclude program code error.
Reset codes with attachment. Upload, reboot in coord w/SX Berne: 02:30 (HKT), 20:30 (GMT)
<file: XRB.886>

Flash Traffic

tdc: +h917-29bco+
Ex: Operations Desk (sub)/SUTF

Eyes Only: Dragon 6/SUTF
Subject: Berlin Station reports enemy comms intercept and decode.

Decoded intercept trace: Rome-Riga
Intercept reads: "Execute Operation Riptide"
Intercept ends.
No further data.
SX Unit analysis: inconclusive.

TWENTY-FOUR

I

KATHERINE HEARD A KNOCK AT HER BEDROOM DOOR.

"Come in."

Officer Jannsen entered the room, closed the door behind her. All the lights in Katherine's room were off, and gray light seeped through rain-drenched windows. Coming to the hallway Officer Jannsen saw a glow of soft, wiggly light coming through the open door to Max's room. She reached the door to Max's room, looked in.

"Was ist das?"

A green rainproof tarp had been hung tentlike from the ceiling. Strung with ten-millimeter climbing rope, slings, and carabineers. The ropes were anchored to heavy dumbbells set about the room. Red plaid blankets had been tossed over the floor under the tent, and on the blankets, huddled around the glowing lantern, were Katherine, Max, and Monsieur Booty. Katherine in the middle wearing Marc Rochat's black floppy hat, a book on her lap, a cup of tea at her crossed legs. Monsieur Booty was sitting to her left, paying rapt attention to the sketchbook. And Max was to her right, propped up in his car seat with his toy hammer in his hand, pacifier in his mouth, and his bicycle helmet on his head. Officer Jannsen dropped her jaw and leaned against the doorjamb.

Max had never seen such an expression on her face and thought it very funny. He giggled, pointed at her.

"Nnnn."

"*Heiliges Kanonenrohr,*" Officer Jannsen said.

"What's that mean?" Katherine said.

"Holy gun barrel."

Katherine rolled her eyes. "Germans—can't just use 'holy cow' like the rest of the world."

"I'm Swiss."

"Yeah, but that was German. The boys told on me, huh?"

"They told me you asked them to come up, then they went and got some climbing gear and weights and Max's car seat. They said they came back and helped you make something. I asked them what it was, they said I must see for myself."

"What do you think?"

"What is it?"

"It's a tribal council of truth."

Officer Jannsen stepped closer, looked at the book on Katherine's lap.

"Is that one of his sketchbooks?"

"You can say his name, Anne."

"Is that one of Marc Rochat's books?"

"It's called *piratz*. I've read it to Max six times so far today. We're working on number seven."

"He likes it."

"A flying giant caterpillar named Pompidou, an evil wizard named Screechy in search of a future-teller diamond, a beautiful princess trapped in an ice castle, and a band of silly pirates wearing paper hats to the rescue. What's not to like? You want in?"

"Yes, I would."

Officer Jannsen crouched down under the tent and sat across from them, forming a circle.

"Why is Max wearing a bicycle helmet, Kat?"

"It's the one he wanted."

"What?"

"I was conducting another experiment."

"What was it this time?"

"Letting him pick things, seeing if he's the reincarnation of Marc Rochat. See, that's how the Buddhists do it. The Dalai Lama dies, monks take a few of his things. Eyeglasses, or a book, maybe a hat. They put them in a bag with toys and other stuff, and they wander the land visiting newly born boys, showing the boys their bag of stuff. The boy who picks up the things of the Dalai Lama is the reincarnation of the Dalai Lama. Easy."

"You've been on the Internet."

"Hey, I'm from Los Angeles. Can't swing a dead cat there without hitting a Buddhist."

Mew.

"Sorry, Monsieur Booty, wasn't talking about you. Anyways, in LA everyone tries it out once in their life."

"You were a Buddhist?"

"Yeah, my sophomore year in high school."

Officer Jannsen looked at Max, reached over and pulled at his pacifier. Max's baby teeth held on.

"Max isn't the reincarnation of Marc Rochat, Kat."

"I know."

"You do?"

"He picked the bicycle helmet instead of Marc's hat. Leaves me wondering who he is."

"Max is your son."

"Yeah, but who's his daddy? For a while I was trying to remember if maybe it was Marc."

"What?"

"Looking at Max's eyes yesterday, I saw Marc's eyes. Got me thinking."

"About what?"

"I didn't get knocked up by the head bad guy in Lausanne. Because his fucking eyes were silver, and the goons with him, their eyes were black. So maybe it was Marc. Don't look at me like that, Anne. You know why I'd think that."

"Do I?"

"Marc Rochat's eyes, Max's eyes, and my eyes are emerald green. Thing is, my eyes were never this green. Greenish, yeah, especially if I wore my fave green cashmere sweater. But not like this. So following that line of thought, I remembered being in the loge of the belfry for days. I remember being out of my mind; maybe a little less than I am now, but I was out there. But I clearly remember, like I can see it, that I thought about fucking Marc so I wouldn't feel bad stealing the money he had stashed in the cathedral. A hundred thousand Swiss francs in a tin with a picture of a little train and Zermatt on the lid. Gets a little foggy, but I know I decided not to steal the money."

"Why not?"

"Because there was a knock on the door, and when I opened it, I saw the man who wasn't there. Before, he was a shadow standing in the corner of a memory. Now I can see him. He's tall, not bad looking, and he's wearing a beat-up overcoat. Guess what else? His eyes are the same color as Marc Rochat's and Max's and mine. Interesting having a conversation with a crazy lady, isn't it?"

"You're not crazy."

Katherine picked up her tea and sipped.

"Better living through chemistry. Who is he?"

Officer Jannsen looked out the open doorway to Katherine's bedroom. The CCTV camera was pointing toward them, but as Katherine and Max were in the room, the camera would be off. Officer Jannsen pulled her mobile from her belt, slid it, facedown, under the blanket. She looked at Katherine.

"He's what we call a deep asset."

"What's that mean?"

"Someone who isn't what he appears to be."

"Where is he now?"

"I don't know."

"Who is he?"

"You have to remember his name yourself."

"Why?"

"Because that's the way it works."

"Fuck's sake, tell me."

"I don't know his name."

"C'mon, you were in the cathedral. You saw him."

"There's a special unit that deals with deep assets. I was in it, but I was assigned to you on close protection after the cathedral. When I was transferred, all names and faces of deep assets were wiped from my memory."

"They can do that to you, too, the mindfuck stuff?"

"You're asking me?"

Katherine stared at Officer Jannsen, thinking how she herself couldn't remember a thing of her life for six months. Didn't even know she was pregnant. Could never quite see the man who wasn't there.

"Yeah, dumb question. Can I talk to him, can you get a message to him?"

"What about?"

"Seeing as I met him in Lausanne a few times, I'd like to know if it was between the sheets once. Or twice."

"It couldn't be him."

"Why not?"

"Deep assets are forbidden to touch locals."

"Locals?"

"It's a code for anyone who's not a deep asset."

Katherine took another sip from her cup, laughed a little.

"What's so funny?" Officer Jannsen said.

"I'm just wondering why it is I'm the one drinking the tea, because you're the one who sounds nuts."

"I suppose I do."

Katherine looked at Max. His green eyes sparkled with lantern light, and they were going back and forth between the two women, wondering who was going to speak next.

"Well, buster, that leaves only two options on the daddy question. Virgin birth, or aliens with an impregnatronic ray gun. With Mommy's beforetimes, Mommy's going for aliens. How about you?"

Max swung his hammer.

"Apposoose."

She turned to Monsieur Booty.

"You?"

Mew.

Katherine looked at Officer Jannsen.

"Alien with a ray gun it is, this side of the tribal council. How do you plead?"

Officer Jannsen pulled her mobile from under the blanket, snapped it to her belt. She stood up.

"I say you, Max, and I should go have some huckleberry pie at Molly's."

Kat sat up like a shot. "Really?"

"I'll have a detail take us in. You can play music and sing badly."

"Are we done with the lockdown drill?"

"No."

"What about being held prisoner in the ice castle? House, I mean."

"Grover's Mill is in the lockdown zone, too."

Katherine eyes widened. "No way. The whole town?"

"And everyone in it."

"They're all working with you?"

"They're all here to protect you and Max."

Katherine looked at Max, Max looked at her, they both looked at Monsieur Booty. Katherine shook her head, Max waved his hammer, the cat sneezed.

"What about the tourist buses? Tuesdays and Fridays, on the way to Rainbow Falls?"

"Supplies and tour rotation of personnel."

Katherine let it sink in. "Wow."

Officer Jannsen nodded toward the door.

"Let's go. Seb and Luc are in the Explorer outside, they'll drive us into town."

Katherine crawled from the tent, reached back, pulled out Max's car seat with him still in it.

"We need a diaper change first, don't we, buster?"

Katherine unhooked Max from his car seat, carried him to the changing table, and gave his bottom a reboot. She sat him up, dressed him in his Converse All Stars, a woolly coat, and a wool cap. She set him back in his car seat and reunited him with his hammer. She handed the completed package to Officer Jannsen.

"Here, hold this."

"Nnnn," Max said.

Katherine reached back into the tent and grabbed the lantern and sketchbook.

"What are you doing, Kat?"

"Max won't go anywhere without the lantern or the sketchbook. And he makes me wear Marc's hat all the time. I'm hoping it's a phase."

Officer Jannsen smiled.

"All right, I'm sure the team in Grover's Mill will enjoy it."

Katherine looked at her.

"You're telling me stuff you're not supposed to tell me, aren't you?"

"You deserve to know the truth, Kat. Let's go, there's something else I want to talk to you about. Away from the house."

They marched downstairs, stopping for Officer Jannsen to put on her coat and Katherine to throw on her cloak. They went to the driveway, climbed into the back of the Ford Explorer. Corporal Sebastianus Fassnacht turned over the motor, and Luc punched a few buttons on the heads-up display. He turned back, smiled at Max.

"Greetings, Captain Picard. We are ready for takeoff, sir."

Max waved his hammer.

"Woof!"

They drove through the forest to Bear Creek Road and crossed Carson Highway to Rainbow Falls Road and into another forest.

"Is there even a Rainbow Falls?" Katherine said.

"No."

"What about the roads?"

"Carson Highway is real. We take that one to Portland."

"What about the ones to the house and Grover's Mill?"

"Those roads are there, but people passing by don't see them."

"Like the boys in camouflage back at the house."

"Something like that."

"How about the doctors in Portland? Max's, mine, the shrink. Are they like everyone else in Grover's Mill? Are they even really doctors?"

"They're real doctors, they're just our doctors."

"Their test with Max. It wasn't an MRI, was it?"

"No. But I promise you, it didn't hurt him, or you."

"Me?"

"You remember, you were with him."

"Yeah, I remember. So what did it do?"

"It read your light levels. You and Max."

"Light levels."

"Yes."

Katherine fixed a spit curl on Max's head.

"This has something to do with my dream in Lausanne Cathedral. The bum on the altar, the light coming through the rose window, doesn't it? It really happened, didn't it?"

"Yes. And the test in Portland showed . . ."

"Stop."

Anne looked into Katherine's eyes. She saw flashes of green.

"What is it, Kat?"

Katherine looked at Max again. As usual, he was paying keen attention to the conversation.

"Whatever Max is to you, whatever he is to those bastards that attacked me in Lausanne, whatever he is to everyone in this Disneyland of a town, Max is my son, I'm his mother. I could give a flying fuck about the rest. I don't need to know." She looked down at Max. "Pardon my French."

"Fench," Max said with a giggle.

Officer Jannsen looked ahead. The Explorer was approaching the edge of Grover's Mill, and the rain eased.

"*Arrêtez la voiture ici. Madame Taylor et moi marcherons.*"

"What about Max?" Katherine said.

"He can ride with the guards. They'll keep him entertained. I need to talk to you alone."

"Okay."

The driver stopped. Katherine looked at Max.

"Mommy and Anne are going to walk, sweetie. You ride with Lieutenant Worf and Seb. And keep an eye out for the Borg. Give 'em a whack if you see them."

"Boog!" Max said.

She kissed the top of his head.

"See ya in a sec. Here's your book, I'll hold the lantern."

Officer Jannsen had alighted, come around the truck, and opened Katherine's door. Katherine climbed out. Officer Jannsen closed the door, and the Explorer drove down Main Street and parked in front of the Candle Lodge, across from Molly's Diner. The diner was packed with the after-lunch coffee crowd.

Katherine looked at the scene, laughed.

"It was all here. People in the diner, right across from the shop. I've been surrounded by an army the whole time. Jeez, who are all these people?"

"People devoted to light."

Katherine rolled her eyes. "Oh, cripes. Which light are we talking about now?"

"I'll explain it all when we get back to the house. There's something else I need to tell you right now. Let's walk."

They walked slowly down the middle of the street.

"I'm quitting my job, Kat."

Katherine stopped in her tracks. "What?"

"I can't do it anymore."

"No, Anne . . . Look, I'm sorry I've been such a loon. But I'm coming around, I'm staying on the teas. Please, you can't leave me and Max—"

"Kat, it's all right. I won't be leaving you."

Katherine took a deep breath. "Then what are you telling me?"

"I can't do this job anymore because I need to be with you and Max. I sent in my resignation this morning."

"What?"

"It will take effect as soon as my replacement arrives."

"But you'll stay here?"

"As long as we're here. Then they'll send the three of us some-where else."

"When, where?"

Officer Jannsen smiled.

"I don't know. I'm already being kept out of the intel loop. That's the way it works when you tell Inspector Gobet you want to quit."

Katherine tried to speak, felt herself shaking.

"Anne, are you sure about this?"

"I'm sure. That's why I'm telling you the truth about you, about Max. Or what Inspector Gobet is allowing me to tell you. There's no going back for me now. But there is something you need to know."

"What?"

"They will wipe my memory of everything I've known about the cathedral, what happened to you. They'll replace it with a cover story. In time, it will take hold. But for a while, I'll be like you were when you first came to this place."

Katherine stared at her.

"But . . . if they wipe your memory . . ."

"I'll have my emotions for you and Max. That's about all I'll have until the cover story roots itself in my consciousness."

"How long does that take?"

"A month or two. What it means is you'll have to take care of me for a while. If that's all right with you."

Katherine felt something lift inside her. She threw her arms around Officer Jannsen's neck, held her tight. She could feel their hearts, beat-ing close to each other.

"Oh, Anne. My lovely Anne."

Officer Jannsen laughed, pushed Katherine away.

"*Excusez-moi, Madame Taylor.* I'm still on duty. For the next few days at least. When I turn in my gun, you can have your way with me. After we're married, properly."

Katherine looked into her eyes.

"Are you really sure?"

"You already asked that question. And I answered. Let's go celebrate with some huckleberry pie."

Katherine spun in a circle, the folds of her cloak fanning out. "Oh, thank you! Thank you!"

Officer Jannsen took Katherine by the elbow.

"Come with me, Madame Taylor, you're under arrest."

"Oh, yes, please."

They walked toward the diner. Corporal Fassnacht was getting out of the Explorer and reaching to open the rear passenger door. He signaled he'd get Max from his seat. Officer Jannsen nodded okay. Katherine was looking around the town. She looked at Officer Jannsen.

"Just tell me I'm not dreaming."

"You're not dreaming."

"Tell me even though this town isn't real, you're real and what you just told me is real."

"It's real."

Katherine looked over Officer Jannsen's shoulder, saw Molly standing in the doorway of the diner. She was waving to the Explorer across the street as Corporal Fassnacht was lifting Max from the backseat.

"Oh look, there's Molly, she sees Max."

Officer Jannsen looked back, saw the scene. Katherine tapped Anne's shoulder.

"One more time before we go inside, tell me it's real. And this time, cross your heart and hope to—"

Katherine felt hands grab her, pull her.

"Get down, Kat!"

She hit the asphalt hard. Officer Jannsen pulled her sidearm and fell on top of Katherine.

"What?"

"Stay down!"

The air was sucked from the sky, the windows of the diner shattered, and a ball of fire exploded into the street.

II

THE BUS BROKE THROUGH THE PERIMETER OF THE PROTECTED zone on a heading of 327° and into a pissing rain. It slammed down onto Pont Bessières, skidded as Karoliina hit the brakes.

"Lausanne Cathedral, dead ahead," Karoliina said.

Harper looked through the windshield. "Bear left onto Rue Pierre-Viret. There's a café a hundred meters on the right. Stop there."

"Stopping for an aperitif, are we?" Krinkle said.

"I could use a bloody drink after that bloody reconnect."

"Wasn't the reconnect, it was the time warp around Lausanne. We're lucky we didn't break apart. Karoliina, what the hell happened?"

"I don't know, and HQ isn't responding."

"Say again?"

"I lost contact just before we hit the PZ. We were committed, and I had to bring us in on manual."

"How far back from real time are we?"

"Can't tell. Temporal sequencers are offline. Here's the café."

The bus screeched to a stop, and the hydraulic door opened. Harper and Krinkle grabbed Astruc under each arm, dragged him off the bus. Krinkle looked back at Karoliina.

"Sister K, get the bus close to the cathedral, find a shadow to park in. Hit the band with green injectors and get them good to go. Do an eye-ball sweep of the cathedral grounds, stake it out if there's no cover."

"What's up, Krinkle?"

"I don't know, sister, but keep your eyes open."

Karoliina gave her *japa mala* beads a twirl, closed the door, pulled ahead and around the bend. Harper and Krinkle stood with the priest hanging from their arms. They scanned Rue Pierre-Viret both ways. Nothing but rain in the road. No approaching headlights, no sound of wheels on wet asphalt.

"Quiet," Harper said.

"And wet. Which way?"

Harper nodded to the wooden steps going up.

"There up the last bit of Escaliers du Marché. Cathedral's at the top."

They hauled Astruc up, and the priest's boots hit the wooden steps with a steady *thump, thump, thump*. They reached the esplanade and saw the rain-soaked façade of the cathedral, lit up with arc lamps.

"Every time I see the place, I think it should be bigger," Krinkle said.

"It's that kind of place."

They dragged Astruc over the cobblestones. Harper pulled at the iron latch of the great wooden door.

"Hang on, what time is it?" Harper said.

"Why?"

"Because the door's locked. And it's dark."

Krinkle looked up into the rain. The cathedral was wrapped in the cover of night.

"Whoa. Didn't even notice."

Krinkle managed to see his own watch. The hands had stopped.

"It was sixteen thirty approaching the protected zone," Krinkle said.

Harper ran the clock.

"Standard lag from real time is five minutes. It should be the middle of the afternoon."

They both looked and listened.

"It's like they stopped the clock in the middle of the night," Harper said.

"And it's more than quiet. There isn't a fucking sound but the rain. I'd say something's way wrong, brother."

"I'd say you're right. How are you at picking door locks?"

"Fucking brilliant, but my tools are on the bus."

"Shit. Let's drag him under the trees, over there, by the fountain."

They hauled Astruc back to the chestnut trees, dropped him on the cobblestones.

"Heavy dude, isn't he?" Krinkle said.

"Like a sack of lead."

Harper leaned under the iron spout of the fountain, took a long drink. Krinkle walked over.

"Drinkable?"

Harper stood up, wiped his mouth.

"Best water on the planet."

"Don't mind if I do then."

Krinkle drank like a thirsty dog. When he had his fill, he straightened up with drools of water dripping from his beard. He squeezed it dry with his hands.

"I'm ready. What's the plan?"

"We get into the cathedral."

"How?"

Harper pulled his SIG from his weapons rig, walked toward the cathedral, pulled the slide, and loaded a round into the firing chamber.

"Hey, bro," Krinkle called.

"What?"

"You can't shoot a cathedral, man."

"Rules and regs?"

"Not that I know of, but who the fuck cares?"

"You sound like a local."

"The locals know shit we don't. And any local would tell you shooting a cathedral is seriously bad karma."

Harper flashed the cathedral job.

"Should've been here the last time."

"I was, but I was outside the time warp working the perimeter. Never been inside, come to think of it. What did I miss?"

"We blew up the place."

Krinkle nodded. "Cool. Rock on."

Harper raised his SIG, let fly with four rounds. He walked to the door, saw the hole where the iron latch used to be.

"Right. Let us pray."

He holstered his gun, walked back. Harper and Krinkle grabbed As-

truc under his arms, dragged him back over the cobblestones to the cathedral. Harper kicked open the door, and they went into the narthex.
The purple curtain ahead billowed in the draft and settled when the
door slammed closed behind them. They waited, letting their eyes adjust. A single, high-above light lit up the stars painted in the dome.

"Holy crap," Krinkle said.

Harper glanced over, saw Krinkle looking up where Headless Mary,
Mother of God, sat on a heavenly throne amid the stars, the child Jesus
torn from her arms.

"What about it?" Harper said.

"*That* is seriously bad karma."

"It's a statue."

"When did it happen?"

"During the Reformation. Why?"

"Looks like the bad guys were doing a bit of prophecy themselves in
our own backyard. And we completely missed it."

Harper looked at the statue. Miracle birth, child conceived of light,
born of woman . . . *When they come, we will find them, we will kill them.*

"Maybe. Let's go."

"Where?"

"Crossing square, under the lantern tower."

They pushed through the curtain, dragged Astruc up the center aisle.
Arc lamps, outside on the esplanade, bled through the leaded glass windows and filled the nave with dull gray light. Up ahead, a shaft of tubular light poured through the great rose window set in the south transept
and fell on the black floor stones of the crossing square in flashes of red
and blue and green. Beyond the square, beneath the scallop-shaped half
dome of the choir, was a marble altar, a cross of iron, and a lone sanctuary candle holding back the dark. They reached the square, climbed
three steps, dropped Astruc on the floor stones in the middle of the
light. Harper and Krinkle caught their breath.

"When does he wake up?" Harper said.

Krinkle pulled a penlight from his coat, dropped to one knee, and rolled Astruc over. The priest's eyes were open, but still. Krinkle shined the penlight into Astruc's pupils.

"He's awake, just paralytic. It'll wear off, but he's going to go in and out for another hour. But where is Monsieur Gabriel? If Father Astruc comes to and he isn't awakened properly, we may have to shoot him for real."

Harper stared at Astruc. The tips of the priest's fingers were twitching.

"I think he heard you," Harper said.

"Good. He's got a lot of explaining to do."

"About what?"

"I'll start with whatever the fuck is going on," Krinkle said.

Krinkle stood up, followed Astruc's line of sight up to the ribbed dome of the lantern tower. He walked around to Astruc's ankles, grabbed hold, and dragged him till his eyes were dead center of the lantern tower.

"What are you doing?" Harper said.

"My form has compulsive disorder issues. Sometimes they manifest themselves."

"How long have you been in your form?"

"1962. He was a roadie for the Grateful Dead. OD'd on some bad smack."

. . . bad smack, bad smack, bad smack . . .

Krinkle's eyes followed the sound of his voice as it rose high into the lantern tower.

"Okay, that's strange."

. . . that's strange, that's strange, that's strange . . .

Harper smiled. "You'll get used to it."

Hollow bells rolled through the nave.

. . . gong, gong, gong . . .

"So, it's three o'clock in the morning in the protected zone," Krinkle said.

Then came six bells.

"Or maybe not," Harper said.

Then three bells, then six again; again and again. Krinkle pulled at his beard.

"Sorta adds to the general strangeness of the place. I'm not surprised you blew it up once."

Harper listened to the sound of the bell.

"That's not Marie-Madeleine," he said.

"Who?"

"Biggest bell in the tower. She calls the hour."

"You know the bells by the sounds they make?"

"You hear Marie-Madeleine once, you never forget her."

"So which bell is ringing now?"

"It's Clémence."

. . . clémence, clémence, clémence . . .

Harper and Krinkle looked at each other, checking if they both heard the same voice. It was coming from somewhere in the nave. A girl's voice; soft, spiritlike. They turned slowly around. Nobody.

"Where are you?" Harper called.

"In the shadows."

. . . the shadows, the shadows, the shadows . . .

The voice was coming from the Lady chapel, off to the left. They turned. Nobody again. They glanced at each other, the both of them reaching inside their coats for the grips of their killing knives.

"Why can't we see you? How are you moving around?"

"I'm not moving. It's a game I play in the cathedral at night."

. . . cathedral at night, at night, at night . . .

They listened for steps. Nothing.

"Why is Clémence ringing?" Harper said.

"Because when she's not the execution bell, sometimes Clémence is the warning bell."

. . . the warning bell, warning bell, warning bell . . .

The sound was coming from the south transept now, by the side doors.

"What warning?" Krinkle said.

"Bad things are happening to the children."

. . . to the children, the children, the children . . .

"What children?" Krinkle said.

"The ones like me."

. . . like me, like me, like me . . .

The voice was floating down to them from the triforium now.

"What is happening to the ones like you?" Harper whispered, letting his voice drift through the shadows.

"They're dying. That's where Monsieur Gabriel is. He's trying to save them."

. . . save them, save them, save them . . .

The sound had circled around to the ambulatory behind the altar. Then came a sepulchral voice wrapped in a French accent.

"You are too late. The Dark Ones are finished."

Harper and Krinkle turned around. Astruc was leaning on his elbow, his eyes wide with terrible visions.

Krinkle moved next to him. "C'mon, brother, talk to me. What do you know, what the fuck have you done?"

Astruc looked up at him, sneered. "I am not your brother."

"In that case you won't mind some of this," Krinkle said, kicking Astruc in the guts.

The priest curled into a fetal position, held his stomach, gasped. "'Lamentation, weeping, and great mourning. Rachael, weeping for her children, refusing to be comforted because they are no more.'"

Astruc's head fell to the stones. Krinkle looked at Harper.

"That's from the Book of Jeremiah."

"It's also in Matthew's Gospel. The Magi trick Herod, leave Bethlehem a different way after visiting Christ. Herod sends in a kill squad; every male child under two years old."

They stared at each other long seconds, till Krinkle finished Harper's thought.

"The slaughter of the innocents."

Harper turned slowly around, his eyes searching the shadows.

"Where are they dying, the children like you?" he said.

"Everywhere."

473

. . . everywhere, everywhere, everywhere . . .

"How do you know?"

"I saw it from the belfry. That's why I started the warning bell. I saw it."

. . . i saw it, saw it, saw it . . .

Clémence sounded through the nave, drowning the voice with sorrow, with grief. Harper let go of his killing knife.

"And after you saw it, you came down here. Because the belfry is profane, the nave is sacred. You came here to hide from the bad shadows."

"But they will come, they will find me like they found the others."

. . . the others, the others, the others . . .

The voice was coming from the south transept. Harper turned slowly around, his face lit in the shaft of tubular light.

"Be not afraid, I know who you are. I've seen you from my balcony, in the old city on Rue Vuillermet. I see you when you call the hour to the north."

"You haven't come to kill me?"

. . . to kill me, kill me, kill me . . .

"No," Harper said, "I'm here to protect you."

Then slowly from the shadows and into the light came a small form dressed in a black cloak and a black floppy hat. The form walked toward them, its eyes locked on the floor stones till it came to the edge of the crossing square. The form stopped, parted its cloak, and revealed a lantern burning with a brilliant spark of flame. The form looked up, and Harper saw a young girl's face and a pair of emerald-colored eyes.

"Bloody hell."

It was the new one . . . *le guet* of Lausanne Cathedral.

III

I N THE NUMBING SILENCE CAME AN AWARENESS OF LIFE.

Katherine opened her eyes, turned her head, saw broken glass and burning debris over Main Street. Then she saw the Ford Explorer, two hundred meters away. It'd been blown off the street and tossed through the front of the candle shop. She saw Corporal Fassnacht hanging from the rear passenger door. He wasn't moving.

"Max! Jesus, Max!"

She tried to get up, but someone was on top of her, talking to her.

"Don't move, Kat."

"Get off me!"

"There could be a secondary."

"I don't care, get off!"

Katherine kicked against Officer Jannsen, heard her moan in pain. "Awhh."

Breaking free and getting to her feet, Katherine saw a piece of jagged glass embedded in Officer Jannsen's leg.

"I'm sorry, Anne."

She ran down the street.

"Kat, wait for me!"

"Max! Max!"

She dodged chairs and pieces of tables, shards of glass, body parts, and blood. Fire trucks rushed from the station, an ambulance rounded a corner, sirens wailed. Something caught Katherine's foot and she went down, held out her hands. She landed hard, scraped the skin from her palms.

"Shit!"

Katherine rolled over, saw a woman's body with its head blown off. Katherine stared a second, trying to make sense of it . . . *Molly, it's Molly.*

"Holy fuck."

She got up, ran for the Explorer.

The motor was off, sides and doors peppered with shrapnel, bullet-proof glass shattered. Luc was still in the shotgun seat, slumped over the heads-up display, bleeding from his head. Katherine listened, whispered, "Max?"

Nothing.

She ran to the right side of the truck; it was pressed up against a brick wall. She ran to the back, tried to open the hatch. It was locked. She kicked it.

"Fuck!"

She came back around to the open rear door, grabbed Corporal Fass-nacht by the shoulders.

Suddenly, hands took hold of Katherine from behind, spun her around, and slammed her against the truck. It was Officer Jannsen.

"No, Kat, I'll do it."

"Let go of me!"

"Listen, I'm trained for this. If Max is badly injured and you move him the wrong way, you could kill him."

Katherine bit her lip.

"Okay."

Officer Jannsen pulled at the corporal, and he fell to the pavement. He'd caught a chunk of shrapnel in the back of the neck, and the lower part of his legs had been sliced off at the knees; he was gone.

Katherine looked in the Explorer. Max's car seat was empty.

"Where . . . where is he?"

Officer Jannsen nodded to the backs of the front seats; they'd been peeled away and were laying on the floor.

"The panels are blast blankets. Sebastianus must have seen it coming, threw Max to the floor and covered him."

Katherine focused her eyes, saw the floor *was* covered. She reached in, pulled aside the blankets. Max was on the floor, clutching his rubber hammer. Seeing his mother, not understanding what was happening, he broke into tears.

"It's okay, Max, Mommy's here . . ."

Just then the air was sucked from the sky again. Officer Jannsen grabbed Katherine, threw her onto the backseat, jumped in.

"Down!"

Another flash of light.

Shock waves slamming shut the door.

A growling roar and a sideways rain of glass and steel.

Quiet.

Katherine raised her head, saw the fire truck and ambulance in flames, more body parts and blood scattered all over the street. Through the shattered glass of the Explorer's windows, the world appeared a thing smashed to pieces. Then Officer Jannsen's voice:

"We've got to get out of here."

"What the hell is happening?"

"I don't know. They've never gotten through the defenses before."

"Who?"

"Who do you think?"

Officer Jannsen jumped into the front, checked Luc's pulse.

"He's alive."

She reached into the glove compartment, took a yellow-colored auto-injector, rammed it into his thigh. She climbed behind the steering wheel. She tried to start the motor. Once, twice . . . each time the radio kicking in with crackling chatter before shutting off.

"... *Zulu Alert* ..."

"... *no contact* ..."

Third try the motor turned over, the radio blared.

"... *do you read? This is Control for Blue Four. Defensive perimeter compromised for thirty seconds, enemy kill squads taking form on compound grounds. No contact with Grover's Mill. All comms down.*"

Officer Jannsen put the truck into reverse, but the undercarriage was stuck. She changed to four wheels, rocked from first to reverse, pressing the transmit key on the steering wheel.

"Blue Four to Control. Are the defenses back up, over."

"*Blue Four, roger, but we have no operational control. What's your status, over.*"

"Suicide bombs in town, mass casualties. Corporal Fassnacht is dead, Luc is alive. Swan Lake and Blue Marble with me. Proceeding to Control. What is your status, over."

"*Kill squads attacking from six-zero and three-three-zero. Repeat, enemy attacking from six-zero and three-three-zero, over.*"

"Is the house under attack, over."

"*Negative, but we will not be able to keep them back. There's hundreds of them, Chef. Maybe thousands.*"

"You sent out a distress call?"

477

"Affirmative, but no response. Repeat, no response."

"Regroup at the house. We need to get Swan Lake and Blue Marble into the safe room."

"Understood. Will order guards to fall back to Defense Profile Delta to cover your approach, over."

"Defense Profile Delta, roger."

"Request ETA, over."

"As soon as possible. Just fucking hang on. Out."

"Roger, out."

Katherine, looked back out the window, saw shreds of black mist oozing over the street, wrapping themselves around the dead.

"They're here," she said.

Officer Jannsen looked back at Katherine.

"What?"

"My nightmares from the cathedral, they're here, and they're real."

Officer Jannsen saw the mist.

"Listen to me, Kat. Those are devourers, they can't hurt you, you're alive."

"What about the other ones?"

"Where?"

Katherine pointed to the swirling black mist.

Officer Jannsen wiped her eyes with her bloody hands, saw twelve shapes take form and step from the mist. Long daggers in their hands, slashing at the throats of the bodies in the street.

"Goons," Officer Jannsen said.

Katherine felt herself wobble at the word.

"What is it, Kat?"

"I saw myself in the cathedral with the man who wasn't there. The way I saw them in my nightmares. He called them 'Goons.' Jesus, they're real, my nightmares are real."

Officer Jannsen nodded toward the blast blanket. "The blanket fits between the back and front seats to form a compartment. Cover Max; we're getting out of here, I promise."

Officer Jannsen turned to the steering wheel, rocked the Explorer harder. Katherine looked at Max; he was crying in shuddering sobs. She saw the sketchbook on the seat, lay it on the floor next to Max.

"Here you go, honey, you can read about those silly pirates. And I'm going to cover you so we can play hide-and-seek, okay?"

She pulled the blast blanket over him, heard his muffled cries.

"Maman, maman."

"It's okay, honey, we're playing hide-and—"

The rear hatch window crashed apart. Katherine spun around, saw a man with dead black eyes crawling into the Explorer.

"Anne!"

Then the side window exploded inward, powerful hands reached in and locked around Katherine's throat . . .

"The child, give us the child that we may feast on his flesh and blood!"

Before Katherine could scream, Officer Jannsen was reaching back with her Glock.

"Don't move, Kat."

Two cracks, and bits of supersonic steel whipped by Katherine's face. The goon's head snapped back and it squealed, its fingers loosening from Katherine's neck. She fell to the seat, rolled over, and kicked the goon from the door as two more rounds exploded over her head. She heard another death squeal. Officer Jannsen dropped the Glock on Katherine's chest.

"Ten rounds left, make them count. Let them get close, two shots to the head between the eyes. Understand?"

"I'll try."

"There's no trying now, Kat. You were right. All your nightmares were real. I've been trying to protect you from them. But now you need to fight with me to protect Max. He's all that counts. Do you understand what I am telling you?"

"Yes."

Officer Jannsen turned back to the steering wheel, floored the motor: *rrrnnnn, rrrnnnnn.* The tires caught traction and the truck jumped back.

Officer Jannsen shifted gears, stomped on the accelerator, and the Explorer raced from the burning town. Max was wailing under the blanket. Katherine stuffed the Glock in her belt, pulled up the blast blanket.

"Come here, honey. Mommy's got you."

"Kat, you should keep him under."

"No way . . . he's a wreck, he can't breathe down there."

"Then lay him on the seat and cover him with your body. Put the blast blanket over the both of you."

Katherine did, dug through her pockets, found his pacifier.

"It's okay, honey, we made another funny tent, isn't that funny? And look, Mommy has Mister Gummy. Where's your book . . . here it is. Let's look at some pictures. Oh, look, here's that big fat caterpillar."

Max settled a little in his mother's arms, sucked on his pacifier, making little choking sounds in his throat. He looked at the sketchbook, tapped Pompidou the Flying Caterpillar with his rubber hammer. "Pomdoo."

"That's right, silly old Pompidou, and now we're going home, and we're going to go for a ride in the yellow submarine, okay?"

She poked her head from under the blanket, saw Luc coming to, pulling himself up.

"Are you with me?" Officer Jannsen said to him.

"Ich bin bei euch."

"Is our heads-up display still working?"

Luc pressed buttons, flipped switches. "All we've got is radio contact with the house and local radar. No comms to HQ."

"Get the Brügger and Thomet, give me your sidearm."

Luc pulled his Glock, loaded a round, handed it to Officer Jannsen. He picked up the submachine gun, made it fire ready.

"What happened?" Officer Jannsen said.

"Just before the bomb, Control radioed flash traffic," the guard said. "Time warps went down in Berlin, Toulouse, Lausanne, and Hong Kong. Light scans picked up thousands of goons taking form and overrunning the orphanages."

"Status?" Officer Jannsen said.

"Offline."

"All of them?"

"*Ja, Chef.*"

Katherine watched Officer Jannsen swallow hard, watched her mouth form silent words. *Mein Gott.*

"What's he talking about, Anne. What orphanages?"

Officer Jannsen didn't answer.

"Hey, Anne, remember the part about you telling me what the fuck's going on because we're getting fucking married?"

Officer Jannsen checked the dashboard, watched the radar sweep from side to side.

"There are three orphanages in Europe, one in Hong Kong. They're for special children we care for."

"Children like Max? That kind of special?"

"No, children like Marc Rochat."

"What?"

"There's no time to explain, we have to get you into the safe room."

They came to Carson Highway. Officer Jannsen stopped, checked the radar. There were blips running left and right across the screen. Katherine looked both ways down the road, saw nothing.

"What are we waiting for?"

"Traffic."

"What fucking traffic?"

"It's there, you just can't see it."

The blips on the screen disappeared. Officer Jannsen hit the accelerator, and the Explorer shot across the road and into the cover of the forest.

"Not that I know what you're talking about, but why are we going to the house, anyway? Why aren't we following the invisible cars to Carson City or Portland? Why are we going where the goons are?"

"Our defensive perimeters are jammed, Kat. We're locked in. We just have to hold off the goons till reinforcements get here."

"Bullshit, let's just jump the fucking wall and blow this place."

"We can't."

"Why not?"

"Our defensive perimeter isn't a wall, it's time."

"Are you telling me we're trapped in time?"

"I'm telling you we have to hold out till we get backup."

Katherine tried to make sense of it.

"Bullshit, turn around, get on the highway, get us away from here."

"Listen, Kat, this is the only chance Max has. The bad guys know who he is. Out there, in real time, there are millions of goons; he wouldn't stand a chance. In here, we can fight as best we can."

"Out there we can hide."

"Kat, there is nowhere to hide in the world. You found that out at Lausanne Cathedral. There's only here and now, and you've got to focus on not letting Max fall into the hands of the goons. Your only chance, Max's only chance, is the safe room."

Katherine saw herself in the belfry again. The tall silver-haired goon with the silver eyes, ramming a knife into Marc Rochat's stomach, raising his crooked body on the blade and dropping him on the ground. She looked at Max, still tapping the pictures of Pompidou the Flying Caterpillar. She suddenly knew she was two places in time at once. She looked at Max, felt herself tremble.

"Get us home, Anne."

Officer Jannsen sped ahead. Goons rushed from the trees, raised weapons, and fired.

"They're trying to cut me off," she said. "Give me cover."

"Roger, *Chef*," Luc said.

He hit a button on the dashboard and a section of the Explorer's roof blew off. He stood on his seat, sprayed a ninety-degree arc of bullets into the trees. The Explorer rounded a turn. A huge log had been dragged across the road.

"Scheisse!"

Officer Jannsen pulled the emergency brake, turned the wheel, and forced the Explorer into a spin. Luc dropped back into the truck as its rear wheel hit a stump—*wham!* The truck flipped onto its side and skidded over the road. Katherine had Max in her arms, covered his head with her hands. Max screamed and from the forest there rose a howl of ravenous voices. Then:

Quiet.

"Everyone good?" Officer Jannsen said.

"I'm good," Luc said.

Kat twisted Max in her arms.

"Yeah, we're okay."

Officer Jannsen crawled over Katherine and Max into the back of the Explorer. She kicked the release and the hatch blew open. She crawled out, reached back.

"Give me Max and come."

Katherine held out Max to her. He waved, kicked his legs, and shrieked, *"Maman! Maman!"*

The goons howled from the trees hearing Max's voice.

Officer Jannsen got her hands under Max's arms, pulled him out. Katherine quickly crawled out, then Luc with his Brügger & Thomet slung over his back. Max flew into Katherine's arms. *"Maman!"* She put her hand over his mouth.

"Shhhh, it's okay, honey. It's okay."

The forest fell quiet again.

She heard Officer Jannsen and Luc whispering to each other in German. He nodded, reached back into the truck, pulled out two bags. One was a medical kit, the other a backpack. Officer Jannsen found a pressure bandage in the med kit, tore it open, and wrapped it around her thigh and the jutting glass.

"Aren't you going to pull it out?" Katherine said.

Officer Jannsen shook her head. "Too close to an artery. I'll bleed out."

Luc fitted the small canvas bag around his shoulders. He reached in the truck again, pulled open the side panels, took out two more Brügger & Thomets, handed one to Officer Jannsen, draped the other around his neck; now he had two. Officer Jannsen reached in the truck, pulled out an ammunition case, and opened it. It was stuffed with loaded clips. They continued to whisper in German, slapping clips into their weapons, stuffing extra clips into their pockets.

"What is it, what are you guys saying?" Katherine said quietly.

Officer Jannsen looked at Katherine.

"The goons are regrouping for an attack. The house is sixty meters through the trees. You and I will run with Max."

Katherine looked at Luc.

"What about you?"

"I will stay and give you cover."

"But the radio said there are hundreds of goons inside with us, maybe thousands."

Officer Jannsen touched Katherine's arm.

"Kat, they're coming at us from all sides. We must cover our rear or we'll never make it to the house."

"Yeah, but how?"

Luc opened the backpack. Katherine saw a timer, watched the guard set it for two minutes, hit the switch. The timer started counting down.

"I will fire double taps for ninety seconds, then stop. The goons will think I am out of ammunition and charge. That will be your signal to get down."

"No," Katherine said. "You can't do this."

"Madame Taylor, it is my duty," Luc said. He looked at Max, smiled, and gave him a salute. "And may I say, Captain Picard, it has been a great honor to serve with you."

Max stared at him as if knowing the true meaning of the man's words.

"Woof," Max whispered.

The guard checked the timer.

"One hundred seconds. *Ich wünsche Ihnen alles gute, Chef.*"

Officer Jannsen grabbed the guard's hand. *"Im namen des lichts, mein bruder."*

"Und du bist, meine schwester."

Katherine leaned to the guard, kissed his cheek. "Thank you."

Officer Jannsen pulled Katherine's arm.

"Let's go."

They ducked into the forest, heard the Brügger & Thomets open fire in succession. Pause, speed reload, fire again. Bullets counting down like ticks of a clock, then the guns stopped and ravenous howls sounded through the forest. Officer Jannsen led Katherine into a gully.

"Get in, get down, cover Max."

Katherine jumped into the gully, lay Max on the ground, and curled her body over him. She covered his ears . . . a great *crump* rocked the earth, and bits of metal screamed through the air and smacked the trees. Katherine looked at Max. His eyes were wide, fear was clawing at his throat.

"We're almost there, Max, we're almost there."

Officer Jannsen peeked over the rim of the gully; Katherine did, too. A ten-meter-wide section of forest was burning. The Explorer had been ripped apart.

"Let's go," Officer Jannsen said.

Katherine picked up Max, his arms dangling from his sides.

"Max? Max?"

Officer Jannsen checked Max's eyes.

"He's falling into shock. Keep talking to him, but keep moving."

They ran ahead, autumn leaves and brittle twigs snapping under their boots. Katherine saw Officer Jannsen wasn't running, she was limping. A burst of automatic fire crackled and echoed through the forest. Katherine got down; Officer Jannsen turned back, pulled at her arm.

"It's outgoing, Kat. It's not coming at us. The house is twenty meters away. Keep moving."

Katherine held Max close.

"It's okay, honey. We're almost there, Mommy has you. Mommy has you, Max."

The guns crackled again, the forest filled with death squeals. Then quiet. Officer Jannsen stopped, leaned against a tree. Blood was dripping down her leg and onto the ground. She tightened the pressure bandage, grimaced with pain.

"Anne, you're really hurt."

"It doesn't matter. All that matters is getting you and Max into the safe room. Let's go."

Officer Jannsen limped ahead. Branches of the trees began to sway, the entire forest seemed to bend.

"Down, Kat."

They ducked behind the widest tree. *Crump, crump.* Then a blast of heat.

Up ahead, through the trees, Katherine saw the house. It was in flames.

"Holy fuck."

Officer Jannsen nodded to the thick of the forest.

"We'll circle around to Control. Come on."

Branches of pine slapped at their faces. Katherine tucked Max inside her cloak as they ran. Two minutes later, Officer Jannsen stopped, called out, *"Hold fire at your rear!"*

A voice answered from ahead in the trees, "Blue Four, where are you?"

"Ten meters out on your one-sixty. Is it clear?"

"They've taken the house, they're trying to take Control. We've held them back twice. We can't do it a third time."

"How many of you are there?"

"Five."

"Post two men at the top of the stairs to the safe room. When they're set, give it five seconds and open up on the goons. We'll come in on your left, copy?"

"Hurry, *Chef*, here they come."

Then the howl of goons closing in for the kill. Officer Jannsen looked at Katherine.

"I'll lead you to the guards, you keep going into Control and down to the safe room."

"What about you?"

"Don't worry, I'll be right behind you."

Officer Jannsen jumped to her feet, hurried ahead, broke through the trees and into a clearing. She called back to Katherine.

"Now, Kat, move it!"

They dashed from the trees. A wave of goons charged from the forest to cut them off. Officer Jannsen dropped to a firing position, let off a spray of automatic fire. She ejected the clip, reloaded, fired again. Something caught hold of Katherine's legs, pulled her to her knees.

"No! No!"

She held on to Max, kicked herself free, saw two goons crawling toward her.

"The child is ours!"

Katherine looked at Officer Jannsen, reloading again, firing into a second wave of goons from the left.

"Oh, Jesus."

She swapped Max to her left arm, covered him with her cloak. She pulled the Glock from her belt, her hand shaking. She fired two rounds wide. Max screamed at the sound. The two goons howled, got to their feet, rushed ahead.

"Fuck!"

Katherine steadied, squeezed the trigger twice. Blew open the first goon's head. The second goon fell on top of her, raising a knife to slice open her throat. She jammed the barrel into the goon's left eye, fired. The goon flew back, black blood and brains splattering a tree; and when the goon hit the ground, Katherine put one more round into its shattered skull.

"Don't ever touch me, you fucking pigs."

Hands pulled at her again. Katherine spun around with the Glock— she had dead aim on Officer Jannsen.

"Jesus."

"That's my girl, Kat."

"Where are the rest of them?"

"They fell back to the house. How's Max?"

Katherine opened her cloak. He was dangling in her arms.

"Max? Max?"

Officer Jannsen checked his pulse and eyes. They were open, but had lost focus. His skin had gone white.

"He's going into severe shock. You need to stabilize him."

"How?"

"In the safe room there's a med kit under your bed. You'll find a silver box with injectors. There's a red one, give it to Max. It'll bring him around. Come on."

An explosion of gunfire and squeals ripped through the air, and a voice called from ahead. *"Chef!* It's now or never!"

"Let's go, Kat."

Katherine got up, held Max with both her arms, followed Officer Jannsen through a patch of trees and onto the driveway. The house was like a funeral pyre. Seven Swiss Guards lay nearby with their throats slashed open. Ahead, three more guards were firing across the back garden.

"On your left!" Officer Jannsen shouted.

One of the guards called back: "We're on our last clips! Make it fast!"

Officer Jannsen looked at Katherine.

"Do not stop until the two of you are in the safe room. Give him the shot, keep him warm. Do you understand?"

"Yes."

Officer Jannsen ejected the clip from her Brügger & Thomet and reloaded.

"Run, when I say."

Officer Jannsen limped up the driveway, took a firing position with the guards.

"Hold your fire for the next charge."

The three machine guns ripped apart the air; Katherine heard squeals and howls.

"Now, Kat!"

Katherine charged from the trees down the driveway. Between the burning house and Control, she saw the garden . . . It was filled with dead goons. And now, hundreds more charged from the trees . . . all of them with knives. Katherine kept running, made Control, ran down one level, through a hall, made the stairs down to the safe room. Two Swiss Guards were posted at the top of the stairs, their weapons targeted at the entrance.

"Hurry, Madame Taylor, get in."

"You, too, get in."

She heard steps shuffling down the hall, looked back, saw Officer Jannsen limping toward her. The bandage had fallen from her thigh and her wound was draining blood.

"Anne, your leg."

"I'm right behind you, Kat, move!"

Katherine rushed down the stairs, squeezed through the guards. At the bottom of the steps the door to the safe room was open. She rushed in as gunfire broke out at the top of the steps. Squeals and howls echoed down the stairwell into the safe room. She rushed into the room, opened her cloak, and lay Max on the bed. Behind her, the hydraulics kicked in and the steel door began to close.

"No, wait! Anne! Anne!"

She rushed to the door.

Goons were mobbing the top of the stairs, crushing one another to get through. Their eyes flaring, their knives dripping blood, black drool dripping from their mouths. Officer Jannsen was running down the stairs, blocking the guards' line of fire. One goon broke from the mob and flew down the stairs. Katherine raised her Glock, fired two body shots. It dropped and the guards finished it off. Officer Jannsen squeezed by the guards.

"Hold your fire till they charge," she ordered.

She opened a panel on the back of the closing door, pressed in a numerical code.

"What are you doing?"

"Overriding the release codes so you aren't fooled into opening the door. You and Max can hold out here for two months if need be."

"No. You have to get in here, all of you."

"There's not enough oxygen. There's only enough for you and Max."

"Anne, wait! Don't leave us!"

Officer Jannsen pulled back her arm as the massive door began to seal. "I love you, Kat."

Katherine heard the goons charge down the stairs. There was a blaze of gunfire, then the guns stopped, then screams and howls and the gnashing of teeth . . . then the vault's hydraulic bolts slammed into their sockets. Quiet.

IV

KATHERINE TOUCHED THE DOOR, THINKING IT WOULD OPEN ANY second and all would be well. She pressed her ear against the door; there was nothing. Then she remembered the door was solid steel, a meter thick. There would be no sound from the other side of the door. But there was a sound in the safe room, a quiet gasping sound. She turned around, saw Max on the bed, staring at the ceiling.

She went to him, dropped the gun on the bed. And though he still had a hold on his rubber hammer, there was a terrible, lost look in his eyes. She saw herself in the belfry of Lausanne Cathedral with the same look in her eyes. It wasn't shock, she realized; Max was slipping into the madness of seeing unknowable things.

"Honey?"

He didn't respond, he didn't blink.

Katherine bent down, pulled the medical kit from under the bed. She dug through it, found a small silver box containing auto-injectors. The top of the box had a list of what colored injector did what. She grabbed the red one, flipped the cap, and pressed it into Max's thigh. She hit the release. Max didn't even jump when the needle punched his skin. She dropped the injector on the floor, leaned over Max's face. She almost touched his face, saw blood on her hands, saw blood on Max's clothes from her holding him. She wiped her hands on her cloak, she combed Max's hair.

"Honey, it's Mommy. We're safe now. No one can find us. Max, look at me, honey. And, oh, look what silly Mommy remembered, here's Mister Gummy."

She put the pacifier in her mouth to clean it, held it to Max's lips. He didn't take it.

"Max, it's going to be all right."

She stood, hurried to the kitchen area, opened the refrigerator. There were bottles of Molly's apple juice in one side drawer. She took one out, poured some in a glass, walked back to Max.

"Hey, look what I found. Some of Molly's juice. And I'm going to dip in Mister Gummy and swirl him around, and here you go, honey. Taste it. You know what it is. It's from Molly . . ."

Katherine choked back tears remembering Molly, how she loved Max. How they all did.

"Come on, honey, taste it, please."

The juice sank through Max's lips, he tasted it on his tongue, and he blinked, saw his mother.

"Mowy jooz," he whispered.

"Yeah, there you go. Here, let me do that again, that was fun."

She dipped the pacifier, set it to Max's lips, and he sucked at it. She stared at him, wet her thumb, and wiped the tracks of tears from his cheeks.

"It's okay now, honey. Everything's going to be—"

. . . *thump* . . .

The room shook a little.

She looked at the door.

. . . *thump* . . . *thump* . . .

The room shook again, then by fractions of inches, the door began to move inward.

. . . *THUMP* . . .

"No way, no way."

Katherine set the glass on the floor, picked up the Glock, pulled the slide. One bullet in the firing chamber. She ejected the clip, one more bullet makes two. She replaced the clip, reset the slide. She got up, walked to the vault door. She slammed it with the palm of her hand, watched her own blood smear against cold steel. She held her hand in place, rested her forehead against the door.

"I swear, on the Holy Mother of God, you will not touch my son. Do you hear me? I will not let you do to him what you did to me or Marc Rochat, or anyone else on the fucking planet. Do you fucking hear me?"

. . . *THUMP, THUMP* . . .

The locking bolts began to groan and bend.

She turned around, looked at Max. He stared at the door, thinking it was a game perhaps, like Whac-A-Mole. He raised his hammer, waved it at the door.

"Borg!"

Katherine felt herself choke . . . She drew a quick breath. "Yeah, honey, it's the Borg. You show those guys they can't scare us. Let 'em have it, Max."

. . . *THUMP* . . .

"Goog!"

Katherine walked to Max, sat down, and rested the gun on the bed. She looked at the door, saw black mist seeping in from under it. She picked up Max and straddled him across her lap, reached down and picked up the glass of apple juice. She pulled the pacifier from Max's lips.

"You know what, buster? You're a big boy now, and you need to learn to drink from a glass. Here you go."

She held the glass to his mouth. He sucked at the liquid, and it rolled down his chin. He giggled, waved his hammer.

"Good try, let's have some more. C'mon, Max, show Mommy what a big boy you are."

He drank again, this time getting it down his mouth properly.

"Good boy, Max. Such a good boy."

He was back and with her now. She could see it in his eyes, and color was coming to his cheeks. She set the glass on the floor, wiped apple juice from his chin, combed back his black hair. The door of the vault groaned louder and began to crack apart. Max looked over his shoulder. Katherine took his chin in her hand and turned his face to hers.

"Don't worry about the silly old Borg, honey. Look at Mommy. Look into Mommy's eyes, listen to Mommy's voice."

Max stared at her, tipped his head, hearing the words. His green eyes sparkled.

"Maman," he said.

She bounced him on her lap.

"That's right, honey, you look at Mommy. Keep looking into Mommy's eyes, listen to Mommy's voice. Everything is fine, honey. We're together, you and me. Everything is going to be all right. Just keep looking at me."

She saw a smile cross his face.

He waved his hammer and giggled again.

"That's right, honey. You get those bad guys, you scare them all away."

"Goog!"

"Mommy loves you, Mommy loves you so very much. *Je t'aime, mon fils. Je t'aime.*"

He touched his mother's face.

She pulled him to her breasts.

She picked up the Glock, slipped her finger through the trigger guard, pressed the muzzle to her son's head.

"Big, brave Max."

✤

TO BE CONTINUED IN
The Way of Sorrows

PART THREE OF
The Angelus Trilogy

❦

ADÆQUATIO INTELLECTUS ET REI:

David Rosenthal; editor, counselor, friend,

Georgina Capel, high priestess of the sacred order of literary agents,

Gilles Thomas, *le cataphile mystérieux* who led me on "unauthorized tours" of *les carrières* beneath Paris,

Locomotora, for the use of their name and song "Older Than Dreams," as well as their persons as characters in the story,

Karoliina Vilenius, Richard "Krinkle" Kreuzkamp & Leo Mates, who also became part of the story,

Burton C. Bell, for the use of his name and music project, *Ascension of the Watchers*; also for use of his lyrics from "Like Falling Snow,"

Immanu El, for the use of their name and lyrics from "Under Your Wings I'll Hide,"

My cats, Zorro and Zeus, for keeping me laughing,

And Afnan, for everything.

ABOUT THE AUTHOR

Jon Steele was born in the American Northwest. He's worked as a keyboard player in a rock band, postman, liquor store clerk, radio disc jockey, and TV news cameraman. His autobiography, *War Junkie*, published in 2003, is regarded as a cult classic of war reporting. *The Watchers* was his first novel, published in 2012 as part one of The Angelus Trilogy.